A Weaver's Heart

The King's Weaver

Book Two

Novae Caelum

For everyone who needs to feel seen.
The magic is in who you are.

Prologue

Irava/Caleb

His brow is smooth during sleep, his face untroubled. His long black hair tousled over his shoulders, glossy in the early morning sunlight shining through our bedroom window.

My husband.

My king.

I'm his king, too. And just now, his queen.

He wakes slowly, eyelids fluttering, and peers hazily at me with his gray-green eyes.

He groans, stretches his shoulders under the covers, then reaches out to brush hair out of my eyes.

I capture his hand—it is mine—and kiss it.

"Good morning, Master Weaver," he says.

"Good morning, Court Mage."

He grins. And flops onto his back as he spreads his hands, the air shimmering above him into a small illusory falcon. It was the first reality construct I wove in this palace, beyond my illusion at the time as Caleb.

He's been determined to make it himself the last week, and he almost has it. The falcon stretches its wings over his hands and flies toward the window, only unraveling at Torovan's will before it reaches the panes of glass.

I prop up on one elbow. "That was good!"

"I'm a court mage now," he says, shifting to prop up, too. Facing me again.

"As of yesterday." I tap the medallion that he wore to bed. Because *of course* he wore it to bed.

I wore mine, too.

He grins, and I launch at him, tangling my hands in his hair, locking him to me. To myself. To my being.

I know we'll be busy today. Me, with helping Master Aldric sort through a large shipment of books on weaving we sent for from Galenda—and my mother learned of and sent as a wedding gift instead.

And Torovan in his endless meetings, trying to wrestle the kingdom into a shape better for its people.

We'll be apart for a few hours. And why does that feel like a lifetime?

I pull back from him, looking between his eyes.

"I want to make something between us," I say.

His brow crinkles. "Like, another weaving construct? I probably don't have time this morning—"

"No, like, the possibility of another...person."

He stares at me blankly for a moment. Then his eyes widen.

"You're sure? It's not too soon? Are you—are you even sure at all, we don't have to—"

"We haven't been *not* trying," I say.

"But—but you're back and forth between your realities as Irava and Caleb."

"Yes, and as soon as I feel a new possibility inside me, I'll stay Irava. I mean, my body will have to—I'll still be Caleb, but my body will have to be an illusion. For a bit."

He moves to sit up further, to caress my face. "Do you want that, Irava?"

I bite my lip. No. No, I don't. I love my body as Caleb, when I'm Caleb.

I reweave my reality as Caleb around me now, settling into the differences, settling, as my inner self moves to Caleb, into myself.

"I will never ask you to do that," he says. Running his thumb over my cheek. "We can figure out—well, when Elsira marries, if she has children, they can be my heirs—"

I have been thinking about this. I have.

Our marriage is a political alliance.

And I believe him when he says that we could find a way around this. There have been other kings and queens who married kings and queens in turn, and let inheritance fall to other family members, or brought a surrogate into their marriage.

I have thought about it.

But I want a child who is his and mine. Something beautiful and sacred that we both made together. Our realities synchronized to create this.

I want to give this to him.

And I want to have this for myself.

I want to hold in my arms a miracle that our willpower made together.

"It's nine months," I say. "And I can wear an illusion of myself just fine." I lean forward to kiss him again. He makes a small sound, leaning into me, his hands in my hair this time. My body stirring with need.

Will it be the last time I'm with him for nine months, in my body now as Caleb?

I'll find a way around this. Surely there have been other weavers who were pregnant—maybe not genderfluid like me, but surely.

It's one of the reasons why I have sent for so many books on weaving.

I've never healed myself with my weaving, but I know it's possible, too. I reweave my reality into another body all the time, surely I can reweave more subtleties within my own.

So it doesn't have to be nine months.

Surely.

"If you're sure?" he asks again, coming up for air.

"Tonight. If I'm Irava tonight, then, yes. And tomorrow if not. But yes, I'm sure."

CHAPTER 1

THE LETTERS

TOROVAN

FIVE MONTHS LATER

My hands aren't shaking, but only because I'm willing them not to.

It's morning in the Great Hall, sunlight streaming in through the high windows, casting some of the courtiers and dignitaries in shadows, some in pockets of floating light.

And it's hard to stand in the Great Hall today, this place that's always been a part of my home, and not see potential enemies everywhere.

In the nobles milling about in small clusters, sharing the latest court gossip or excitedly talking about the seven nights of the Harvest Festival to come.

And in the dignitaries from neighboring kingdoms, too, in their gowns or their waistcoats or their frills—or in their simple finery, too, according to their own customs. A sea of faces and nationalities and friends and possibly foes.

All of their voices combine to make a happy roar that echoes to the vaulted ceiling.

We hold the Harvest Festival every year in Barella. It's a time when all of our allies, our neutral neighbors, and some of our enemies converge to form new alliances, new trade deals, and shore up existing treaties. It's a time when Barellan nobility come to renew or form their own alliances, too, which will last throughout the year. As king, I'll ask the gods' blessing on our kingdom's harvest and on our next year.

It's when the whole of us can see each other as people and not just the interests we represent.

This will be my first Harvest Festival as king. Last year, my father died shortly after the harvest.

And I'm clasping my hands in front of me tightly to contain my nerves.

Not at the Festival itself—that would be normal, that would be easy and expected of me as a king still new to the throne.

I carefully don't think about the letters tucked into a hidden compartment in one of the meeting rooms nearby— one Caleb seldom goes in. Locked into a small box, with the only key around my neck, tucked inside my shirt.

One letter I received this morning. One the morning before that, and one the day before. And the feel of those letters still numbs the tips of my fingers.

I know the nobleman talking to me just now, Lord Navirat, a Council member, is saying something I should be hearing. Everything is important when you're the king. Ever more so when you're the king of a kingdom you're trying to change for the better.

But I look up at my husband across the hall, who's

standing in a gray and gold embroidered coat and burgundy trousers, his light-brown hair neatly pulled back to frame his delicate pale face, his spectacles slightly askew. He stands at the center of his three apprentices, his hands raised and gracefully plucking on the threads of reality around him. A small crowd of onlookers has gathered to watch, though they've given Caleb and his apprentices a wide circle in which to work.

I can see those threads he's weaving now, pulled lazily from the air around him, winding their way into the illusion of a small tree, its top branches reaching just above him, a few autumn leaves falling toward the floor.

Caleb stands back, his whole posture satisfied.

"There. You see? Not so hard. It's all in the—"

Someone closer to me calls to a friend across the hall, and I catch my breath. I'm not there with Caleb, I'm here. I'm here, supposed to be listening to a Council lord, not watching my husband. Not with my husband.

But I look back to Caleb and watch as his three apprentice weavers raise their hands to try the same, darting looks around them at the watching crowds. They're not used to an audience, and Caleb insisted their last practice before their display at the first feast of the Harvest Festival be here, to help them know what they're getting into.

He's not always a patient teacher—that I know. He has too much life in him sometimes to slow down enough for anyone to catch up. But he is a *good* teacher. He can pull apart concepts so they're easy to grasp. He guides, and he doesn't criticize.

Caleb moves around one of his apprentices to point up at the illusion the apprentice is weaving.

And he looks up across the room, his eyes meeting mine. And his gaze heats.

I rake him in again, all of him, every last inch.

But he turns away.

And what is showing on my face?

Can he hear the racing of my heart from here? I know he can't. And still, it sounds thunderous to me.

He will always have all of my heart. Always.

But I turn away, back to the Council member I've been talking to. Or trying to listen to. Or...not trying.

"—why I'm recommending that we send a troop to the border with Akreal to find out what's actually going on."

My attention sharpens. Akreal.

It's a large kingdom that shares a small stretch of border with Barella to the north.

The kingdom I'm almost certain my mother fled to after she escaped the palace dungeons, though I don't have solid confirmation yet. Akreal doesn't trade or share information well with Barella.

"Why should we send a troop?" I ask. "We're not at war with Akreal."

Yet.

But I already have an idea of what he'll say. I've been tracking the rumors, that villagers near the border to Akreal have taken a sharp distaste to weavers in the last month.

And weavers aren't common enough for every village to have one, but, the fervor has grown to where people are accusing their neighbors of forbidden magic.

Of the kind of dark soul weaving that Lord Nikolai Metrial used on me.

That he's trying to use again on Caleb.

"Excuse me," I say to Lord Navirat, because I can't take it anymore.

I signal most of my guards to stay here, because Caleb, I think, is in more danger than I am.

If Caleb has noticed that I've assigned more guards to him in the last few days than is normal around a big event like this, he hasn't said. Yet.

I've mostly had the guards keep their distance, not be obvious about it.

And Caleb's not unaware, he isn't. He does know that tensions have been building.

But he's been so distracted lately, so busy, that I'm not going to add to his worries.

My own personal bodyguards follow me out.

And I'll find out what happened this time on the border, I will, and maybe I will send troops. But the letter I received this morning—I have to see it again.

I push into one of the side chambers off the main corridor, and my guards, at my signal, stay outside.

I shut and lock the door, and for a moment fight the boyish urge to lean against it, to block out the entire world.

But though the crowds gathering in the palace for the Festival have been taxing, the threat...the threat is in this room.

I look around, then gather a breath and look with my weaver's senses.

The meeting room has a normal amount of reality. As they all have since Nikolai was arrested. Since my mother fled.

But Nikolai isn't in our palace dungeon anymore. And he isn't dead. Much as I'd wish it on the man who murdered my father.

No, this room is normal. And I don't sense the reality of anyone else in it.

Should I have waved my guards back so quickly?

What if I had been wrong that the only threat here is in the letters?

The autumn sunlight from the arched windows is less hallowed than in the Great Hall, more immediate in this room.

I stride to the wall to my left and press gently on one of the carved panels of wood set between plates of swirling green and gold wallpaper. The panel sticks a little, but I slide it upward carefully, just enough to reach inside the hollow and pull out the box with the letters.

My fingers hum again as I touch it. Even not touching the letters themselves yet, my fingertips buzz with the unreality within.

I pull the key from my shirt and angle the box so I can unlock it. Then I slide open the box's lid, and shake the letters into my hands. I've folded them to fit in the box, and I've opened them when they arrived, but I haven't dared do anything more than read them and inspect them with every weaver's sense I can bring to bear.

I pull out the letter I received today, and let the others drop back into the box. The letter feels to my senses like it doesn't exist, like it shouldn't, like it was never made. Like no one has ever held it.

An unreality weaving. I can sense the threads that I still can't see, or rather, the lack of those threads. It's a numbness, an absence in my senses. A heavy sense of wrong.

The only other time I felt anything like this before was in my father's bedchamber. The room where he died.

And later, as Caleb was teaching me, in my mother's bedchamber. Which was the lesser of the two traumas. Maybe.

I carefully unfold the plain parchment, the black ink smudged as if it was written in haste. But this letter wasn't prepared in haste, a weaving like that couldn't have been done without thought.

There are eight words on the paper, scrawled in a cramped hand.

I don't know if it's Nikolai's hand, but I don't assume.

I can't afford to think he's working alone.

He wasn't before.

"I will kill him if you tell him," the letter says.

That's it.

The same message as the day before.

And the day before that.

I stare at the words as if staring can make them tell me more. Tell me what the danger is, exactly, to show me how I can unravel it. I can't feel anything more on these letters than the unreality—I can't feel beneath it, like Caleb could.

And that's the point. These letters are a taunt. Caleb could unravel this puzzle, but if I tell him...

I don't think they're an absent threat.

I fold the letter again and tuck it back into the box, tap the box lid shut, shove it back into the wall panel, and slam the panel back down into place.

I never needed to ask who "he" is—Nikolai knew Caleb as Caleb, mostly, not Irava, too. Caleb is who Nikolai hated. First with jealousy when Caleb saved his life from a careless weaving when they were court mage candidates, and then...because Caleb stood in his way.

His way to controlling me.

Caleb stopped him, it was Caleb who stood between me and Nikolai's mind control magic.

It was Irava who finally subdued him, yes. But he only saw her for minutes, not the weeks before.

"I will kill him if you tell him."

No more demands than that. Just a threat.

I allow myself a moment to shudder. Then draw myself up, because I have to go on.

And I can't stop the Harvest Festival now. Too many people have been traveling to Barella for days. Many have already arrived, some will be arriving this afternoon, before the Harvest Festival officially starts this evening.

I don't even know if the threat is distant or already here. There is no return address on the letters, only the stamp in one corner of having come into the palace. They could come from Nikolai's estates in the north, or they could come from anywhere.

They could have been written in the palace and sent from outside it. But I don't know.

I have to tell Caleb of the danger.

Caleb is the most powerful mage in this palace—in this kingdom. He can defend himself, and I have my guards around him. I know that.

Surely he could defuse whatever traps Nikolai laid for him in those letters.

And I should be near him, too. I'm not the master weaver he is, not for a long time yet, I think. But he's been teaching me for months now, when I have the time. I'm a weapon in my kingdom, too.

But if I tell him...

If there's even a chance Nikolai can back up that threat.

Oh, gods of the autumn rains, I can't tell him.

I swallow, and stride back out into the corridor. There isn't a Council session today, not when everyone is concentrating on the Harvest Festival, but I tell my guards, "Get Valtair. Send runners to the Council in the palace—we meet in a half turn of the glass."

I hesitate, then call after the guard turning away, "Tell Valtair to get Caleb."

At least near me, away from the crowds, he'll be safer, won't he?

I used to love the Harvest Festival. But now I can't ignore my rising dread.

CHAPTER 2

PRACTICE

CALEB

Torovan's watching me from across the Great Hall, I know he is, I can feel his eyes on me even when I'm not looking. Warming me.

He's supposed to be paying attention to the Council member who's cornered him, not making eyes at me.

Not that I'm objecting.

And I'm supposed to be paying attention to my three apprentice weavers. Just now, they're all making another attempt at the illusions that we'll display tonight at the first feast of the Harvest Festival, dazzling the guests with our showy displays.

I watch one of my apprentices, Aria, stretch her long arms out, her brow furrowed as she works on her illusion of a tree. So far so good.

The tree she'll weave tonight will be much larger, towering to the ceiling of the Great Hall, but for now, with everyone here, we're keeping them small.

Aria is a few years older than me, the daughter of a high

noble. She's willowy with loose black hair, light-brown skin, and a dancer's build. She always sways with her magic, as if every weaving is a performance, every plucked thread of reality a note in a symphony.

I catch Torovan's eye and bite my lip when his gaze lingers, then his gray-green eyes rake over me.

And I linger on him, too. The way the sun from the high windows has half of his light-brown face in shadow, the other half in blazing light, putting the planes of his strong brow and chin in all the right angles. All of them.

His black hair is bound back today, but a few strands, as usual, have escaped their enclosure. His lips are parting, and I can almost feel his desire growing from across the room.

I flush, blink hard, and turn back to my apprentices. One of whom is trying not to smirk at me. His own illusion has fallen apart, but at least he safely pulled the threads back into place.

I raise my brows. "Well? Try it again, Kian. Eyes on your work this time, please. Your branches have to breathe."

Kian wipes away his grin. He's the oldest son of a high general, gangly, with a halo of coiled hair framing his youthful brown face. He's not quite grown into his height even at eighteen. "Yes, *Your Majesty*."

He does not act his age, and I know it's deliberate. I well know what it's like to grow up with a parent's crushing expectations. Though his stubbornness has proven formidable in his willpower for weaving reality.

And I scowl. I don't like when they call me that. And maybe we have all become too familiar for court manners, but they're my apprentices, and I can't teach them to wield their willpower if I'm constantly suppressing it.

Still, I glance around to see if anyone heard that subtle dig, and while the palace staff is busy hanging up gold and green banners and draping garlands from the carved stonework around the pillars, I don't think anyone else is near enough to have heard.

I smile at one of the noblewomen watching us and receive a polite series of bows from her and her companions in return.

I've been royalty all my life, but it still unnerves me, knowing I'm their king. Well, technically, king consort, though Barellan custom doesn't tack that qualifier onto a title.

Torovan might be the king, but when I'm Caleb, I am a king, too.

I glance back toward Torovan—and he is leaving, I just see the swish of his long coat as he marches out through the side doors, followed by a few of his guards.

He leaves the bulk of his guards in the Great Hall, though. And probably wise for that—while the conversations I've heard around me have mostly been happy, and mostly been civil, I know the rivalries that will be descending on this palace yet today.

My own two personal guards are still by the heavy carved oak doors propped open to either side.

"Shit!" Kian says. "Aria—"

I turn back to my apprentices just as Aria's threads of reality begin to knot and then unravel.

She's had trouble holding more complex illusions together before. And maybe she's trying too hard now, maybe I was too distracted to realize she was taking on too much, but my stomach clenches as the edges of her weaving spark, then roar into a cascading flame.

Aria yells and ducks, and I thrust up my hands, grabbing

hold of the swiftly unraveling strands, quickly weaving them into a different illusion, a massive butterfly, because it's the only thing I can think of in the moment.

The butterfly takes off across the room, bleeding sparks and fire, but the reality around it is stabilizing.

Mostly.

I watch my rewoven illusion for a moment, tensed to reach for it again if it still proves unstable. But I've set it to unweave itself naturally, its threads easing back into the reality around it.

Aria is trembling, her hands still stretched up to try to save a weaving that's no longer there.

I open my mouth, but my third apprentice, Sabella, gives me a look and approaches Aria, wrapping a sturdy arm around her.

Sabella is short and with pale pink skin, prematurely graying but with a handsome round face, and dresses mostly in men's clothes, preferring women. She's also a former kitchen maid, and when she helped another younger servant out of what could have been a drunken tirade by talking him down with sheer, steady will, I asked if she would like to be trained as a weaver.

Because weaving shouldn't just be a magic that the nobility learns, if the commoners don't often have access to books or teachers. Because Torovan's efforts to give more power to the people should be echoed in the palace, too.

And because I need more weavers. We all need more weavers. Nikolai might not be in the palace anymore, but he's still out there.

"It's all right," Sabella says, patting Aria's back. "It's okay, Caleb unwove it, we're all safe, everything's fine. We can try again later."

They use my name. Not my titles—usually—or, gods forbid, "Master Caleb."

No.

Torovan tried that once, and it sounded far too much like Master Aldric for me not to swat that down.

Master mage or not, I just want to be myself.

I bite my lip and start toward Aria, too, but catch someone else stepping up beside me.

I tense, and I'm not sure why I'm jumpy just now—yes, that could have been a dangerous unraveling, but it wasn't. I was here. I knew it would be fine. I push my apprentices, because I know it will be fine.

And I'm sure, too, that Nikolai is training apprentices of his own. Gaining more power of his own. He's out there, in his family's estates.

His influence is growing, I've seen his influence in the unrest about weavers in the countryside.

And we can't be caught unaware again.

But just now, it's not an enemy who's stepped up beside me.

Just Valtair—well, Prime Minister Valtair, with the enamel gold and emerald seal of office settled over his heart. His eyelids are shimmering with green in his handsome, clean-shaven brown face, his dreadlocks tied back in a thick tail today.

"Gods, Caleb, what happened? What did you do to traumatize your weavers?"

Valtair is one of the truest friends I've ever known.

I would step in front of a sword for him.

I would face Nikolai again right here, just for him.

I know he would for me.

And he can also be an ass. And right now—right now I'm not in the mood.

But he sees it, because that's also Valtair. His demeanor shifts. His voice lowers.

"What happened?" he asks again.

I shake my head and watch as both Kian and Sabella help Aria up.

"One of their weavings unraveled. I had to fix it."

"Ah, so that was the fiery butterfly. I'd wondered if you were going to try that at the Festival, and I was going to warn you that some of the nobles might take objection to sparks falling in their food."

I glare at him, and he shrugs.

Then touches my arm.

"Torovan's asking that you attend Council today. Both of us, and I know it's an off day with the Festival starting, but we have more news from the border." He glances around us. And that's all he's going to say here in this crowd.

Heat spikes in my stomach.

And, extremely unwanted, bile rises in my throat. My cheeks must twitch, because Valtair leans even closer.

"Caleb. Are you well? Do you need help on your way out?"

I breathe through the nausea. And keep glaring at him.

"Well enough."

I step back, putting distance between us. Giving myself more room.

"Aria, no harm was done," I say. "You did well. We'll go over what we're doing for the feast again when I get back to the common room."

"Can I do the main display?" Kian asks, bouncing on his toes.

Gods. Do I have time to deal with my apprentices' egos right now?

But then, egos are part of willpower, too.

Kian's eyes are sparkling with anticipation, and Aria won't even meet mine.

"Kian," Sabella scolds. Then turns to me. "We'll be in the mage's common room." She ducks a bow and begins to herd them all out. Thank the gods for Sabella, who's unofficially decided to mother it over the rest.

It has not been easy trying to marshal three very different people with different backgrounds and skillsets and personalities, all with blazingly strong views of themselves and their own wills.

I have maybe the tiniest bit more sympathy for my mother, who had to corral my own will for most of my life.

The tiniest.

I glance up at the empty air where I just unwove the unraveling illusion. But that's a mistake—the crowd gathered around us follows my gaze.

So I put on my court smile again, swallowing hard against the bile still simmering in my throat before I say to the people around me, "If you attend the feast tonight, you'll witness a demonstration to remember."

Gods. But that's probably what they're afraid of, too.

I feel the mood in the Great Hall changing. What was beautiful and wondrous a few minutes before has now turned the crowd wary—they know the dangers of a weaver who can't control their own magic, too. They know that too well, and know what it ultimately led to, with Nikolai.

Nikolai might have fled to his family's estate, with help

from his supporters, and much of the kingdom's opinion might be against him.

A weaver who can control minds? A weaver who can create the illusion of someone else within a person, until that illusion overrides that person's will.

Those are the weavers of nightmare, of old legends, and they're not the heroes.

And I worry—I worry that people are beginning to forget there's a difference.

I shrug my shoulders in my coat, straightening as I turn to Valtair.

He raises his brows and waves to the doors. "Ready?"

I fall into step beside him.

Yes, it rattled me that Aria lost control of her magic. Because that means I haven't taught her well enough.

And while the people's opinions of me are generally good, their opinions of weavers in general have been growing... troubling.

I miss a step and have to pause as my stomach surges again.

Shit. The worst of the morning sickness eased a month ago, but my stomach has still not settled. My body certainly hasn't settled to carrying another raging ball of potential reality and possibilities within me, and I'm always aware of it. Always. It's slowly becoming more and more real.

"I can tell Tor you're sick," Valtair says, looping his arm in mine. Some of the dignitaries not familiar to the court might remark about the husband of the king walking arm in arm with the court's most notorious rake, even if he's been trying to reform that image now that he's the Prime Minister.

But, the Barellan court knows we're only friends.

I haven't told anyone but Torovan, his sister Elsira, and Valtair that I'm pregnant.

Valtair looks troubled, and I wonder if he's thinking about trying to sense the growing child with his elemental magic—but he's the Prime Minister of Barella. If it was forbidden for him to have elemental magic before as a high noble, it would be a disaster for the court to discover it now.

And I pull my mouth tight. Because I got my happy ending. I got Torovan, I got to be fully myself, I got to love him as his king and his queen.

I got to be a court mage as both a man and a woman, a master mage, and I'm teaching more weavers to weave the threads of reality, too. To protect Barella. To ultimately surpass me, because that's the hope of any teacher, isn't it?

I got all of that.

But every elementalist born to a high family still has to hide.

In the corridor outside the Great Hall, Valtair checks my face again, then lets go of my arm and tugs on the ends of his waistcoat, touches the Prime Minister's seal resting over his heart.

"All of this is bullshit," he says beneath his breath.

Torovan was absolutely right in choosing him to be the Prime Minister. He's good at it. He's patient, he listens, he doesn't dismiss things out of hand.

That doesn't mean Valtair likes the responsibility.

"It's necessary bullshit," I say, clapping his shoulder before I step past him and keep walking toward the Council chamber.

I hear his deep sigh as he catches up.

CHAPTER 3

───────

THE COUNCIL CHAMBER

TOROVAN

I have to fight to keep my hands from fidgeting as I enter the Council chamber. Sunlight shines in from the windows lining the dome overhead, showing a still mostly empty semicircle of tables and chairs around the lectern at the front dais. And behind the tables are the chairs where the general audience would sit.

There is no audience today—I only called for the Council members. Which is happening more often of late, and I don't like that. But I don't want panic from the public on the first eve of the Harvest Festival, either.

Where once I'd been hesitant to claim my place at the center of my kingdom, I stride without hesitation to the lectern now, gripping its sides, ignoring the curious or guardedly annoyed looks from the Council members as they filter in.

They're not happy that I've interrupted their Festival break. But the wiser souls among them don't show it.

Lord Navirat, who I was speaking to earlier, enters and gives me a grim nod, his black mustache twitching. He doesn't take his place at his habitual table, but stands with his arms folded near the edge of the dais. He knows he'll be giving a report.

I watch the doors for Valtair and for Caleb, trying to staunch my impatience.

Caleb is not fond of Council meetings, though I can't say that I am, either. But they're necessary. And my father's work—my work now, to give more power back to the people—is working.

If slowly.

In fits and starts.

And going vastly backwards some days.

Not a week ago, I stood here and argued for hours to build a university on the border between two of my kingdom's districts, and representatives of the commoners from one of those districts argued back that they didn't want it.

That district holds some of Nikolai's father's lands.

I am not willing to see that as a coincidence.

Caleb enters like he's on a mission, and on his heels Valtair calls, "I have a brunch with a lovely man from Cardalan in an hour, and I'd hate to miss it."

But if he's trying to make light of his tension, of the unease in the room, no one is buying it. Least of all Valtair himself.

Everyone knows I wouldn't call a meeting today if it wasn't urgent.

And Valtair's flippant delivery falls short, too, with the pendant of office he wears. He's been trying hard *not* to be seen as the court rake, and a slip now betrays his nerves, too.

I catch Caleb's eye and almost expect him to roll his eyes, his own break of tension, but he doesn't.

Which makes the moment seem all the more potent.

Valtair and Caleb don't know about the letters, and even still they're on edge.

But then, even though the atmosphere of the palace is festive, we all know there's more going on than that.

Valtair approaches me at the lectern and lowers his voice, all humor gone. "Tor, what's the crisis?"

"We're about to find out." I glance at Lord Navirat and feel a twinge of guilt for not truly listening to him earlier, Caleb holding my more urgent attention.

But Caleb always holds my attention, in danger or not.

And Lord Navirat's information is urgent, too.

I have the worming feeling in my gut it might be just as dangerous to the kingdom. If not to my own heart.

My hands curl around the sides of the lectern.

"We'll start soon," I say to Valtair, and he nods, descending the few steps to the floor to take his place at the tables.

And it's taking all my willpower not to run back to the room where I hid the letters and look at them again, look for some way to defuse whatever traps are in them. To see if there are any traps at all. To see how bad the danger is.

To tell Caleb about the letters, because he's the only one who might have a chance at unraveling their traps.

I swallow.

Caleb sits at our table in the front row, beside where I usually sit when I'm not at the lectern. Valtair takes his place one table over—a slight formal distancing here so that he's seen as the head of the Council and not just under my command.

He does now have the authority to oppose me with a Council vote. I made sure of that, when I chose him to be Barella's Prime Minister. The Council wasn't fond of my choice, but they did like the idea of having more say in the decisions of the kingdom.

And since Valtair took office four months ago, the complaints about handing over a large portion of the government to a court rake have mostly disappeared.

He's *good* at what he does. He helped me manage the kingdom when I was lost in my fog of grief, and he's doing it officially now.

Caleb folds his hands together on the table, soft wisps of hair falling loose around the fine angles of his face, bright in the morning sunlight.

His brows are drawn in a concentration I'm growing to hate, a concentration to keep his stomach settled.

My own gut tightens in sympathy.

I desperately wish for all the months between now and when he has our child to be quick. I don't like to see my husband in pain.

And I want to meet our child. But that's yet on the horizon, and right now—right now Caleb sees my grimace and sits back, doing his best to smooth out his features and appear less queasy.

Lately, we've met more across a distance than we have been together. We've been busy.

But.

I glance around and decide this is as many Council members as we're likely to have, with many preoccupied with dressing for the night, or in the nearby town to make last-minute purchases, whatever their needs—wait, I see Master Aldric hurrying in, carrying his staff rather than using it, a notebook tucked under one arm.

All right.

"I was given urgent news this morning," I say to the scattered double handful who came, "and I wish the Council to hear it."

I nod to Lord Navirat, and he approaches the lectern, bows to me.

"I brought this news to you first, Your Majesty," Lord Navirat says.

Further guilt twinges. But I hold my face impassive as I step back from the lectern.

"Then, Lord Navirat, if you will."

He bows again, and I descend to the main floor to take my place beside Caleb.

Caleb glances to me as I smooth down my coat and sit, then reaches for my hand beneath the table.

I give mine back, and he squeezes. The tightness of his grip is the measure of his discomfort right now, and I ache with it.

I stroke his thumb with mine and relax a little at his soft sigh. Then turn my hand so I can interweave my fingers with his.

Valtair, at his own table, isn't making any of the usual disarming gestures he uses to keep people off balance and underestimating him. He does still do that.

But just now, he's focused and alert.

His eyes meet mine, and his gaze is troubled.

"I had word not an hour ago," Lord Navirat says, leaning against the lectern as his lips twitch with nerves. "A weaver has gone missing at the border to Akreal."

CHAPTER 4

THE BORDER

TOROVAN

"As I was telling Your Majesty," Lord Navirat says, "we've heard the rumors about the unease around weavers near the border to Akreal. I've asked the merchants I work with to send news of any more unrest in the area, and a merchant convoy that just arrived for the Festival brought word. It's a secondhand report, but the merchant who came to me talked to a villager himself. A village weaver from the border village of Iren went missing three days ago. One Gardellan Mar, seventeen years of age—"

Beside me, Caleb stiffens. His hand clenches mine.

"He's not even as old as Kian," he says under his breath.

His apprentice.

We share a look.

Because the world looks a little different when you have a child on the way.

Lord Navirat pauses, waiting for if Caleb wishes to speak.

Caleb tilts his chin up. "Is the weaver dead? And was it the villagers who hurt him, or the Akreans?"

Lord Navirat waves a jeweled hand in a fending off motion. He looks to me, back to Caleb.

"We don't know, Your Majesty. The merchant also said he heard there's another man missing from a neighboring village, an older man this time, but that report is less sure. But the rumor is that other missing man is also a weaver, though the merchant thought that might be speculation or accusation. Which itself is troubling. The first young man was confirmed to be a weaver, but the second, if it's true, we don't know."

There's a murmur of unease from behind us, from the tables around us.

My jaw tenses, and my knee wants to start bouncing again. I keep it still.

"And more," Lord Navirat goes on, "the young weaver's hut was heavily ransacked, but no one in the village seems to know who did it. And there have been frequent sightings of Akrean soldiers crossing the border in small groups, maybe testing how permeable our borders are. These villages are between our own border garrisons, we don't have a strong presence there."

We haven't needed to. But I denied a request for more troops two months ago because I didn't want to escalate the tensions with Akreal.

If I'd sent more troops to the border then, would these missing villagers still be missing?

"So I respectfully suggest, Your Majesties, that we send a full troop to the border to investigate," Lord Navirat says. "We know the Akrean opinion of weavers of late, or at least suspect it." And the Council knows my suspicions that Akreal is the kingdom where my mother fled, though we still don't have any confirmation of that. Yet.

"If Akreal is in any way involved in kidnapping weavers from our kingdom—Your Majesties, those weavers are a valuable asset to our kingdom. As you both know and demonstrated in this very room."

He meets my eyes, just briefly.

And my stomach knots.

If this is an Akrean attack, it's not subtle. Is my mother done with being subtle?

And what about Nikolai?

Is Akreal taking weavers now so that Barella can less defend itself when Nikolai does decide to come for me again?

But these aren't weavers who are trained for war. They're a young man, and an older man who might not have been a weaver at all.

Whatever's going on is fear. And I don't know what direction that fear is coming from.

"Do the villagers themselves fear the weavers?" Caleb asks, his posture still rigid. "Is it as bad as we've heard?"

Lord Navirat shakes his head. "It's not good, I fear. The merchant said the villagers are glad the young weaver is gone. They aren't owning up to having done it themselves, but they were hostile to the idea of the weaver coming back. They would already have taken the weaver's home, the merchant said, if they weren't afraid of mind control traps—which makes the ransacking doubly suspicious."

"Was this young weaver a soul weaver, then?" calls a new voice from behind me, Lady Sima. I glance back to see her already in her Festival finery, her long braids wound up and held by gold and ruby pins. She was one of the Council members who Nikolai had under his control on that day we'd confronted him here in the Council chamber.

And I remember the feeling of being outside of myself all too well. Of *wanting* to carry out his will, not mine.

I don't ever want to feel that way again.

"I don't know," Lord Navirat says, which isn't the answer I want to hear. "The merchant didn't say there were any signs, but then, are there always signs?"

He looks to Caleb, and Caleb's mouth is a grim line.

"No," he says. "Though I'm always looking."

The tension in the room shifts from unease to an acrid tang of fear.

"We'll send a troop," I say, keeping my voice calm. Pulling my hand from Caleb's to place both of my palms flat on the table.

"Perhaps even two," Lord Navirat says cautiously. "If Akrean troops are crossing the border, we might encounter them—"

"Done," I say. If I wanted to avoid escalation with Akreal before, they're not trying to avoid it now.

And is it coincidence that this is happening now, while the Harvest Festival is about to start?

While Nikolai's letters have been burning my soul every morning for the last three days?

Valtair taps his table. "Any troop we send should include a weaver." He looks sideways at me. "But not you, Torovan. Or Caleb. Respectfully."

"No," I agree.

"I will go," Master Aldric says, sitting back where he sits several tables to my right around the circle. His thinning gray hair is bound back in his usual braid today, his jaw set. He's abandoned some of his grandfatherly persona in the last few months and now just looks...haggard.

The chamber quiets.

Aldric nods to me, magnanimously respectful as always. "I don't see any other weaver qualified. Forgive me, Caleb, but your apprentices are not ready for any work outside these walls."

Or, unspoken in the air, within them.

I narrow my eyes at Aldric, who might give me his respect, and even his loyalty, but he's never been my ally. Is he suggesting Caleb is incompetent as a teacher?

But then, Aldric has *nothing* to say about that, with how he taught me.

Caleb opens his mouth to protest, then closes it.

No one here thinks the apprentices are ready.

Master Aldric going to the border is probably a good idea. Aldric is one of the most educated weavers in the kingdom. He knows what the dark threads of soul weaving look like, and he would be an asset.

But...he *is* one of the most educated weavers, and I have three letters now that I can't show to the most powerful weaver in the kingdom.

Gods. I can't let Aldric go. What if this is a distraction meant to split our weavers apart? Meant to pull my resources away from me when I need them here?

And *do* I need them here? Exactly where is the threat?

What if Aldric leaving means I lose Caleb?

What if Aldric staying means I lose the border? Lose the trust of the people, my enemies eroding at the edges of my kingdom?

But...Caleb.

"No," I say, a little too sharply.

Caleb turns to me, frowning. He adjusts his spectacles.

Aldric blinks, the picture of courtesy, though I can tell he's annoyed. "Your Majesty?"

"No," I repeat. More firmly this time. "You're most needed here. The Festival influx is already straining the palace's resources. I can't spare you."

That's not a lie, technically, but it's not enough truth to be an actual reason.

But Aldric slowly lowers himself back into his seat, the tips of his fingers steepled.

"We'll send a master elementalist instead," I say. "If weavers are the ones in danger, we shouldn't send another. Master Getran, I believe, has commanded troops in the field before."

Master Getran, a man close to Aldric's age who wields fire, isn't in Council today.

Valtair considers me, nods. "I'll ask him, and make sure it's done." He makes a note in his own notebook, slipped from his jacket pocket. "Torovan, we shouldn't keep in session longer than necessary, and I don't believe we have further information to add to this? Most of us have Festival preparations to attend to."

And he has his lunch date. Though I doubt he has much of an appetite now. I know I do not.

And Valtair's bringing things back to the mundane. Because this *is* supposed to be a time of celebration, even if the Harvest Festival's always been a place of political tension, too.

I hesitate a moment, though I know they're all waiting for me to dismiss the Council.

If weavers on the border are in danger, should I issue a call for weavers in that district to come to the palace? Should I call in weavers kingdom-wide, should we train them, should we prepare for...whatever will come?

Are the rising threats enough for me to justify that?

But weavers descending on the palace would be a sure sign of either fear or aggression on Barella's part. Maybe that's what my mother or Nikolai are hoping to provoke. A reason to move their own plans forward.

Caleb's still watching me, troubled.

I meet his eyes and rise.

"Yes, we've finished. Do we have more business for the Council?"

I'm already standing, and so are most of the other Council members. If anyone wants to raise more issues now, they won't be well-loved for it.

"I want a more thorough report of what is happening at the Akreal border," Lady Sima says, smoothing down her orange and red gown. "Lord Valtair, can you task Master Getran and the commander of the troops with seeing that happens?"

"Yes, I will. And there will be a delegation from Akreal arriving later today, I believe." Valtair looks sideways at me. "We should all keep our own watch throughout the Festival."

"That I can do," Master Aldric says.

"Good." I hold out my arm and Caleb rises too, his face taking on that queasy cast again. "I will see you all at the Festival this evening."

Chairs that haven't scraped before do now. Hands slide papers and notebooks into cases.

Only Valtair casts a final glance my way, the tilt of his head saying he knows something is going on with me, something I haven't told him.

Should I tell him?

But what if there's the smallest chance that the "him" in that letters could mean Valtair, too?

I know it doesn't. But that might not stop Nikolai from using it as an excuse.

That might not stop a trap, if there is a trap, from triggering if anyone else opens it but me.

Am I overthinking this?

Am I foolish to heed this threat at all, was it just meant to get into my head?

I look to Caleb as we make our way toward the doors, but Lady Sima approaches on my other side.

"Your Majesty, may I have a word about the university project? I know this is the first day of Festival, but I heard from my people that a spiked fence went up one night around the land where we hope to build. It's easily taken down, but not without losing the will of the people from that district."

Gods.

Why would my people try to fight against the power I wish to give them?

Are they all under Nikolai's control?

Or am I failing at what I set out to do, on the eve of my first Harvest Festival as their king?

Caleb's frowning. "I want to see that fence. And I want to see the people who built it. I could tell if this is Nikolai's influence. Can you have one of them brought here?"

But Lady Sima's already shaking her head. "No, and Torovan, you know we can't arrest the common people for doing no more than saying no to help."

Well, we could, but that wouldn't win the good will of the people.

And no one was suggesting Caleb go there himself. Or me. That was too close to Nikolai's influence.

I still my restless need to move. This is important, it is.

But not as important at the moment as making sure the Harvest Festival is successful. So many of the alliances for the next year will be brokered at this Festival. So much of the mood of the kingdom will be set.

And this will be the time that many of my subjects, and many of our neighboring kingdoms, see me as the king. And Caleb as my king, too, or queen when he's Irava.

Yes, the Barellan court has accepted him readily—accepted him and her—but we will be dealing with other nations tonight and the rest of this week. We may be dealing with people tainted by the opinions of Nikolai's family. And their own traditions.

And do I dare give Nikolai's family even that small bit more of a foothold in the university project, even on this Festival day?

I lean toward Caleb. "I'll meet you in our chambers before the feast."

He licks his lips, something that draws all of my attention for that singular moment. And I know he didn't mean to do that, but he sees it, his lips twisting up in half a grin, half a grimace.

"Tonight," he says, brushing my cheek before he pulls back. And because he knows I'm worried, he adds, "I'll keep my own watch for trouble."

Or maybe he thinks it's still his duty to protect me, not be the one protected.

But he strides off after Valtair in a swirl of his knee-length coat, and I'm not about to call after him and correct that assumption, though I want to. Oh, I want to.

I watch to make sure his guards follow him out before I turn back to Lady Sima.

CHAPTER 5

ILLUSIONS

CALEB/IRAVA

I storm out into the corridor behind Valtair, fire churning in my soul.

Nikolai's reach keeps haunting us.

I thought we'd won that day in the Council Chamber, when we gave Master Aldric our combined wills, and he made sure Nikolai was subdued.

I thought the danger had ended when Torovan arrested his mother.

And even when she escaped, and when Nikolai's family's influence was too great for Torovan to hold him, too, I thought that distance would matter.

I thought my love for Torovan, and his love for me, would be enough to hold a kingdom together.

But now, on this first day of the Harvest Festival, Nikolai's reaching across the distance from his family's estates to our palace. Lady Sima's news might not point directly to him, but why else would the common people refuse the help that Torovan wants to give?

And Torovan's mother's reach, too, if he's right, and she's behind the reason behind Akreal crossing the border into Barella, and maybe kidnapping weavers. Torovan said Akreal wasn't friendly before, but they weren't hostile, either.

And everywhere I look there seems to be a rising fear.

Of us. Weavers, like Torovan and me.

That fear shouldn't be spreading. Nikolai's soul weaving was defeated. We won.

We *won*.

But Nikolai's still out there.

And Torovan's right, he has to deal with this. He has to deal the only way he can—as the king. And that means talking with Lady Sima, even though I wanted a stolen moment, just a moment after what happened with Aria's weaving earlier to ground myself in his nearness, to reassure myself, because I'm off balance today.

And I can't be. I can't be anything less than perfect tonight as his king.

And when my mother arrives.

I catch up with Valtair and lower my voice. "What is up with Tor the last few days?"

"What do you mean, what is up with Tor?" he asks, though I know he's seen it, too. I saw the look Valtair gave him when he said—emphatically—that Master Aldric shouldn't go to the border.

It wasn't his dislike of Aldric, or, I think, his fear for Aldric's safety. And I don't buy his excuse that Aldric's needed desperately here.

It makes sense on the surface, but that's not why he said it.

"He's worried," Valtair says. "He's anxious about the Festival—it's a big deal, you know, you haven't been to one yet.

It's the biggest feast of the Barellan year, I think equivalent to your new year's celebration in Galenda? A lot is depending on it going well. A lot of good will toward Barella, and from the nobles to Torovan—and you—is dependent on how this Festival goes."

Which is nothing I don't know. And a whole lot of words to cover Valtair's own anxieties.

I bite my lip and straighten my spectacles.

I know Torovan's nervous, I do. But I know what he's like when he's nervous.

And this is more than just that.

And even though what's happening with Akreal and the weavers at the border is not good, he was anxious before then.

Maybe I thought it was just the Festival, too. But I'm not thinking that now.

And I'm worried about him. What is he carrying that he thinks he's protecting me from?

I slow and grimace. I'm feeling the tug toward being Irava right now, and I'm in a public corridor. I can't drop my illusion as Caleb and reweave my illusion as Irava—not if I don't want people to see my pregnancy.

"Valtair, I need to change my illusion."

He looks around us, then heads to a nearby alcove with a statue set into it.

I raise my brows, but shrug. There's just enough room behind the statue for me to slip behind it, and Valtair positions himself in front of the alcove, crossing his arms.

I slip behind, my sleeve brushing the leg of the green marble goddess, and quickly unweave my illusion as Caleb. I'm wearing the same clothes, though with my illusion, I'd made them look filled out in different ways.

My growing belly, now, is the first thing I see, and I briefly wrap my hand around it. Letting myself fully feel the growing possibility inside me that's always in my awareness. My lips twitch, briefly, into a smile.

Then I weave another illusion of myself—this time myself as Irava.

But myself *without* my rounded stomach. Without the slight puffiness to my face, without the tired rings beneath my eyes.

I straighten the gray knee-length coat with its gold embroidery, one of my favorites. Now it appears to fit slimmer and more tailored around my waist—at least, in my illusion. It'll be fine as long as no one actually touches or brushes against my stomach, because they'd touch something solid before they reached what looked like the edge of my coat.

I've been careful since my pregnancy started showing that no one touches me, though. No one who doesn't know, at least. I've learned how to turn myself away from any potential danger.

It wasn't Torovan's idea to hide this, but mine. I know our enemies are out there. I know their influence is growing, even before this news today. And I'm still determined to find a way to reweave my reality as Caleb around this growing child inside me, to be able to bring all of my powers and attention as a weaver to bear. While I'm always maintaining an illusion, my attention will always be partly on that.

I learned that during the storm, when using all of myself stripped my illusion away.

But I haven't yet found a method of reweaving myself as Caleb that I think is safe.

There just haven't been that many pregnant weavers, and so very few women weavers written about at all.

No one, that I can tell, who moved between different genders in their realities.

If I can find enough time and patience, I want to fix that, to write something of my own. But not yet.

I haven't stopped looking, though. And though the stacks of books for me to read through has dwindled, I haven't given up hope.

When I show I'm with child, I want it to be fully as myself, as Irava and as Caleb. I want that.

I need that.

"I'm done," I say, and Valtair looks back, sees me, and steps aside to let me back into the corridor.

His eyes go to my stomach, which is annoying. I've let him, with his small elemental healing talent, check the sense of the growing child twice.

But I can feel the growing possibility on my own. I would know if something was wrong, and it's fine. Beyond the queasiness that still hasn't left me, it's fine.

I push my spectacles up on my nose and head off again.

"Your mother's coming tonight, right?" Valtair asks.

I shoot him a glare. That's his idea of small talk?

Then I slow again. I don't even know where we're going. I was headed to the mage quarters—and yes, we're headed that way, the corridor growing more crowded around us as we near the Great Hall again.

"Yes."

I'm trying not to think about it.

Maybe it did bother me more than I'd thought seeing Aria's weaving unraveling in the Great Hall today—it was far too close to that first day in the palace, when I had to save Nikolai. Not that I can compare her to Nikolai at all. At *all.* Aria's nothing at all like him. But it rattled me all the same.

And maybe it bothers me a lot that Torovan is upset about something he's not telling me about.

And it terrifies me that our enemies are successfully turning some of the peoples' minds against us.

Against Torovan and me.

But right now, the thought that makes my hands go clammy and my heart pound in my throat...is my mother.

She knows I'm both Caleb and Irava. I did tell her that, in a letter after we married.

She wrote back, very polite, and addressed the letter to Irava and Caleb. But I know my mother. I know how she likes the people around her to be who she wants them to be. She's a queen, and she likes to rule in her own household, too.

I know she wasn't happy that we moved up the wedding, and she couldn't attend.

I fear she won't be happy about a lot of things.

"Well, my father is coming, too," Valtair says with a grimace. "He wrote a letter about how pleased he was that I'm now *actually* one of the most powerful people in the kingdom and not just steering Torovan around."

I make a face. "Oh gods. He said that?"

"Not in as many words, no, but I know what he's thinking. You've met my father. He is delightful, you know."

I have met Count Valtair, the former Minister of Finance, which was one of the highest positions in the kingdom before Torovan formed the position of Prime Minister a few months ago. While Lord Valtair takes after his father in his handsome features and natural grace, the count is aloof, and far too obsessed with things being done the way he thinks they should be.

Valtair's father, too, likes to rule his own household.

I softly tap my fist on Valtair's arm. "We check in every day. If one of us needs to explode, we explode."

He nudges me back. "Deal. I'm going to have to explode at least twice. A day. My father's here all week, just like your mother. No, maybe three times a day. We should just schedule it in now."

I snort. "Are you walking me back to the mage quarters now? Are you going to help me convince my apprentices they're ready to demonstrate their illusions tonight?"

"Hmm, well, do you think one of them should sit out? What with...the difficulties we've been having at the border?"

"No," I say firmly. "The people need to see what weavers can do, that it's accessible—"

"But they saw a weaver nearly lose control today." He looks around as someone passes nearby, then signals to our guards to form a wider perimeter around us.

"Most of them will have only seen a butterfly," I say stubbornly. "There were only a handful of people actually watching us."

"It was more than that."

"Valtair—it will be fine."

He lowers his voice as we pass out of the main corridor and into the relative calm of the passage leading to the mage's quarters, the common room, and my study.

"Irava, I'm concerned that if there's another incident at the feast tonight, especially with the delegates from Akreal there, there might be...trouble."

I touch the master weaver's medallion over my heart, rubbing the edges through my fingertips.

"I'll have illusions ready," I say. "If something starts to go wrong, I'll take the weaves and weave my own illusions around them, make it look like nothing is happening."

"That sounds too risky to me," he says beneath his breath. And gives me a pointed look. "If you drop your own illusion, it might be less so."

I speed up my steps. "You know my reasons. You know that's my choice, and Torovan's."

He shrugs, but it's stiffly. And I know he cares—I know he wouldn't be pushing if he didn't care.

"Please let it go. I'm fine. I'll—I'll figure out how to do that after the Festival, all right? I don't want to distract from the Harvest Festival—"

"Gods, Irava, that would hardly be a distraction, or at least it would be an excellent distraction. Maybe we all *need* that distraction. Some very good news."

"And you really think it's a good idea to tell the court now, with what we just heard?"

To give our enemies more leverage over us.

He opens his hands. "Okay, maybe, point. But—"

"After," I say.

But I don't say when after.

I'll figure out, somehow, how to reweave my reality as Caleb after. I *know* I will. I have to.

And Valtair knows, doesn't he, that I'm the master weaver I am because of my stubbornness and willpower?

He sighs dramatically, but nods. "After. I'll see you at dinner tonight. And let us hope both of our parents are late, and we can get in a decent meal before we have to face that...

that…" He waves for words that aren't coming. Because the polite ones won't do.

I grip his hand, briefly. If Torovan and I are worried about how the Festival will go, I know he's worried, too.

"Agreed," I say, before we part at the entrance to the mages' common room.

Chapter 6

Apprentices

Irava

I really don't feel like uplifting the willpower and egos of my three apprentices just now, not with the worry gnawing in my gut, pushing at the already queasy feeling.

But we have to make this show at the Harvest Festival tonight, we have to show our allies—and our enemies—that weavers are just people. That we can do amazing things, that we aren't the corrupted weavers like Nikolai wants everyone to believe we are.

Am I fighting the wind?

In the mage's common room, Aria is standing with her back braced, arms up and poised, threads of reality flowing gracefully around her. Even her magic is graceful.

Sabella watches like a spotter for a tumbler, but though Sabella has formidable willpower and control, she hasn't yet been able to harness that into raw power.

Aria has the power, but she can't seem to contain it with her will.

And Kian is watching sullenly, leaning against a table, while one of the elementalist court mages reads by the hearth. The elementalist only barely looks up when I stride in.

"Good, Aria, good," I say. "Hold that, and you will do excellent tonight."

She looks up, and I twitch as her control on her weaving starts to falter. But she furrows her brow in concentration and her weaving steadies. It's still not the towering tree she'll make tonight, but more compact for this lower space.

Her concentration slowly turns to a grin, which she flashes at me as I watch.

She never grins at me that openly when I'm Caleb.

Torovan and Elsira and Valtair don't seem to care, don't treat me any differently between the two halves of myself. But I have sometimes seen others' reactions shifting. Taking me more seriously when I'm a man. Or, like Aria, being less intimidated when I'm a woman.

I'm already tense for the day and try to shrug it off, stepping closer as Aria, more confident now, continues her illusion.

And it's good. It's very good, the tree branching out to roll across the ceiling, giving the illusion in the moment that there is no ceiling, that there's a sky overhead, the sunlight casting onto Aria's upturned face.

"We'll need stars tonight," I say softly.

And Aria hums, flicking her fingers to pluck the threads of reality into a glittering starry sky.

I stare up, for a moment arrested.

Because I know my own power, and by now I know Torovan's too—his own weaving more direct, more practical than mine. But Aria's is as graceful as she is herself.

"Beautiful," I whisper.

She turns to me, and her grin widens, and now her weaving does start to fall apart.

"Aria—"

She catches it, though, but the fumble is clumsy, and it takes a nervous minute until the threads are all under her control again.

The night sky has turned into a glittering fall of stars all around us, the tree's branches unraveling into ribbons of bark.

I reach up and gently tug some of the illusions away from her as she struggles to unweave what she can.

Sabella's face is pinched. "Irava," she says slowly, and it always sounds like she's saying my name with hesitation. Like she doesn't deserve to say it. And I hate that.

"Maybe we should do something simpler?" she says. "Like, imaginary fireworks? Or, a flock of birds. Or, like the butterfly."

Aria cringes, finally dropping her arms as reality flows back into the way it had been before she started weaving. "I'm sorry. Irava, I'm sorry, I've been practicing, hours a day—"

"I know," I say. "And you've been doing so well. No..." I pass a hand across my forehead and feel the sweat I'm not letting show through my illusion. "No, I'm sorry, this is too soon. I pushed you all to do this too soon."

I've been teaching them for months. But it took me years to learn to be a competent weaver.

And maybe Valtair is right, maybe a display of weaving now isn't the best idea. Not with what's happening at the border to Akreal.

"No," Kian says, launching himself away from the table he'd been leaning against. "No, Irava, we've been practicing—"

I hold up my hands. "I'm not saying no, I'm not."

And I know this public display is important to them, maybe as important as the mage demonstrations had ultimately been to me.

For them, this is a chance to show their progress. And yes, a chance to show that weavers can make beautiful things. And not just do the destruction that Nikolai wrought.

That is important, yes.

And, Master Aldric said to me when he brought up the idea a few weeks ago, having this reward of public approval will go far to keep their loyalties with me.

I hate that he thinks about people like that, as pawns on his board, but I don't think he's wrong.

Not with seeing the crease in Torovan's brow.

Having loyal weavers right now is a very good thing.

But that only works if nothing gets out of hand.

"So—so yes, we'll simplify a little, for now. And work on practicing our full demonstration for the last day of the feast. Yes, I think that will work, I'll tell Valtair. Tonight—let's show a display of, yes, fireworks. We can all make fireworks."

That was one of the first things that they'd all taught themselves—Aria first, then Sabella reluctantly before she took to it, and then Kian as soon as he'd barreled into my training. I'd only had Kian for the last two months, though he was already near Aria's level with his illusions.

And fireworks were always a hit. We'd had a few demonstrations for the stable hands at night, nothing formal, nothing big enough to draw attention, very close overhead. But, high enough that the ceiling of the Great Hall should do fine as a backdrop.

And I can make the ceiling glitter with stars while they all launch their fireworks—yes. Yes, that will work. And be enough of a spectacle that no one will be concentrating too hard on the weavers making the illusions.

And Aria can handle fireworks just fine.

Aria is biting her lip, but at my look, she draws herself up and nods. And opens her hand to shoot a tiny blue and white umbrella of sparks into the air.

"Like that," I say. "Yes. All right, let's practice how we want this to go. Aria, if you can handle the blooms in the center of the hall, Kian toward the high table, and Sabella toward the far end."

We move around the smaller space, with me staying nearer Aria—and I know she knows why I'm staying near, but she doesn't protest.

And we get to planning out a fireworks show.

After a minor mishap with Aria's and Kian's weavings colliding—in which the elementalist closed his book and made a hasty retreat from the common room—I stand back and watch them run through it again, holding my own illusion of the night sky with little effort.

But my illusion falters when I feel a sharp jab inside my stomach.

I catch the falter, I don't think Aria and Kian, focused as they are on their bright displays, even notice. But Sabella, between her weavings, does.

She turns, and I can't help my hand straying toward my stomach before I jerk it back to my side.

I only brushed the edge of where the illusion hides my stomach, but.

Sabella freezes, her eyes locked on me.

Gods. Gods, she can tell. She knows. That small mistake

was enough—I know she's putting together the nausea I've had sometimes, though I do my best to cover it.

She is a mother, her twelve-year-old son an apprentice to an apothecary in a nearby town. She takes a few days to visit him sometimes.

Slowly, Sabella pulls her gaze from me, but not before it dips once to my stomach.

I swallow.

And why do I suddenly feel cold that someone outside of the very few I've told knows now, too?

I told Valtair I would announce my pregnancy...at some point after the end of the Harvest Festival. I hadn't said soon.

And I trust Sabella. Of all of my apprentices, she is the most trustworthy, the oldest among them, responsible to a fault. I asked her to train with me, not the other way around.

Gods, I'm stressed. I know she won't tell anyone, that's not who she is.

This won't go beyond this room until I want it to.

But I feel like a piece of my armor has cracked. And my throat is tighter than I'd like.

The fireworks display ends, again, and I give my apprentices the praise they're due, because it was excellent. And I know it will go very well tonight.

But my anxiety for the day has already soured into a foreboding I can't name.

CHAPTER 7

———

MORE GUARDS

TOROVAN

It's two hours before the first feast of the Harvest Festival starts. In our bedroom, the waning light casts long shadows across the floor as I rifle through my wardrobe.

I already know what I'll wear the first night of the feast, it's been planned for over a month. But I'm still sifting through various coats and shirts and pants as if something new might appear.

Caleb sits on the edge of our bed, undoing the buttons of his coat with careful fingers. Which isn't like him. He usually has his coat off in seconds, tossed aside on the bed, waiting to be cleaned up by the staff later—not out of carelessness, but because he simply forgets.

I ache with everything in me to pause him with a touch, to run my hands through his hair, to tilt his chin up to me. Straighten his spectacles, or take them off altogether.

I will kill him if you tell him.

I curl my hands tight, force myself to release the tension

again, because I know Caleb will see it, and I can't have him asking questions.

I can't.

And I know the bounds of his body are different beneath his current illusion. I can't see the illusion, even with my weaver's senses, but I know it's there.

I love him no matter his body. All of his body, whatever body.

But it bothers him not being able to be fully himself when he's Caleb.

And gods, though I want this child, our child, with all that I am, though I'm excited for our child to see the world and grow with us, I wish—

I wish Caleb hadn't had to know pain in the making of this.

He looks up at me. I've stopped, and I'm staring down at him.

His look back is a little defiant, his shoulders tight, his jaw set.

I curl my fingers back into my hands.

"The Akrean delegation arrived an hour ago," I say, because it's within reach. "Valtair's getting them settled in the east wing. Which is where we're lodging most of the foreign delegates. Gods." I run a hand across my mouth, my own nerves spiking.

I need this Harvest Festival to go well. I need...I need there not to be danger in my home and among those I love.

Will I ever know a life without enemies?

But then, I'm a king.

And because of me, because he couldn't defeat me, Nikolai is threatening Caleb.

Caleb nods, shrugging the rest of the way out of his coat. "Any trouble so far?"

"Not yet." I finally pull the clothes I'm going to wear tonight from the wardrobe and hang them on the canopy of the bed. "I'm assigning you two more guards. I want you to keep them close—no dodging them in the corridors or using your illusions to slip away." I look at him askance. "I know you do that sometimes."

He smirks. We haven't talked about it, because until a few days ago, there hasn't been a need to. I know Caleb—and sometimes Valtair—take it upon themselves to be their own spymasters in my palace, too. It was how they discovered the truth about my mother.

Caleb stands and begins unbuttoning his shirt. And I have to look away, because we have to go to the feast soon. And I know he's not in the mood.

He's watching me intently, though. Not quite taunting. In a weird mood.

"I don't need more guards," he says. "I've saved your life three times, Torovan—I'm as much your guard as—"

I turn back, my temper heating. And because I'm tired, and because tonight is wearing on me, I let it.

"You stopped being any kind of guard when you married me, Caleb Braise. And when you—"

"When I started carrying our child? Is that it?"

"I was going to say when you assumed the duties of a master weaver—but yes, that too."

I know it's the wrong thing to say, I know it. His pregnancy has been a sore spot since shortly after it started.

And it had started off well enough. We had been so happy.

We'd spent moments lingering in the quiet places of the

garden. We'd spent hours tangled up in the sheets, just watching each other.

Caleb strides up to me, glaring up into my eyes. "I don't need a guard. I don't need *more* guards—the ones I have are fine, they trail me everywhere, that's all I need. And your guards are all over the palace anyway, and wherever you are. I can protect myself, Tor, and if you're afraid of the threats from the border—"

My shoulders twitch.

"I'm always afraid. Our enemies aren't giving up, they want to see us, to see me—and you, Caleb—hurt. They want my plans to fail. They want to condemn weavers. You know this. We just had the Council meeting—"

He steps back, and something I've been seeing more often, and liking less and less, descends over his face.

It's a wall.

It's a wall he's building between us, and I don't know how to scale it. I don't know why he feels the need to put it up.

"I love you," I say, spreading my hands. "I only want to protect you, because I love you."

He's shirtless now, still in his illusion, and turns to his own wardrobe to pull out a black silk undershirt, tugging it on in short, angry motions.

I step toward him, because I often help him dress. It's what we've been doing since we asked the servants not to dress us five months ago, after he became pregnant.

But I stop, because the lines of his body are tight with anger.

"Just two guards," I finally say. "Just two more. And only until the end of the Festival, because of the delegates from Akreal."

Not just because. But I can't tell him more than that.

"I'll assign Reveyan to you," I say into the stretching silence as he pulls on a dark green velvet coat embroidered in gold vines. "And Morgan. You like them both. They're highly attentive, should anything happen—"

"I don't need guards," he says again. "Torovan, it just shows our enemies that we're afraid of them. I'm not. We defeated Nikolai, we both did. The whole court knows about him, he's not going to take us on now. And you're much stronger as a weaver now, too. We're not in any danger from another weaver."

I don't think he actually believes that. I've seen his fear, too. It's part of why he hasn't wanted to show his pregnancy, I know that.

But gods, I know my husband has a formidable will. And just now, it's aimed at me.

"What about the Akrean delegates?" I insist.

"What are they going to do in your court? With all of your guards, with everyone here?" He struggles with a top button, and I twitch to help, but instead fold my hands in front of me.

"Can you get this one?" he asks with a huff.

And I cross quickly to him.

"That's my point," I say quietly. "The more guards you have around you, the less chances anyone will have. Even if those chances are small. Caleb, please—this will help me not to worry about you during this Festival. So I can concentrate on making it a good Festival, my first Harvest Festival."

He purses his lips, and his gaze softens a little. He grips my arm as I finish the last button.

"You'll do fine, Tor."

I straighten. "I know that."

I don't know. Maybe a few days ago this felt like something I could handle just fine. But with the letters sitting hidden in that meeting room? With how weavers are being treated at the border?

He presses a warm palm to my cheek. His eyes darting between mine.

I lay my hand over his. I don't ask him again, but I ask with my eyes.

My heart is pounding, and while I've been able to keep the fear of those letters aside for most of the last few hours, knowing that we'll be at the feast tonight, knowing so many of our allies and some of our enemies will be there, too, is like a fire inside me, scorching away any calm.

"Okay," he says finally. "Morgan and Reveyan. That's all."

I lean to kiss him, and he stretches up to kiss me back.

CHAPTER 8

CROWNS AND MEDALLIONS

CALEB

"And now you have to dress," I say, pulling back from Torovan, wetting my lips, tasting his taste. He had something with honey earlier, his lips are still sweet.

I move around him, because my body's already heating, and I can't deal with that right now. I can't deal with wanting him, and not being sure of my body, and being nervous about my apprentice's demonstration tonight. And nervous about my mother.

And now nervous about his insistence on more guards for me, because I feel like it's something more than what we learned today about the missing weaver at the border, though that's probably bad enough.

But I do know it's more, and that he's keeping something from me. Torovan is not the best liar in the world, and I *know* him.

He thinks he's protecting me from something.

So, okay. Maybe I go along with this. Morgan and Reveyan are fine.

Though I wonder at his choice of Morgan. Morgan is an excellent guard, yes. But Torovan told me months ago that he had a man among his guards who'd also been born a woman. He's never said who, that's not who he is. But I know it's Morgan. I know.

Does that mean anything with his overprotectiveness just now?

He skims out of his coat and trousers, undressing to his underwear in a quick shucking off of the old, preparing for the new.

I grab his trousers from where they hang with his coat and shirt, but he takes them from me, his smile tugging up.

"We have limited time," he says.

And I heat again, gods, and have to squeeze my hands together to keep from reaching for him as he dresses.

He watches me, his own eyes hooded as he carefully and deliberately does up the buttons on his cream silk shirt. He doesn't get anything stuck.

Then tugs on his deep burgundy coat with its knee-length panels and gold and diamond trim.

I move to the stand beside his wardrobe and retrieve his heavier ceremonial crown. A band of gold with rubies and sapphires inset around diamond clusters, fine gold sunbursts ringing all sides in a perfect symmetry.

I hold it up and he ducks his head as I carefully settle in on his hair.

His black hair is pulled back and secured with a gold clasp, a little mussed from the day, but I'm not going to tell him to fix it. Those loose strands framing his face are *entirely* the point.

He grimaces and adjusts the crown. "Gods of the harvest, this is heavy. It will dig in all night."

"You said you wanted your ceremonial crown for the Harvest Festival."

"This night at least," he sighs. "I did."

Then he reaches and plucks one of the two crowns sitting on black suede forms beside my own wardrobe. Not as ornate as his, no. One meant for a queen, more delicate gold and emeralds. The other, the one he takes now, with a thicker band, set with rubies like his crown now.

He carefully places it on my head. And it digs, too, I know it will dig all night.

But it's a crown made for a king, made specifically for me. And the weight of it, the meaning of it, settles the part of my soul that's been jittery about my illusion of Caleb these last days. More jittery than usual.

Torovan winds his fingers into mine, facing me.

"You look amazing," he says, his eyes roaming over me.

He reaches to the bed and grabs my master mage's medallion, and then his own mage's medallion. He loops mine over my head, then carefully navigates his own over the crown and settles it over his heart.

As I settle mine.

We're both weavers. We're both mages, and visibly so. And I know that visibility has been making some of the courtiers more uneasy lately, too.

Even if they know the history, even if they know that we're weavers, not elementalists—for royalty to be an elementalist, in many's eyes, would be unthinkable.

It's why even Valtair hides his elemental talent. And I know he's not the only high noble who does this.

Weaving is learned, not something you're born with. It's forged with willpower and determination and strength, and it's dangerous for anyone to learn. Let alone someone who grew up a princess. And someone who is sometimes a king.

But that's not why they fear us now.

I squeeze his hands. "Everything will go fine tonight."

Because it has to.

He squeezes my hands back.

"Your seeing your mother will go fine, too."

He doesn't know that. Oh, he can't promise that.

But I nod anyway, letting out a sigh.

It's the first Harvest, too, that many will see me as the king at Torovan's side. And they will see me as the queen as well, as the Harvest Festival goes on. Barellans have accepted this, yes. No one blinks at all whether I'm Irava or Caleb.

But it won't only be Barellans at the feast.

I've felt at home in the two halves of myself, mostly, since I married Torovan. At home in who I am, at least, if not quite my changing body now.

But Barella hasn't received dignitaries in force like this since last Harvest Festival, and more have come this year than usual to welcome Torovan as the new king.

I bite my lip as I stare up into his eyes, trying to hold his reassurance as my own.

I nod and finally let go.

There's a soft rap on the bedroom door. Torovan's valet, who's been mostly barred from dressing him for the last months. The excuse was that I like to dress in privacy, and because I am sometimes a woman, maybe that excuse works. Maybe.

We haven't told him I'm pregnant, but I wonder sometimes if he knows.

Now, the valet's sturdy voice calls through the door, "Your Majesties, Prime Minister Valtair is waiting in the king's study."

"We are coming," Torovan calls back.

We do a last-minute check of clothes and hair, straighten a few things, and then we both hesitate.

He eyes me and his expression changes, a subtle shift. He steps toward me again, and I find myself bracing myself—and why?

Why do I not want him near me right now?

I love him. I want to shudder out of all of these clothes again and pin him to the sheets. I want that so badly it burns me all the way through.

His fingers reach toward my stomach, then he stops.

Maybe he registers that I've frozen.

I bare my teeth and grab his hands and bring them to my stomach, to what looks like the empty air covered by my illusion. I feel his touch on my stomach and close my eyes. And the touch itself is...healing.

"Caleb," he says gruffly as I lean against him.

A tremor runs through me.

"I'm *sorry*," he says. As if everything now, all of it, is his fault.

"I'm not." And it's true. I'm not sorry we're making a family together. I will never be sorry for this child when they are born. Never.

"Tell me how to help. Anything."

And what do I tell him? I don't know what I need, beyond needing to find a way to rebuild my reality as Caleb around this child growing within me. To feel like myself again.

But I still haven't found the references I need in all the books I've read. I have more to read yet, and I quietly sent for a few more, with Master Aldric's help.

But though I have ideas and vague theories, none of them yet are solid enough to risk a growing life.

Though there was one suggestion in a book I read the day before that I've been quietly turning over in the back of my mind.

And maybe I've been a little scared to even think about it. To hope it might prove to be an answer.

And if I haven't wanted touch the moments before, suddenly I crave it now.

I wrap my arms around him, pulling in tight, not caring if I rumple my Festival clothes.

His fingers clutch into my back, his own anguish, I know, at mine.

"Four months," I say as I stretch up to him, my smooth cheek, beneath my illusion, brushing against the rough stubble on his. I am always covered by an illusion now. Always.

"Would it help...should we tell the court about our coming child?" he asks. "Tell them that we're going to be parents? At the Harvest Festival. Should we make this more of an event?"

I can hear the hope in his voice, but also, beneath it, more fear. It's that fear he's holding back from me.

"You don't have to protect me," I say hotly, pulling back enough to glare up at him.

But he brushes the hair out of my eyes, and I lean into the touch.

"Not yet," I say. Which is what I've been saying for the last two months, past the quickening. "After. When the Akrean delegates are gone."

Like I said to Valtair. But...I'm not sure Torovan will take it as vaguely.

He breathes out. In relief?

Maybe I've just made a promise. Maybe I'll have to keep it.

And maybe it could be a relief for people to know, to not have to hide this part of myself, too.

Maybe.

But he holds me tighter a moment before letting me go.

And, with a frown, he straightens my collar, and I try to brush a crease out of his coat.

His frustrated face must be a mirror to mine, because he vents a small laugh.

"Valtair is waiting," I say.

"Valtair can very well wait. Caleb—I know what happened in the Great Hall today, with your apprentice, Aria—"

"It won't happen tonight. We changed to a simpler demonstration."

He nods. Trusting me.

Then trails a hand down my arm before letting go, out to meet with Valtair.

Chapter 9

The Start of a Celebration
Torovan

I stride out through the short hall toward my study.

Caleb never moved into my mother's old apartment.

I never moved into my father's.

My apartment has a second small bedroom we can use for a nursery, but if we have more children than this, we will have to move to one of the larger royal apartments.

Have to.

"Did I interrupt a tryst?" Valtair calls as I push into my study. He eyes our rumpled clothes as Caleb comes in behind me.

"No," I say shortly. "What do you need?"

His brows raise. "To accompany you to the feast. And tell you another Festival guest reported a secondhand account of another village weaver, a woman this time, who's been missing for more than a week. That weaver's from a village a dozen miles within the border."

Valtair's eyes flick to Caleb, who's crossed his arms over his chest and is doing his best to look unbothered.

But I know he's not.

I'm not.

And after the moment we just had in our bedroom, I'm feeling less than steady, less than prepared to handle this just now.

But I'm a king. I can't tell a crisis to wait for my own timing.

I tighten my hands and release them again.

"Do I need to see the guest? Who is it?"

"No, like I said, it was secondhand. He's a minor lord, traveling in the company of a small trading party. He was talking with one of Lord Navirat's traders, who mentioned he's interested in news from the border, and that made its way from there to me." He pulls a folded sheet of paper from his fine coat and hands it to me. "One of Navirat's staff recorded the testimony."

I unfold the paper, reading the few lines quickly. And why does my heart pick up, like I'm afraid this will say something like the letter from Nikolai?

But it was written here in this palace. Taken from a testimony.

And it's exactly as he said. A weaver went missing from a village farther in from the border—and it's a strong rumor, but not a confirmed fact. The minor lord apparently did not know about the other missing weaver—possibly more than one— closer to the border.

All of which is troubling, yes, very troubling. But not quite an immediate threat to our Harvest Festival starting tonight.

I hand the paper to Caleb, and my gaze lingers as he reads it, too.

Our eyes meet.

We are, at some point soon, going to have to do something about my mother.

Or Nikolai.

Or both of them still working together—and are they?

They have to be. Too much is happening in too many places for this to be a coincidence.

My mother wants this kingdom back for herself, but what claim can she lay on it? I will not obey her, and neither will my sister.

Nikolai doesn't have the approval of the people, as a known weaver of the darkest soul magic. But then, the people farther from the palace have been turning on even ordinary weavers.

And where will that end?

I glance at Caleb's stomach, which isn't showing beneath his illusion, and a queasy wave washes through me.

I've had a bit of sympathetic morning sickness, but it mostly ended weeks ago.

And I never told Caleb.

But what if my mother got a hold of our child?

How will I ever rest when this child is born?

We will have to do something about my mother, if nothing else.

And I don't know if that something will mean war.

Caleb hands the paper back to Valtair. "My apprentices are improving quickly." Improving enough for eventual war?

That was never the hope, in training new weavers. But that was always in mind, knowing our enemies.

"Not there yet," Valtair warns. "Not even close. Not to play on the level of kingdoms."

Caleb pulls his lips tight. "Then I'll have to train them harder."

I'm not sure if that will work. I've found with my own weaving training with Caleb that my biggest leaps tend to come after self-realizations more than any training for control.

In letting myself embrace my own willpower, and trusting in my place in reality. I anchor myself and make reality bend around me.

So does Caleb, in his own specific way—every weaver is different. And that's why weaving is so hard to teach.

"Don't push them beyond their means," I say. "But yes, we may need more weavers soon. I will talk to the elementalists, too, for a more vigorous training regimen for our newer elementalist court mages, too."

Was it a mistake to focus so hard on implementing my father's plans the last months and not on preparing for this?

I stop short of saying we need to be on active watch tonight, at the first night of the Festival.

Because we're all already thinking it.

I already assigned Caleb those two more guards, and I wish I could give him more, even if he'll be in the Great Hall. Even if we'll be surrounded by people.

But the influx of people into the palace is part of the problem.

And I don't want...I don't want to bring more attention from the gods to Nikolai's letters. To the possibilities that might spring from them. I don't want to think the unthinkable might happen.

I can't, and still walk into the feast tonight with my husband on my arm, and make a show of being cheerful for the harvest.

I smooth down the front of my coat, and Valtair's demeanor shifts, too.

"I'm sorry to bring this on the eve of the first feast, Tor—"

"You're doing your duty," I say.

He frowns.

"And I'm doing mine." I stride to the door where I know my guards and Caleb's are both positioned. "I'll be a moment, then we'll go to the feast."

I step into the corridor. "Morgan, Reveyan. A word, please."

Both guards, who've been part of the four who've been close by my side these last weeks, in the current rotation, glance at each other and approach.

Reveyan is tall and built like a wall, his handsome light-brown face nicked with a training scar on one cheek, his dreadlocks neatly bound back. Morgan is shorter but solid, his brown hair neatly trimmed short, his pale, sun-tanned face flushed.

There's little danger in this corridor, guards posted at every way in or out, but Morgan and Reveyan still give both ends of the corridor a check before approaching.

"You'll both be accompanying Caleb from here out—" And I see the shift in Morgan's dark eyes, the upset. "Because I trust you both. Guard my husband with your lives. Guard him over mine, if need be."

I don't tell them that Caleb is carrying our child—we've still told no one but the very few we trust implicitly.

And maybe, with the threats escalating, that is for the best right now.

Maybe.

Morgan straightens alongside Reveyan. "Yes, Sire."

I see Morgan's brow crease. "Is there a heightened threat, Sire, that we should know about?"

The letters never said if I told anyone else that Caleb would die.

But I'm not taking that chance, either.

"The Akrean delegation will be at the feast tonight, and you're aware of the rising tensions with Akreal." They'd both been within the Council Chamber earlier. "And not all of the other delegations are as friendly to Barella as they might be."

The two guards share another look. "Yes, Sire."

"Good. Tell Kas you're pulling Shiyan and Hiran into my personal guard rotation. Four for me, four for Caleb."

The door to my study opens again and Caleb steps out, surveying the guards. Surveying me.

His lips are pressed thin, but he's not arguing now.

And maybe we should tell the guards he's pregnant. Would it make a difference, that extra vigilant edge, in keeping him safe?

My hands stretch with the need to pull him close.

I close them again.

Valtair comes out after him, and did they just have a short argument, too? Both are looking peeved and not looking at each other.

I take a breath.

We're all tense tonight.

And tonight is *supposed* to be the start of a celebration.

Gods let it be just that.

I hold out my arm and Caleb takes it, and we start down the corridor to collect my sister, Elsira, then join the waiting feast.

CHAPTER 10

THE HARVEST FESTIVAL
CALEB

I've been watching the staff get the Great Hall ready the last few days, hanging the decorations and setting out the extra lamps.

But tonight, on the first feast of the Harvest Festival, stepping into the familiar hall feels like stepping into another world.

All the candles on the high chandeliers are lit. All the lamps placed on extra stands around the rooms glow until the space is bright and warm. Garlands of autumn leaves wind around the massive stone pillars, glittering with gold dust.

The tables gleam with silver, orange and gold tinted glass plates rimmed in silver too, the tables draped in the gold and olive green of Barella.

Ah. And Barella is a harvest kingdom, isn't it? This is the most important feast of the year, the time the gods bless the kingdom with the greatest bounty. The time the king pledges the kingdom back to the gods to be bountiful another year.

My throat closes.

My arm in Torovan's tightens, and he looks at me with a question.

But he can't let his focus stay on me, because a swell rises from the nobles and dignitaries already seated at the lower tables as Torovan and I enter, with Elsira and Valtair behind us.

There are grinning faces all around, people happy and excited for the start of the Festival.

I breathe through my panic, and I don't quite know where it's coming from.

The weight of the crown feels heavy on my head, and yes, the edges are digging in. Is that why this hall suddenly feels too bright, too open, too full?

I scan the tables—is my mother here yet? But no, she would be seated at the high table if she was. And the high table is still empty and waiting for us.

And my mother's not among those still waiting for the palace staff to seat them, either.

Some of my panic eases. I manage to paste on a smile.

My mother's not here yet. Gods, she's not here.

She's late in her travel, maybe, or long on the road. Maybe she got a late start. Maybe a carriage wheel broke, or a horse was injured. Or—or—anything could have happened. Not every delegation will make the first feast, though many have tried.

Should I be worried?

No, I decide, I'll be relieved. For now.

"Thaddeus!"

An older gentleman, stiff in his out-of-date court finery, hones in on Valtair behind us.

I hear Valtair's sharp inhale, even in the noise of the crowd. And though I'm still annoyed with him about his pressing me again to postpone the weaving demonstration tonight, I grimace in sympathy for an overbearing parent.

"Father," he says under his breath, and fixes his own smile on his face. It's not quite up to his usual charm.

And maybe I'm annoyed with him that I think he's right. That another weaver going missing makes this demonstration tonight more dangerous than the good it will do.

But I can't disappoint my apprentices now. That's also part of the training of a weaver, I'm finding—you have to show a weaver you know their value, always. *Have* to.

Count Valtair dips a shallow bow to Torovan and me. His resemblance to his son is strong, though his graying hair is short and thinning at the temples, and the lines on his handsome dark brown face crease more with his scowls than his smiles. "And Your Majesties. It is good to see you both well." He clasps Torovan's forearm. "How are you, my boy?"

The count, at least, is smiling now.

Torovan's own smile breaks through the tightness he's had all afternoon. He grips the count's arm back, and I feel my tension easing a little more as his eases, too.

Torovan might not have his father for this Harvest Festival, but he does have the count.

And I haven't been paying as much attention as I should to that, either, I know—I know Torovan's missing his father. I shift a little closer to him.

"And Elsira," Count Valtair says, reaching as Torovan's sister slips around him to give the count a hug. "How have you been? You look more like your mother every time I—"

He stops. His eyes meet Torovan's in a brief, pained grimace.

Torovan's hand, resting on my arm, tightens.

Elsira does strongly resemble her mother, with her black hair swept up tonight in an elegant flow of ornaments and pins, her face, a shade darker than her older twin's, carefully placid.

Though her mother, the Dowager Zinara, was never placid.

"I'm well, Count Valtair," Elsira says. With perfect poise, because she's dealt with the discomfort around her mother for months. Which doesn't mean it's not painful. "Is the countess here as well?"

"She's already seated. It was a long trip, and she wearies from the travel. We will both call on you tomorrow, however, be assured." The Count turns his attention on me. "Caleb."

He nods, and I nod back. It's not a snub, it's just how he is. He doesn't know me well enough to linger.

Behind me, Valtair is standing rigid, though I'm painfully aware he's trying not to.

I don't know all of what's between Valtair and his father, but I watch his father's eyes linger on the pendant of the Prime Minister on Valtair's chest. He gives a nod. Of approval? He's seen his son with the pendant before, Valtair's not so new to his position as that.

"Thaddeus," the count says again, moving toward his son. "I would like to meet tomorrow, too, can we arrange that?"

It wasn't a demand, but just barely.

Valtair stiffens and takes his father's hand automatically. "Of course. I will have my—my secretary arrange it."

"And I will let you go to your table." The count smiles, lets go. And Valtair exhales. "Happy Harvest Festival to you all."

Torovan leads us on to the high table, but I watch Valtair, my earlier annoyance at our argument ebbing. He's still not relaxing, but he sees me watching and makes a visible effort to gather himself as he sits on Torovan's other side.

His lips twitch, like he wants to say something biting, but his eyes flick to the crowds, and he presses his mouth thin. Then puts his pleasant smile back on and gives me a pointed look to do the same.

Right.

Right. Because he's wearing his pendant of office, and I'm wearing my crown. And it doesn't matter if our families make our stomachs churn, it matters that we show ourselves steady to the watching crowds. This isn't really our Festival tonight, it's the people's.

Valtair will track me down later and blow up then. Or I'll track him down, once my mother arrives.

Gods. And my nerves are ratcheting up again.

I sit to Torovan's right, Elsira on my other side. And I focus all my attention, for a few moments, on her.

Torovan's younger sister—by all of a few minutes—is wearing a deep blue gown tonight with fine beading down the bodice. She is dazzling, as usual, and less tentative than when I first met her.

That, also, is thanks to her mother.

She grips my hand, shooting me a look of empathy. She knows my mother's arriving tonight, too. And she knows everything about having to deal with a mother who is also a queen.

And worse. For her, so much worse, and I try to tell myself that my mother at least wishes me well.

I hope.

Then again, she did betroth me to Torovan when there were rumors that he'd killed to gain his throne.

Elsira leans in to my ear. "The kitchen left three glasses with only grape juice, same color as the wine."

I slowly turn my glass, watching the carved crystal spin. I've been drinking only juice for months now, and both Torovan and Elsira usually join me in that.

If the kitchens have speculated over that longstanding request for the three of us, maybe they think it's because Torovan and I are weavers and need our wits about us? Or maybe that it's a habit of royalty?

But, we have more eyes on us than usual tonight. And many among the kitchen staff will be new.

"Thank you," I say, and manage a smile back at her. Though my stomach still turns as the first course is brought in, a lightly spicy fruit and white meat dish.

I will get through this feast without being sick. Without showing I'm sick. Without any of that.

My nerves aren't helping, though.

I catch a glance from Torovan, checking on me, and I straighten, forcing myself to eat. Forcing myself to look as relaxed and festive as I can.

While my mind drifts, as the meal goes on, as the conversation continues. I listen only vaguely as Elsira talks about a new horse she's having trained. She wants to accompany Torovan on his hunts—I've never found the hunts enjoyable, though Torovan's definitely tried to show me how to enjoy them.

He loves the thrill of the chase. He comes alive, becoming a primal force that has nothing to do with his duties or manners around the court.

He is *beautiful* on a hunt, and if I've enjoyed them at all, it's in watching him ride like he and his horse are one being, his eyes intently focused ahead, every bit of him taut and alert.

I want to be near him. But not while I have to concentrate on not being sore while riding, the bushes catching at my clothes.

Elsira, though, has decided that it's her newest passion.

Well, and maybe she wants to spend some actual time with Torovan, I know she hasn't had much lately.

We've all been too busy for our own good. All of us, really, except Elsira.

I shift in my chair and tell myself I should make more time for her, because Torovan and I got busy after he arrested his mother. But Elsira...did not.

But by the third course, my stomach is threatening to make a scene, and I only nod and respond when it's required now, trying to distract myself by thinking about a passage in a book I read yesterday.

If I told Torovan that I'll tell the court about my pregnancy after the Festival ends—and that's more than the vague promise I gave Valtair—my time to find a way to reweave my reality of myself as Caleb is shrinking.

And no, maybe what I read isn't a full solution to my problem, but the book talked about a weaver encasing an object in their will to protect it from that will, and then wrapping a new weaving of reality around that encasing.

I have to try it—I haven't had the time. But I have to try, to experiment. Not on myself, on inanimate objects. To see if it's even something I can remotely adapt to my situation.

And am I fooling myself by even trying? Will I ever dare to risk the child growing within me to see to my own comfort?

Could I be that selfish?

Torovan's chair scrapes on the dais floor.

I look over to him.

And then freeze as he bangs against the table, knocking over his glass, his arm thrust out in front of him, fingers spread wide.

What?

"Torovan—"

I follow the length of his arm to see a gleam in front of me.

Hovering, in midair.

What am I looking at?

What am I looking at?

It's silver, rippling, shuddering.

A dagger. Still humming with its spin, caught within Torovan's bracing threads of reality.

I stare, for a moment not comprehending.

A dagger.

Then I feel hands on my shoulders, dragging me out of my chair, pulling me down.

Shouts, and more guards pulling Torovan down.

"Get off!" he roars, and wrestles his way back up, then stops fighting his guards and reaches for me. "Caleb!"

I grip his hand back, shock giving way to burning, igniting rage.

Did someone just try to kill me?

Someone just tried to kill me.

Or did they try to kill Torovan?

No, the silver was in front of *me.*

Someone just threw a knife at me, and Torovan stopped it.

Torovan.

With his weaving.

And whether whoever threw that knife knew it or not, they would have also hurt our child.

"Tor," I hiss, gripping his hand tightly as pandemonium erupts around us.

I extend my senses, all of my senses, feeling for any corrupted weaving around us. Any weaving at all. Any sense of reality that will tell me what the hell is going on.

I feel chaos around me, an eruption of shattered illusion—the illusion of safety.

Torovan's eyes are as dark and deadly as I know mine are, too.

He lets go of me and launches up, fighting down his guards, who try to stop him.

CHAPTER 11

THREADS OF REALITY
TOROVAN/CALEB

TOROVAN

My world narrows to the shimmering, shuddering threads of reality I hold clenched in the fist of my will. I strain to hold the dagger in place, to counteract what the dagger wants to do.

The blood the dagger wants to take.

Is the dagger's will born of soul weaving? Or just the will of its wielder imprinted into its action?

It's hovering not a foot away from Caleb's heart, still trying to spin forward.

I push the rest of my senses out in a frantic, sweeping wave, looking for more danger, for a second throw, for anything.

I hunt through the chaos of the hall, sifting through the panicked threads of hundreds of guests, searching for the slippery rot of soul weaving or the cold, dead void of an unreality construct.

I expect to find Nikolai's signature tainting the air. So familiar now from the letters.

I brace for it.

I find nothing.

And do I find nothing because there is nothing to find, or because I'm not yet good enough to find it?

I feel the dagger's momentum slowing within my reality weaving.

And as I hear a shout and Caleb flies backward, pulled down by the guards, I finally let the dagger drop.

It gives a clang as it hits the edge of the table and skids across it.

I feel hands pulling me down, too, and my shoulder hits the dais hard.

I shout at my guards, I don't know what I say. And twist around, looking for Caleb, oh gods, did Morgan—it was Morgan—pull him down too hard, what about the child—

We should have told the guards. They needed to know this to protect him.

But Caleb is rolling over, pushing up on his hands.

I reach for him. "Caleb!"

I have so much power. So much power in my person, in my title, in my will. I stopped that dagger. I saw the glint in the air and reacted without thinking, summoning the full force of my will that said my husband will not be harmed.

But I feel powerless now.

That this happened at all.

I grip Caleb's hand, and he grips it back, his eyes wide, his spectacles askew.

His illusion shimmers, goes hazy, then solidifies again. And that lack of control from him rattles me more.

Fuels like fire in my veins.

Someone tried to kill my husband. That dagger wasn't aimed at me, but at him.

Someone tried to kill my *husband.*

"Tor!" he rasps.

Whoever tried to kill my husband is about to be fucking *dead.*

I try to shake off my guards, and when that doesn't work, push up against their strength as I rise again, bracing on the table.

The Great Hall, stunned a moment before, has erupted into chaos.

I roar into the maelstrom, "Seal the hall! No one leaves! Find who threw that dagger!"

CALEB

Reality crashes back over me in waves.

Someone tried to kill me. Here, surrounded by hundreds of witnesses, foreign dignitaries, our own people—someone hurled a dagger aimed directly at my heart.

I touch my master weaver's medallion. Would that have stopped it? I don't know.

I try to picture how the dagger looked again, and no, it had been aiming actually for my heart, not the center of my chest.

My head swims. The world is a blur of motion and screaming. My elbow throbs from where Morgan slammed me to the dais floor, his weight still holding me down. He'd cushioned the fall with his arm, and I didn't hit my head, but it was still an impact.

Rage, sharp and hot, burns through the shock.

Someone just threw a dagger at me.

At *me*.

Torovan is rising, a furious, avenging king, and I try to rise with him. We should be facing this together.

"Stay down, Your Majesty," Morgan grunts in my ear.

"Get off me," I snarl, struggling against him. My magic wants to lash out, to throw him off, but it's a chaotic storm inside me, uncontrolled. "We have enemies in this room! I have to—"

"Which is why you will stay down," he insists.

I twist my head, trying to find a target, a direction for my fury, and see Valtair across the dais, his face tight as he directs other guards. Our eyes meet, and his are wide with terror. Sharp with questions.

Then I look back to Torovan. He's staring past me, toward the main entrance to the Great Hall.

I see him swallow.

"Fuck," he breathes.

That's all it takes.

I shove against Morgan with all my strength, wrestling up enough to see above the table, see what has stolen Torovan's focus.

And I gather enough of my scattered will to hold my magic close, ready to strike.

I see the guards first, moving through the hall, their voices raised as they question nobles and servants alike. Panic ripples through the crowd—foreign delegates looking alarmed and suspicious of each other, Barellan nobility pressing back against the walls, servers dropping their trays in their haste and fear.

Weeks of careful diplomacy undone by one thrown blade.

But that's not what has Torovan's attention.

Through the growing commotion, I catch sight of a familiar figure near the main entrance. The great doors are being shut, guards herding anyone trying to get out back in.

My mother, Queen Sevine of Galenda, stands frozen just inside the doorway, still wearing her traveling cloak. Road dust clings to her usually immaculate appearance, and her composed queenly mask has cracked completely as she stares at the scene before her.

Her eyes go to Torovan, narrow, then flit to me.

Oh, gods.

I'm Caleb. I'm Caleb right now. Will she recognize me—

She does recognize me. I see it in the storm in her eyes.

The doors to the Great Hall slam shut and are barred with a resounding clang.

I draw enough breath to shout, "Valtair!"

I point toward the doors. "My mother! Get her out of here. Through the side doors, take her to Torovan's study and stay with her."

His lips part, a question, and I can see his concern, too.

But right now, I can't be his friend, I have to be his king.

Because this was an assassination attempt on me.

And my mother's here. I have to know she's safe.

Valtair nods once, then turns to snap orders.

While Torovan starts toward the end of the dais, like he wants to wade into the crowd.

"Shit," Morgan says beneath his breath. "Your Majesty—Caleb—stay *here*. Stay down."

"Yes, go." Because yes, I will stay in place if it means Torovan doesn't throw himself into that mess.

I don't know what I can do to help. Not in this chaos.

Chiran, one of my two original guards, and Reveyan, push themselves in front of me, gently but firmly herding me back toward the private door behind the dais.

"Get Torovan to safety," I snap. Because we don't know that I was the only target. We don't even know if I was supposed to be the distraction.

"Yes, Your Majesty," Reveyan says. But he keeps herding me.

I twist around to look between him and Chiran—Valtair and a few of the hall guards are escorting my mother at a quick walk to the side doors. And maybe I should have said that she should use the private door here and passage behind the dais, but—but I need a moment.

I'm going to need a moment before I talk to my mother.

A long moment.

I see Torovan's guards bringing him back toward me and breathe out a small relief. His eyes are razor focused on me— and then roaming again for threats before they come back to me.

He's been nervous the last three days.

He saw that dagger and stopped it before I even noticed it.

Was I that distracted, or was he that attuned to the danger?

He saved *me*.

I swallow bile.

The private door opens—Elsira, who I'd lost track of and must have gone ahead, beckons.

She grips my hand, pulling me inside.

CHAPTER 12

CHAOS

CALEB

I barely feel Elsira's cool fingers gripping my arm as she pulls me deeper into the cramped private chamber, shutting out the chaos in the Great Hall with a decisive thud of the door. I can still hear the frantic shouts, the roar of voices outside this room, but they're muffled now.

Though I barely hear anything over the pounding of my heart.

"Caleb," Elsira says, her voice trembling, "are you hurt?"

"I'm—" My voice threads and cracks, and I have to clear my throat. "I'm fine."

Her eyes go to my stomach, and I press a hand there, too, my hand wavering my illusion.

I let go. I don't feel any pain, and I don't feel any difference in the growing possibility inside me.

That means everything's okay, right?

That this, at least, is okay?

But I'm not fine at all.

I can still see the dagger hovering in the air before me, silver glinting in the light of the many candles in the hall, stopped inches from my chest.

Stopped only because Torovan's magic caught it. His arm outstretched and teeth bare in his strain.

A moment slower, and—and—

Elsira looks me over, her breaths coming fast, but she nods.

"Stay here, with your guards. My guards are already checking down the passage. I'll see about Torovan. Was he behind you?"

He was. Gods, what's keeping him? Morgan was supposed to be bringing him—

My nerves spike all the way up again.

I look to Reveyan and Chiran. I start back for the door.

Reveyan blocks me. "You can't go out there, Your Majesty."

I'm a master mage—watch him fucking stop me.

I extend my weaver's senses, preparing to weave the air into solidity beside him, and shove him aside on my way out.

"Caleb!" Elsira's rushing to me. "What are you doing—"

I stop.

Just freeze, and tremble.

Am I under attack again?

Or is my body, drenched in adrenaline, betraying me?

My knees start to buckle, and Elsira catches me.

And she shouldn't be that much better off than me, she was beside me. That dagger could just as easily have hit her.

Though there's no question at all who it was aiming for.

I choke, fighting for air in a surge of panic so strong it turns me toward the door again. "Tor—"

My concentration slips, and my illusion falls.

And that shocks me back into some semblance of sanity.

I look at the guards crammed into the room with us—there are two oil lamps on the walls, the light isn't bright. But it's enough to see the bulge of my stomach.

My eyes dart to Reveyan. To Chiran.

Chiran, I know, has a family. Has a wife. Knows exactly what a swollen belly means. He looks down, looks up at me, and his eyes narrow in anger.

I flinch back.

Reveyan looks to me, starts, then spins as the door bangs open. He doesn't draw his sword in the tight space, but his long dagger leaves its hip sheath.

"Torovan—" I rush toward the door, and he's there. His gray-green eyes flaring, mouth tight in his anger.

But he sees me and stops, slows.

I'm not Irava right now, though I'm not wearing my illusion.

I make a face and threads of reality swirl around me, my will yanking them back into my illusion as Caleb. The effort winds me, and I bend over my knees, panting.

"A healer," Torovan says, his voice choked. "You need to see a healer. I need to get you to, or get a healer to—"

He crosses the few steps to me and crushes me in his arms before remembering he probably shouldn't and eases his grip.

He buries his face in my hair, holding me to him. Holding himself to me.

And I cling back, feeling tears track down my face. Trembling again, and I can't stop.

The crown on his head and the crown I've almost forgotten is still on mine, both of which made it through our various tackles from the guards, clink together.

He growls and pulls his off, then mine, and hands them to

Morgan, who came in behind him. Strands of black hair cling to the sweat on his brow. His eyes are raw with panic.

"Caleb. Gods. Are you—are you—"

I manage to shake my head, though my throat feels scraped raw. "Just...I'm just..."

He exhales sharply, shoving back his messy hair. He pulls back in his own shudder. "The hall's sealed. Guards everywhere. No one claims to have seen the assassin yet, though I don't know—I don't know what the guards will find. I want to protect you, but I need to be out there, I have to find—"

He glares at Morgan, who glares back, holding both crowns.

"A dagger that close," Torovan hisses. "In my palace. In my hall, at my feast—"

"You caught it," I say.

"I didn't catch who threw it," he growls.

"I wasn't paying attention," I say. "I knew—I knew I should be more vigilant, and I know you've been scared, is this what you've been so afraid of for the last few days—"

He rears back as if I've struck him. "No," he says. Then, "Yes."

I shake my head. "Do you know who it was—was it the Akreans?"

"I don't know."

But is that the truth? Is he lying to me right now?

I open my mouth, but he says, "Your mother. I saw your mother. She saw what happened."

Not that she wouldn't have heard of it anyhow when she arrived. But, yeah. She was there. She saw it all.

And she saw me as Caleb. As this part of myself.

Bile shoots up my throat.

"I'm going to be sick," I manage, but I choke it back down, and swallow for several moments.

Torovan sways, his own face pinched.

I glare up at him. "I know you get queasy when I'm queasy, too."

His brows twitch down. "I can't help it."

"Can you stop trying to protect me?"

But he gives me an incredulous look.

And I deserve that. He just saved my life.

I rub my face in my hands, and I feel his arms around me again, closing tight, holding me close. I shudder into his shoulder, inhaling the familiar scent of him. Wood smoke, cedar, and roses.

"You saved me," I whisper.

He shivers. Gods.

"But you're safe," he says.

It sounds more like a hope than a fact.

"You'll tell me what you know?" I ask, glaring up at him.

He nods. But he doesn't offer anything more.

I can't press him on it now, or why he thinks he still has to keep whatever this is from me even now, after someone just tried to kill me. Unless this was what he was expecting?

But why didn't he warn me?

My nerves are too raw, too wide open.

And my mother is, almost certainly, pacing the rug in Torovan's study. And if Valtair is with her—gods, poor Valtair.

I groan and step back.

"My mother. I can't handle her. But I have to handle her."

"Can I talk to her?" Elsira asks. "I handled our mother."

Torovan and I both jump. I'd forgotten Elsira was still here.

I rub the illusory stubble on my cheek. "No, I have to. I do have to. I just—I need a moment to breathe."

"I'm with you, Caleb," Torovan says, bracing my shoulder. "I'll be with you."

No, I don't need a moment to breathe. Every second now is ratcheting up that different panic.

My mother came in at the absolute worst possible time. And I have to deal with her now at the worst possible time, when I'm already unsteady and don't have my defenses in order.

"Valtair will be there, too," Torovan says.

I snort. Try to shrug the tension out of my shoulders, try to steady the shakiness in my hands by squeezing them together.

Can I weave the illusion around myself of someone who is not currently losing his shit right now?

No. I barely have the concentration to maintain my illusion as Caleb now, and that hurts, that sits with me like a visceral punch that this can't be my reality just now.

My failure to figure out how to be myself, my lack of awareness of what was happening around me, almost got me killed.

My mother can't know I'm pregnant. Whatever else happens in the meeting we're about to have, that can't be it. It's too much, it's too close, it's just...not for her.

Not yet.

Not now.

Torovan slips our fingers together, holds tight.

I look up again, and his eyes are steady, if still blazing.

"You did well, Court Mage," I say softly, anything to stall the meeting just a moment more.

His lips twitch, not quite a smile. "Anything for you, Master Weaver."

I shudder again and close my eyes in the pain of knowing that I'd failed tonight.

"We unwove a vortex together," I say. So why couldn't we have stopped that threat before it became a threat tonight?

He stopped it. Torovan stopped it.

But not me.

I'm supposed to be the one to protect him, not the other way around. That's how it's *supposed* to be. That's how I want it to be, that's what makes sense.

"Caleb, this isn't your fault," Torovan insists.

And I nod.

I know. I know he's blaming himself, too. That the words are just a cover for his own blame—but he saved me.

Gods.

The lump in my throat is tightening too hard.

"Let's go see my mother."

Chapter 13

The Queen

Caleb

I don't realize my hands are still shaking until I'm outside Torovan's study, watching my fingers tremble against the seam of my coat.

I shouldn't be this nervous. Or maybe I'm still shocky from the attack.

I was hoping to greet my mother in a way that I could control, not this. To walk her into who I am as Caleb. I wanted her to see me being happy.

Not this haphazard meeting while my head is swimming, and I'm struggling to keep my myself steady.

Valtair stands beside the study door, arms folded over his dark emerald coat. His scowl doesn't bode well at all for what I'll find with my mother inside.

When he notices my trembling hands, though, his expression softens.

"She's inside," he says, nodding to the heavy, carved door.

My heart clenches.

There's been no time for me to gather myself, let alone

figure out how to explain all that's happened in Barella since I left Galenda. All that's happened to me.

Even if she knows some of it, I know my mother. She'll need the whole of it from me before she softens any of her snap opinions.

I exhale, trying to steady the wild energy still coursing through me. At my side, Torovan is a warm anchor, his palm pressing gently at my lower back.

I want to lean into him, to let him carry this conversation, I want to slink off down the corridor and curl up in a ball and hide.

I'm thinking of pulling Valtair into the nearest linen closet for that mutual parental scream we both need right now.

I widen my eyes at Valtair, but he shrugs. And looks away.

I can feel Torovan's tension, too. This will be the first time he's met my mother officially as a king—they brokered the treaty by correspondence.

And the first time since we were married, too. And had the wedding without her.

"Thank you, Valtair," Torovan says. "Please coordinate with the guards. I want to know everything."

Traitor, he said Valtair would be here, too. I need all the buffer I can get.

But...I know that someone needs to handle the chaos below.

Torovan's voice is low, but he's calmer than he was in the side chamber. I can still almost taste the coil of fear inside him, though. Nothing about this night is over yet.

I inhale sharply. "Valtair, my apprentices."

Oh gods, I forgot—I forgot to even worry about their safety.

I am failing this night on every count—

"I'll see they're safe," he says, and looks back to Torovan. "And manage the fallout. You handle the Queen of Galenda."

And then he's gone, his quick boot steps echoing down the corridor.

I stare at the closed door for a long moment. Behind those thick wooden panels, Queen Sevine of Galenda—my mother—waits with all the regal composure she's built over years of ruling a demanding court. I know it. And I can imagine her exact posture of controlled anger, too.

But I also know she's a mother who used to brush my hair in the candlelight of her private chambers, her voice soft and exacting as she explained court politics to me.

She's cold and logical in one moment, fiercely protective in the next. And now, she's just watched me narrowly escape death.

"Ready?" Torovan asks in a low voice.

I look up at him. "No. Are you?"

He gives a small huff, then opens the door.

Torovan's study is familiar and homey, but it feels like the space has been invaded, set off from the warmth it usually brings.

But the walls are still lined with the shelves of texts about government and history and weaving, local laws, logs from the palace historians. The dimmed lamps flickering on wall sconces still give a warm glow. The fireplace to the left hums with a small, crackling fire.

My mother stands near the hearth, half-turned toward us. Her traveling cloak lies abandoned in a heap on a chair. Her gown is a vivid crimson that sets off her light-brown hair—always elegant, even when she's dusty from the road. She came to the Great Hall straight from her travels, not even taking the time to clean up.

My mother, the queen of her kingdom.

And I have to remind myself that I'm a king of mine, too.

She looks up. Her brown eyes flick from Torovan to me and narrow at my appearance as Caleb. I can almost hear the gears in her mind turning, evaluating every detail: the fact that I'm still standing here as a man, wearing my regal court coat with the master weaver's medallion at my chest. That I know my hair and clothes are a little mussed, that I didn't take the time to fix it.

I'm no longer wearing the crown, and I almost wish I hadn't taken it off.

Though wearing a crown in her presence now might have felt like a child trying to play at ruling a kingdom.

My throat knots, and I know I'd feel small if Torovan wasn't beside me. If he wasn't the anchor to the truth that yes, I do have power here. And no, my mother's temper can't take that from me.

Torovan closes the door behind us, and for a moment, there's only the low crackle of the hearth. The soft swish of my mother's skirts as she steps closer.

"So," she says. She doesn't look away from me. "This is my son?"

The tension in the room goes taut as a drawn bowstring. I can almost feel reality curdling around me.

Torovan bristles, stepping forward in that subtle, protective way of his. Which warms me even as my nerves threaten to spiral.

"Caleb is my husband," Torovan says firmly. "And Irava, when he is Irava"—he glances at me—"is my wife. That was the agreement when you and I signed the treaty between Galenda and Barella. Or did you not agree that I should marry your child?"

I stiffen. And yes, that treaty had a happy ending. No, I wouldn't want to be anywhere but here right now, with Torovan, beside him.

But this marriage still was made without my permission, or me playing any part in that treaty at all beyond being bargained for.

Torovan sees my anger and grimaces. He knows how I feel about having had my choice taken from me. But he doesn't apologize for bringing that up, not here in front of my mother.

My mother, her gaze flicking between us, makes a dismissive wave. "Treaties. My child was nearly murdered tonight. Is that how you protect the treaty, Torovan Braise?"

She's treating him like she'd treat one of my brothers, like she'd treat her own wayward child.

Is that a good thing? Does that mean that she's accepted him as her son as well?

Torovan's jaw tightens, and I hope to everything the storm of his temper won't get the better of him now. Here with my mother, who can absolutely match it.

But he pastes on his semi-pleasant court face and says, "I'm sorry you had to see that, Queen Sevine. You deserve to know what's been happening here."

My mother considers him. "I've had your letters. Both of your letters. And I've heard the rumors. There was a mind control weaver in your court, and you arrested your own mother for the murder of your father. But reports didn't mention the threat continued to the point that I would walk in to see a dagger suspended midair a hair's breadth from my son's heart." She presses a hand over her heart, as if in echo. "I want all of it. You owe me all of it, both of you."

Her *son's* heart, she said.

I swallow around the rising lump in my throat. She's angry, yes. She has a right to be. I know that.

If not quite the right to berate me for the choices I made to counteract hers.

But she called me her *son*.

I wet my lips and reach up to resettle my spectacles, which don't really need fixing.

Yes, my mother deserves answers, but the sum of all we've faced—Nikolai's weaving, my illusions, the late king's murder, and Torovan's mother's betrayal—all of that feels too big right now. Too close to the danger we just faced.

I just want to crawl into my bed and pull the covers up over my head. To curl around my stomach. To have Torovan beside me, his arms wrapped around me, holding me close and safe.

His heartbeat at my back in a steady rhythm.

My hand fixing my spectacles is still trembling, and my mother sees it and frowns.

She steps closer, and I flinch.

Why do I flinch?

She stops, her lips going thin.

"Torovan," my mother says. "Can I have a moment with— with my son."

I close my eyes, feeling the prickle behind them as my cheeks burn. I don't know why I'm embarrassed. Like her saying I'm her son is something shameful, even if it still sends warmth through every layer of me.

Torovan touches my arm, and I want to tell him to stay.

But I do need to talk to my mother. And I can see the signs in her face that she's barely holding her composure together.

"I'll be in the bedroom," Torovan says. With a clear warning to my mother that he's still close, and a clear message to me to call if needed.

My mother frowns after him, but then turns back to me. She looks me over, and I cross my arms, lifting my chin.

I feel the weight of the master weaver's medallion over my chest.

In the illusion, my chest is flat, but that's not my reality just now, and I feel that all the more intensely under her stare. I feel my stomach and the growing possibility within it, I feel what she can't see.

She opens her mouth, and I don't know what she's going to say. I'm braced for anything.

"Do you need to leave?" she asks.

That isn't what I was expecting.

I sway. "What?"

"Leave Barella," she says, stopping in front of me. "I can take you home."

I shake my head. "The treaty—"

"To hell with the treaty," she hisses, and I recoil. "I didn't know I was sending you into this. I didn't know about the danger. I'd met Torovan before, when he was younger and still a prince, I didn't believe he had it in him to kill his father. I would not have betrothed you to a man I thought capable of that. But I certainly never thought Queen Zinara would have done that, either. Irava—"

"Caleb," I bite out.

She frowns. "Caleb. This clearly is not the situation Barella was in when that treaty was signed."

I hold my arms to my sides, because holding them to my stomach would betray me.

"I'm fine."

Which is becoming my frequent mantra.

"You had a dagger hurled at you tonight—"

"I'm fine, Mother. I can defend myself. And—and if I can't, Torovan can. He caught the dagger, he's also a weaver, I told you that—"

"No one should have to see their child mid-assassination attempt!" my mother hisses back, and I shiver, step back.

She stops, watching me. Then holds up her hands.

"I want to know everything. I deserve to know what I sent my child into."

She shouldn't have sent me here at all. She didn't send me —I came on my own to try to undo the marriage she'd promised me into. We were only supposed to be married two months ago, not almost six now.

I changed her plans. I changed everything—Torovan was in danger before I came, yes, but my saving Torovan from that danger made two powerful enemies, driving them into the shadows.

Those shadows are coming back for vengeance.

And *now* my mother's unhappy about that.

I want to have that argument with her. I want to yell at her with the full force of my anguish and my willpower about how could she have done this to me, when she'd promised I could marry who I want?

And how can she try to take me from this now, when my place is here? Even with the danger.

I have to stay by his side.

I know he'll stay by mine.

Yes, I want this marriage now. Yes, I love Torovan with everything in me.

But she didn't know it would end up this way.

She couldn't have.

And she has no idea what she's trying to interrupt now.

She pulls me away from Barella—and Barella falls.

It's why I can't fail. It's why I have to be better than I am and not distracted as I have been.

It wasn't a mistake to want a child with the man I love and a family together—gods, I will never regret that. I do not regret that.

But it was a mistake to think it wouldn't distract me.

That it wouldn't make me less effective of a defense, and my apprentices aren't ready yet, and Torovan is stronger, yes, but—but he's not the master mage that I am.

I'm all that stands between this kingdom and the storm.

And tonight the storm almost won.

I'm shivering again.

My mother watches me, the corners of her mouth drawing down. She picks up her travel cloak and drapes it around me. I hastily incorporate it into my illusion, even as she tucks a lock of hair behind my ear. Presses a hand against my cheek. Like it's her motherly due.

"We'll talk tomorrow," she says. And I don't know if that's a promise or a threat.

She hesitates, still in front of me, and I can't quite look up and meet her eyes.

"I'm not going back to Galenda," I say.

She runs a hand down my arm, and I wonder if she notices the slight edges of my illusion as Caleb.

It hurts to even think she might.

"You're a master weaver," she says. She touches the medallion with one manicured nail.

I do look up now. "Yes."

I dare her to say I shouldn't be.

"I never liked that you taught yourself weaving. I shouldn't have had those books in the library, they should have been locked away. It's too dangerous by far."

"I saved Torovan's life. Three times, Mother."

She meets my eyes. "And he's saved yours? With his own weaving? I want you to live a life where you don't have to save each other. Either of you."

She sighs and rubs her mouth, her fire cooling until she just looks tired. "But that is not often the life of a queen. Or a king." She eyes me. Eyes my hair where the crown had been when she first entered the Great Hall.

Then she moves toward the door. "Goodnight, Caleb."

Chapter 14

Not Fine

Caleb

My mother's crimson gown is the last thing I see as I pull shut the door to Torovan's study. I yank off my spectacles and press the heels of my hands to my eyes.

I open my mouth in a wordless scream.

My magic responds and ripples the threads of the air around me, a tremor throughout reality.

And I rein myself back in, because I have to. I *have* to pull myself together.

I carefully put my spectacles back on, straighten them.

I take off the travel-worn cloak my mother draped around me and sling it over the back of a chair near the hearth. The cloak puffs as I set it down, giving off a scent that I've never thought *was* a scent, the mix of pine and perfumes and spices that is the Galendan court.

And all of it—all of my anxiety, all of the raw fear from the dagger, all of my struggles with finding a way to be myself again

—all of it pools in my throat and stays there, stuck, and for a moment I can't breathe.

The inner door to the study bangs open, and Torovan looks in. "What happened? What was that?"

I exhale in a rush. Gods. Had he been the only one to feel my tremor of reality? I hope.

"I was upset, I'm fine—"

"You're *not* fine, Caleb."

He hovers his hands on either side of me, his face shifting through pain and rage and distress.

I drop my hands to my sides.

And sniff hard, and blink back the sting in my eyes.

I drop my illusion because it's an effort I can't make right now.

"I'm still Caleb."

"I know."

I know he knows. I collapse into the chair beside the hearth that I draped my mother's cloak on, and Torovan drags over a chair from another corner, and we sit. He sighs as he leans his elbows on his knees, head bent as if the weight of everything is entirely too heavy.

He reaches across the space between us, and I grab his hand. Sniff again.

His hand squeezes mine.

"Why couldn't we have a normal life?" I ask. To no one in particular.

He lets out a long sigh. "You thought we'd have a normal life. Us. With the way we met, the way we carried on, and the way we married each other."

I shrug and let our hands stretch between us as I sit back, until it's a strain and I let go.

He makes a dissatisfied sound, looking up at me. "I'm sorry."

"Why."

If he's going to try to say it's his fault again for why I can't be myself right now, I...I don't have the energy for that yet tonight.

I watch him, half of his face edged in firelight. Is he going to tell me what's had him so scared, or that this attack *was* what had him so scared? And how he knew about it?

"I mean, I'm sorry it's still dangerous. I'm sorry you have to live with that—that we have to live with that. That we're bringing a child into that."

"I knew what I was walking into, Torovan."

"No, you didn't," he says, and leans forward again. "I didn't think when I made that treaty. I didn't think about you."

We've had this conversation before. But with Mother here —I know it's enflamed those old wounds.

Exhausted, I rest my head in the crease of the chair and watch him.

"I'm glad you did, in the end," I say.

"But it wasn't—" He swallows. Looks at the fire. "Maybe it was fate, I don't know. That it was *you.* That you came and had the power to stop Nikolai and my mother. If you hadn't—I might be a puppet. I might be dead."

We both look into the fire, at the crackling embers.

"I love you," he says. "Caleb, I can't lose you. I *can't.*"

"And I can't save you right now," I say, bile rising in my throat. "If that dagger had been aimed at you, Torovan—you would be dead."

And saying that...saying that, my whole body shudders.

That's what I've been afraid to admit.

"You're not my guard, Caleb."

"But I'm what's standing between you and your mother and Nikolai taking back the kingdom. You know that, Torovan. I know that. We've known that since they both fled. The only reason they're not here now is because of me. Because they're *afraid* of me. And if I'm not—"

My voice gives out. The lump in my throat is too tight.

He shifts to the edge of his chair, reaching for me again.

I shake my head.

"Why don't you just tell me what's going on?" I ask. "I know you knew about this attack."

"I didn't."

"Torovan, don't—"

"I didn't know about this specific attack," he says. "But—"

He snaps his mouth shut.

He straightens, like he has to still project his kingly presence here, with me.

"But you won't tell me," I say. "You don't trust me."

"I *can't*, Caleb! Can't tell you!" He takes a gulp of air. "And danger is danger, no matter the source. I will find who threw that dagger." He tries to glare at me, but his eyes are shining. "And *you* won't go looking for who threw that dagger."

He's still protecting me. And the problem is, maybe he's not wrong to protect me. I hadn't seen the dagger in time. I hadn't felt anything amiss, any shift in the realities or possibilities of the room, because I wasn't watching. I wasn't vigilant, I was distracted by my own problems. My own fears.

I close my eyes. "I'm a terrible king. I'm not who you need at your side."

"Gods, Caleb."

I hear a thunk and open my eyes to see him on his knees in front of my chair, reaching to grab my hands again.

"You will always be who I need."

"I'm not—" I start to say I'm not the person he married. That I can't be that person right now, I *can't* be all of who I am. And guilt wraps around me because yes, even now, even *now* I still want this, I still want this child for us, to come into this world.

Why does it feel like I have to choose between my husband's happiness, and my husband's life? Between my happiness and my own self.

I close my eyes again. "And I'm failing at being pregnant. At being a good parent, I'm failing at—"

He stands, and I feel his arms slipping beneath my thighs, my back, as he starts to lift me up.

My eyes widen.

"Torovan—"

I'm not Caleb in reality just now, and I haven't rewoven my illusion yet, but I'm still not light.

He staggers a step.

"Torovan, set me down, you're going to hurt yourself!"

But he manages to steady and carries me into the hall beyond the study, into the bedroom.

Banging my foot on the doorway, which he apologizes for.

The fool.

My fool.

He sets me on the bed, then starts tugging me out of my court clothes, stiff and wrinkled now.

Not like he wants to be with me, not just now, there isn't any heat in his eyes. The fear is drowning it out. And there's a quiet determination as he pulls off my brown leather boots.

"Tor," I say softly, and reach to touch his cheek.

He's crying again. And that makes my own throat close up again, because he so very rarely cries.

"Let me take care of you."

He seems to need this, so I let him. He helps me undress down to my underwear, then helps me pull on night clothes. Then goes to his side of the bed to pull off his own ornate coat in short, angry jerks.

His shoulders are shaking. His teeth are bared. And he's not saying anything, but I know him too well.

"It's not your fault, either," I say. "The dagger."

We had this conversation before, in the panicked moments after the attack.

But some conversations you need to have more than once. And we're having a lot of those tonight.

A noise escapes him, a sob.

"I'm not good enough," he says. "I need to be a stronger weaver, and I'm not good enough."

"But you caught the dagger."

"I have to protect you, Caleb!"

He turns, only in his pants now, his chest heaving.

"I *have* to protect you. I know you don't always like that, but I have to."

I sigh and reweave my illusion as Caleb around myself.

His face twists, and he waves at me. "And watching you struggle is not protecting you!"

"I'll figure it out," I say.

"But you haven't yet, and I don't know how to help you."

I bite my lip, my whole chest aching, burning with all the things I'm not sure how to say. Things I don't have names for. Private pains, private joys.

Torovan sits down in his own exhaustion. "I'm sorry. I didn't mean—I don't want to press—"

"It's four months left," I say. "I'll be okay. I'm not worried about me as much as I'm worried about the kingdom."

But he shakes his head, as if that's nothing.

"I trust you. Whatever you need to do to get through these months, do it."

I look away.

"I *trust* you," he says again. "I trust you with my life, and with our child's."

My hands knot together. But I don't.

Nikolai isn't my greatest enemy. And neither is Torovan's mother.

The only person holding back my power right now, my ability to protect him and all I love, too, from any threat against us, is me.

Just me.

But I have to protect the child growing within me, too, and that's the problem. I will protect that child with all I am. I *am* protecting that child with all I am.

It's not a matter of trust, it's a matter of safety, and if I don't know if it will be safe, I can't do what I need to do.

Can't he see that?

Like he thinks I can just solve this.

Can't he see I've been trying, with all I have, to find a way?

After a long moment, Torovan pulls off the rest of his clothes and puts on his own night clothes, then slides into bed beside me.

I know he really should be out showing our people that he's fine, and I should be, too. I should be beside him, being the steadiness to his turbulence. Showing our enemies we will not fear them.

Showing them the combined strength of our willpower.

But we're not in sync right now, and I don't know where it went off.

It's not just that I feel off in myself, I feel like he feels off in himself, too.

And I don't know how to fix that, either.

He sighs again as he settles, and I feel the softness of his breath near my shoulder.

I turn, and he turns his head, too.

I love him with everything in me.

I know he loves me the same.

I lean in as he leans in, a slow and searching kiss.

Our fires are still ignited.

So why can't we flow in the same movements right now?

Why do we both seem so caught in private pains?

I lean against him and let him hold me close as I drift to sleep.

CHAPTER 15

EARLY MORNING VISIT

TOROVAN

I wake up in the early morning and can't sleep again.

The silence of the palace is broken by the distant sound of carriage wheels in the palace courtyard far below the window to our bedroom, more Festival guests arriving in the early hours.

Caleb lies sprawled beside me, his illusion holding even in sleep. I want to brush the hair out of his eyes, to reassure myself that he's okay. That I'm okay.

But I don't want to wake him.

That moment, that flash of light before I realized what was happening and reached out to stop the dagger plays over and over in my mind.

What if I'd not been looking in that direction? What if I'd been turned away?

Or worse, what if I hadn't been able to stop it?

I still don't know what I did. I reached out, and I made reality *stop* around the dagger. With...with *something*.

I will have to talk it out with Caleb—sometime. A time that isn't now, and likely isn't soon.

He is so ready to take the blame himself.

Gods of all the seasons, he thinks he's the only reason that Nikolai and my mother haven't outright attacked to take back the palace.

But I don't think he's wrong.

I haven't wanted to see it. I've been hoping that somehow —somehow I would just outlast my enemies. My betrayers. That the new policies to help the people would strengthen Barella so much that it would prove them irrelevant.

I've wanted that so much that I hoped it was true. How could I be so naive? I didn't think that was who I was, either.

Maybe I've just been too happy.

But my enemies are attacking on the level of the people.

We're on a battlefield I never thought I'd face.

I have to get stronger. But until then, I have to find out who threw a dagger at my husband.

He can't carry the weight of a kingdom and also carry its future—both things together are driving him under, and I can't let him fall.

And I don't think his mother helped any of that.

I glance at Caleb again in the dim pre-dawn glow from the windows, then finally ease out of bed.

He's used to my restlessness some nights and doesn't stir.

I don't dress, but pull on a dressing robe against the night's chill, and slip out toward my study.

The fire is banked—my valet must have been in and out again. The oil lamps are out, but I light one, nurse its flame, and settle heavily behind my desk.

It's not enough light to work by, but though my desk is

full, as always, of the stacks of papers and correspondence I need to see to, I don't make a move toward any of it.

So was the attack from my mother, or from Nikolai?

Was it the Akreans working for my mother?

Was it a hired agent, who could be anyone?

Caleb knows I'm keeping something from him, and that itself is dangerous. He's been relentless in pursuing answers before.

And will his life be in any more danger if I do tell him about the letters? Let him see the unreality there, and maybe actually unravel that part of the threat?

I need to tell him.

This nightmare has to end, I need my husband, I need him to be safe.

Will he ever be safe?

Will either of us, will our child?

I can't sit here.

And I don't care that I'm only in my night clothes and a robe, I grab a pair of shoes I'd set near the bookshelves one night and slip off my night slippers, put on the leather shoes. Shivering slightly as my feet hit their chill.

The letters. I can't yet bring myself to tell Caleb, but I have to tell *someone*. It's no longer enough for me to know this is happening, I need help.

And maybe that help will be able to tell me if I *can* tell Caleb.

Because no, I know that he won't be safe while Nikolai draws breath. While my mother schemes from whatever hole she's crawled into.

Not while enemies circle us like wolves, waiting for any sign of weakness.

And I've been too busy trying to build my father's dreams while my own have been crumbling around me.

I don't know what to do about Caleb drawing in on himself, I'm doing all I know how.

But this—this threat of the letters I need to try to handle. Somehow.

I ease open my study door and step into the silent corridor beyond.

It's an exhausted looking Morgan on duty outside the door, and my own Kas.

I look between them. "I'm going to Master Aldric's rooms, stay here. Guard Caleb."

Kas says, "Respectfully, Sire, I'm coming with you. Morgan can guard Caleb. Please stay here, I'll get two of the others down the hall."

I'm too tired to argue and nod as he hurries off.

Morgan shuffles beside me, but stills back into a guard's professionalism.

"Thank you," I say quietly, "for pulling him down."

"It's my duty, Sire."

"Thank you all the same."

He looks up, his eyes intent.

But Kas comes back with two more, one to stay and one to go with us.

I can't help but say, "Guard him with your life."

As if that wasn't already their jobs.

"Yes, Sire."

I reluctantly leave. I want to protect my husband, I don't want to leave him alone. But what I'm doing now is part of that protection, too.

"I need to retrieve something before we go to Aldric," I say, and lead the way to the meeting room where I've hidden the letters.

We pick up another pair of guards at the end of the residence corridor.

And we pass a few other people in the corridors as we enter the common areas of the palace. I'm regretting now that I didn't take the time to dress at least in simpler clothes, rather than my night clothes and robe.

But it's my palace.

Kas and his partner insist on clearing the meeting room before I enter, but there's no one inside.

I leave them out in the corridor, lock the door behind me, then stride to the wall panel where the letters are and hastily retrieve them.

The numbness of the unreality weavings on the letters burns my fingertips.

What if the attack tonight was Nikolai's warning? What if it was meant to fail?

No, that attack was not meant to fail.

I don't open the letters—I certainly don't need to know what's inside.

And will I get another letter today? Will that letter gloat?

I tuck them into a pocket inside my robe.

My guards fall in around me again as I leave the meeting room, striding toward the palace mage quarters.

The corridors in this section stretch empty and cold, light from the sparse lamps along the walls casting deep shadows. Our footsteps echo on the stone.

And as we near the door at the end of the master mages' quarters to Master Aldric's apartment, a different unease settles in my bones.

Aldric spent years trying to undermine my own willpower in favor of his own. He almost succeeded.

Which is, in its own way, as evil as Nikolai's attempt to control me, too. If not quite as malicious.

I haven't forgiven him for it. I don't ever intend to.

But I know he's loyal, in his own way. He thinks he's doing right by the kingdom.

And I'm so glad now I didn't send him off to the border.

He was deceived by Nikolai too. He has his own reasons to want Nikolai Metrial stopped.

I rap on Aldric's door with more force than necessary, urgency overriding courtesy.

Silence. Then shuffling sounds from within, a muffled cough.

A servant opens the door, his sleep-heavy eyes looking like he's been up, but not for long. He takes a step back when he sees me.

"I'll get the master mage," he says. "Do you wish to come inside?"

"Yes. I'll wait inside."

The servant hesitates as I step in, then turns up a guttered lamp to give the sitting room some light and hurries further into the apartment.

I wait. The apartment is small, and I hear the sounds of voices further in. The air is musty, smelling faintly of medicinal poultice. Aldric's used his staff for years as a political prop, but I've seen him leaning more heavily on it of late. I've seen his slight limp.

He's aged more than I thought he would since we took down Nikolai. Since he lost his status as the most powerful weaver in the kingdom.

It's several minutes before Aldric comes out, wrapped in his own dressing robe. He doesn't have his staff, though his steps are measured.

"Your Majesty," he says, his eyes red and puffy, his long gray hair loose and disheveled. "How can I help you?"

"Forgive my interrupting your sleep," I say, because I know he'll expect that.

"It was nearing time to rise anyway," he says, waving that off, but he's growing more alert, his gaze sharpening on me. "What is it?"

He knows this has to do with the attack last night. How can it not?

"I wish to speak alone. Can you dismiss your servants?"

Aldric nods and says a quick word to the servant who opened the door.

The younger man goes into the back hall, then comes out with another man in night clothes, who's barely awake, leading him out.

I look to my guards, who step back outside.

The door shuts.

"We are alone?" I ask.

Master Aldric frowns. Because his sending his servants out should be enough.

"We are. What's wrong, Torovan? Besides the fact that there's an assassin in the palace, and no, I don't know who it is. I would surely tell you if I did."

I pull the letters from my inner pocket and move the lamp to a table near the hearth.

I sit to get closer to the light, and Aldric, reluctantly, sits on the chair across from me.

I unfold one of the letters, scan the eight words I know by

heart again, and then, my hand shaking more than I'd like, hand it to him.

Aldric takes the letter, tilting it to let the lamp light catch it.

He goes still as he reads.

Looks up at me.

"Did you just receive this?"

"No. Yesterday morning." I hold up the other two letters. "And the morning before that, and the morning before that."

I hand the other two letters over, and he studies them, too.

"The 'him' in this meaning, Caleb?" he asks.

"No one else makes sense."

He nods, inspecting the paper, the handwriting. All things I've done before.

"It's not in the paper," I say. "It's in the lack of reality within it."

Aldric's breath hitches, and I know he's looking again with his weaver's senses.

He knows what unreality feels like, yes. But his senses, while highly trained, are considerably less sensitive than my own. His own weaver's power much less than mine. And far less than Caleb's.

"Nikolai," he says, and he's holding the letters now like they might catch fire in his hands. "Yes. Gods. I do feel it. Or, don't feel it."

"Can you see the weavings? Can you find the threads to unravel them?"

He turns the letters over, his heavy brows drawn down. "I don't dare try. The only person I know who can hope to do that safely is—"

"Is Caleb," I say.

And he looks up. Rests the letters on his knee with a sigh.

"Yes." Aldric stares down at the letters still in his hands. "I don't want to give these back to you. I don't know what dangers they hold."

And the part of me that was hoping he could tell me what to do with them, that he might possibly have enough experience to see through any traps Nikolai put on them, dies.

I reach, and he does give them back. Because his sense of self-preservation is probably stronger than it should be.

"Gods, Torovan. You think the attack last night was Nikolai? Nikolai himself?"

"I don't think it was actually Nikolai throwing the dagger, it was far too blatant an attack. But he could be behind it."

Aldric leans forward. "Is he in the palace? Under an illusion? Could he put himself under an unreality illusion and we'd never see?" He rubs at his eyes. "I'm sorry, Torovan, I don't have the ability to see through the unreality weavings like Caleb can, though I have grown more sensitive to them after studying the weavings in your mother's bedchamber. And I see your problem. The danger is real and present, but so is this threat."

He waves at the letters in my hands. "And politically? Strategically, this is masterful, because he undercuts your effectiveness with paranoia, while taking away your greatest asset in Caleb's ability to stop him."

"I know," I say. "And I don't know if he's here or not. The letters are delivered each morning with the regular correspondence."

"Have you traced back where they came from?"

"No. No, I've been—well, I haven't wanted to try, in case—"

He holds up an understanding hand. "All right. So we know Nikolai is actively making threats. And the Dowager likely has a hand in what's happening near Akreal. And now there's been an attempt on Caleb's life."

"Yes," I breathe out. "And Aldric, I don't know how to protect him. Except stay by him every moment, but I can't do that. I *can't* do that. I can't show my own fear, and he wouldn't let me."

"And he's carrying your child."

I freeze.

But then, Aldric, even if he isn't a strong weaver, is still a weaver. I can feel the possibility of a new life within Caleb if I'm paying attention. And Master Aldric has always been aware of the people around him, if only to know how to manipulate them.

He holds up a hand. "I haven't told anyone what I've seen, I know you haven't wanted to announce it yet, and that's probably wise."

My shoulders fall, I can't help that. Because I don't want it to be true. I don't want Caleb's instincts to be right.

I don't want this danger to be my reality.

"Yes," I say, "he's carrying our child."

Aldric looks at the fire, his mouth a grim line.

I tuck the letters back into my inner pocket, though having them that close to my heart again makes my skin prickle.

"Can you help me?" I ask. "Help me find out where the threat is? Help...somehow. Find any other signs of a weaver in the palace—because someone had to have put the unreality weavings on those letters, and while this might have been planned in advance, and Nikolai might have sent those letters from afar...and the attack might have been a coincidence..."

Aldric shakes his head. "I doubt it was."

"Then if Nikolai is *here.* If he's already in the palace— Aldric, I can't investigate on my own as the king. And I fear any move will make him take it out on Caleb. We don't know where he is, we don't know where to look, and we don't know what he'll do if we try." I look up. "Should I tell Caleb?"

He rubs his chin in thought. "Caleb already knows there's danger. And he's already vigilant for soul weaving. I think the lesser threat might still be in not telling him. Not yet. You will have to tell him soon, though, Torovan. If Nikolai's in the palace, Caleb's the only one who even stands a chance against him."

I nod, sitting back in my chair, exhausted.

But Aldric leans forward, frowning. "You were right to come to me. And I'll do all I can. I'll watch everything today— today is the reception in the Great Hall this afternoon, and the trials of strength on the Festival grounds this evening. Will Caleb be there? To either event?"

"To the reception, yes, I think so. But not to the strength trials, no. He'll have to attend to his apprentices, anyway, and he's not overly interested in games of sport. I won't be attending, either—it's never been a strong tradition that the king attends the first day's more common activities."

But then, my father sometimes did. And if I'm supposed to be the champion of the common people, shouldn't I be there, too?

But I have to stay near Caleb.

Aldric nods. "All right, then I'll remain in the palace, too, and see what I can find." His eyes narrow at me. "Be careful, Torovan. Be so careful. That attack might have been aimed at Caleb, but really, it was meant to hurt you."

"I know," I say, the words clogging in my throat.

Because that's what I can't stop thinking about.

Yes, Caleb is the strongest weaver in the kingdom.

Yes, he's a threat to our enemies, who want to bring me down.

And yes, he's the one thing in the world that, if I lost him, it would defeat my spirit entirely.

And my own willpower.

Nikolai doesn't just want to defeat me, he wants me to suffer.

And then there are the weavers going missing, and the common people siding against them. Fearing them.

I swallow hard and stand. "How do we win this?"

I shouldn't be asking him that, I shouldn't be showing this much vulnerability of myself and my kingdom to this man who once sought to keep me small.

But he helped me defeat Nikolai before. He knows what we're up against, and that it will take every weaver on hand to stop Nikolai again.

I lost my father, but Aldric also lost a king to Nikolai and my mother, too. He lost a king who favored him.

Aldric does have a stake in this game.

His mouth is set in a thin line.

"By being vigilant." He meets my gaze and his hardens. "And by not giving into that bastard's attempts at fear. We'll find him, and when we have a target, Caleb can strike. Nikolai will regret having walked this close to the fire."

I can only hope it will be that simple.

But I fear these are the opening blows of a war.

Chapter 16

Support

Irava

He's gone when I wake up. His side of the bed empty, though still slightly warm.

I press my hand to the warmth and sigh.

I really don't want to venture to the Great Hall this morning, despite that I probably should, to show the people that I'm not afraid. That a thrown dagger will not stop me.

But I dress quickly for the day and ask the guards to have the kitchen send breakfast to my study in the mage's quarters.

I have to fix this now, I have to sort through my notes again, I have to be at my highest concentration. I can't be so distracted again.

Not ever again.

But still I reweave my illusion as Irava, covering the roundness of my stomach.

And walking the corridors, even with my guards this morning, feels exposed.

I've been under threat of danger before—when I first came

to the palace, Nikolai had threatened me. The Dowager, too, had threatened me. I collected all my enemies up front.

And which one now was behind the attack last night, and does it matter?

I know, with the clarity that comes with the early morning chill, that the attack on me was meant to hurt Torovan, and I hate that. I hate that I am something his enemies are trying to use.

But they still wanted me dead. Because I am a weapon, and they need to disarm the kingdom before they can take it for themselves.

I can't be the weapon Torovan needs unless I'm as sharp as I can be.

I narrow my eyes as I reach the mage's common room. I have never taken kindly to threats. And I'm not about to back down or hide myself away now.

All three of my apprentices are in the common room, and some of the elementalist mages as well. Some brought food from the Great Hall—the mood seems jittery, faces tight or dour.

"Irava!" Kian rushes over to me. "We couldn't see you last night, the guards wouldn't let us."

I glance to Morgan and Reveyan, who are trailing me now, while my two other guards station themselves in the corridor.

Both of my new shadows look haggard—I doubt either had any sleep. I don't need to ask if most of the palace guards were up all night—they would have been overturning the palace to find the assassin, I'm sure.

I haven't yet worked up the courage to ask if anything or anyone was found, though the frustrated feeling in the air makes me think not.

"I'm fine," I say to Kian. "Truly, I'm fine. Tired—a little tired."

One of the elementalists who became a court mage at the same time I did approaches.

"We're on watch, too, Irava. We'll be on watch for anyone who's trying to harm you."

"Thank you, Rani," I say, and I want to tell him that it's not necessary, I want to say that I have this under control.

But I don't.

He gives a wan smile.

"Yeah," another calls. "You have all of us. We will smoke anyone who tries to hurt you."

And he demonstrates with a puff of flame over his hand.

I bite my lip to hold back a smile. And it does my soul good. I hate that it's necessary, but it does my soul good to know they're with me in this.

"We didn't get to do our demonstration last night," Kian says. "So can we show off our weaving in the mage trials in a few days?"

"Kian!" Aria snaps. "This isn't the time."

"But it would help!" Kian protests, a little too loudly. "You're always saying we need to show people that weavers can do excellent things, Irava, so this would show that, too. You're going to be weaving, aren't you?"

I rub at my eyes. "I don't know. I don't know if that's a good idea now."

Rani, still standing nearby, says, "I don't think you can back out. My family is minor nobility, and I get the prejudice about people having magic that other people don't like. You can't back down from that."

It's not quite the same thing, but I get his point. It was the same point I argued with Valtair the night before, wanting my apprentices to make their demonstration before the court.

If we stop showing what we can do because of our enemies' pressure, then our enemies win. We show that we think what we do is harmful, too, don't we? We show that we're ashamed to be who we are.

"We'll all be there," Rani says. He looks back at Drayan, another elementalist who became a court mage when I did, who I know he has a crush on. "We'll all be watching for trouble. Stay in the center of us, Irava. But you have to be there, as one of our master mages. And I'm sorry, but, especially now."

I nod and give him the best ghost of a smile I can muster. "All right. I'll still weave in the trials."

Torovan's not going to like it. But we hadn't said I shouldn't participate. He's still almost certainly going to participate in the trials of combat near the end of the Festival.

It's Barellan tradition, and that tradition, I think, is more important now than ever.

"So can we do it, too?" Kian insists. "Wouldn't having every weaver who can demonstrate be a good thing? We'll show them they can't stop us. Torovan caught the knife, so—"

"*King* Torovan may not be participating in the mage's trial," I say. And we hadn't discussed that, either, but in the few times we'd talked about the mage's trial before, he'd as much as said that I would be the one showing royal abilities, not him. Which had sounded smart to me, because of the people's view of magic and royalty.

My magic was already established when I came to court. But though Torovan wears a mage's medallion, he hadn't demonstrated his magic in public before last night.

After that, should he demonstrate, too?

I don't know.

Gods, I don't know how best to handle this, I'm not a politician like Aldric. Not a *good* politician, anyway.

But Kian does have a point. Even if apprentices and mage candidates traditionally aren't supposed to compete in the mage's trial.

And it's less a trial and more a show for the crowd, we all know that. Whoever has the showiest elemental conjuration or weaver's illusion wins, the vote decided by a panel of the nobility. It's for entertainment, and to subtly show Barella's strength to our allies and our enemies.

Kian's eyes are lit, but intent. He knows what this demonstration is for, too. Though his ego is certainly driving him on.

"All right," I say again, holding up my hands. "It's in the daytime, so fireworks aren't going to work. We'll have to come up with something else."

Kian bounces. "We will! Oh, we will."

"Sire," Morgan says. "The food from the kitchen has arrived."

I look back to see two servants carrying heaping trays—and how they think I'll eat all of that food on my own is beyond me. But the kitchens send up the same amount every time I've ever asked.

I glance to Kian, who's eyeing the steaming trays now with interest. And Aria's perked up, too. Even Sabella, who's hanging back in a dour mood today, cranes her neck to look.

Have they eaten? Not likely, if they were hoping to find me here.

"Come on," I say, and wave them toward my study. "We'll eat and go over plans for your demonstrations. If we're going to put on a show, it has to be a *good* show."

CHAPTER 17

SWORD FORMS

TOROVAN

I should have gone back to sleep.

Instead, I left Caleb and borrowed a shirt and trousers from one of my guards who's near my size. And went out into one of the more private palace courtyards to practice my sword forms.

I'm not the best swordsman. It's never been the king's or a prince's place to openly carry a sword, but I do know how to use one. And right now, I need the vigorous exercise, I need the biting autumn morning air, I need the silence of movement.

And it's here that Valtair finds me. He's looking haggard, too, and I wonder if he got even less sleep than I did.

I stop when I see him crossing the courtyard to me, and hand my practice sword over to one of my guards, accepting the towel he hands me back to wipe my face. It's too cold to go shirtless, but my thin undershirt clings to me, making the chill more biting when I stop.

"Tor, have you had breakfast?"

He doesn't open with his usual sarcasm. And that has me

handing off my towel, taking the borrowed guard's coat one of them offers me, and following Valtair back inside.

"No. Are you headed there?"

"I ordered some to my office. And looks like a lot of people have done the same, the Great Hall was only half full when I passed it a few minutes ago." He looks at me, frowning. "Did you even sleep? Gods, did you sleep in the guards' barracks? Why are you wearing a guard's uniform?"

I can see more questions waiting to spill out and say quickly, "No, I just borrowed clothes. I was up early. What's the mood of the court, besides not wanting to be in the Great Hall?"

He eyes me a moment more, then shrugs it off.

"Not good. There's sympathy for Caleb, of course, and anger about the attack. That I expected. But there's also an ugly sentiment that if Caleb wasn't wearing the medallion of a master mage, that maybe that dagger wouldn't have been thrown."

My blood heats up, and Valtair nods.

"Yes. My thoughts exactly. Tor, I'm not sure how much of this is superstition, or the usual unease around weavers that Nikolai inflamed earlier this year, but it's not good. Or, how much is being stoked by Nikolai's agents. Or your mother's."

He stops as a group of courtiers comes too near, and I put on my courtly mask as much as I can just now and nod to them. Never mind that I'm not even remotely presentable just now.

It *is* still my palace.

We pass the entrance to the Great Hall, and it's as Valtair said, only a scattering of people inside, not the packed bustle it should be on this second day of the Harvest Festival.

But we take the stairs on the other side of the hall up to where the Council offices are.

In Valtair's office, he pulls out a chair at his desk. There's already a large tray heaped with food on the desk, and my stomach growls despite my mood.

Thankfully, there's more than one plate.

I lift the lids and start heaping mine.

We wait until we're both settled to speak again.

"There's the reception in the Great Hall today," Valtair says, "the first official political reception with all the nobility and dignitaries. Then, there's the trials of strength in the Festival fields later today. I suggest you go to both, Tor. At very least, Caleb should be with you for the reception, though I think it's less important for the strengths trials."

I stuff my mouth full of eggs with minced fillings. I'd told Aldric that I wouldn't attend the strengths trials, but that was bothering the back of my mind.

Because I *do* need the connection with the common people just now, I absolutely must have that. If Nikolai is trying to fracture that trust, I must work to strengthen it.

"Fine. Yes. I agree." I'll have to talk to Caleb about the reception—but then, he knows the schedule, too. I need to convince him to stay near his guards while I'm down at the trial.

And maybe it's the coward's move, but I ask, "Can you send to Caleb to make sure he'll be in the Great Hall, at—what—two turns after noon?"

Valtair gives me a look. "Are you fighting?"

"No. I'm busy."

"So busy you took several hours to exercise this morning and you're wearing your guards' clothes?"

"Valtair."

He sighs. "I'm avoiding my father. You're avoiding Caleb. He's avoiding his mother, presumably."

"He is. I'm sure."

"So, we're all avoiding someone. But you'll have to make a show of it this afternoon, Tor, have to. The both of you together. No, I'm not going to send to Caleb. You ask him, you figure that out."

My mouth pulls tight, but I don't press. I know he's right. Though I don't want him to be.

"And the assassin?"

"Dead ends. A few people saw who threw the dagger—a middle-aged man with pale skin and a thick brown mustache, wearing a blue tunic that was well-made, but worn. That's the description I have. But no one seems to know who this is, or know where he is. I suspect a disguise."

I meet his eyes. "An illusion?"

"I don't know, Tor. Every weaver we know in the palace was accounted for. But there are a lot more people than we know in the palace right now. If it was a weaver, it could have been anyone. Did you sense anything?"

I shake my head, spearing a sausage. "No. It would have been easier if I had."

"Maybe," Valtair rubs the back of his neck. "We need to increase the palace guards, should I call in some of the auxiliaries?"

"Some," I say. "Not all. I don't want to cause alarm."

"People are already alarmed. I think they'll want to feel safe." He hesitates, and I look up, knowing I'm not going to like what he says next.

"When Caleb saved your life, the people praised that. Of

course they did. Caleb is an excellent hero—he's the son—or daughter—of foreign royalty, he's the outsider, he's a person of intrigue. All of that. And handsome."

I raise my brows. "And?"

"And...when you saved Caleb, the same isn't also true."

"That I'm not handsome?"

He doesn't even smile. His look is flat, and tired. "You're a Barellan king, Torovan. You know what the people think about royalty having magic."

"It's weaving. It's learned, not something I'm born with."

"I know that. You know that. Mostly everyone *does* know that, but it's the stigma, isn't it? The gods-damned stigma."

I clear the rest of my plate and reach for a small helping more.

"So?"

"So, there's unease around it. I've had reports of rumors that people are uneasy that their king has visible magic."

"Gods, Valtair, I've been wearing a mage's medallion for months. Every day. It's not like they haven't known—"

"But they haven't seen it in action, Torovan, and that's different. You know it's different."

I swipe at my mouth.

"So what am I supposed to do, not save my husband when someone tries to assassinate him?"

"I'm saying—I'm just saying what's happening. I'm not saying you can do anything about it."

"While my mother is busy getting a foreign kingdom to kidnap my weavers—"

"You don't know that's what's happening. You can't make that accusation yet, Tor."

"And Nikolai is inciting the people in his district against me, and inflaming anti-weaver sentiments."

He waves his fork and talks around a mouthful. "That you probably can say."

"Gods, Valtair. Why is it always a tangle? Why can't people see that I'm trying to do good by them? I'm giving everything I have to do good by them. It's put my own life in danger, it killed my father—"

"I *know*, Tor."

I hold his gaze.

"And I know this Harvest is important," he says. "I know you have to make a good show of things, we all do. Our enemies don't want that. And they want our best defenses uncoordinated and pressed into being ineffective. I don't know the best way forward, but it's not in fear, and it's not in hiding, and it's not in giving in. But we have to be aware."

Which was more or less what Aldric said, too.

My jaw flexes as I grit my teeth, looking past him to the sky outside his window.

All of me, the entire whole of me, wants to punch something. To make people see that what they're fearing isn't what's actually going on. That they're being manipulated by a dark weaver, not in any danger from me, or Caleb, or the weavers of this court. Or any ordinary village mage, for that matter.

"I think your mother and Nikolai both have agents in this court," Valtair says. "No, I know they do. We know. We *have* known, and maybe it was a mistake to not more aggressively find them before."

I take a breath. "I've talked with Aldric, he's keeping an eye out for weavers of any kind."

"Good. You and Caleb should do the same. Not actively, I think, but—"

"Yes."

"And, I suspect, ordinary people either paid or coerced. Those will be the most dangerous, I think. Already are. Tor, some of the court sentiments this morning are too regular not to have been seeded somewhere and then nurtured into thorns. Even on this short notice."

I grimace. Gods. This is the part of politics and being a king that I hate. I am good at action, I am good at straightforward responses.

But this is where Valtair excels. He does understand the nuance and what to do about it.

"Handle it," I say, rising. "You're already handling it."

He stands, too. "Be at the reception, you and Caleb both." He tilts his head, considering. "Don't wear your ceremonial crowns. Actually, don't wear your crowns at all. You must be more relatable today."

"Fine. Yes. It's heavy anyway."

His mouth lifts in half a smile.

"We'll figure this out, Torovan, we will."

He hesitates again, like he wants to say more. And does he see what Caleb saw, that I've been afraid of more than I'm saying?

If I told Aldric, can I tell Valtair, too?

But my chest tightens, and I keep my mouth shut.

At least Aldric knows, and it was a risk to say even that.

Yes, we will figure this out.

We'll find Nikolai's agents, we'll find my mother's, we'll get them out of my court.

I don't exactly have a plan how, but at least I'm in motion.

I nod to Valtair. "I'll see you at the reception."

CHAPTER 18

FAULT

CALEB

Sometime in the late morning, I reweave my illusion as Caleb.

And while I talked and planned with my apprentices for several hours, now I have as many open books as I can fit across my messy desktop, and I'm reading passages I've read before, searching for something new.

Anything.

Some connection I didn't see before.

Anything. Anything to convince myself that even attempting to weave around the growing child within me won't be dangerous.

I even try what I'd been thinking about the night before, weaving a shell around an object—one of my books—before weaving an illusion around that. It does work. It even stays, and maybe that does have promise.

But I have to dig deeper.

Torovan says he trusts me, but he's not the one with another life in his hands.

And he would never forgive me if something went wrong.

I would never forgive me.

My eyes are half crossing as I reread and read again another passage in a book I studied and set aside months ago, which hardly told me anything at all.

There's a tap on the door. Tentative—not one of the guards, then.

I look up, rubbing at the bridge of my nose beneath my spectacles. "Come in!"

The door opens slightly and Aria peaks in, her loose hair hanging down as she cranes through the doorway.

I sent them all to practice in the common room, and hoped they'd be at it for another hour at least.

But maybe—gods, I'd been studying all the rest of the morning and it's almost noon.

Do I dare brave the Great Hall for lunch?

There's a breakfast roll left on the discarded and mostly eaten food tray. I can eat that.

Aria slips all the way inside and looks at the books scattered across my desk.

"I can help with that, with whatever you're doing," she says.

Which...might not be a bad idea. But a few of the books, the very oldest books, do talk about mind and soul weaving in a way that hasn't always made it sound bad. I'm not sure I'm ready to expose my apprentices to that yet.

Or, ever.

"Maybe," I say. Then lean my arms on my desk. "What do you need?"

She shrugs, slipping into the chair across from me.

I'm Caleb just now. I know she's more comfortable around

me when I'm Irava, but I'm not going to reweave my illusion just for that.

Aria doesn't look at me when she says in a rush, "It's my fault, I'm so sorry."

I sit back. "What's your fault?"

"That you were attacked!"

She's looking at me now, and she's serious. "If I hadn't lost control of my weaving—"

"Oh, gods. No, that's not your fault. There's—"

And how much do I share with my apprentices of just how deeply our enemies have been manipulating the people?

Of how subtle and insidious the danger to weavers is?

But then, she is in danger as a weaver in this palace, too. My apprentices are all aware—weavers have to be.

"There's enemies of Barella who are trying to make the people afraid of weavers," I say.

"I know that." She juts up her chin. "We've already talked about that. That's why we needed to do the demonstration in the first place. And why my losing control—I know that was like what happened with Nikolai's, Lord Metrial's, demonstration before the king. The demonstration that you stopped. I know that made the people more afraid."

I breathe out.

Well.

I've been trying to protect them, to shield them from the worst of it while they're still in training. But they *aren't* unaware.

And maybe I'd best stop trying.

Like I've been asking Torovan to stop trying to shield me.

"There are weavers going missing on the border," I say. "There's unrest in Nikolai's family's district, and there's obviously now someone in the palace who either works for Nikolai or Torovan's mother, or another party who wants to see me dead."

"And it's my fault," Aria says again, hitting each word separately, as if that will make me believe it this time.

I bite my lip.

My apprentice, Sabella, saw my pregnancy yesterday.

Reveyan and Chiran, two of my guards, saw it, too, though I don't think they'll have shared that information anywhere. That's not the men Torovan picks to be his guards.

Dare I add one more to that list?

I am bone weary of secrets.

I stand and drop my illusion.

Aria just watches me, used to my shifts in appearance. Then her gaze drops to my stomach. To the roundness that definitely wasn't there before.

"That is why it's not your fault," I say, waving down at my stomach. "I was distracted last night, otherwise—"

Aria's gaze snaps back up to mine. "But that doesn't make it your fault," she says, "the attack wouldn't have happened if I'd kept my magic under control!"

I pull my illusion as Caleb back around myself, frowning.

"It was likely planned," I say. "Aria..."

She's crying now. She plops back in the chair, her face in her hands. "I'm never going to be able to control my weaving, not like you can, or like Kian can, I can't protect you!"

"I don't need you to protect me."

"You do! That's why you're training us, I know it. I know you have enemies. It took *weeks* to convince my parents to let me train with you, Caleb, but I did. I know what's at stake. I know I have to get better."

And maybe I haven't successfully kept anything from my apprentices at all.

"Then we'll train," I say. "You and me. We'll train after hours. We'll work until we find your blocks and get past them."

She nods. "Yes. Yes, please. I want to help Barella, not hurt it."

"Aria, you didn't—"

But she waves her hands. "I made things worse, I know I did, you can't tell me I didn't. But I want to make it better."

There's steel in her eyes.

"Teach me how to protect the kingdom, Caleb, please. And I will."

I know she will. I know that.

I nod. "Let me get through this day. Maybe this week, because my schedule with the Festival happening is tight—"

I straighten.

Oh, no.

I almost forgot there's supposed to be a political reception today, and I'm supposed to attend it. It's in, what, two hours? Less?

I need to dress for it.

There's another knock at my door, this one firm.

And I already know who it's going to be before he pushes open the door.

Torovan looks inside. He's—wearing a guard's uniform?

He's sweaty. He must have borrowed clothes.

Because he hadn't come back this morning to dress.

His hair is disheveled in a way that makes me want to run my hands through it right now. And I kind of like the uniform, even though it's a little short in the sleeves.

"Caleb, you'll be attending the reception? I'm going to get ready." Implying I should do that, too.

I exhale.

"Yes, I'm coming." I glance at Aria.

"You three need to get ready, too—please tell Kian and Sabella. This is formal, and you have an official place in this court. Be ready within an hour, and be at the Great Hall at the second turn of the glass."

Aria straightens and eyes Torovan. But says to me, "Yes, Your Majesty." And makes a courtly bow, and again to Torovan. "Your Majesty."

Torovan frowns, but he doesn't contradict me. He steps back into the corridor, and when I follow, he falls into step beside me.

And he keeps looking at me again, like I'm breakable.

Like he didn't leave me in the middle of the night to wake up to a cold bed this morning.

To go do what, practice in a guard's uniform in the courtyard?

"What?" I snap.

His face pinches. "Are you ready to face the court today?"

I give him a sidelong glance. "It's not like I haven't faced the court after danger before. Or disaster."

He tenses, and I slip my hand in his.

"I'm sorry," I say. "I'm just...yesterday was a lot. And I'm pretty sure my mother will be there."

He hisses through his teeth. "This week is supposed to be enjoyable. That's what a festival is *supposed* to be."

"It was fun when you were a prince, not a king," I say.

"Ha. Yes. *Yes.* Were festivals actually fun in Galenda when you were a princess?"

"Sometimes." I give a half a smile. "I never really behaved enough for the fun to outweigh the consequences."

He snorts. "I do believe that."

He stops near the back stairs leading up to the royal apartments and turns to face me.

He's looking between my eyes, his face intent.

"Can you trust me? Trust that everything I'm doing right now is to protect you, and the kingdom?"

My stomach churns.

But then, maybe I'm not the one to judge keeping secrets.

I stretch up to kiss him, and he huffs out a breath between kisses.

"I'm a mess," he says. "I need to clean up. No time for a bath, either."

"I've seen you worse," I say, around him kissing me back. "I've made you sweatier than this."

He makes a noise deep in his throat, a noise that I like.

Gods.

I don't want whatever snarls have come between us.

I want this, right here. I want my king's hands tangled in my hair.

I want us close, not always dancing off each other's rhythms.

Can I still have that?

I trust him, yes, but that's not really the issue. It's that, for whatever reason, he doesn't trust me.

He pulls back. "Stay close today?"

I try not to bristle, but I know how distracted I've been lately.

And I know the danger.

"Yeah, I will."

CHAPTER 19

THE RECEPTION

CALEB

don't want to be at this reception. I know I told Torovan that I'm used to the crowds looking at me like I'm different, a magnet to danger as a master weaver, but I never said it was comfortable. More comfortable in the last months, as the Barellan court is used to me now. And there hasn't been any visible danger for them to worry about.

But it's not just Barellans here today.

I'm by Torovan's side as we walk in, but the eyes on us today don't hold as much warmth as they did the night before.

It's less of a welcome, and more silence than I'd like.

Because the people are reminded of why someone might have wanted to kill me?

Because Torovan showed his weaving?

I glance behind us at my three apprentices, who we stopped to collect again before coming here.

They're all dressed in the best they have, and even Sabella is wearing the court-worthy coat and trousers I quietly gifted her last month. Because I know what it feels like, too, to be the village mage in a court of glittering people.

I'd said to them in the mages' quarters:

"You will be polite, you will present yourselves as courtiers, as my apprentices. You will *not* do weaving of any kind. None. This is a diplomatic function only."

This with an eye to Kian.

But they all nodded solemnly and gave off a ripple of "Yes, Caleb." After talking with Aria earlier, I think they all know the weight of this reception today.

And the parallel to my own early days at the court isn't lost on me—how Aldric warned us mage candidates to be seen and not heard, to avoid drawing attention or causing disruption.

But I do want my apprentices to be seen—that is the point. I want people to see them as ordinary, likable people. I want them to mingle and gain more of their own connections. Not just to their families, and not just to me. Sabella especially—she is not a servant of this court anymore.

"My mother is here," I say to Torovan, spotting her talking across the hall. She's wearing a pearl blue gown today, her light-brown hair pulled up in rolling curls, a lightweight crown sitting atop it all. The very picture of a queen.

Torovan and I aren't wearing crowns today. He said Valtair said it would be better to look relatable.

But seeing my mother, is that a mistake?

The long tables haven't been moved, but the chairs are all pushed in, and only light snack food is set on platters around the hall. Knots of courtiers and foreign guests are clustered everywhere.

"We can make a circuit in the other direction," Torovan says. "Away from your mother."

"She'll notice that."

"Well, would you rather we walk toward her?"

We share a look. And I follow him in the opposite direction from my mother.

I move with Torovan from conversation to conversation, smiling, practiced by now in the manners and ways of the Barellan court. And most of the people we're talking with are those I've met before, some I see often.

But their nervousness is palpable at being close to me today. Do they think by being near me that makes them a target? By just talking to me?

Or are they nervous, too, about Torovan?

Just how deep does the fear of weavers run here? I thought this court saw me as its protector.

But then, they saw last night that I hadn't protected even myself.

Some, though, aren't afraid. Count Valtair is booming in high form about a country game he's trying to build a stadium for on his estate. His cologne today is also in high form and isn't at all helping my unsettled stomach.

I spot Lord Valtair across the hall, and he tips his head to me. In irony—or sympathy, maybe. Or both.

And through it all, my weaver's senses are as open as I can stand, feeling all the currents of willpower around me. People shifting their own inner weights to draw others toward them. Or to repel others away. The shimmering threads of reality and possibility dance around this hall, sometimes with eagerness, sometimes with friction.

I don't usually keep my senses this open with so many people around, but I'm scanning, constantly looking for any signs of weaving—or soul weaving.

Or even pockets of malevolent intent, which I've found sometimes I can see before it's acted on. A stable boy pushing another down, a noble parent berating their child.

I see some of that here, yes. And my gaze lingers on members of the Akrean delegation, longer than is politic, or polite. One woman from that delegation turns to look at me, her pale face stern, her black hair pulled back with a tightness that makes my scalp ache.

But I see no malice around her. She meets my eyes with a nod before we both look away.

Everything I'm feeling right now, everything in this room, is what I'd expect to feel.

But there's also so much to sense here, too, that I don't know if I'd feel another attack in time to stop it. I don't have foresight, I'm just highly attuned.

But Torovan and I are moving on from one clustered group of nobles to another when I do sense weaving from the other end of the hall.

I keep myself from visibly reacting but turn in that direction.

To see—gods. To see a spiral of threads above Kian, his hands outstretched to try to control them.

I *told* him not to weave.

Torovan follows my gaze and stiffens.

"Go," he growls. "Get that under control."

I push through the people around us, trying not to run, trying not to attract more attention than necessary.

What the hell is Kian thinking, weaving here? In this crowd of people already nervous about weavers today?

Yes, he's ambitious. I know that.

But he's not a fool.

And even though his father the high general isn't at the court right now, Kian knows whatever he does publicly will get back to him.

I spot Morgan and Reveyan cutting through the crowd with me, and now I'm definitely attracting more attention than I should.

But so is Kian.

A shout goes up, then a scream.

I break into a run.

Kian's arms are up, trying to contain a shuddering mass of reality expanding above him as people rush to get back. He's holding it, but barely.

I reach out and pull on the threads he's trying to gather back in, tying off loose ends, weaving reality back together into a pattern it can handle.

He sees me, and I watch his face fall first in relief, then terror.

I'm concentrating now, but I'm not trying to hide my fury, either.

Kian fully lets go of the weaving, and I'm only dimly aware of more shouts around me as I concentrate on unweaving the mess that Kian's made before it explodes.

And I do, moment by agonizing moment, calming the maelstrom of reality that was threatening to unravel into chaos.

I'm still holding my own illusion, too, I don't dare let go of that now in this very public space.

But I still have enough concentration to unweave what Kian's done.

And I'm not sure what he was trying to do, but by the time I got here, it wasn't coherent. And now, I'm not even pulling it into constructs, just soothing reality where I can, trying to put the threads back in their places, or at least new places that will hold them.

I'm panting by the time I lower my hands. And my mouth is pressed thin with my own need to not explode as I turn to my apprentice.

Apprentices. Aria and Sabella are near Kian, too, Aria rigid but moving to Kian's side, Sabella's face a stormy mask.

Was it just Kian, or all of them?

But I don't have time to ask what happened before someone nearby shouts, "We need a healer!"

I turn and see a cluster of people around a young nobleman I've seen around the court the last few months, a second son of a minor lord. His handsome brown face, usually confident, is now contorted in pain. He's clutching a trembling, burned hand.

"He did it," the man gets out around chattering teeth. "The weaver tried to kill me!"

Nodding toward Kian.

Gods.

I turn and find Morgan nearby.

"Get them *out*," I hiss to him, and jerk my head toward my apprentices.

His own fury is plain even in his guard's professionalism, and he grips Kian's arm, waving to Aria and Sabella.

"It wasn't his fault," Aria says to me, pleading.

"Was it yours?" I snap.

She flinches, and I check myself. This isn't the way to handle this, but everyone is watching now.

Everyone.

"Come on," Sabella says quietly, pulling Aria back. She

gives me a look, and yes, we're all going to have to go over what happened later.

But now, now I have to try to mitigate the damage. If I even can.

What was Kian *thinking?*

But it has to be more than it seems. It has to have been an accident.

Kian, looking shocky, goes with Morgan without a fight.

And the crowd around us collectively takes a breath as the apprentices leave.

That's not good, oh that's not good. They don't seem afraid of me, at least, I'm still being seen as the protector.

Valtair arrives, pushing through the re-gathering crowd, now that the apprentices are gone.

"What happened?" he asks in a low voice.

"Kian—somehow his weaving got out of control. There's someone injured."

Valtair turns toward the young nobleman, his own hands twitching.

I catch his arm. Catch his eye. No, he can't help that man here. Valtair showing he's an elementalist right now would be the disastrous end to another disastrous day.

Valtair presses his lips tight. Then turns, calling for a healer, sending two of the hall guards running.

"Why by all the seasons was he weaving?" Valtair asks under his breath.

Then Torovan arrives. He didn't run—he'd be expected not to, even if I took off. Even if I've been here six months and more now, I'm still the outsider.

And he is expected to act like a king.

Heavy silence descends as Torovan surveys the scene and

the injured man. Like people are waiting for him to mete out punishment.

On my apprentices?

The eyes around me are cold, fearful, unyielding. There was a clear danger in their midst, and they want to know it won't happen again.

And whatever reason Kian had for weaving—and it had better be a *damned* good one—I'm not going to subject him or the rest of my apprentices to the court's wrath any more than I have to. His heart has always been in the right place, even if his ego and ambition are often just as big.

I turn to Torovan. "I take responsibility for my apprentices—this will not happen again."

He frowns at me, but he can't contradict me now, not in front of everyone here.

"Master Weaver," he says carefully, "thank you for protecting the court." He holds my gaze, his own troubled.

"Is this how Barella treats its guests?" someone calls, their voice heavy with an unfamiliar accent.

One of the Akrean delegates, the woman who caught my eye earlier.

My weaver's senses are still narrowed in my focus to stop disaster, but I widen them again now. Something is off here. But though I'm looking for signs of weaving, signs of mind control weaving, even, I don't find any.

The Akrean meets my eyes again, then her gaze slides past me to Torovan.

Another voice, familiar this time, joins the fray.

"My son moved quickly to stop an accident from getting worse," my mother says, and I stiffen as she joins us.

She nods to me.

"In my court, that is when we'd say, 'thank you.'"

And now Torovan's shoulders are tightening up again, too, but he nods to my mother.

Then turns back to me.

"Master Weaver," he says. "Please attend to your apprentices."

There's a bustle at the doors—the guards coming back with a man in healer's blues.

Torovan moves closer to me and leans in. "I'll see you tonight at the feast."

Should I even come?

But I have to. Despite the danger, despite this chaos now, I'm still the king by his side. I have to be, especially now.

I nod to him and stride out.

CHAPTER 20

THE ENEMY

CALEB

Every step toward the mage's common room is another notch upward in my anger.

I *told* them not to weave. Specifically, Kian.

What by all the gods of *all* the seasons would possess him to start weaving at that reception?

And if Aria knows much of what's really going on with weavers in the kingdom just now, he does too.

He's smart, he knows how many ways that could have gone wrong, which it did.

I'm wondering, with a tightening chest, if I need to dismiss him from my apprentices—

But then that's the point.

That is the whole point, that weavers will follow their hearts, no matter what. Their own wills, their own ways. That is why we wield the power that we do.

And, gods, I wouldn't do that to him. Not even mad as I am.

I will not do to Kian what Aldric did to Torovan—I will not tell him he's not good enough. Because it's not true.

I need to get the rest of the story.

Frustrated, I don't stop as Reveyan opens the door to the mage's common room ahead of me.

I storm inside, pause to see my apprentices all sitting huddled near the hearth.

Kian looks up, rears back, his whole body broadcasting his dismay. His court coat is unbuttoned, his hair messy like he was grabbing at it.

He stands as I stride over, they all do.

Sabella is bone pale, her hands clasped behind her back. Aria's arms are braced around her middle.

Kian—

Kian launches at me, and Reveyan, still near me, and still on alert since the attack last night, tenses. But Kian wraps his arms around me.

"Caleb, I'm sorry! I know I shouldn't have—"

Then he draws back, looking down.

"What is—why is your stomach—"

He's touching my illusion.

I close my eyes, breathing through a moment of the most *profound* frustration, then drop my illusion.

But I'm still Caleb, so I reweave my illusion as Caleb with my pregnancy showing.

There's no one else in the common room but my apprentices, and my guards. Two of my apprentices already knew. So did two of my guards.

Now, they all know.

"This *does not* go beyond this room," I say.

Kian nods.

And his demeanor has shifted in his surprise, and in his curiosity, to something else. His shoulders are squared again, his whole penitent posture gone.

I narrow my eyes and look between him and my other two apprentices.

He would never be that apologetic on his own. He would be defending himself if he had been the one to start whatever it was that had just happened. He had been weaving, yes, but had it been his idea?

Aria shrinks back from my gaze, and I do my utmost to soften it.

Sabella—Sabella meets my gaze head on, her mouth a thin line.

"What happened?" I ask, more quietly this time.

Sabella shifts, then exhales, bringing her hands around to clasp in front this time. Where she was pale before, she's flushing now.

"I don't know what happened," she says. "I don't know why I reacted how I did. I thought I felt something, like an instinct, and then I was weaving a shield to my side to defend myself. Then, the weaving...sputtered. I didn't lose control, but it shifted in a way I didn't expect. Kian saw it and tried to weave around my weaving to contain it, but then both of our weavings flared up, and caught the hand of the man nearest to us. Which, I believe, scared Kian, so his weaving flared even more, and that's when you came in."

I blink slowly. Sabella is steadfast. That is her predominant trait—she is immensely stubborn, immensely determined, and immensely kind.

Was she trying to take the blame for Kian, or for Aria?

"Is that what happened?" I ask Kian.

He exhales explosively. "I tried to stop it, whatever the threads were doing. But I couldn't. I'm sorry—"

I shake my head. "You did well, Kian." I grip his shoulder. "Truly."

He doesn't look happy. But he nods. "And Sabella?" he asks.

I turn back to Sabella...and understand why Kian was trying to protect her. She's not a noble. She doesn't have noble parents, or a general father, like Kian. If she's blamed for this, the court will want her blood.

Sabella faces me squarely, braced for rebuke, or dismissal, or worse. And that bracing is curdling my insides.

But the story is still not adding up.

"What did you feel?" I ask. "What made you react, can you describe it?"

I hadn't sensed anything from across the hall, anything that would have spelled danger, or another weaver, but then I had been sensing broadly. How much had I missed?

She shakes her head. "I don't know. It was just an instinct, like I said. Like, the feeling when you're in a dark corridor and you have to whirl around to see if someone is following, or watching."

Cold slices through my lingering anger, rapidly chilling my blood.

I step closer to Sabella, and she holds her ground, but I pause when I see her gathering fear.

I hold out my hands and, as gently as I can manage just now, say, "I want to check for signs of mind control weaving."

She stiffens, but after a moment, nods.

"You mean Nikolai?" Kian asks, moving close, still protective.

"Like his magic, yes. Kian—I'll need to concentrate."

He huffs, but backs off a step and doesn't say more.

And I widen my weaver's senses again, seeing the threads of Sabella's reality, her willpower, her soul.

A human soul is a blaze of reality. And the resonance between her and me, her and Kian, and her and Aria, hums in the air between us. Not quite seen but felt, and known.

It's the other side of soul weaving. If Nikolai sought to disrupt a soul's willpower with his own will, to overwrite it, to control, then these quiet connections defy that unnatural interference.

I've been very careful not to try to weave them, even after I first saw this resonance in the fight with Nikolai. I gave Torovan my willpower through that resonance, and it strengthened the connection between us enough to interrupt Nikolai's control.

But that was a surrender of my will to Torovan, and his will that used mine to strengthen the connection between us.

These connections are forged through relationships. Through both people's will.

Trying to manipulate them would skirt dangerously close to Nikolai's kind of magic.

But now, I have to fight Nikolai's kind of magic again.

Again, here, in this palace that's become my home.

I don't know that I know what I'm doing, but I don't know anyone else who can do this, either. Who might be able to see if Nikolai is controlling my apprentice, my friend.

If Sabella losing control today, or having the impulse to weave at all, was an act of sabotage.

I carefully follow the resonance between myself and my

apprentice, trying to find the sense of her soul within her threads. Her own symphony.

And here's where I pause.

How do I see the threads of her thoughts without crossing that line between the glow of resonance and actual soul weaving?

How do I see past the possibilities around Sabella to the actual threads of her reality that drive those possibilities? To the thoughts that make Sabella who she is.

Torovan and I discussed this before. We both trained ourselves to see but never touch.

But as I listen to her sense of reality, I can almost hear… there are notes in her symphony that feel off.

There's something unbalanced, the pattern of her reality pushed out of true.

She's looking up into my eyes. And maybe she sees my hesitation.

"Whatever it is," she says, "get it out of me."

I don't see anything causing the unbalance. But the feel of it…the feel has a ghost of familiarity.

Of unreality.

Of holding space for something that is no longer there, but was.

It feels eerily like the quiet of the late king's bedchamber, the absence of evidence.

It's the empty spaces that violence left behind.

Something happened in Sabella's mind, something that wasn't her own will. And her mind has subtly shaped around it.

With the hands of my mind's eye, I carefully nudge one of the threads of her mind that seems slightly out of tune.

Sabella shudders, and I pause, check myself.

I unweave my illusion around myself and give my full concentration to this now.

"Sabella," I ask softly. And I know she's attuned, I know she senses, at least on some level, what I'm doing. "Can I fix this?"

She nods.

Carefully, so very carefully, I touch one of the threads again with my own mind's hands, nudging it back into where it seems to want to go.

Sabella flinches, but her eyes never leave mine.

Trusting me completely.

I nudge one more thread that feels out of place, as if something else recently occupied where it wants to be.

Her symphony goes back in tune.

Sabella lets out a sob, which is so unlike her for a moment it stuns me.

"Are you done?" Kian asks, angrily.

I swallow, and retreat from Sabella's mind.

Should I have done that?

Did I feel what I thought I'd felt, that Nikolai messed with her mind before?

Does Torovan have those same mental scars?

Gods. Gods, what have I done?

I should not have touched her mind.

"Yes," I manage, before Kian pushes me aside, wrapping his arms around Sabella, holding her tightly while she clutches him back, sobbing into his shoulder.

I back away, struggling to catch my breath as my own eyes fill.

I meet Aria's burning gaze.

"That was mind control weaving?" she asks. I have never heard her voice so flat, or so full of potential violence.

Is she asking if I did mind control weaving, or if I fixed it?

But I didn't try to impose my will, just fix what had been done before.

"It's not there anymore, but it was there," I say. "I saw where it had been, and where it had disturbed some of her threads."

"Then Nikolai Metrial *is* here," Aria says. "He's here, in the palace?"

I freeze as the implications of all of this start to hit me.

I hadn't felt anything in the Great Hall.

And Sabella said her feeling was an instinct, not anything she could name.

How long has it been since that weaving was done to her? And what exactly was done?

I don't know enough about mind control weaving to know if time is a factor, or distance, if a weaving is made and then the weaver goes away. Did the weaving trigger at the reception and now it's gone, only leaving the absence of it?

The unreality weaving in Torovan's father's apartment had to have been there for months. And likely the same for his mother's, before I found it. It's still there now.

At what point does a mind control weaving just become... reality?

Become instinct?

Sabella's mind seemed to be off from where it should have been, but not by much. Was that a fresh wound, or a scar on her mind?

And should I be looking for more signs like this, in the people around me?

I look to Aria, then Kian. He's still comforting Sabella, so I gesture Aria close.

She swallows, but steps close enough to touch.

I don't, though. My mind's eye is enough.

But though I'm looking as deeply as I dare, I don't see any sense of wrongness in her mind.

"No," I say, and she bites her lip, stepping back, her eyes filling with relief.

Kian turns his head just enough to see me. "Can you check me?"

He's entangled with Sabella just now, but I try.

"No," I say a few moments later. "No, I don't see anything."

"Then it's just me?" Sabella asks, pulling away from Kian. Sniffing loudly.

I have never seen her so vulnerable, and it makes a hollow depth open in the pit of my stomach.

"Yes. Sabella, I'm sorry. I did my best to fix it." I bite off the "but." But I don't know if I made it better.

I've been worried about weaving my own body with my pregnancy, but I just wove her *mind*.

Sabella nods, sniffs again, then wipes her eyes on the embroidered sleeves of her courtly coat.

Kian fishes in his pocket for a crumpled handkerchief, but she fends him off.

"So what now?" Sabella asks.

She seems okay. She truly does seem okay, beyond the emotion.

I shake my head, my panic rising like a slow but inevitable tide.

I knew there was a threat.

I knew we had enemies.

I even knew my life was in danger.

But what if the person who threw the knife was controlled, too?

What if anyone around us, at any time, could be controlled?

What if seeds were planted long ago, and are only now coming to the forefront?

What if Nikolai's not even here, but his agents are every-where? Unknown to even themselves.

What if he has apprentices, too, and what if they are here, too?

I don't know enough about how this works.

And maybe I should have been finding and studying books on soul weaving and mind control instead of trying to fix my own concentration problem.

"I don't want this to happen again," Sabella says. "Or—or to Kian, or Aria, or *anyone* else. Caleb, you've shown us so much, but not how to see the mind control weavings. We have to know. You have to show us that."

I hadn't wanted even a chance of them getting ideas on how to use them. What I did just now is walking the line close enough.

And I can't show my apprentices actual mind control weavings, no. I will not do them.

But I can show them unreality. And that is a different varia-tion of the same kind of magic.

Torovan and I left his mother's apartment untouched, beyond my carefully showing him exactly how that weaving works. And I worked it out for myself, I know I can weave that unreality weaving if I want to.

But I *never* want to.

"We want to protect you," Aria says, swaying slightly as she hugs herself.

I swallow. I've been trying to protect my apprentices from the silent, gathering danger.

But it's already found them.

I reweave my illusion as Caleb again and watch Kian flinch. They're all too keyed up.

But they're watching.

"This," I say, and slowly unweave and reweave my illusion again, flattening my stomach this time, "is how to create an illusion around yourself. You've all seen me do it, but I always do it quickly. Have any of you seen enough to figure it out on your own?"

Kian—of course—immediately weaves himself into an older, slightly taller, much more heavily muscled version of himself.

Even with all of this, I can't stop my smile, and he makes an embarrassed shrug, but he doesn't unweave it.

"I haven't," Aria says. "Can you do it again?"

"I can show you how," Kian says, bouncing on the balls of his feet.

"Let me do it, Kian," I say gently, and he reluctantly nods.

I show them all four more times, talking them through all the steps, what it feels like, what they should be looking for in the reality around them, how they should be shaping their will into it. I'm going slowly as I both weave and unweave my illusions.

And I'm bending the reality of light around me, but not reality itself. Not my own reality.

My throat tightens with every reweaving until I have to

stop. Because this is the one thing I still can't do—safely weave my reality around my growing child.

This is the one thing that's holding everything back.

But Aria's now carefully weaving an illusion of Sabella around herself, Sabella being her closest reference point. She's going slowly, and I watch her threads, correcting her once, and she catches the slip. Holds steady.

Sabella frowns at Aria in her Sabella illusion.

"I'm not that dour," she mutters.

Then, with a bemused tilt of her head, she starts to weave herself into Aria. But she's taking it too far, she's pulling in reality itself, and Aria trembles.

"No!" I say, reaching out in case I have to grab the threads. "No, Sabella, let it go, let the threads relax."

Sabella's breathing heavily now, her face ashen again. "What did I do? Aria—I'm sorry, what did I do?"

Sabella lets the threads go, safely at least, then sits heavily in the chair behind her. She grips her hands tightly together.

"You were pulling in Aria's threads of reality, not creating the illusion," I say.

Which was a mistake I might have thought from Aria, but not Sabella. Sabella has the control, though she often lacks the raw strength that Aria has.

Did Nikolai just mess that up?

Did I, if Sabella was watching what I'd just done in her mind, shifting her own reality?

"Gods," Sabella says, scrubbing her face. But she stands again. "Can you please, Caleb, show me one more time?"

I swallow, but do so. She watches intently, then points at the place where her own weaving started to go wrong.

"There. Okay. I have it." She watches my full process of weaving my illusion, then unweaving again.

Then weaves herself into...me.

Well.

But she did it, and the weaving is sound.

Sabella breaks into a relieved grin, which is weird to see, because it's still my face as Caleb.

But then she unweaves it again, looks to Kian, and then makes herself look older, her hair lighter, longer, all things within easy reach.

"Did I get it?" she asks, and turns to look at herself in the mirror over the hearth, standing on her toes to see better.

I exhale. "Yes. You all three have it. That's an illusion you can wrap around yourself, or someone else, though that takes a bit more practice because you aren't just dealing with your own will around yourself.

"And here," I say, "is how to obscure your presence altogether, make it look like you aren't here. It's harder in the open, much easier in the shadows or corners, where people usually don't look."

They watch as I obscure myself as best I can in the open, which is not particularly well. I step toward the far end of the room and the shadows farthest from the hearth, and show them again.

This time, they all pick it up on the first try.

And then, when they've unwoven their obscuring illusions, we stand a moment in the silence.

I glance back at my guards, Morgan and Reveyan. They've stationed themselves inside, with the others guarding the other side of the door and out of hearing.

Morgan's expression is...intent. Like he's studying the lesson, too.

He couldn't have seen the weaving, it takes weeks or months of practice to be able to see the threads of reality around you, or another weaver's weaving.

But I mark the interest.

And...maybe it wouldn't take him so long. He's already, in some ways, rewoven his reality with his will.

Reveyan's hand is still resting, lightly, on the pommel of his sword, but his attention is toward the door, not us.

I need to not have an audience when I ask my apprentices to do what I'm going to ask. Because Torovan's not going to like it. I'm not sure *I* like it, but what other choice do I have?

Our enemy is here, and active.

And I just taught them the means to be spies in this palace.

That will be their first task, as court mages.

They all just got promoted, though they don't know it yet. I know they can sense that things have changed, though.

Gods help us all.

I turn back to my apprentices. "Come on. We're all going to the Dowager's chambers. The back way." I eye Morgan and Reveyan again, and they nod, Morgan moving toward the outer door to get the other two guards.

If we go the back way, no one but the guards will know where we're headed.

Should I examine the minds of my guards?

I shudder.

No.

No, I can't let that panic overtake me, I can't.

And I don't want to do what I just did to Sabella to anyone

else, not before I think it through, not until I have a better handle on what I'm doing.

I need to do more research, and soon.

CHAPTER 21

UNREALITY

CALEB

I've been here many times now, but though the Dowager Queen Zinara hasn't lived in this apartment for over half a year, I still carefully push open the back service door into her bedroom.

As if making more of a sound might disturb all of the pain that she's brought to this palace. Might ignite it again.

I'm not in the mood for feeling pain.

I stride to the heavy curtains and yank them back with a poof of dust to let the afternoon light inside.

I don't want to be here at all, not and remember every bit of every private agony Torovan has poured out to me over the last months.

But, this is necessary.

My apprentices are quiet and self-contained. They know the weight of this room, too, though not the entire history of it.

There are some things Torovan and I haven't told the

court. The court knows the king was killed by Nikolai at the dowager's request; they don't know how.

Morgan, who's been here before with Torovan, glances around for threats, but then settles at the corridor door while Revayan heads into the rest of the apartment to make sure it's clear.

But these rooms have been locked up for months. And I have absolutely no intention of occupying them myself.

The feeling of unreality in the bedroom, familiar now, hums at the back of my senses. That old feeling of wrongness, the lack of life in this room.

And yes, it has the same flavor as what I just found in Sabella's mind.

My stomach quickly sours, and I place a fist to my mouth, waiting a moment to see if it passes.

It does.

I meet Sabella's eyes, and she gives back a tight smile. Not really a smile.

And maybe this room feels less wrong now than it did the first time I felt it. It's been unoccupied for the last six months, and the stifling stillness is more believable.

Kian shivers as he looks around.

"Can you feel it?" I ask.

He hunches his shoulders.

"It's like nothing's in here," Sabella says, turning around to look at the dusty chair, the dusty four poster bed.

"It's creepy," Kian says. "And she was a murderer."

"Is," I say. "We think she's partly behind this new mistrust around weavers."

I center myself in my magic and tug on the unreality weave,

finding the anchor thread in the corner of the room, then unraveling it enough to see beneath it.

Kian jumps. "What did you—oh!"

Aria, still quiet, focuses on the fireplace.

Yes.

She finds the loose brick and tugs it out, pulling out the pouch beneath it.

The magical poison is gone—we destroyed that months ago.

But the scraps of the books are still there, in their pouch with its own unreality weaving.

I watch as Aria pulls it out and looks over the scraps of paper.

She turns to me, her mouth tight.

Kian and Sabella move close to see the paper scraps, too, and she passes them around.

Then, silently, the apprentices hand them back to Aria, having seen enough.

Aria replaces the pouch in its place above the cold hearth.

I carefully put the room's unreality weaving back in place, and Kian shivers.

"What do we do?" Aria asks, her dark eyes blazing. "How do we fight this, if it feels like nothing?"

"But it doesn't," I say. "It's meant to, but it still feels wrong, doesn't it? Emptiness is a tangible thing, too."

Aria holds out her hands like she's trying to sense the air itself. "It's like—it's like something you're waiting for that hasn't happened yet. Like you know what it will feel like, but you can't actually know until it happens."

"Is that what you felt in me?" Sabella asks, and the others go quiet.

I shift.

"It's the same kind of magic," I say. "It's a narrowing of possibilities, I think. In a person, or in a room. I can't show you the kind of soul weaving, of mind control magic, that Nikolai does. But yes, this has the same flavor."

Sabella looks away, toward the window, her posture rigid.

I know the sense of violation she must be feeling—not from myself, but from Torovan.

How will he react when I tell him Nikolai isn't just a threat gathering resources on his country estate, but that he's already here?

His reach, at least.

I've seen the time it's taken Torovan to fully regain his confidence again. He's kept busy, yes. But I've seen the toll.

He almost lost himself at the hands of those he trusted.

Kian hunches, scuffing one booted heel on the rug. "Can we go?"

His usual bravado is gone.

Aria and Sabella are tensed, too.

And we've already seen what we came to see.

I lead the way back toward the service corridor, then take them out into the main royal apartments corridor and into Torovan's study.

It's the safest, most grounding place I can think of just now, and I need that.

Torovan isn't here. He's almost certainly still at the reception, which feels like a lifetime away now. On the other side of seeing Nikolai's mind control weaving again. He'll be trying to smooth over the damage done to weavers' reputations today.

Gods, and that was a good place for Nikolai to strike.

I twitch with the need to rush down there, to try and search everyone in that room, to see if they have an illusion.

But a weaver's illusion can't usually be sensed past when it was first made. Or I would have been found out a lot sooner when I came to the palace in my illusion.

I shut the door to Torovan's study, but don't lock it.

Maybe I should have asked if he'd be okay with my bringing my apprentices here, but—well.

We all did cross that line today, between students and teacher and...gods...soldiers and general? Did I dare even think that?

Spymaster and spies.

Torovan won't like that, either. But we no longer have the choice of keeping my apprentices apart—one of them was used against us today. At least, that's still how I'm reading this.

And that can't happen again.

I won't let it.

All three of my apprentices turn to me inside, looking around themselves, waiting.

They're all solemn, all ready in their own ways.

And I wish there could have been more time to show them the joys of weaving without the terrors of a reality where weavers are already locked in a silent war.

I glance at Sabella, trying not to be obvious about check-ing, again, if she's okay. If there's any signs that what I did caused her pain.

But she catches my eye and holds it. Her own gaze hard as granite.

She wants to fight back.

Okay.

"What happened today was meant to cause panic and fear

against weavers," I say. "And meant to undermine Torovan's and my authorities, as weavers, and as kings. And Sabella—I'm truly sorry this happened to you. I don't know, from what I saw, when it happened. But we must assume that either Nikolai or other soul weavers are already in this court."

Kian's face twists as he fidgets. Aria worries her lip.

Sabella doesn't meet my eyes again.

"But," I continue, "our enemies have told us they're here, which is something. And now you know both how to weave illusions and misdirections around yourselves, and what an unreality weaving feels like. I think you'll be able to see soul weaving, too, if it's aimed at you again, though it might be subtle. You'll have to be extra vigilant."

"I will be," Kian says, his eyes burning. "He's not going to get me."

I don't know that Kian will have the strength to stop Nikolai.

It took Torovan's, Aldric's, and my own will to subdue him.

It took every shred of willpower that I had to break his hold on Torovan.

I was a lot more confident in my ability to stop Nikolai when he was half a kingdom away.

But I nod. Because they have to believe they can.

"Good. So, I want the three of you to gather intelligence."

Kian's eyes spark with interest, though Sabella seems to have already worked out what I'm asking them to do. Her expression doesn't change.

"Starting *tomorrow*," I say, looking at Kian. "And then for the remainder of the Festival, you'll take a few hours each day and move among the guests and staff. Observe. Listen. Become invisible—socially, I mean, not actually invisible. You can't be obvious about it, you know, be the staff. Be whatever makes sense in the moment.

"We'll practice yet today, we'll go through how not to be obvious. Then, you'll tell me each night what you've seen and heard. Or as soon as is safe, if you find something significant."

Which I'm hoping they will.

My gut twists again, because what if Nikolai finds them out, what if they're not good enough at hiding their intentions, they aren't trained for this.

But I can't search the entire palace on my own, and I know that's too dangerous. I know my life is more precious now that I'm a king at Torovan's side.

I know that the new possibility I carry within me makes it more precious still, and dammit, I know Torovan's not wrong to want to protect that.

I know.

But I'm sending my apprentices into danger.

Yes, I wanted to train more weavers for the sake of training weavers, especially women. I wanted that badly.

But yes—I'm ultimately training weavers to be able to fight. To be able to defend the palace, and the kingdom.

Kian's father understood that. I don't think Aria's parents do, but Aria herself does.

Sabella knew what she was walking into, and walked willingly, too.

Being a weaver has never been about being safe. Just learning to weave is dangerous, though I've been with them every step of the way, averting that danger when needed.

And I will still join them in spying on the palace guests, as often as I can. I won't make them do this all on their own.

Because my enemies tried to kill me, and tried to control one of my apprentices, and I am not going to let any of that happen again.

And anyhow, if someone's trying to kill me, I'm more likely safer if I'm disguised with an illusion than I am on my own right now.

So, there's that argument.

Which I will carefully present to Torovan.

When he finds out what we're doing.

I glance at the door to Torovan's study. I'm not sure how long he'll be at the reception, but he'll stay as long as his duty as the king requires.

But I am a master weaver, and the duty of a court mage is, ultimately, to protect the king, the palace, and the kingdom.

So this, right now, is my duty.

And now, it's my apprentices' duty, too.

"You're all court mages now," I say.

Kian inhales sharply. Aria's eyes go wide.

"Because I'm not going to trust this responsibility to apprentices. And because you are all ready."

Aria hunches back again.

"All of you," I say, and she meets my eyes. Straightens.

"You won't get your medallions now. Because that's part of what we must do—act out the fiction that I'm upset with your demonstration today, Kian, and that I'm giving you less responsibilities, not more. That I'm giving you more to study. That will help carve out more time for your, uh, spy work."

And, I'll have to find a way to tell Torovan that I already promoted them, because that's supposed to be his choice. And they're supposed to take their oaths to him.

Well, we will figure that out later, after we've found our enemies and driven them out of the palace.

Is it impossible to hope that we can do that before I have to tell Torovan any of this? That I can spare him that very personal fear?

Then again, someone did try to kill me, and I'm leaning more and more toward Nikolai's direct influence there, too.

My apprentices exchange glances with each other. They've become close these last weeks and months. We all have, though I know I stand apart from them as their teacher.

I wait until I see resolve on all of their faces.

Because a weaver's resolve, once found, is nearly unshakable.

"All right. We'll practice the rest of the afternoon—but we should move to my study. Then, tomorrow, you will start."

"Can we still go to the mage's trials?" Kian asks, and I let out my breath in exasperation.

"No," Sabella says for me, glaring at him. "Really, Kian."

I hold up my hands. "I'll be participating, yes. I have to be visible as a master weaver. But, your time is better spent finding out just who is trying to kill and sabotage weavers in this court."

"He wants to kill you," Aria says. "And control us. Nikolai."

That straightens Kian's shoulders again, and he nods.

"And your best defense, at all times," I say, making sure I meet all of their eyes, "is knowing who you are, and what you hope for, and what you fear. Think on that. Think on it hard."

And I will, too. Because I have so much more to fear for now.

"Right," I say. "Let's go to my study and run through what you'll need to know."

I'll teach them for the next few hours, until I have to go to dinner—which will be late tonight, because of the reception this afternoon. My apprentices will have to eat in the mages' common room, tonight at least. I don't have to know exactly what's going on in the Great Hall right now to know that.

And what should I tell Torovan, if I've already made up my mind that I'm not going to tell the whole of this yet?

My gut is doing a *fantastic* job of churning today.

I know I should tell him. I know he's in danger, too.

But if Nikolai preys on fears, telling Torovan Nikolai's here isn't going to help.

And I know he wouldn't want me or my apprentices near this if he knew Nikolai was here. Nikolai *or* one of his apprentices.

Torovan is keeping his fears from me—he asked me to trust him. And I do.

But he has to trust me now, too, as a master weaver.

Because I can't protect him and this kingdom if he's fully focused on protecting me.

CHAPTER 22

HAPPY

TOROVAN

Four letters now. Four identical letters, all of which threaten Caleb, but are aimed at me.

And an attempt on Caleb's life that almost succeeded.

And now one of Caleb's apprentices injured a courtier in a public display of weaving that should not have happened.

I spend the afternoon being polite, talking to people I both like and don't, trying to do what I can to show that the court carries on. The king carries on. And the fact that I'm a weaver, too, shouldn't matter to any of them.

But I see them eyeing the medallion of a court mage on my chest. I almost regret wearing it today.

Almost.

Caleb's mother stays by my side through the rest of the reception, and that—I don't know what to do with that.

Is it helping my cause to have the Galendan queen silently —or not so silently, often enough—reinforcing my authority as king? Is it a good reminder to the court that Caleb, a master weaver, is also the son of a queen?

Or does it say to the court that I would have less authority without her?

Without Caleb, by my side, being the silent promise of protection?

I stay in the Great Hall until the servants start to clear out the half-empty trays and prepare the hall for dinner. Maybe I should have gone to the trials of strength being held this afternoon, which have always been more of a draw to the common people rather than the nobility, and might run past dinner. But I couldn't bring myself to leave, and leave the court to work themself into a state about what happened earlier.

The setting sun has cast the hall in a faint pink glow, and staff has already lit the chandeliers and are lighting the extra lamps around the hall, too.

Musicians test their lutes and zithers in one corner.

Most of the guests from the reception have filtered out. And maybe it was a good thing I kept them here this long. That they didn't flee at the first sign of a weaving gone wrong.

I just want to sit. And I need to talk to Caleb about what happened, desperately need to know how he handled it on his end.

But it's nearly time for the meal, and guests that have gone off to change are filtering back in again.

It's Irava I see when she steps back into the hall, and while she did change her clothes, now wearing a calf-length, split-panel indigo coat with a high ornamental collar, she isn't wearing a crown.

She spots me and smiles, and I smile back, making my way over, offering my arm, which she takes.

She's still wearing her master weaver's medallion.

Which, for a heartbeat, makes my breath squeeze tightly in my chest.

Then I let it go.

Because it doesn't matter. In the end, what the court thinks of us doesn't matter, if we know our own minds, our own wills.

Doesn't it?

We have forged our own paths before.

"My apprentices will take dinner in the common room tonight," she says in a low voice, adjusting her spectacles as she looks around.

She notes the people staring, I know. Then focuses on me, her mouth a hard line before I watch her consciously try to soften it. To put on the royal appearance, the fiction that everything is fine, she's happy to be here right now, and doesn't care at all what other people think about her.

"Good," I say, and I know we can't talk here, not really. "It is well?"

She gives a tight nod, shrugging both her shoulders, trying to relax them again as a social necessity.

I grip her arm on mine. "Don't."

She looks up at me. "Don't what?"

I glance around. I spent the afternoon showing everyone just how fine everything is.

My heart can't take much more of it.

"Don't be anything other than who you are."

Her mouth twitches up, bemused. "I don't think I ever am."

But she tenses up again, her smile fading.

Especially when her mother steps into the hall again, now

regal in an all-gray gown embroidered with roses, her hair braided, not coiffed. Not wearing her crown.

"Queen Sevine," I say, calling out before she can make this meeting hers again. "Will you join us at the high table?"

Her eating at the high table was never in question. But she nods graciously as if the invitation is a gift and crosses the hall alongside us.

I glance around for Valtair—he headed off some time ago, and I haven't seen him back yet.

My sister is crossing the hall to us now, though, wearing a knee-length tunic and trousers, her hair in a fraying braid.

"You missed the carpenter Jenarran from the town lifting a table with six men balanced on it," she says, and grins at me. "Granted, one of them was only thirteen."

But she looks between Irava and me and quickly sobers. She doesn't ask what happened yet, but I know we're not the picture of happiness now.

Then, news about Kian's weaving getting out of control hasn't reached the Festival grounds below the palace, or at least, not that Elsira heard.

And maybe she hasn't heard precisely because of who she is, no matter if her clothes tonight aren't as fancy as she usually wears. Elsira's guards are hovering near mine, far enough away to give us some space, close enough to be here in a few strides if needed.

"Princess Elsira," Sevine says, "it's good to finally meet my daughter's sister."

Irava beside me gives a soft exhale and settles more. She lets go of my arm.

"She has been very good to me," Irava says, and pulls Elsira on her own toward the high table. Drags her, more like.

Queen Sevine makes a small huff.

"Is she happy?" she asks in a low voice, looking up at me.

I'm not prepared for the weight of that question just now. And I'm exhausted from the day.

So I think it's the truth that comes out.

"Mostly. I wish there wasn't as much danger. But there would be more danger here without her. And that does seem to make her happy, too, that she has that role in the kingdom. She likes being a master mage."

The Queen of Galenda watches her daughter as Irava and Elsira take their places and pointedly do not look our way.

"I didn't know she was training herself to weave until she was already a weaver," Sevine goes on, her voice lower still. In this crowd, with the space around us afforded by our guards, no one can hear us.

I turn to her. "You don't approve of her being a weaver?"

She frowns. "It suits her, actually. I never watched her weave before today, not in any concentrated effort."

She meets my eyes. "I don't like the air of this court around weavers, Torovan. And I don't like that she's at the center of it."

It wasn't a threat, not quite, and wasn't an ask, either.

But I nod all the same.

It's nothing I can change, this danger we're in. Nothing I can change quickly, at least.

What would Queen Sevine think of the letters Nikolai sent?

Am I fooling myself that I can solve this without putting Caleb in any greater danger?

I stride toward the high table before Sevine can go first and force me to follow.

CHAPTER 23

PALACE SPIES

TOROVAN

I tell Caleb I'll be to bed late. That after the disaster at the reception this afternoon, I have more work I have to do.

I don't know that he believes me.

But it's not that it's untrue.

I asked him to trust me.

Is he trusting me?

And he hasn't said much more about his apprentices than that he's handling the situation. That he'll be spending more time with them in the upcoming days, and less time at the Festival.

Which, I guess, I can't complain about.

It's better that he stays in safety, around people who can—mostly—protect him.

At least, until I find out just what the hell is happening in my palace. And who threw the knife. And why.

And at whose command: Nikolai's, or my mother's?

And does it, ultimately, matter?

My hands slowly squeeze into fists as I stride through the

corridor toward Master Aldric's study. My boot heels striking the stone floor, and the anger that I had to put off at the reception earlier, the anger I had to curb during the dinner, and after, when Caleb was looking tired and vulnerable—that anger surges up in me now.

It's a familiar friend, if not exactly wanted.

And why do I feel echoes now of the days after I first lost my father?

Haunting my palace like a wraith.

But that Akrean delegate. The way she looked at Caleb after Kian's magic went wrong—like my husband was personally responsible for endangering her and her delegation.

Not that she was even close to Kian's weaving.

Like Caleb hadn't just prevented a disaster but started one.

How Barella treats its guests, she'd said.

And then Caleb's mother, stepping in. When I hadn't yet had the chance.

I open my hands again, stretch my fingers out.

I told Aldric about the letters this morning, about Nikolai's threats against Caleb. But today's incident at the reception—the way that Akrean delegate spoke, the timing of Kian's magical failure right in front of foreign witnesses—it feels too convenient. Too orchestrated.

Like someone has their hands in the hearts and minds of my palace again.

And with the letters...I'm starting to believe it's true.

If there's one thing ruling this kingdom has taught me, it's that I can't afford to believe in coincidences.

Was Kian provoked into whatever he did?

Caleb hadn't said. And he was looking tired enough that I hadn't pressed.

I reach Aldric's study and knock once before entering. The older weaver sits behind his desk, surrounded by the neat stacks of books that always seem more for display than actual use. The lamplight silvers the gray in his thinning hair, still tied back in his braid, making him look every inch the harmless scholar.

But he's neither a true scholar, nor harmless.

His eyes are sharp and alert when they meet mine.

"Your Majesty." He rises, but I wave him back down.

"We need to investigate the Akreans," I say, closing the door firmly behind me. "Tonight."

Aldric's eyebrows barely raise. "That's a quick escalation from suspicion to action," he says dryly.

"Did you see how their delegate responded to Caleb unweaving Kian's magic?"

"No, I was on the other side of the room."

"It was like she was just waiting to use that jab." I begin to pace the small confines of the study. "So now there are weavers going missing at the Akrean border. I have threatening letters sent to me every day—another this morning. Same thing. And maybe Kian's mishap was a mistake—"

"Or maybe not?"

I face him. "Can we absolutely assume that Nikolai is the only dark weaver in Barella?"

"Nikolai Metrial is one of the most ambitious mages I've ever met. He might not want to share his power, if you're saying he's teaching other weavers."

"But other weavers would increase his power, wouldn't they? Yes, he's ambitious, but he's too spiteful not to use every weapon he can find. He was already trying to make weapons of us in the Council meeting."

"So you're saying he's controlling people in the palace again?"

"I—don't know."

He sits back, his chair creaking. "Do you think Kian Devarial is being controlled by Nikolai?"

"Do you?" I fire back.

He considers. "I would hope Caleb is able to sense if he is. But Caleb doesn't know about the letters."

"And he can't know. Not yet."

Aldric spreads his hands. "Then what do you want to do, Torovan? If it is Nikolai already here, you and I can't hope to stop him alone. If he has his own apprentices, that's even worse, isn't it? You will have to tell Caleb, whether there are traps in the letters or not. I think this chaos has gone on long enough, and it's only escalating—"

I press my hand to my heart, brushing my own mage's medallion.

"I *can't.*"

Because even if there's a *chance* I might lose him, I can't take it.

Aldric sighs, wiping a hand across his face. He looks up at me, and looks tired, showing every year of his age.

I don't like this man. I truly don't want to ask him for anything, but do I have any other choice?

If I can't tell Caleb, and the apprentices aren't ready, by any means—who else do I have?

"So you want to investigate the Akreans?" Aldric asks.

I lean on the back of one of his chairs. "I want to know if they have a weaver with them. If that's the angle we should pursue."

"Why would the Akreans have a weaver if they are known to despise weavers?"

"Because I need something to make sense, Aldric, and I need to know if they're working with Nikolai directly, or even sending those letters on his behalf. I need to know—I need to know *something*." I grasp at the air, trying to pull together my scattered, frantic thoughts.

I take a breath.

"I have to start somewhere. Or else, I don't know where to start."

"Whoever delivers the mail," he fires back. "I thought about sending one of the elementalists to watch the palace mail exchange this morning, but I didn't want to alert whoever was bringing the letters."

Which...isn't a bad idea. It's one I've had before, though I've been afraid, as he said, to tip off the sender. To escalate the threats.

But he's right. It's one of the only leads I have.

I nod. "I'll look into that, too. But tonight—I want to look into the Akreans."

"It's late, Torovan. Are you just going to put on your crown and knock on their doors?"

"Illusions," I say. "You know how to weave an illusion around yourself?"

He makes a sour face. "I know how, yes. It takes most of my concentration to hold it."

"Caleb taught me how."

But I haven't really used it, I haven't had the time. And that was months ago. Can I remember exactly how it's done?

I haven't fully thought this through, but I picture who I want to be—pulling up the face of a kitchen server I'd seen at dinner tonight, who's been with the palace staff for years. He's about my size and build, if a little bit shorter.

I haven't used these illusions, but it isn't like I haven't *thought* about using them.

I hold up my hands, carefully, very carefully, pulling the threads of reality into a different shape around me. Weaving the light, as Caleb would say.

Surprise flickers across Aldric's face. "Your training has progressed this far?"

Heat prickles up my neck. Even now, even when we're working together, there's that dig in his voice, that doubt of my willpower.

He's told me for years that I lack the willpower to be a weaver.

But he'd lacked the courage to be outpaced, and so he'd tried to tamp my willpower down.

"Yes," I say. And pause. I'm still speaking with my own voice, and I don't remember how to change that. So, I guess I'll have to be as quiet as possible.

I tilt my chin up. "Can you hold an illusion? For a few hours?"

Aldric shuffles some of the papers on his desk. "I can manage subtle changes. Nothing as dramatic as Caleb's transformations, but enough to avoid anyone recognizing me." But he stands, moving to clear a space in the center of his study. "Shall we see what we're capable of?"

I watch as he raises his hands, his movements precise and controlled. The air shimmers around him, and slowly his appearance begins to shift. His hair darkens from gray to brown, his face becomes slightly fuller, his clothing more common in cut and fabric. But the changes feel...strained. Held in place by careful will rather than natural power.

Then he lets it all go.

"We can't walk out of here like this," he says, and waves at me.

I reluctantly let go of my illusion weaving.

Apparently, I didn't do it wrong, or he wouldn't be acting like we're actually going to do this.

And anyway, it should be enough to avoid recognition in dim corridors, especially if we're careful about who sees us.

And if we're caught?

Well. This is *still* my palace.

I nod and open the door.

My guards outside follow us into the mages' common room. Which has never been a place where I feel particularly welcome, even if I am a mage. This is Caleb's domain. Even though he is still a king, still my husband and royalty, the people do treat him differently than they treat me.

No one is in the common room tonight, though, and the hearth is only a flicker, banked and letting the autumn chill seep through the walls and the floor.

I turn to my guards. "Stay here. We're going out with weaver's illusions."

They look at each other, and I can see a protest forming.

I hold up my hand. "We won't be ourselves, we'll be safe enough."

I don't know that. But I carefully reweave my illusion around myself to demonstrate.

My guards' frowns deepen. One glances to Master Aldric as he painstakingly changes his appearance, too.

He isn't carrying his staff. And after he weaves his illusion around himself, I wouldn't think he's anything other than a palace guest, an elderly low noble. And I'm palace staff, maybe guiding him through the palace. Maybe he was lost.

That sounds like a good enough excuse if we're asked.

We slip outside the common room and join the night hush of the palace.

The corridor outside is quieter now, most courtiers having retired after the long day of Festival events. On any other Festival in any other year, the halls might still have been over-flowing long into the night. But this night—people are wary. The atmosphere of the palace is hushed, like a held breath. Just waiting to see what disaster will happen next.

The few servants moving through the halls barely glance at us as we make our way toward the guest quarters on the other side of the palace. Up past the administrative offices—Valtair's, and the other members of the Council.

It feels strange to walk within an illusion. And stranger still to be unnoticed within my own palace.

And maybe I can see why Caleb likes this, likes walking within the palace with anonymity. I'm not sure what I'll find ahead, but I find myself relaxing more than I thought I would. No one is looking at me just now.

No one expects me to fix anything. And maybe that strain, that expectation of having to fix, has been wearing on me more than I'd thought.

And no one is trying to tell me I shouldn't fix things they don't thin are broken. Even if they are.

After a few minutes, though, maintaining the illusion starts to feel like a low drain on my energy. And Caleb does this constantly? Whether he's Caleb right now, or Irava.

We pass a pair of my guards heading into the guest quarters, and I carefully don't look at them.

But I don't know if that's suspicious, and I tense up again as we reach the first of the guest suites.

I near Aldric. "Do you know where the Akrean quarters are?"

He gives me a look that says that I should have known that going in.

And I brace myself against the shrinking back I used to do as a boy.

"No," he says. "But I'd think we should sense for weaving throughout this whole section. You don't know it's the Akreans."

But now that we're here, too, I wonder how much good we can do sensing closed doors. Maybe Caleb's senses would extend that far, but I don't trust that mine will.

Aldric waits for my decision. And I feel the heat in my face again—he's humoring me. Indulging this whim, because I think he does genuinely want to help. Even if he thinks this late-night mission is pointless.

And not well-planned.

I swallow, and push on, opening up my senses as I go, trying to feel for anything out of place.

Aldric follows me without a word.

And I don't know what I'm looking for, that's the problem. A weaver like Nikolai isn't going to broadcast that he's here, and that's also the problem.

But we've gone around a corner, and I slow as I do feel something ahead.

A low buzz in my awareness.

It's coming from a door ahead, toward the right.

I glance back at Aldric—does he feel it, too?

Then I approach the door. There is a weaving overtop of the doorframe, a shimmer of expectant reality.

Aldric looks up at it, then waves me on, and we walk past.

"It's a sound-dampening weaving, to discourage listeners," he says when we're several doors past. "It needs to be rewoven every day, sometimes several times, depending on the strength of the weaver. And yes, I will find out who that door belongs to. There is another weaver in the palace—one at very least."

I glance back at the door but keep walking. Because even if I haven't done this before, I know enough not to pause here. "Yes. Find out."

We take a service stairway down to the lower level of guest quarters, which sits behind the main palace. This is where lesser nobility and dignitaries are staying. But though we pass a few people still up and walking the corridors, we don't find anything else suspicious.

"It's late," Aldric says, and by the set of his mouth, I think he's straining the edges of his ability to hold his illusion in place. He's gained the slightest limp along the way, too.

So I nod, and we work our way more slowly back to the mages' common room.

My guards are still waiting. And both visibly exhale when we come back inside. The common room is still empty—and maybe my guards kept it that way.

But I unweave my illusion, fatigue starting to pull on me now.

I truly don't know how Caleb holds his illusions all day, every day.

But I know he must hold them, too.

I know he's trying with everything he has to find a way to reweave his reality without harming the child.

And I wish with all I am that I had the strength and skill to help him with that.

"It was the sixth door on the right, from the end of that corridor," I say to Aldric as he lets go of his illusion, too. He gives me a look, but nods.

We know precious little more now than we did a few hours ago, but knowing there's another weaver in the palace isn't nothing.

"Good," I say. "Find out, and we'll meet again tomorrow."

CHAPTER 24

INFORMATION

IRAVA

My books lay in a scattered mess across my desk, piled higher than before, giving no more answers. I spent the day in places I did not want to be, talking to people I did not want to talk to, because I want to be searching the palace for my enemy.

For Nikolai.

If he's here.

I dreamed restless, queasy dreams, and woke up to Torovan asleep beside me, his face pinched even in his sleep.

He's afraid. He's so afraid, and he's not telling me why.

And now, I'm not telling him what I know would terrify him more. That the man who haunts his nightmares, the man who killed his father, might be here again.

This morning, in the dark, I watched my sleeping husband and wondered if I should try to reach out and find any signs of mind control within him again.

If the reason he's not telling me everything is because he can't. Because he's compelled not to.

But he asked me to trust him.

And now I'm pacing my study, after a blur of meals and meetings I hardly remember, some of them on Torovan's arm, my mind all the way bent on searching everyone, anyone, for signs of mind control weaving. Not looking closely, no, but alert. Looking for anything inconsistent.

Anything.

Because I'm drowning in a sea that has no answers.

I want to tell him, I want him to tell me that we'll figure this out, that it will all be okay.

But I'm the master weaver, and he's the king.

And he has to stay steady enough to keep being the king, so that means I have to do my duty as a master weaver.

At least through the rest of this Festival week.

Because I haven't been doing it well enough if Nikolai is already here.

I straighten when I hear the knock on my study door and adjust my spectacles.

I'm Irava right now, but I'm not showing my pregnancy, even to those who know. My illusion is my armor, it has to be.

"Enter," I call, my voice coming out harsher than I intend. I swallow and try to steady myself.

My apprentices aren't my enemies, gods.

And they were my other worry all day. I sent them out to spy on the court with only a few hours of practice, hardly enough. Knowing the enemy we're facing.

How could I have done that? Yes, they're all skilled weavers. But are they truly ready for this? When Aria lost control of her magic only a few days ago, when Sabella still lacks the raw strength needed for significant weaving, and Kian's ego gets the better of him at least several times a week.

No, that's not fair. It's not actually fair to any of them.

And none of it is as true as it seems from the outside.

My apprentices file in, and the sight of them sends a fresh wave of anxiety through me.

Aria's mouth is pulled tight, and she won't meet my eyes. Sabella's tension is a palpable presence, and Kian is vibrating with a restless, angry energy. I force myself to settle back behind my desk as they arrange themselves in the chairs across from me.

And, catching two of the volumes open on my desk, I shut them. I know, too, that if the court knew I was studying Taishe and his book that praises mind control weaving in my spare moments today, they would only find more reasons to fear weavers. To fear me.

But I have to know more, I have to know how to defeat Nikolai this time—not just subdue him, but make sure he's never a threat again.

My research into how to reweave my reality can wait.

Sabella's brows flick up as I shut the books. I usually leave my sprawl when they're here.

"Are you all right?" I ask, ignoring her silent question.

Aria grimaces. "I heard more people are leaving the palace—the man that was burned yesterday? He's left, too. They're saying...they're saying what happened with Kian's weaving wasn't an accident. That weavers can't be trusted."

"We didn't do anything today, Caleb," Kian says, his voice tight with frustration. "We walked around all day and found nothing useful. If Nikolai is here, we're just walking around while he plots against us." He pauses. "Can you, uh, check us again?"

I swallow. If Nikolai is here, would my apprentices have

given him the chance to weave their minds? Did any of them slip up, or put themselves in a place where they could be compromised?

I lean forward, and look to Sabella and Aria for permission, too. "May I?"

I know that this kind of looking into the threads of their minds is invasive. And I hate that. I hate what Nikolai is doing to us again.

Sabella and Aria nod, though, and I concentrate my weaver's senses, trying to see the shapes of their souls and minds, trying to see if they've been tampered with.

But I only see *them*.

The connections between us, the resonance of their souls.

The temptation is there to dig deeper, though, to be absolutely sure.

But I let go of my concentration again, and sit back, shaking my head.

I don't like that I'm spending so much time looking at souls through my weaver's senses, either.

How much time has Nikolai spent looking at souls, if he's learned how to manipulate them so deftly?

I pull off my spectacles and rub at my eyes.

And look up to see Kian's anger as a mirror to my own restless energy.

He feels as powerless as I do.

And that feeling is poison.

That—that we must change at all costs.

"Okay," I say. "You all did well. Thank you. I couldn't join you today, but—"

"But it wouldn't have made a difference," Kian says, his

eyes intent on me. "Irava, we have to find him. Before he tries to kill you again."

"I don't know that he's the one who threw the dagger," I say.

"But he might have controlled who did."

And he's not wrong.

"We *have* to protect you, Irava," Kian says. "What we heard about weavers today—after, after I messed up in the Great Hall yesterday—"

"Which is not your fault," I say. "None of this is any of your faults."

"No." Sabella's eyes are hard. "But it doesn't make it any better. And no one is going to step out and say they tried to kill you. Or, tried to control me."

She's right, too.

I put them into danger in spying on the palace today, but I didn't give them everything they'd need.

Gods. I don't want to do this. I need to be at the Festival events, I need to be at Torovan's side. But I should be doing this on my own, not putting my apprentices in this position.

Kian looks like he's going to start pleading for a better plan. Or he'll go off and make one on his own.

"All right. Today wasn't enough," I say.

I pull a fresh sheet of paper out from under a stack of books. My hand is a little unsteady as I sketch the palace corridors, the service passages, the patrol routes of the royal guards. I know them by heart. I know how to be a ghost in this palace when I want to be.

They watch me in silence as I draw.

"This," I say, pushing the map across the desk, "is how you actually become invisible. This isn't about avoiding the guards you see. It's about knowing which corridors are truly empty so you can listen at a door without being seen by anyone."

They all look at the map. None of them even suggest that what I'm showing them is treason, of a sort.

It's nothing that should ever be on paper, the blind spots between the guards. It's what I've found after months of careful observation.

And maybe I haven't felt as safe as I should in this palace if I've been collecting this all along.

But if Nikolai is here—we're past the point of caution.

Kian picks up the map, his earlier frustration replaced by a steady resolve.

I've been in Council meetings with his father, High General Devarial, when he's in from the garrison at the eastern border. The high general makes that same face when he's digging in on a point.

Aria watches Kian, her shoulders tight, but she nods.

"I haven't prepared you enough for this fight," I say. "Sabella—you should never have had that happen to you."

She glares back at me. "We'll say the same thing to you—this is Nikolai's doing, not yours." She looks at the others. "We know why you're teaching us. It's not just to teach us—gods, Irava, we know that. We know Nikolai is a threat, and he'll be a threat again."

She takes the paper and carefully folds it. "We're going to study this, then we're going to *actually* get good information tomorrow."

I tap my desk. "Tomorrow is the Harvest Ball. I will need to attend, but—"

"But it's best if we don't," Aria says, "so we can do what we have to do anyway. And we won't make the courtiers nervous."

I don't like it, but I nod.

Then I stand. "I'll give you another weapon to use. Kian, I'm going to weave around you now, watch what I'm doing, please."

I raise my hands, gathering the threads of reality, then weave a sphere of absolute night around him. The light in the room seems to bend into it, swallowed by the perfect, silent darkness.

"Fuck!" Kian hisses. Then, "This is amazing."

Aria inspects the weaving from where she is, but Sabella approaches.

"This is useful," she says.

And more importantly, they're not likely to hurt each other or anyone else with darkness.

But it might be enough to let them run from danger.

Might be.

I hold the construct for a long moment before letting it unravel.

"Your enemies will have a harder time attacking what they can't see," I say. "If you're caught—use this. Will the construct to follow your target, and run. Then find me."

"This won't stop Nikolai," Kian says.

"No."

"Then will you teach us to do what you did for Sabella? To undo the mind weaving? Can you show us, please, how you defeated him before?"

I swallow. Because I don't like that I did what I did to Sabella yesterday. And I still don't *know* what I did exactly.

I've added it to my stress around being able to reweave my reality around my growing child—because I can't protect those I love with my weaving if I'm not sure it's safe.

I shake my head. "Mind control weaving, soul weaving, preys on your fears. It tries to reweave the reality of your soul and your willpower so that you want to obey the weaver instead. It tries to replace your will with theirs. And you have to resist that. You have to know who you are. If anything—focus on that. Be sure of yourself."

That isn't what Kian wants to hear, but he nods slowly and doesn't push me.

None of them do.

They murmur thank yous and file out.

And I collapse back behind my desk, scrunching my hands into my hair.

I want to scream in frustration.

I want to talk to Torovan, to tell him everything.

I want to talk to Valtair and have him yell at me for not telling him last night.

But yes, part of being a master weaver is knowing the tensions of reality around me, and I'm so afraid that Torovan's tension is about to break.

I've seen it in him. He's barely sleeping. His eyes dart, and with good reason.

He only barely caught a dagger spinning toward my heart.

And he won't tell me what's going on.

So I've given my apprentices all that I can, all that I dare.

Tomorrow, I'll be more vigilant in my searching the court for signs, but—but I know I won't find them. Not in the open.

And I'm not willing to search people's minds without a clear sign of coercion. Because that feels like the slippery slope toward the disregard for minds and souls that Nikolai himself has.

My gaze drifts back to my books, and the thought of everything I don't yet know threatens to overwhelm me.

I stare at the place on my desk I just cleared enough to sketch the guard rotations.

I trust my apprentices. I *know* them.

I'm doing the right thing, aren't I?

By not telling Torovan yet?

By telling more than I probably should to my apprentice weavers?

I huff out a sigh and put away the most damning of the books I've been reading, locking them in the bottom of one of my bookcases, then pause to reweave my illusion as Caleb.

Then I stride for the door. Because maybe I can get some surveillance in tonight. Maybe.

Or is it too late?

Gods, yes, the glass I set has already run out. Torovan will be expecting me in our apartment.

Not that we'll do anything but dance around each other, each lost in our own problems.

I swallow.

Outside, I catch sight of Morgan, and then hesitate again, a new and different thought rising up.

"You were watching my weaving yesterday."

He stiffens, eyeing me before looking away with a guard's blank stare.

I need more weavers. I need more people on our side. I need more people to tip the balance of Nikolai's control.

"Would you like to learn?" I ask.

His gaze snaps back to mine, and I watch a flush creep over his sun-tanned cheeks.

Oh gods, does he think this is an insult? He knows that I'm

wearing an illusion right now, and that I weave my reality into my body as Caleb when I can. And yes, I'd thought about teaching him anyway. I want everyone who wants to know how to reweave their reality to know how to do this.

"I'm asking," I say quietly, "because I think you'd be good at it. And it would strengthen your ability to guard us."

I wet my lips. "My child will need all the protection they can get."

He does meet my eyes. Looks away. "I'll think on it, Your Majesty."

Chapter 25

Relentless

Torovan

"It's the Akrean delegation's suite," Aldric says to me at the archery trials. "That's where the weaving is."

I'm supposed to be paying attention, and even more so with my sister is up to compete in this round, but I turn to him.

"You're sure?"

He gives a nod, then gathers his robes to sit in Caleb's vacant seat beside me, leaning his staff on his shoulder.

I grimace but let it pass. People are already giving us looks, wondering what's so urgent that a master weaver had to interrupt the king during the trials.

But when they see Aldric settling, they settle, too. He is still an important figure in this court, even if Caleb has, in many ways, overshadowed him.

Aldric sighs. But he keeps his thoughts mostly to himself throughout the rest of the competition, only making the occasional comments for appearance's sake. This isn't the place to talk about hidden and desperate things.

He knows I don't like him, but he seems to have made his peace with it. And he is helping, in his way.

And he's still the only one I can rely on to help me with this.

But what do I do with the information that there's a weaving to stop eavesdropping on the door of the Akrean's suite? Does that mean there's a weaver among them after all?

I got the fifth letter today.

And I wish they'd say something different.

Vary the threats.

Make it anything but this slow, relentless, onslaught.

When the archery trial ends, I award Elsira the third-place medal, and that is a highlight. That is one singular bright point during this day.

And I keep my eyes on the members of the Akrean delegation as I dine in the Great Hall, as I talk to the courtiers who wish to speak afterward.

Caleb is distracted, too.

Can he see just how afraid I am whenever we're together?

He can't see that. I can't let him see that.

So I do my best to be the king that I need to be during the Festival, even if some of the courtiers and dignitaries left after the weaving at the reception the day before.

And Caleb is doing his best, too, despite the appraising looks his way. I'm watching the strain, and understanding more of it now that I know the physical toll of holding an illusion for so long.

And now, at the end of the day, I'm with Caleb in bed, watching him sleep in the pale moonlight from the window. Watching him in this moment of peace. He's still holding his illusion, he's learned to keep it during sleep.

Gods.

I could ask him to do what he always seems to do anyway—spy on the palace for me. To find out just what is going on with the Akreans.

He'd even like if I asked, I know he would.

But what if he would run straight into Nikolai?

What if he would run straight into his would-be assassin?

What if he wouldn't be prepared?

So I watch my husband sleep. And wonder, as I'm starting to wonder every day now, if it will be the last time.

My eyes sting, and my throat burns, and I clench my hands into fists.

I tell myself, again, that I can't tell Caleb what I know. Not until I fix this, or know more, or the danger is past.

He was distracted all the last day, tense and not saying more than he had to.

And I know he's dealing with his apprentices, and the public humiliation of Kian's loss of control, and I wish I had more time to help with that.

I wish I didn't have to sit through archery competitions and diplomatic meetings, with or without Caleb. Though they're always better with.

Though, yes, I did enjoy watching my sister defeat grizzled veterans on the archery field. I hadn't known she'd gotten so good with a bow. I will have to go on more hunts with her, with an aim like that.

I lay awake until the pre-dawn glow, bleary but unable to stop my rushing thoughts, then slip out of bed.

Caleb stirs, his eyelids fluttering, but then he curls around himself, burying his face back in his pillow.

My hands spasm with the need to hold him.

But I have to protect him, first.

I don't want to see that tension in his shoulders, even in sleep.

So I get dressed, quietly, and freeze when my belt buckle clanks against the bedpost.

Caleb stirs again. "Tor?"

"I have to do some work before my meetings today. I'll see you at breakfast?"

He groans. Mumbles into his pillow. Makes a little wave before flopping his arm back down again.

I wait, but he doesn't stir again.

I rub my hand over my face, then pad out into my study.

Another weaver went missing near the border to Akreal yesterday, I did register that much in the blur of the day. It's escalating to a crisis, and I don't know what to do about that, either. And what does it say about the state of the kingdom that this crisis feels like the lesser threat, the much more distant threat among many?

I got that news the night before. I didn't tell that to Caleb yet, either.

He's carrying enough with his apprentices right now.

And how can I protect him when keeping him safe means I have to keep pushing him away?

I'm shuffling papers on my desk without sitting down, without proper light to look at them, because I know what I want to do next, and I'm stealing up my courage to do it.

I have to investigate where the letters are coming from— *have* to.

But I hear the inner door to my study creak, and Caleb pads out, his hair still messy, night shirt hanging low on one shoulder.

I catch my breath.

And open my mouth to say something, anything, to interrupt the need building up in me, alongside my desperation.

But Caleb yawns hugely, bending over in the effort.

I love him. With all my soul, I love him.

And in that vulnerable moment, in that space between what we say and what we know, I almost tell him everything.

But he stands up and grimaces, pressing a hand to his back. His illusion right now shows his pregnancy, and he looks up, and stills.

What does he see in my face?

He approaches and carefully uses his sleeve to wipe around my eyes.

I blink. Yes, my eyes have been welling.

"We'll find the assassin," he says. As if that's the only thing worrying me, and normally—normally it would be. If any of this was normal.

He tilts his head. "We have the Harvest Ball tonight."

"Yes."

"We haven't practiced the dance."

We haven't had time.

"Are you saying you want to practice now?" I ask.

He smiles, but it's a wan smile. "It's basically just the sun dance, but we'll mirror each other instead of one of us leading."

"Yes. Basically."

He's trailing a hand down my neck, and I swallow.

He leans in to kiss me, and I hungrily kiss him back until he breaks away, pressing a finger to my lips.

"Later," he says. He smiles again, and there's something forced about it this time.

And he turns around, studying me. Like he wants to memorize my face.

Like...like he's accepting that an assassin might succeed.

And that this might be the last time he sees me, too.

"Caleb--" I reach after him.

"I'm going to dress and go to my study. I'll meet you before the ball. We'll do one practice dance. Okay?"

My throat's tight, but I manage, "Okay."

I have to go. I have to leave right now, or I will tell him everything.

CHAPTER 26

UNSORTED

TOROVAN

I grab a coat from a hook on the wall—it's my shabbier older coat I've had for years, that I've always worn when I'm chilled, but not out into the public places of the palace.

But I'm not going to have to be myself where I'm going, and I'm starting to understand Caleb's fascination with that, too.

I can't stop replaying the kiss, and the look he gave me.

Or, does he expect an assassin to take me away from him?

It's almost happened before, though not quite in this way. Nikolai almost took my will from me, and he might have succeeded if Caleb hadn't been brave enough to show me who he really was.

My actual betrothed.

But once I'm out in the corridors, my purpose today starts to clear the haze in my head.

It's motion.

It's a direction.

And I've always done much better when I'm in motion. When I'm on the hunt.

I lead my guards down the stairs and into a lesser meeting room, one with no one else around at this hour of the morning.

Then, I weave the illusion of myself into someone else.

This room has an ornate gold leafed mirror on one wall—and it's unsettling, looking into it and not seeing who I am. I don't know the servants' rotations enough to not accidentally run into one of them, so I choose the face of one of the garrison soldiers I sometimes train with, who I know is at the Akrean border right now.

No, that won't work, he's known here. So I do my best to shift my features away from his, too. I end up decidedly unattractive, but then, I don't have to be attractive to do what I need to do today. At least I'm not myself.

I shrug my shoulders in my coat, and decide it looks shabby enough to fit this person in the mirror, so I leave the rest of myself as I am.

Then I head out again past my guards.

It's the same pair from the night before, with the outer guards across the hall, looking for incoming threats if there are any.

"Stay here," I say. I still haven't figured out how to weave an illusion over my voice. But I'm not about to run back and ask Caleb how.

No.

One of my guards, Kas, a tall man with a medium-brown, pock-marked complexion in his middle-aged prime, leans in. "Wherever you're going, Sire, you should not do this alone."

"But I can't do it with you."

He pulls a sour face, but nods. "I'll tell the outer pair, we'll all four go back to your study as if you're there." He hesitates. "Whatever you're about, Sire, be careful."

I nod. My safety now is in obscurity.

I know another letter will be delivered to me this morning, to be handed to me among other letters, or handed to me by an unwitting messenger. So I make my way toward the palace's mail exchange.

Out into the sunlit outer courtyard, striding past people already bustling with either the day's festivities or the day's chores. Courtiers and staff both.

And I have to remind myself more than once to slow my stride a little, to not act like I own this palace.

No one stops me, though, as I enter the outbuilding where the mail is sorted.

And the mail chamber is bustling despite the early hour. Which makes sense with so many guests here for the Harvest Festival.

Though less guests now than there were when we started. There should be more guests as the Harvest Festival goes on, not less.

And that's not a good sign for my people, either. I know they'll note it.

And note it as one of my failures as king.

Inside the mail chamber, three clerks sort through bags of letters and parcels, their movements efficient despite obvious exhaustion.

"You're early," one says as I approach, barely glancing up. "Bless the gods of all the seasons. We're drowning here."

They're not even going to ask if I belong here?

"Where do you need me?" I ask, and try to drop my voice

into a gruffer accent. It comes out weird, but the clerk doesn't seem to notice.

He gestures to a pile of unsorted mail. "Start with those. Separate by kingdom, then by district of the sender, then by priority. Mail originating in the palace always gets priority. Red seals go straight to the top."

I nod and get to work, scanning every piece that passes through my hands. Looking for something that feels wrong to my senses. Looking for the numbness that means unreality.

Or even the same paper, the same handwriting.

But there's nothing. Letter after letter, all perfectly normal. Trade agreements from Cardalan. Social invitations from visiting nobles. Reports from border garrisons.

Nothing that hums with the wrongness I've come to dread.

I try to get closer to one of the clerks to see the mail he's sorting, too. Because I'm only seeing a fraction of it.

"Busy night?" I ask casually as I work.

"Always is during Festival," another clerk replies. "Though most of the urgent stuff came in yesterday evening. This morning's been lighter." He spits a seed he's been chewing into a cup. "I think all the misfortune's rattling folks. But when our kings dance tonight, that'll set them all right again. That'll make sure the harvest is prosperous for the next year. Bad business, though, with the dagger and the magical attacks."

My hands slow as I sort, absorbing that, before I force myself to speed up again.

I shake my head. "Yeah. Bad business."

And maybe, if I'm trying to help the common people of my kingdom, I should actually get among them more often.

It's a weird feeling, being within sight distance of my own

apartment, but feeling like I'm a world away here, working with these clerks.

I keep searching. But as time passes, and the sun rises, and the clerks turn down the oil lamps in favor of the morning light, my pile dwindles.

I've found nothing.

Again.

Nothing but an earful of rumors that make me think that Nikolai has been busier playing with the hearts and minds of my people than I thought.

The unease around weavers is...stifling.

And, when I reach the end of my stack, I stand and say, "I need to check on...a letter's seal." Without having a letter in hand.

I quickly dart out before anyone can protest.

I return through the palace corridors, keeping my illusion until I'm in the corridor of the royal apartments, and only my guards are in sight.

Kas looks toward me, taking a visible breath of relief, which isn't something any of my guards show often.

"Did Caleb leave?"

"Yes, Sire, a while ago."

But I knew that.

I'm jittery, and bump into my study with an uncoordinated fluster that's more like Caleb than myself.

I pause in the empty, quiet room.

I was so sure I'd find something. Some trace of how those letters reach me.

But whoever is delivering them to the palace isn't using normal channels.

Which means they have access to the palace staff directly, they have to. Or are paying someone off. Or coercing them.

And at this point, how can I think it's not Nikolai himself here in the palace?

Just taunting me.

I move to my desk—and freeze.

A space has been cleared in the center of the desk, my papers pushed aside. Sitting squarely in the center, all on its own, is another letter.

Same paper.

Same black plain wax seal.

My blood turns to ice.

I stride back to my door and swing it open.

"Did you deliver a letter to my desk?" I ask, looking between my guards.

"No, Sire. No one has been in or out—is there something wrong, Sire?"

I slam the door shut and rush back to my desk, my hands shaking as I reach for the letter.

It takes me two tries to crack the seal and open it.

The familiar wrongness of the letter buzzes in my hands. Hums in my blood.

The words blur for a moment before snapping into focus.

"I will kill him if you tell him, and your heir."

My heir.

Our child.

The letter slips from my nerveless fingers, fluttering to the desk. I stumble back to my chair and sink into it, all the strength leaving my legs.

He knows. Nikolai knows about the child.

And he's been in my study. In the heart of our private

apartments. Close enough to touch our belongings, to see where we sleep.

He got past my guards—I don't know how. I look toward the door that leads into my father's old chambers—he had to have come in that way. But that way is also heavily guarded.

Do I tell my guards?

I hesitate a long moment.

And I'm still sitting another moment later.

How many people know about Caleb's pregnancy? Five, maybe six. Caleb, myself, Valtair, Elsira. The guards who witnessed Caleb's illusion drop after the assassination attempt have suspicions but no confirmation.

That's it.

Which means either one of them is feeding information to Nikolai, willingly or not, or...

Or Nikolai has found another way to spy on us.

I think about the missing weavers at the border. About the mind control magic he wielded before. About how easily he could twist someone's thoughts, make them forget they'd ever seen him.

Has he twisted my mind again? Is that why I feel this nameless terror, has he been in my apartment before—

I slam my palms to my desk top.

Breathe, Torovan. Just breathe.

The letter lies open, like an accusation.

All my attempts to protect Caleb have failed. The secrets I've kept to shield him have only isolated him, made him more vulnerable.

And now our child is threatened too.

I can't keep holding this all alone, or even just with Aldric. I can't protect them by myself.

I need Caleb's strength and skill.

And I need to stop trying to be the sole protector of everything I love. I know that doesn't even make sense—Caleb was the one before who protected me.

But I just...I wanted to keep him safe.

I know my reasons for not telling him about the letters are shattering, even while the necessity of telling him is warring with the threat of telling him.

My feet carry me toward the door without conscious decision. Down the corridors again to Master Aldric's study. Each step feels like I'm walking toward the loss of everything I love, but also toward the only hope I have left.

Aldric opens the door at my pound, takes one look at my face, and steps aside to let me in.

"What happened?"

I pull the latest letter from my pocket and shove it at him. "This was left on my desk in my study. While my study was guarded and I wasn't there."

Aldric's eyes lock with mine. He understands what that means and quickly opens the letter.

He scans it, his face grim. "And now he threatens the child."

"Aldric." My voice cracks on his name. "It was on my *desk*. In my *study*. Someone walked into the heart of my apartment and left it there."

Aldric carefully folds the letter.

"You must tell Caleb. Tell him now. This isn't even a question anymore."

I take the letter back, tuck it back into my coat, which is still—gods—the shabby coat I wore out before.

I hope no one puts it together with the man who helped sort the mail this morning.

And—and I remember the conversation of the clerks, that so many people are looking to the Harvest Ball this evening, and the dance I'll perform with Caleb. With my first Harvest Ball as the king, and his first as my king, or my queen if he's Irava. That dance is an offering before the gods, a renewal of agreement, a sign the people need to know there will be prosperity ahead.

A sign that I need, too. I need to know that everything will be okay.

"I'll tell him after the ball," I say.

Aldric frowns. "And if that's too late? Torovan—"

"After the ball," I say again.

Do I risk the wellbeing of my kingdom, the goodwill of my people, for my husband and my child?

Do I risk my husband and my child for the wellbeing of my kingdom?

I don't think it's an accident this letter arrived today.

"Caleb knows to stay vigilant," I say, remembering his look this morning. Oh gods of all the seasons, that look.

Like he knew the danger was ready to swallow us both.

Well. But of course he knows. It's only been days since he watched a dagger spinning in front of his chest. I forget that my greater knowledge of the threat doesn't outweigh the fact that someone still tried to steal him from me.

Aldric grips both of my shoulders, and, startled, I look into his eyes.

He's always been grandfatherly to the court, and I've always hated it. Because I know the person he is. The person who tried to steal from me my own inner strength.

But his eyes are shining now, intent on mine.

"Do your dance. Wait only the acceptable amount of time. Then *tell him*, Torovan. Tell him."

I stare back into his eyes and slowly nod.

And it's just now, this moment, that all the grief I've been holding back this week comes rushing in.

Right now, when I have the least capacity to deal with it.

This is my first Harvest Festival without my father.

My first as the king, and I would never be the king without my father being gone.

I close my eyes, stay very still as I try to rein it all in again. I have to. I have to be strong right now—Caleb, and my child, and the entire kingdom depend on it.

Aldric is still bracing me, and I open my eyes but don't meet his. I pull back from his grip, and he lets go.

"Tonight," I say, because he seems to be expecting an answer.

I don't feel like a king just now.

I feel like a prince without his father.

I feel like a boy adrift.

I back out, hardly seeing where I'm going, but manage to straighten as I reach the corridor. I glance down the hall to the closed door to Caleb's study.

And my heart kicks into a pound.

I could tell him now.

But I don't want the fight that I know will happen. I don't want him charging off after Nikolai—not yet.

Not when people are already leaving, when the mail clerks are casually saying that weavers are a threat, when so much—*so much* depends on the people still believing in weavers, because I *am* a weaver.

And this is my kingdom.

There's more than one way to take a kingdom from someone, isn't there? There's more than one way to control it, if you can control their hearts with your own lies.

And I can't seem to gain enough foothold again with my truths.

But...tonight. I'll tell Caleb tonight.

I *will* tell him tonight. Despite the risks.

I can only pray that it won't be too late.

CHAPTER 27

THE TELLING

IRAVA/CALEB

My mother finally corners me in my study on my third day of avoiding her.

I've been dreading this conversation for three days now, ever since she arrived and found me with a dagger spinning in front of my heart. Three days of careful maneuvering around the palace, of sending polite excuses through servants when she asks, of making sure I'm always with other people when she's near.

And with everything else going on, this isn't a conversation I think I can handle with care right now.

But Queen Sevine of Galenda didn't raise a fool, and she certainly didn't raise a child who could evade her forever.

I look up from yet another stack of weaving books scattered across my desk. I'd been diverted for most of an hour from trying to find more about soul weaving to a Taishe passage that talked about changing the shape of a thing without changing the state of it.

I'm not quite grasping it yet, but I gather it's about making more than an illusion, but less than a reality.

There's a soul component to it, though, which feels...troubling. I don't know if this is the answer I need.

I look up to find my mother standing in my doorway, having invited herself without knocking.

Her arms crossed, wearing the expression I remember from childhood—the one that means I'm about to explain myself whether I want to or not.

I'm Irava right now. And though she's seen me move back and forth between Irava and Caleb, it feels like less than the armor I want.

"Mother." I set down my book. "I wasn't expecting you."

"I'm sure you weren't." She closes the door behind her with a soft click. "You've been *expertly* avoiding me."

Her brown hair silvers in the afternoon light outside my window, pulled back in a severe knot that makes her look every inch the queen she is. She's dressed for court in deep blue silk with the golden seal of Galenda at her throat, and the way she moves toward my desk—this is my mother in full interrogation mode.

I straighten, smoothing down my own gray coat. Which I realize now I've worn more than once this week, a definite social blunder in the court.

"I've been busy, Mother."

"Well, yes. You're a queen now." She settles into the chair across from my desk, her posture straight as a blade. "And that's exactly what we're going to discuss. All of it."

My stomach clenches—from nerves more than the lingering morning sickness this time. I glance toward the door, toward the stacks of books, toward anywhere that might offer an escape route.

But there isn't one. There never was with her.

"I don't have a lot of time," I say.

Which is true. I should be heading up to my apartment shortly to change for tonight's Harvest Ball. And I'm feeling the pull toward being Caleb again. I'm feeling that more often these days, my time spent as Irava growing less. Is that the pregnancy, or something more?

But I can't change my illusion now, I'd have to show her my pregnancy.

I want to get back to my research. To my surveillance plans. To finding out how to draw Nikolai out, and how to defeat him.

"Make time," she says simply. "I need to know what's actually happening in this kingdom, Irava. I need to know why someone tried to kill my child three days ago, and why you look like you haven't slept since your wedding day."

I swallow against the sudden tightness in my throat.

Because she's not wrong. I am tired. I'm tired of the constant low-level nausea and the strain of maintaining illusions. I'm tired of feeling like I'm failing as both a ruler and a protector.

And most of all, I'm tired of the disconnect between Torovan and me, the careful conversations and worried glances that we pretend the other doesn't notice.

He looked at me this morning like it might be the last time.

Like he's terrified that an assassin will succeed in killing me.

Not that I'm not afraid of that, too, but I don't have time to be afraid.

I need to figure out how to fix all of this, defeat Nikolai, because I just want the danger to end so we can go back to being happy.

I shrug, hunching my shoulders. "I—I'm—things are just complicated right now." Well, and she knows that. "There are threats on the Akrean border—"

"This isn't about politics," she says. "And I'm not some visiting dignitary you need to manage like all the rest. I'm your mother. And I can see that something is very wrong here."

I start to protest that the Akrean threat is part of all of this. It's a lesser threat now that Nikolai is active in the palace, yes, but—

But my mother leans forward, her brown eyes, so like mine, fixed on my face.

"Start from the beginning. All of it. Now, Irava. You have put me off long enough."

I close my eyes, just for a moment.

And it's like I'm back in the palace in Galenda, standing straight under my mother's withering glare. Her disapproval.

Or is it worse now, with the weight of everything pressing down on me? Nikolai. The mind control weaving. This pregnancy that's keeping me from being myself, Torovan slipping away in the night.

Torovan, with dark circles under his eyes.

Torovan, who I have to protect at all costs.

And my child, who I have to protect at all costs, too.

We said we'd practice the dance tonight, before the ball.

And I want to be in his arms, I ache to be in his arms.

And also...it's so much.

So much.

When I open my eyes, my mother is still waiting. But then, I hadn't really hoped she'd be gone.

"Nikolai escaped," I begin.

"No," she says, "I know that. I want to know everything. Start from why you came here without telling me."

My shoulders tense, my anger rising. I want to bite out that it's because she betrothed me to a stranger, when she promised me she wouldn't.

I almost swallow that need. I don't have time for a fight, and I know she knows that. This meeting, despite her support the last few days, is my classic mother.

I look up and meet her gaze.

No. No, this is not the time to swallow this back down.

"I came because I needed to know if you actually betrothed me to a murderer."

Her eyes narrow. "I told you, I would never have—"

"You promised," I hiss. "You promised me I could marry who I want. And then you signed a treaty, marrying me to a stranger—"

"It worked out," she said. "You do love him."

I half rise, leaning on my desk. "You asked me to go back to Galenda with you, you obviously don't think it worked out."

She holds up her hands. "I should have asked you about the marriage."

"Yes!" I roar. And pause, my voice echoing off the walls.

I close my eyes, sit back down.

"Let me tell you all of it, if you want to know all of it, but I'm going to tell you why, and you're not going to like it. But don't interrupt me, or I won't get this out."

I look back at her.

Her expression is still, nearly serene. She's angry, yes. But, she nods.

So, I start from the beginning.

She listens as I tell her about becoming a court mage candidate. About unraveling Nikolai's out of control weaving. Torovan asking me to help him, and what we found in his father's bedchamber. And what Valtair and I found in his mother's. About unweaving the vortex with Torovan, side by side, and accidentally showing him I'm a woman, too. About standing with him, shielding him with my willpower, shielding him with my life and my name and the whole of who I am. And breaking Nikolai's control of him.

About telling him I'm both Irava and Caleb.

I look up at my mother with that, but she only nods.

So I try not to squirm and rush through the rest.

Nikolai's family protecting him from real justice, and his flight to his estates. Torovan's mother escaping, too, and that we think she's in Akreal. The rumors of anti-weaver sentiment Nikolai's spreading throughout the countryside, the missing weavers at the border with Akreal. And that Torovan's doing his best to carry out his father's reforms, but the people are pushing back against it. And that we think that might be Nikolai's influence, too.

I don't need to tell her about the assassination attempt.

And I absolutely don't tell her about the mind control weaving I found in Sabella's mind.

That's a threat I need to handle myself.

When I finish, she's quiet for a long moment, her fingers drumming against the arm of her chair.

"And Torovan?" she asks finally. "There's tension between you two. I've seen it."

My cheeks flush hot. "He's trying to protect me, but I'm the master weaver—"

"And you're pregnant."

I sit back as if slapped. My hand moves toward my stomach before I can catch myself.

"How did you—"

"I'm your mother." Her expression softens, just slightly. "I carried you for nine months, Irava. I know the signs. And I know you well enough to see when you're actively hiding something."

I stare at her, biting my lip.

And what will she do, knowing this?

"Yes," I say quietly. "Yes, I'm pregnant."

"How far along?"

"Five months." I shift in my chair. "And Torovan knows, obviously, and Valtair and Elsira. My guards know, and my apprentices. But we haven't...I haven't told the court yet."

She stills her drumming fingers. "Telling is both a vulnerability and a shield. You're losing ground, Irava, by being a weaver right now in a court that is growing hostile to weavers. I know it's a risk, but telling them will show you're still one of them. It will bring empathy back to you." She pauses. "I saw you weaving at the reception."

I stiffen.

"And you did well to handle that incident before it got worse," she goes on.

I let out my breath. "But you still want to take me back to Galenda. Mother, I'm not going."

"Of course I want to take you home," she snaps out, before making an effort to relax again. "But yes, I also see how critical you are to this kingdom's balance. How much they need you, even the ones who are afraid of you." Her brows draw down. "And how much he needs you. And how much you need him."

She looks down to my stomach again, back up to me.

"How are you doing, Irava? Really. I know you're Caleb often, and I see that. I see—I see I have another son, when you're Caleb. But the pregnancy—"

To my horror, my eyes start to fill with tears.

Oh, gods. Not now.

But Torovan checks on how I'm feeling, yes, and Valtair's hovering has become more stifling than not, but this...this is different. This is my mother, who I've spent months expecting to disapprove of everything I've become. And now she's asking about the part of myself that she hadn't met until a few days ago. Like she truly cares about my life as Caleb, too.

I press my hand to my mouth, and the careful control I've been holding for days starts to crack.

I'm straining at needing to change my illusions—I'm Caleb again now.

Well, but she knows about the pregnancy now, too.

With a glance toward my mother's face, I drop my illusion, then quickly reweave it as Caleb, and, like I did with my apprentices, I weave the pregnancy in as part of it.

My mother's gaze drops to my stomach again, but when she meets my eyes, I don't see—well, I don't know what I expect to see, but I don't expect the softening around her eyes.

And something in me, something I've been holding tight for months now, breaks.

"I don't know who I am," I whisper, and then the dam breaks. "I can't be myself, Mother. I can't be with him like— I'm just an illusion right now, I'm not real. And I'm too distracted, and I can't protect him, and I don't know how to fix this, I've been trying, I've been studying, but I can't find—"

My mother has never been affectionate. But she bumps her

hip on her way around my desk, and I push up into her embrace.

She holds me tight.

She holds me, while I shake against her, baring my teeth against the sobs.

I'm a grown man, and she holds me like she hasn't held me since I was a child.

She doesn't say anything, just lets me cry it out.

And my face burns as I finally pull back from her, but she gives me a wan smile. Pulling out a lace kerchief from a hidden pocket in her skirts to dab around my eyes.

"Mother—"

"Gods, Caleb. Let me care for you. I'll stay a week after the Festival ends, let me actually spend some time with you. And with Torovan."

I shake my head, sniffing hard. "But you have to get back."

"Your brothers could use the practice at ruling a kingdom."

And she could use the break, I hear but she doesn't say. And I understand that now, I do.

"You are so much stronger than you think," she says, adjusting my collar, smoothing down my sleeves. "Though, from how you said you won against Nikolai, I think you do know your strength." She meets my eyes. "And pregnancy isn't forever. And the rewards are usually worth it."

A half smile.

"But you have to stop trying to carry everything yourself—I see you trying to do that. I recognize it from myself. Even if you're not carrying the management of the kingdom, I know you're carrying its safety. But you have a husband who loves you, allies who respect you, and a mother who didn't travel all this way just to watch you struggle on your own."

She squeezes my hand once before releasing it.

"I'll see you tonight at the ball." She hesitates, then nods at my stomach. "I'm not going to tell you to rest, because I know you won't. But I was nauseous through every single one of my pregnancies. It never got better. But rest did help. Stress did not."

She gives a shrug. Then smooths down her skirts and moves toward the door.

"Thank you," I say softly.

She pauses at the door.

"I'm proud of you, Caleb."

I don't move.

She leaves and shuts the door behind her, and I stay, rigid, one hand braced on the desk so I don't sway.

She's proud of me?

She's never said that to me.

That's always been reserved for my older siblings, my brothers and my sisters.

If even.

My eyes fill again, and I sit heavily in my chair, my hands spreading across my stomach.

Is she proud because I'm pregnant?

Proud because I managed to make her betrothal into an actual family?

I lean back in my chair, letting myself feel the growing life inside me. All of its possibilities and potentials.

Will I be proud of them, too?

I need to make a world that's safe for them to live in.

And I still have some time before I must go with Torovan to the Harvest Ball.

So I spread out my books again.

C H A P T E R 28

T H E W E A V I N G

C A L E B

After the talk with my mother—gods, after the *cry* with my mother, and I'm growing more and more mortified about that now—I can't focus on what I'm reading.

So I get up to pace, moving about my small study. It's smaller than Aldric's, even, because I might be a master mage, but I'm the least senior of master mages. No one in the mage's quarters will give me more than my due because of my title.

They never have. I'm one of them.

But the space is mine. It has a window, and I pull back the half-drapes to peer out into one of the palace's back courtyards.

A group of young boys are bouncing a weighted bag between them.

Nearby, courtiers in clothing that's definitely not Barellan talk to each other, waving their hands around. One of them doubles over in laughter, supporting himself on the man next to him, who's also laughing.

I smile.

I would think, knowing that Nikolai or his agents are in the palace, that life would suddenly just...stop.

But it never stopped when he was here before. Not for anyone but the late king.

And...Torovan. It almost stopped for Torovan.

And me.

A sharp knock interrupts my brooding, and I turn, praying it's not my mother coming back. But no, she'd likely just come right in again.

And I'm not happy that my guards let her in the first time. Though I know my mother well enough to know they hadn't had much choice.

I expect one of my apprentices—the knock isn't Torovan's.

But it's Morgan who steps inside, his leather armor softly creaking as he turns to shut the door behind him. Quietly, like he's disturbing the room with his presence.

"What's wrong?" I ask, my pulse kicking into a pound.

Morgan straightens and turns back to me. He starts to say something, then hesitates.

He bows.

"Respectfully, Your Majesty." Then, with his cheeks flushing, he blurts, "You need to tell the king about the mind control weaving. I know you haven't."

Because if I had, the tension of the palace security would be something else entirely.

Morgan wets his lips and steps closer. "I know it's not my place. But, I was in the Council Chamber when Nikolai tried to control you both before. I was near the back—I was paralyzed. I could not move to help anyone."

I step back toward my desk to give myself a moment to think, and he tracks the movements.

Gods. I hadn't even thought—well I hadn't considered that he and Reveyan might tell Torovan what I wasn't telling him. Because that isn't the kind of men Torovan surrounds himself with, and me with. They are loyal to who they're protecting.

But that's the problem—they're *loyal to who their protecting.* And even if Morgan and Reveyan are assigned to me, they are, ultimately, still protecting Torovan above anyone else.

I wave to one of my chairs. "Please, sit?"

Morgan's eyes dart a moment, but then he slowly lowers himself into the same chair my mother just left.

"Torovan has scars from that day," I say. And I'm not going to ask Morgan if he knows what Torovan's not telling me, too. I know he wouldn't tell me.

And that's why he's here—because he *is* loyal.

"And the surest way for Nikolai to control someone is to play on their fears."

"Respectfully," Morgan says, sitting stiffly, hands braced on his knees, "isn't that what Nikolai, Lord Metrial, is doing to you?"

I bite my lip.

Morgan sits forward. "I want to be a weaver. We need more help—that is so clear. I know you're busy now, and I'm happy to learn from books, or be taught by your apprentices."

But from the lackluster tone of that last statement, no, he doesn't want to be taught by my apprentices.

And my scattered thoughts pull back to the present, because I think I know what he's asking, too.

He's like me. He's a man all of the time, and I'm a man part of the time, but we're both men who weren't raised to be men.

My pregnancy is still showing.

Am I that tired, getting that careless? But I don't feel like hiding it again just now, and Morgan already knows.

And he wants to be himself, too. Fully himself. Maybe I can't be that right now, I can only have my illusions, but Morgan's never had the chance.

I nod. "Yes. Of course I'll teach you. I've already offered."

He relaxes the fear in his posture, but not quite the wariness.

"I don't know if I want to be a court weaver," he says, drawing back, "or an actual apprentice, or if I'd be good at it. But I like being a guard. And—" He meets my eyes. Looks away again, then brings himself to meet them again.

"You're going to be a father," he says, more softly. "And you won't be able to keep your full attention on keeping the palace safe. I know you do—and I don't know if I'll be enough to help with that. Or if your apprentices will be better. But I want to try."

I shift in my chair, considering him. "You were watching my weaving with the apprentices. What did you see?"

He flushes again. "I want to understand what's going on around me."

"Can you see the threads of my weaving?"

He tilts his head. "I can see where I think they should be, according to your hand movements."

I hold up one hand, and with the other, weave a small reality construct above my palm. A butterfly again. Slowly, with deliberate emphasis on the threads I'm weaving.

Morgan watches intently. "I don't understand what you're doing. But I feel like I understand why."

I know what he means—not why I'm weaving the construct, but why I'm moving my hands the way I do.

I don't always need to move my hands, but it does help with the focus. And it's certainly helpful to teach.

I stand, an idea rising, and along with it, both misgivings and a sudden hope.

"Morgan, I can't reweave my own reality right now, because of the child. At least, I don't yet know how to do it safely. But—"

But some of the snippets and hints I've read over the last days and weeks snap into place in my mind.

I think it's possible to weave someone else's reality. Not just an illusion—their actual reality.

Is that a soul weaving?

No, I don't think so.

And this would be with Morgan's permission. I don't even know if that would be possible otherwise.

His face blanks, and he stands as I come around my desk.

What makes me think I might be able to do this—that I *can* do this—is how I nudged the threads of Sabella's mind. How I was able to hear her full symphony and know where it needed to be nudged back to true.

So, maybe it's a little bit of soul weaving. But not anything against Morgan's will. Working with his will, not against it.

Can I...do that?

It doesn't feel wrong.

I'm not going to weave the threads of his mind. But if I can hear where the threads of his body are out of tune with himself, can I weave the reality of his body to match them?

Would it remotely be safe?

He turns to face me as I approach him. "You're asking if you can...weave...*me*—"

His face is lighting with a hunger I understand.

I swallow.

I've done this to myself hundreds of times. I know how.

What I've done to myself is instinctual, though, and maybe I did look at the threads of my body and match them against my mind, and found where they needed to be pulled into true.

Did I?

I've never read about anyone in the books who rewove their reality, either. That was one thing I found in my studies—there is no map for what I want to do.

And if I can control my weaving in such a way that I'm only affecting one person, not me...can I do it in a way that only affects me, and not my child?

I shouldn't have offered this to Morgan, I don't know for sure it will be safe.

But then, I didn't know that when I rewove myself the first time, either.

I just did it. And it was right.

I hold up my hands, hesitate.

Morgan nods quickly. "Yes. Do it. Do I need to—" He twists in his armor.

But he's already muscular. He'll fill it out a little more, but I don't think by much more.

"Just loosen it," I say, and he does so.

And I think through what I'm going to do.

And his trust in me.

Torovan says he trusts me. He says I should do what I have to.

But weaving *is* dangerous. It always will be, because realities are forged with willpower—with the collective pressures of society, with the self-assurances of a soul's knowing who they are and who they can be. And who they should be. With the gods' wills. With the possibilities of everything.

I watch Morgan as he loosens the buckles on his armor, taking everything out two notches. And I start to see the possibilities around him, but they're not seething and unformed like many men's are. His focus is intense, his knowing of who he is. He absolutely *knows* who he is.

I can see the outline of the body that should be his. And before I can lose it, before he's fully done loosening everything, I weave it into reality.

Morgan gasps. And I know the feeling—it's not pain, but it's a shift, a different reality from the one he stood within a moment before.

"Shit," he says, then stills as he hears his deeper, rougher voice. "You did it."

Morgan holds up his hands, shakes out his shoulders, his legs. Looks...down, expectantly.

Well, but he's still wearing his armor.

I grin, a little shaky, but I grin.

I'm still looking at his threads, the threads of his mind and the threads of his body, and they are *humming* together in a harmony they hadn't had before.

"Go," I say. "The Harvest Ball is—gods, we need to get back to my room, I need to dress. Okay, no, you have to come with me. But you can go into the spare bedroom, tell me if everything's okay."

But I know it will be. His sense of possibilities in my weaver's senses have honed into a knife's point. That humming energy is still growing as he's aligning himself to possibilities that are suddenly his.

I want that again. I want that with an ache that rocks me where I stand.

Morgan turns, eager to go.

"I'm not sure if it's permanent," I say. "I'm always weaving and unweaving my own realities. But—we'll train so that you can keep it permanent."

He hesitates at the door, but nods. "Thank you. Thank you, Caleb."

I meet his eyes and nod.

And gods. I'm quaking inside. I just rewove *his reality.* I just did that.

Do I dare even attempt to reweave my own?

Do I do it now, and have my senses about me, all of my concentration, for the Harvest Ball?

But—but.

But if there's even a chance I might fail.

If there's even.

A chance.

I swallow.

What if I had harmed Morgan?

What if I'd been wrong?

I hadn't been, but, what if? What if I placed more trust in my abilities than I should?

Should I have taken that risk, even if he'd trusted me with it? Even if I'd trusted myself?

A yawning chasm opens inside me.

Because I can't. I can't take that risk again.

Not if it could harm my child.

I follow Morgan out into the corridor, my hopes sinking again.

CHAPTER 29

THE HARVEST BALL

TOROVAN/CALEB

TOROVAN

I stop in the doorway to our bedroom when I see Caleb dressing.

He looks over at me, his eyes already shimmering with gold and orange shadows. He so rarely wears makeup. And is it actually makeup? Is it part of the illusion?

I don't care.

He's not an illusion to me.

His light-brown hair is pulled back, and he's just now wrestling himself into a knee-length green coat.

"Let me help," I say, and he does, holding still as I button up the front.

He's still watching me with that intensity he had this morning, but it's softened a bit.

My hands shake between one buttonhole and the next. Has he softened into acceptance of the inevitable?

No.

No, I can't believe that. Caleb would fight until the last breath, I know he would.

I finish the buttons and straighten as he turns away, then move toward my own clothes, which were also picked out before the Festival. Every part of the Festival meticulously planned.

I pull a russet coat from my wardrobe, and blue-gray trousers.

I eye the cosmetics jars that Caleb left sitting on the bed and pick them up until I find a gray and golden brown that's close enough to what I'm wearing.

I hear the rustling stop behind me, and Caleb's approaching. "Let me."

I surrender the jars, and he inspects them, then swaps the brown for something more golden, too.

I hold still as he carefully brushes around my eyes.

And I study his.

I open my mouth and almost ask if he's all right.

That constant question.

But then I press my lips tight again.

Tonight, after the ball, I know I'm going to shatter what little peace we have left. And I don't want to shatter that now.

Caleb pulls back and nods, then steers me toward the standing mirror in one corner.

"What do you think?"

He's spread the powder broadly around my eyes, like he has his own. I turn my head, watching the metallic shimmer. And smile.

"Caleb—" I turn, but he's not still behind me, he's capped the bottles and is already moving toward his crown.

And I can't name why, but that sits heavy in my soul. Watching him place the crown on his head, adjust it slightly.

Like I'm the one who put him in this danger.

Because I am.

I turn back and pull my own crown off its stand.

Then go back to the bed to get my coat and tug it on.

Caleb silently helps me do up the buttons. Straightening the collar.

He trails his fingers, briefly, across my mouth. He looks up and leans to kiss me.

There is so much silence between us tonight, so much that's heavy and unspoken, but I'm not willing to break it.

"Do we have time for one round of dance practice?" he asks.

I glance out the window—the sun is almost set.

"We're the kings," I say. "They'll start when we arrive."

One side of his mouth quirks up.

And he lets me lead him out into my study, which has more space in which to not bruise ourselves by bumping into things.

There's no music. But we position ourselves for the start of the dance, then slowly bow to each other, the formal start of the dance. Then we circle, dip, spin, come together. Step back apart. Circle in the other direction, dip, spin. Then the second rotation of the dance facing apart, before we come back together again, facing each other.

His steps aren't perfect, but he does have it. He knows how to lead this dance, he's done it before, though not both of us leading together.

If there's any disaster tonight, it won't be because we fumble the dance.

We end with a last bow to each other, then Caleb breathes out.

"Okay. Torovan—"

"Stay close again tonight," I say, because I can't help it. Because the fear is rising in me again. Because this is the room where our enemy delivered another more potent threat, only hours ago.

Here in this room, which is supposed to be safe.

He frowns, but he nods.

"Be watchful tonight," he says, tilting his head at me. "All your weaver's senses."

I notice—I finally notice—that he's not wearing his master weaver's medallion. I touch the mage's medallion over my heart, and then slowly pull it up over my head.

He sighs explosively. "Yes, that's a good idea, but I hate this, Tor."

I set the medallion on my desk. Then, because this space already feels violated, snatch it back again and slip it into my coat pocket.

Nikolai doesn't get to take that, too.

"I know," I say. "We'll—we'll wear them again after the Festival ends. We'll have to think about how to regain the peoples' trust in weavers."

Caleb looks bleak, though. And I feel the same.

Neither of us say what I think we're both thinking, that—how to do we win against enemies who're already stealing the hearts of our people?

Enemies who can invade our most private spaces and threaten those we love.

I look at the long glass, sitting on top of a lower shelf.

"Time to go."

I hold out my arm, and Caleb takes it.

CALEB

The air is thick with music, expensive wine, the murmur of a hundred conversations. But the mood is brittle. Far too bright.

Everyone at this court knows that the Festival has gone sour. And there aren't as many people here, at the Harvest Ball, as there should be. Even with its importance.

Musicians in the orchestral band fill the space with flowing melodies, while the nobles watch each other like they're all secretly enemies. Every delegate is glaring at every other delegate, even if it's over a smile and a nod.

Maybe it's the lingering threat of the attack from the first night, or Kian's out of control weaving—or both—but I'm glad I didn't wear my medallion tonight.

Not that it fools anyone that I'm not a weaver.

Gods. I want to do this dance with Torovan and leave.

I've never much liked palace balls, and the need to be on display. The eyes on us now are colder than usual, wary, far too assessing.

Like Torovan and I might snap at any moment, and suddenly weave danger at all of them?

I widen my weaver's senses, but I don't see the threads of mind control weaving here. Not obviously so.

Whatever's going on is far more insidious than that.

My grip on Torovan's arm tightens.

And somehow, we smile and get through.

I spot one of the Akrean delegates watching me, the same

woman who snapped at me at the reception the other day. Do I see contempt in her eyes?

But then, it's well established that they don't like weavers.

The mage trials are supposed to be tomorrow, the combat trials the day after, the last day of the Festival.

And maybe I should ask Torovan if we should cancel both trials. Because we've been trying to hold this Festival together, but just now, it feels like the biggest farce.

Knowing that Nikolai is here.

And even if everyone else doesn't know that yet, Nikolai's presence is palpable in this room.

He's here. He's orchestrated the events that have led to this night, this tension. Even if he hadn't thrown that dagger—and it could have been him.

I still don't know.

I still can't look and not see enemies everywhere, too.

Every single face around me—any one of them could be him.

I know how to weave myself into an illusion of someone else, I'm sure he does, too.

Am I being paranoid?

But Torovan beside me is tense, too.

Somewhere in the bustle of the ball, of the many people we have to greet—some of whom seem genuinely glad to see us— my resolve to keep Nikolai's presence in the palace from Torovan crumbles.

I've told myself it's for his protection, but he's not in much better shape than I am. We're both rigid, and haggard, and the gulf between us feels wide enough to fill an ocean.

Torovan's eyes keep sweeping the crowd like he's expecting an attack at any moment.

Which, probably, he is.

And so am I.

I spot my mother across the hall. I see Valtair laughing with an older man, one of the foreign delegates, and Elsira looking like she wants rescued from a conversation with a dour noble matron.

My apprentices, if they are here—and they might be, too—won't be faces I recognize in this crowd.

And will I recognize Nikolai, if he chooses to attack?

The dagger was thrown the first night, a significant night of the Harvest Festival.

Kian's weaving—well, publicly Kian's weaving—went out of control at the reception. Which was important diplomatically.

If there will be a third incident, or attack, tonight would be the most optimal time.

Because the dance Torovan and I are fast approaching is important to the hopes of the people.

I'll tell him tonight.

I'll tell him about Sabella, and the mind control weaving.

I'm just...I'm tired.

I'm so tired.

And I want my husband wholly.

And if he still chooses not to tell me what he's holding back...well.

"How are you holding up?" Torovan murmurs against my ear, his breath warm against my skin. It's the first private word he's spoken to me in over an hour.

Nausea, my constant friend, sits in the back of my throat, more jittery tonight than usual.

And do I feel better knowing my mother had that nausea, too?

Or does that just make me feel even more like a stranger in my body?

"Well enough," I say. Though it's not true. And he knows it.

I look up at him, and he looks at me.

Then the chords strike for the beginning strains of our dance.

And the crowds move aside to clear the center of the hall.

CHAPTER 30

THE DANCE

TOROVAN/CALEB

TOROVAN

The music starts for the ceremonial dance, where the king is supposed to help usher in prosperity for the year to come.

But I hardly feel like I have any kind of good luck these days.

Except for Caleb. Caleb is all of the luck I will ever need in my lifetime.

I pull him toward the center of the floor, and his mouth is pressed tight, his face a little pale.

Is he nervous? Or is it the nausea again?

But he faces me in the center, tilts his chin up. The metallic gold makeup around his eyes shimmering in the light of the hundreds of candles and lamps.

The music hits our starting point, and we bow solemnly to each other, then start to dance.

We circle, dip, spin, come together. Step back apart. Circle to the left now, then dip again, spin.

I don't want to do the part where he's facing away from me. And I feel my own fears rising, because now—now would be the time to disrupt the kingdom again, wouldn't it? While I'm circling, stepping, dipping, spinning, and can't see any threat that would come his way.

I'm straining not to look behind me and only look during the spin. When he's spinning, too.

But then we're turning to face each other again.

And nothing yet has happened.

We go through the motions of the last part of the dance.

Circling each other, dipping, and spinning.

On the last spin, Caleb wobbles, his hand going to his mouth.

Oh, no.

The nausea. The *spinning*.

I tense, but he does complete the spin, his fist curled against his mouth, and moves to the center again to bow to me. More shallowly than he should, but he does complete it.

We've finished the dance.

The music slows, and plays its final chords in fanfare.

Then, silence.

There's usually a cheer at this point, a successful dance completed for the next year.

But Caleb's swaying, his fist still pressed to his mouth, obviously struggling.

I move to him.

His shoulders twitch, and I move faster.

His eyes meet mine, a mix of desperation and fury.

And his illusion drops.

CALEB

Gods. *Gods.*

I'm going to be sick. Why now? Why is my stomach heaving now?

But the nerves, the tension, the dance, the movement, all of it. *All of it* is threatening right now to erupt.

It's taking all of my focus not to be sick. My entire world narrowed to that one single point: *don't be sick.*

We've finished the dance, that is done. But if I'm sick now, at this dance which is supposed to hold all the hopes for the next year—

My illusion as Caleb presses in on my focus.

And suddenly, it's too much. One thing too many, stifling me, crowding in on me.

I'm tired of the lies.

I'm *so* tired of hiding.

So I let my illusion go. Even though I'm not Irava. I'll reweave my illusion as Caleb when the nausea passes.

But right now, that one pressure less is the relief I need.

I breathe carefully, stand still as Torovan braces my shoulders.

I feel him in my senses, lending his willpower to me.

It's not what I need to calm my stomach. But the thought of it, this selfless man, steadies my nerves.

I anchor myself in his gray-green eyes.

And slowly, the nausea ebbs.

Slowly.

He sees the relief in my eyes and gathers me to him.

I hear a murmur around me, like the wind at night.

The room was silent, but now voices are rising.

"—pregnant!" I hear someone say, a single surprised voice rising above the rest. More voices begin to break out.

I jolt away from Torovan, my whole body heating with the realization of what I've just done.

I see Torovan swallow, visibly, and try to pull together a smile for the court. Try not to quake in my own fear of what they will do, what they will say.

If they'll say I shouldn't have this. Because I'm also a man.

If they'll try to use our child against us.

If Nikolai will—

I turn and look at the faces around us, mixes of surprise, distress, and...joy?

I press my hand to my stomach, turning as I take in the people around me.

I see my mother, who's smiling slightly, though her eyes are tense.

She knows, she understands, that I've just given our enemies a greater lever against us.

But I hold my hand to my stomach, fighting back against the fear.

Because yes, I *do* see joy.

Count Valtair is standing tall and proud, his eyes shining like Torovan is his own son.

I watch Torovan see this, watch some of his knotted-up tension ease as he nods to the count. He looks genuinely happy for the first time in a while.

Torovan looks back to me, and his grin widens, then fades. Then widens again.

I laugh, a startled sound, not exactly mirth.

But the nausea is easing back into a background noise, and I reweave my illusion as Caleb, letting my pregnancy show this time.

Letting my soul breathe.

Gods, I can *breathe.*

And nothing yet has happened.

Torovan lifts my hand with his. "We are going to have a child!" he shouts.

And the crowd around us roars, buffeting me. Making my eyes sting.

And maybe...maybe I've been afraid to show them because I was afraid I wouldn't have this.

That their approval of who I was would only go so far, and not this far.

Not so far as to embrace a man who is also going to have a child. Their next king, or queen.

Torovan squeezes my hand tightly, bracing against that roar, and I squeeze it back.

I hadn't intended to say anything tonight, or any time soon.

But there's a weight lifting that I hadn't known was as heavy as it was.

I stand in the growing adoration of a people who just moments ago were looking at me like I was a curse, a danger to them.

They're not looking at me like that now.

Or at Torovan that way, too.

Gods. My mother said my pregnancy could also be a shield.

Was this the remedy?

Is the remedy to the kingdom's fears something else to hope for?

Torovan

How can I feel so much joy and so much dread at the same time?

I hold our hands together and shout again, "We are going to be fathers!"

And I feel my people's hearts coming back to me. When all night, it felt like I was swimming in a sea of strangers.

I don't know if Caleb meant to drop his illusion. I did see resolve in his eyes, but he certainly hadn't meant to feel sick.

But the people will forgive those signs of sickness at the end of the dance, now, too.

It seems like much will be forgiven, the fears of the court diverted, for now.

And maybe, gods maybe, the rest of the Festival can be a celebration.

For everyone else, at least.

I have to tell him tonight.

But for now, we have this moment of joy.

CHAPTER 31

THE NURSERY

CALEB

I hold Torovan's hand tightly as we walk back down the corridor of the royal apartments, stopping at his study door.

We're both flushed. Heady with the good will of the court. Buzzing with their celebration—so much wine was shoved at Torovan, and absolutely none at me, which was...for a time... wonderful.

Like the first days after I married him, when the court was full of giddiness at being saved from disaster. Full of celebration, and celebrating *us.*

But happiness doesn't take away the dread rising in me. Because now Nikolai, or his agents, know I'm pregnant, too.

Torovan pulls me into his study and looks around before we go in further.

And more, his guards move inside, into the rooms, clearing them before they allow us to go further.

I glance at Morgan and Chiran, who hovered dutifully at a distance all night.

Morgan's usually blank guard's expression is now troubled.

"Tor," I say. "Why are your guards clearing the apartment?"

Is it because of the child? Does that now warrant greater security? Will Torovan be thrusting more guards on me?

But I couldn't in good conscience refuse them now.

"It's just a precaution," he says.

He's tensing up again.

And this has to do with what he's not telling me, doesn't it?

And—and I've had enough of that, too.

He asked me to trust him.

But trust goes both ways.

I let go of his hand and move around to face him.

"Tor. What is going on?"

His face is so grim that for a moment, I wonder if I even want to know?

I don't know if I have space in my heart for more dread.

I see a war playing out on his strong features, and I'm not sure he's winning. Or which side of him.

He takes my hand again. Then turns as his guard, Kas, comes back out to the study.

"Clear, Your Majesties. Have a good night."

The guards file out, leaving us in silence.

And mounting, growing, tension.

Torovan leads me toward the room we've been calling the nursery, snagging an oil lamp from a wall sconce as he does so.

He's stalling, I know. Maybe gathering his thoughts. Maybe trying to find a way to put me off again.

And I'm feeling my own bitterness rising.

Because whatever it is, why won't he just tell me?

And I'm too tired to demand any more from him tonight.

So I let him lead me into the nursery. Because that's a room that's full of hope. And I want that hope again just now.

I did tell the court.

And despite everything—oh gods, despite everything, that does feel good.

I hold my stomach, looking around the unfinished space. The sheets of wallpaper that still need to go up. The crib, which was pulled from palace storage. Torovan's when he was younger.

Or maybe Elsira's. There were two cribs, as they were both twins. Neither of them knew which crib was which.

Bile rises in me again, this time like a bile from my soul.

When I first came to the palace, I was full of my own secrets. And Valtair kept telling me to tell Torovan.

And I did, eventually. When I had to.

But how much pain would I have saved both of us if I'd just...trusted him, too?

Because trust goes both ways.

And I'm holding secrets from him again, too.

With good reason, but...

Those reasons are feeling flatter by the second.

I wet my lips. "Torovan—"

I spy something shimmering in one corner of the room, hovering at the edge of my awareness.

I've been distracted, but now my senses snap back into focus, expanding, searching.

This room feels wrong.

It feels *wrong*.

I take a step forward.

"What?" Torovan asks, gripping my shoulder. Steadying himself? His eyes are wide and scared.

"There's an unreality weaving here."

Torvan shakes. Physically shakes.

"Where?" he asks, his voice tight with fear. "Where's the anchor point?"

But that's what I saw in the corner. I reach for it, and even still across the room, I pluck it away from the wall.

Unravel it enough to feel reality seething again beneath it.

And that reality has an air of malice about it.

Torovan stiffens, and I see where he's looking. I'm still holding the threads of the unreality weaving, but I quickly start to unravel them. It's not a complex weaving, not like what was in his father's bedchamber.

But I watch as Torovan reaches for something in the crib. Something I hadn't seen before, which the unreality weaving had kept hidden, or maybe told my eyes it was not worth seeing.

A folded and sealed letter.

"What is it?" I ask.

He holds it a moment before he breaks the seal.

And his breath goes out.

"What does it say? Who is it from?"

I almost have the unreality weaving unraveled now, and I'm moving toward him, trying to see.

Torovan doesn't move. His breathing is fast and heavy.

I finally see the words scrawled across the page. "You told him."

"Told me?" I ask. "Or I told you? Who is this meant for? What does it mean?"

Because he obviously knows what it means.

"I didn't," he says, shaking his head. "I didn't tell you. I *didn't tell you yet.*"

He turns to me, swallowing, his face painted with anguish. With terror.

Nikolai.

No, I don't need to ask who this is from. What I know is catching up with what I'm seeing.

The unreality weaving.

Nikolai was here.

In this room.

In our apartment.

In our *nursery.*

And he's been threatening Torovan, hasn't he?

That's what Torovan hasn't told me.

Because this obviously isn't the start of the conversation, but the middle of it.

Or maybe the end.

"Let me see it," I say.

He snatches the paper out of my reach.

"It's a trap," he says.

And I focus on the letter, and the sense of unreality that's in his hand.

I examine the weaving, then unravel it.

Torovan hisses as the letter catches fire. He drops it—I catch it in the air with my weaving, quickly examine the threads of a reality of heat around it, and then unweave those, too.

The letter falls to the floor as ash.

I see the panic in his eyes, I see what I was trying to protect him from.

I was trying to keep him safe, but he was suffering all along.

I move to him, press my hands to his cheeks until he focuses again on me.

"Caleb. I'm sorry—"

"We will get him," I hiss. "We will get the bastard, he will *not* threaten you. Or me. Or our child."

He stares at me a moment, and the panic starts to retreat. And fury starts to replace it.

How long has this been going on? How long has he been carrying whatever this threat is?

I asked Valtair what was happening with Torovan, but I don't think he knows about this, either.

It is just like Torovan, exactly like him, to try to carry all of this himself.

I pull him tightly to me, and he grips me back, shuddering.

"I can't protect you, Caleb."

And I'm still struggling to protect myself.

I just outed my pregnancy in front of the court, because I couldn't hold myself together.

I'm struggling to protect him, too.

And Nikolai knows that.

He already knew about my pregnancy.

And that...that turns my blood to ice.

"Tell me," I say. "Tell me everything."

CHAPTER 32

POWERLESS

CALEB

We take off our crowns. Because it feels profane, somehow, to be wearing a crown when I feel so powerless.

Torovan says he needs to show me, not tell me, so I follow him back down to the common areas of the palace, and almost forget that I'm still showing my pregnancy.

So we have to stop, several times, and while late night and tipsy courtiers congratulate me. Again.

My face feels like my smile will be permanently baked on by the time we get to one of the meeting rooms beside the Great Hall.

Torovan takes a lamp off the wall to bring in with us, and locks the door behind us.

And there's another pressure inside my soul that needs to come out.

Now.

"I found mind control weaving in Sabella's mind," I say.

Torovan's stepped a few paces into the room, but he hasn't gone any further.

He turns to me, and I see his anger rising again, this time aimed at me.

And maybe I want to see that more than the fear pulling the light from his eyes.

Yes, be angry at me. Be *anything* other than the man who's fading fast, going back to the broken state I found him in when I first came to the palace.

"When?" he asks.

"After the reception. It was Sabella who was weaving and lost control, Kian tried to help but that went out of control, too. I think she was following a suggestion to weave, or at least a suggestion of danger that she felt she had to stop. From—"

"Nikolai," Torovan says, his voice going flat.

I nod.

He stares at me, his eyes burning. "You didn't tell me."

Then he pinches the bridge of his nose. "Because I wasn't telling you—gods, Caleb. Gods!"

He turns and strides to a random place on the left wall, the lamp's flame flickering wildly as he walks.

So...I follow.

He yanks off a panel on the wall and pulls a small wooden box out of an opening inside.

"Give me the lamp," I say, and take it before his quick movements blow it out and we're left in darkness. I place it on a nearby table.

Torovan slides the lid of the box open and pulls out a folded stack of papers.

No, a stack of *letters.*

I start to reach for them, but he yanks them back from me. Like he did with the letter in the nursery.

"They're all from Nikolai?" I ask.

"Yes." He pulls one open and shows it to me.

In the dim light, I can just make out, "I will kill him if you tell him."

I'm already on edge, already wrung out, but the adrenaline surge hits me again now, making my heart race.

I look up to meet his eyes, but he's not looking at me.

This is why he hasn't told me.

Because Nikolai said he'd kill me if Torovan did.

Fuck Nikolai Metrial.

He knew exactly where Torovan was most vulnerable.

He's messing with everything we hold as sacred.

I hold out my hand, and I can feel the unreality weaving on the letters even from here.

Slowly, he hands me the open letter, but holds the rest of the stack back, still away from me.

"How many letters?" I ask.

"Five. Five days. I don't know where they're coming from. The last one—the last one was in my study today. That one said that he would kill you, and my heir."

I stiffen before my hand reaches the letter. Then steel myself and grab it.

I feel the unfolding of reality instantly, and weave it away from the letter, like pulling a poisonous snake off my arm.

"Caleb!"

I hear a pounding on the door, one of the guards asking if we need help.

But all my focus is on unweaving the trap away from me.

It's unreality, and it's not. It's another kind of weaving that

I've never seen before, like it wants to burrow into my skin. To...rewrite me.

Like I haven't been able to do to myself for so long now.

Oh, no.

I *do* know what this is.

It's not that different from how I wove Morgan earlier today. But—but it's *so* different. It's aiming straight for my soul.

I find the threads that are holding the weaving together, a mix of regular light reality threads and sinewy soul magic. But they're intertwined tightly with the light threads, and I'm able to catch them. Hold them. And start to unravel them.

I *will not* be rewoven into what Nikolai thinks I should be, whatever that is. Whatever that means.

I can unweave this trap.

And after a few minutes, and Torovan striding toward the door to keep the guards from kicking it in, the trap is unwoven.

The normal weaving threads easing back into reality, and the sinewy soul threads, with nothing to hold onto, fading.

I'm on my knees on the floor, panting.

That was just one letter.

Just one.

The guards rush in as Torovan opens the door. Morgan and Reveyan come straight to me.

"Sire," Reveyan asks, kneeling down. "Are you injured?"

I shake my head, and stare at the paper fallen on the floor, straining to find any remaining danger.

Then I try to search within myself, as best I can, to see if any of that weaving did get...inside me. Attach to me. Whatever it would do.

I don't feel anything, though. Nothing feels out of place

except the dissonance between who I am right now and my body beneath my illusion.

And that's all too familiar.

Torovan strides back to me. "Caleb."

He pulls me up. He's still holding the letters, but back behind him, as far away from me as he can.

"I'm sorry," he says, "I'm sorry." Like a mantra.

"Don't apologize," I growl. I reach for the letters.

"No!" He trips back, away from me.

"They have to be neutralized—"

"Not when it almost drained you, Caleb! Or, or killed you! Whatever it was trying to do!"

I am exhausted.

And I don't know if I would have unwoven that trap as fast as I had if I hadn't woven Morgan's reality earlier.

I look up at Morgan, and his brows draw down in concern.

His reality is still holding.

I take a shaky breath. But, I still would have unwoven that trap, I know I would have.

And maybe that's what these letters are, Nikolai's attempt to neutralize me. So that when he actually attacks in his full strength, I'm not a threat to him.

But the threat of the letters still remains.

"You told me," I say finally, looking back to Torovan. "And I'm not dead."

And that letter in the nursery—Nikolai assumed that Torovan already had.

He stares at me. "How many people knew you were pregnant?"

But he shakes his head, then. "No, Aldric knew. He said he

could feel the possibility of another life, so Nikolai could have known."

"Aldric knew?"

Gods. He hadn't said anything.

But—

Oh, gods. Nikolai was in our rooms. And I outright drew a map for my apprentices of how to get around the guards in this palace. I taught them how to become as close to invisible as it was possible to get.

Did Nikolai catch one of them, and use them? Did he pull information out of them?

I push up with Morgan's help and start for the door.

"Caleb—" Torovan follows. "Where are you—"

"My apprentices." I glance at him. "They know the guard rotations, the palace blind spots. I have them out...uh...spying to try to find any signs of Nikolai."

"You *what?*"

He comes around me before we reach the door.

"I promoted them," I say. "They're court mages now."

I glare at him, and he glares back.

"You don't have that authority to—"

"I'm a master mage—"

"You should have told me!" he roars. "We are supposed to make these decisions together!"

He's still holding the letters. He looks at them, and his face crumples. And I'm watching all the careful willpower my husband built back up over the last months crumble away again.

I catch his arm.

"Tor. This is what he wants. This is what Nikolai wants. He's attacking where we're weak."

"You're not a weakness, Caleb—"

"Yes, but he sees your love for me as weakness, as something to exploit. And my apprentices, gods, he's exploiting that, too. He's trying to hurt me through them. He's trying to hurt us, by making you keep this from me. Because we can't fight him if we're not in harmony, Torovan. We can't. That's how we unraveled his storm, that's how we beat him in the Council Chamber."

"You beat him," he says, and strides back to the open wall panel, shutting the letters inside the box, shoving the box inside the wall, but then carefully placing the panel back on, his temper running out. He leans his head against the wall.

My apprentices will have to wait. Just a few moments more.

And I tell myself, I don't even know where they are. They might still be out among the palace guests.

When Torovan needs me *right now*.

"You defeated him, Caleb," he says as I approach. "I...was losing."

"But you won't lose now."

He turns back, looks past me to our guards. "Please—"

"Yes, Sire." The guards hastily retreat, leaving us again in our private silence.

Torovan spreads his hands wide. "Maybe Aldric was right, maybe I'm just fooling myself that I have any willpower at all—"

I grip his hands, bring them back to me. "No. Torovan Braise, you followed your father's plans and made them your own. Because you knew it was *right*. Despite everything, you did that. You are seeing it through. You are changing this kingdom for the better."

"And what good is it, if the people are resisting that change, the common people don't want it—"

"Nikolai doesn't want it," I snap back. "Your mother doesn't want it. Do you know what they do want?"

His arms twitch like he wants to pull away from my grip, but I hold fast.

"They want to break you, Torovan. Because they know that's the only way they can control you. And you don't have to do what your enemies want."

And that...finally gets through.

He stills, breathing heavily, looking away from me.

And I know his wounds are deep. He has been healing, yes. But it hasn't been a year yet since he lost his father.

It hasn't been six months since he found out his mother was *why* he lost his father.

Since Nikolai tried to control him, and maybe—maybe that left deeper scars than I'd thought.

Maybe, in my own private troubles, I haven't been paying attention.

As much as I'm not close to my mother, at least I have her. She came to me, she sought me out—she's trying to support me as best as she can. I know that.

Torovan only has me. And Valtair and Elsira, but none of us are his parents. I know he sees Count Valtair as a father figure, but that's still a distant figure. I don't think Torovan's told him about this, either.

And our enemies know exactly where to throw and twist the knives.

His mother *is* one of his enemies.

I press a hand to my mouth as my stomach surges again.

Gods, not now.

That pulls Torovan out of his reverie, though, and he exhales.

"Do you need a bucket? I think there's a waste basket."

I shake my head and slowly lower my hand.

Torovan rubs his face again. "How do we find Nikolai? How to we flush him out?"

I bite my lip. "I sent my apprentices—"

He shakes his head.

"Torovan—"

"They're not ready, Caleb. And you sent them against *Nikolai*—"

"I sent who we have. Would you rather I go myself?" Which I was still planning to do anyway.

He makes a face. "I found weaving on the doorway of the Akrean delegation."

I blink, then frown. "Unreality weaving? Do you think the Akreans are behind these threats, then, not Nikolai? But I found the signs of mind control weaving in Sabella—"

"No. Not the letters. Or the mind control, gods of all the seasons. No. That is Nikolai. But—"

He opens his hands. "We're out of time, aren't we? And we can't have loose ends that we don't know about, we can't afford them. I want to talk to the Akrean delegate. I want to know why there's a weaver among them, if they're so against weavers —if it's not something meant to throw us off from Nikolai. I want to know what place my mother has in Akreal, and I want to know if they support Nikolai."

"And you want to just *ask* them?"

"We don't have time for diplomatic games, Caleb."

I sigh. And feel the roundness of my belly.

And think about the letter that was left in our crib.

"No," I say quietly. I want to go after Nikolai with all I have right now. But I'm following where Torovan is going with this—it's easier to follow the leads we do have than the ones we don't, even if they might not lead straight to what we're after. They're still a part of the whole.

Every thread in a weaving is important.

One thread ignored could mean the entire weaving unravels. Or blows up.

"But—I want to check on my apprentices first. They usually report to me by now, but I haven't been in my study. The ball."

Torovan starts for the door.

"Can you still make an illusion around yourself?" I ask.

He looks back. "Yes."

"I think we'll want that, when we go to the Akreans."

Because still, even now, we have to think about how this looks. How everything looks.

Maybe I bought us some time with the court by showing my pregnancy. Bought us more good will.

But I know us going officially to see the Akrean delegation, knowing how the Akreans feel about weavers, might look like we're giving in to those beliefs.

I touch the space on my chest where my weaver's medallion should be. And I'm regretting not wearing it now.

Of giving in even that much.

Torovan pauses, considering, then nods.

And he's woven someone else around him before he's reached the door.

Despite everything, I break into a grin at that.

My weaver.

CHAPTER 33

THE DELEGATE

TOROVAN

It's not nearly as late as when I walked these corridors the night before. Wrapped in my illusion then, too.

And I've used the illusion of the palace servant again—I'm more than a little paranoid that we'll run into the man.

But we don't.

Caleb has assumed the illusion of a man I don't recognize, dark brown hair a curly mess, clothes that are well-made but a little shabby, disheveled as if he was at the ball earlier, too.

And despite all of the fears driving me just now, I can't help but watch my husband work with a warmth in my chest.

He's *good* at this.

I can't think of any illusion he could wear that I wouldn't find appealing.

That I wouldn't want to back him to the nearest wall and kiss him until our lips are both bruised.

But...the letter.

The letter in the crib.

And the letter he just opened, with threads I could only just see writhing out to attack him.

I should have helped him, given him my strength, but I just stood there. Frozen.

How can I call him my husband if all I do is stand by when he's in danger?

Yes, I caught the dagger at the feast. But I haven't yet caught the hand that threw it.

As we near the stairs leading up to the administrative offices, I spot Valtair coming out of his.

His eyes glaze past me but lock on Caleb with recognition.

Oh, no.

Then come back to me and look between us.

He falls into step beside Caleb, leaning in.

So whoever Caleb is now is either a real person that Valtair knows, or an illusion Caleb's used on their sometimes palace adventures before.

I haven't had time to fill Valtair in.

Well. That's not true. I've decided not to. Not yet.

He glances back at me again, then takes the lead ahead of Caleb, apparently inviting himself on this mission.

And maybe it's not a bad idea—whoever Caleb is supposed to be, he doesn't have nearly as much clout as the Prime Minister of Barella.

And a prime minister can more easily talk to a foreign delegate without controversy than a king.

It's Valtair who knocks on the door to the Akreans' suite.

And it is late, yes. Very late. Though the ball has wound down, the celebration has carried over, I suspect, into the upscale taverns and socialite clubs in the town. And into various meeting rooms and noble's quarters.

Am I glad that we added to that celebration tonight with Caleb's pregnancy, with the promise of an heir? Can I still be glad after we found the letter in the crib?

The weaving is still over the Akreans' door.

And the woman who opens the door is still dressed.

I did see her at the ball, though only on the sidelines. She's tall and severe, her black hair bound up tight.

She reminds me, in her demeanor, of my mother. And I haven't yet spoken to her directly, but she very well may know my mother, as one of the lead Akrean delegates.

She might be here on orders from my mother. But how a weaver fits into that—I don't know.

Is it a taunt? Is it a threat? They had to know that other weavers might see it.

Other weavers meaning Caleb, or me.

"Prime Minister Valtair," the Akrean delegate says, drawing the words out in her rolling accent.

"May we talk, privately?" Valtair asks. "It's a matter of some urgency."

"All of you?" she asks, narrowing her eyes at Caleb, then me.

Then her head tilts. As if she catches what's going on. She steps back inside.

"My colleagues are still out," she says. "We may talk here."

The suite inside isn't large—a tight sitting room which looks to lead to several small bedrooms.

She waits until we are all inside, and Valtair's closed the door, before she says, "I am Lady Denya, if you do not know. Your Majesties."

I straighten, unweaving my illusion. Valtair isn't surprised, so, he did know who we were. Beside me, Caleb unweaves his, too, then reweaves his own illusion as Caleb again.

"Congratulations," Denya says, glancing at Caleb, who's still showing his pregnancy. "I did not have the chance to say."

"Thank you," Caleb says quietly. And looks to me.

And I take a breath. Because no, we don't have the time for niceties, but this does need to be delicate.

And if Valtair knew all the details, he could navigate this better than me, but he doesn't. Not yet.

I focus on Lady Denya, who's watching me steadily.

"You have a weaving on your door," I say. And I hope it won't be a relations-breaking insult.

She tilts her head back. "I do. Yes. I put it there."

"You're a weaver?" Caleb blurts.

I feel my own temper rising past my fears. "Yes, are you a weaver? Akreans are *kidnapping* weavers at the border—"

"I don't know about that," Denya says. "I know that my government sent me, along with the others, to continue our friendship with Barella."

She says friendship like Akreal hasn't been pushing Barella away for decades.

Valtair spreads his hands. "We mean no offense at all. But we have our own reports that say Akreans are not friendly to weavers. So if you are a weaver, and you're showing us you are, we want to know why."

She turns back to me, her lips thinning. "Dowager Queen Zinara Braise has set up her own court within the Akrean court, though that's not yet widely known outside it." She pauses for me to nod that yes, I've heard those rumors from my information network. And now she's confirmed them. "There are a number of those in the Akrean court, myself included, that do not like this. Or her leanings."

"You've met with my mother?" I ask.

And have to keep myself from asking if she's well.

Because I don't want to know that.

And...I do.

She's still my mother. Even if I've had to write her out of my life completely. And out of anything I'd call love.

"I have seen her sitting with the queen in the palace's more private meeting rooms," Denya says. "But I have not spoken with her. She tends to favor those who oppose my political views."

"And what are your political views?" Valtair asks. "Do you oppose weavers, too, even if you are one? Because those reports are well documented, that the Akrean queen and her court have high contempt for weavers, and elementalists, too, though I think that's to a lesser degree."

"I believe the sentiment toward elementalists will eventually reach the same contempt for weavers," she says. "And no, as you can obviously see, I don't agree with that. Superstition and suspicion of anyone who can use magic has long been a part of Akrean culture, but only lately has it risen to the point of restricting magic altogether. I was included in this delegation because even while it is known by the court that I am a weaver, I have never shown my weaving in court. I do not wear a medallion." This with a glance at Caleb's chest, where his medallion would be if he was wearing it.

"And, I have a long reputation of diplomacy," Denya goes on, as if this is a given.

But she was the one who publicly mocked Barella when

Kian's weaving got out of hand. She doesn't seem to like us. But she wanted to signal us, didn't she, by putting that weaving on her delegation's door?

"I want to know what's happening in Barella," she says, turning to me. "And I want resources to stop Zinara Braise from further steering our kingdom in a direction we don't want to go."

Ah. "You want an alliance, then?" I ask. "Not between Barella and Akreal, but myself and your political faction?"

"I thought you didn't like how Barella treats its guests," Caleb says.

I nod in agreement with that not so subtle jab.

Denya scoffs. "Your weavers were out of control."

"Because they were pushed," Caleb fires back, crossing his arms.

"What about Nikolai Metrial?" I ask, watching Denya's face for her reaction.

But Denya frowns. "I have heard of Lord Nikolai Metrial's actions, yes, and how he tried to overthrow your own court. I thought he was defeated."

"Stopped, yes," I say. "But not defeated. His family is a powerful merchant noble family. He has been threatening us throughout this Festival." And I'm still watching her when I ask, "You didn't hire the man who tried to kill my husband?"

I see Valtair shifting, annoyed that I asked that outright, but Denya's gaze on me grows appraising. Maybe appreciating that I'm not dancing around this. She seems like an overly direct person herself.

She reminds me less of my mother now, and more like Lady Sima of my own court.

"No, I have no wish to see either of you harmed. But I'm not the only member of our delegation, and I am the only member from my own political faction."

I nod.

"But you believe that attempt was tied to Nikolai Metrial?" she asks.

"Yes. And any information you have on his ties to the Akrean court, or to anyone in your delegation, would be helpful to me personally, to find my husband's attacker. We believe he is in this palace, and we must find and stop him."

Denya steps back, folding her hands together, looking troubled.

"I would tell you what I know, but I have little to tell. As I said, I have heard of him, but do not have personal ties to those who deal with him or the Metrial family, though Metrial trade caravans are well known in Akreal as reliable sources of food and goods. We can't directly oppose the Metrial family in Akreal without fear of shortages."

She hesitates, then goes on more slowly, "Some of our other main sources of food into the country, from the north, were met with blight this last year, so we have more dependence on merchants from the south than we'd like. And that is not something I should have told you. That is given as a sign of my wish for cooperation between us."

I glance at Valtair. He gives a slight nod. He'll look into that bit of information.

"And my mother?" I ask. "How far has she influenced the Akreal throne?"

I have never met the Akrean Queen Inzana. She ascended three years ago, replacing her aging father. She's old enough to be my mother but has never been much in the public eye. And she's never, as the rumors say, been in good health.

I don't know about her personality, but that's the kind of person my mother could fixate on and make her own. If Queen Inzana let her.

"We fear her influence is only growing," Denya says. "Which is why I wished to speak with you here." She pulls a small card from her pocket, with an address handwritten on the back.

"You may send to this address, and it will reach the right people. Be circumspect."

I take the card, slipping it into my own inner coat pocket.

And this—this is something.

Maybe this is the first shred of hope I've had in how to fight my mother's influence since she escaped six months ago.

And even if that's not helping fight Nikolai right now, it *is* something.

So not everyone in the Akrean Court is on my mother's side. Not everyone wants to be.

"And be warned," Denya says, "There are many in Akreal who do believe that all magic and magic users should be purged from our kingdom. That sentiment is growing, despite my faction's attempts to stop it. It's well known that Zinara Braise despises weavers, saying that weavers stole her kingdom. And are controlling her son."

She looks between Caleb and me. "She has vilified Caleb Varandre Braise in the public discourse greatly. But I don't see any evidence that her claims are true."

Her look intensifies, as if she's looking through us, and I start, even as I bristle at her—well, my mother's—accusation. My mother's accusing Caleb of *actually* controlling me, with mind control magic. Exactly what she herself was trying to do through Nikolai.

And Denya's looking right now with more than her eyes.

"You can see soul weaving?" I ask. "Mind control magic?"

"Yes. We had a problem, years ago, with a young man who tried to control his village by mentally enslaving them to work for him. We contained that incident as best we could, but the rumors of it have greatly hurt the crumbling trust in weavers. But yes, I was one of the ones who brought him down. His attempt to control me was not a pleasant experience."

"No," I agree. "If we are to confront Nikolai Metrial in the open—"

She holds up her hands. "I cannot help you in your own internal affairs."

"Even if it's to stop a threat against us?" Caleb pushes. "And you're asking for our help with your kingdom, too?"

Denya shakes her head. "I can lend no public aid. Privately, through information, I will do what I can."

I share a look with Caleb. And I still don't entirely know what to make of this. Denya seems sincere. But I've trusted sincerity before.

I turn back to Denya. "Is there anything you can tell me that will give leverage over my mother's supporters here?"

Because though some of them fled with her, I don't think they all did. That's been a growing worry, too.

"She came with some of her own retinue," Denya says. "They are popular in the court. Beyond that..." She spreads her hands. Though she doesn't exactly look regretful that she doesn't know more. "Beyond that, I could not say."

I want to ask more, but I've been in enough Council sessions by now to know when someone is done talking.

So I nod. "Thank you, Lady Denya. I appreciate—and Barella appreciates—your help in keeping our kingdom safe."

It's an official sounding line, I know it as I say it, and her mouth tightens ironically.

But, she nods. Because keeping Barella safe from my mother is also a priority, even if not my highest at this moment.

And time is still running out. We don't know when Nikolai will escalate—he's already escalated his threats.

I start for the door, but see Caleb reweaving his illusion around himself, and I have to stop to reweave mine.

Which is more than nerve-wracking, with Denya, a foreign weaver, watching.

But when I meet her eyes, she nods again. As if we are still all just doing business.

"Thank you for your time," Valtair says, before opening the door.

We're silent on the way back to his office, and I know that's where we're going. Because he has questions.

And he deserves the answers, he does. But they will have to be quick.

We're not two steps inside Valtair's office, Caleb closing the door behind him, before I hold up a hand.

And as quickly as I can, tell him what we know.

Valtair's face grows grimmer and grimmer. His hand starts tapping at his side, his own impatience with the situation, with the time it's taking to explain.

"So now we need to find the apprentices," he says. "Gods, Caleb, I wish you'd told me—Tor, I wish *you'd* told me."

But he sighs. "All right. I know I can't parade around the palace with you and not draw attention, and I can't weave myself into someone else. So, let me know as soon as you know more. All right? Please?"

Caleb, looking a little chagrined, nods.

"We will," I say.

Then Caleb and I are out and headed back toward the mages' quarters.

We pass a young man hurrying down the corridor as we walk out, looking distressed.

I frown, then stop as he knocks on Valtair's office door and pushes inside.

Caleb looks to me, and I back to him.

"Kian," he says. Then hurries back toward Valtair's office.

And it is Kian inside when we come back in. He's unwoven the illusion he was just wearing.

He whirls, and I just barely sense the magic he's already preparing to release on us. Whatever that might be.

"Kian!" Caleb says, and drops his illusion again.

The young man freezes.

"Caleb. Caleb! I couldn't find you, so I thought I'd come here, if Lord Valtair knew where you were—it's Aria. Sabella and I have been looking for the last hours, and all during the ball, but we didn't see her this morning, and we haven't all day, then we started to get scared—"

Aria. The apprentice who lost control of her magic in the Great Hall just before the Festival started.

Like how Nikolai couldn't control his magic?

Kian's still talking, but Caleb's looking over at me.

"If she's missing, it's not because she wants to be," Caleb says in a low voice. "It's because he has her. Or coerced her."

I meet his eyes.

"I trust my apprentices." Caleb's watching me intently, and I know he's willing me to trust them, too. Wanting me to.

"Trust *me*," he says. "Trust my judgment. Trust me for *once*, Torovan."

And that stings. I do trust him. But I haven't been, lately. I haven't been able to.

Or is that only what I've been telling myself?

"All right," I say. "We'll search for her. For any signs of her."

CHAPTER 34

THE SEARCH

TOROVAN

First, because Caleb says it might get better answers, we pull our illusions back around ourselves. I'm not willing to let Caleb out of my sight, and he doesn't seem willing to let me out of his, either, so we go together, while Kian goes off again to search on his own. We ask the staff if they've seen Aria. We ask any guests we see, though most, at this hour, are either drunk or besotted.

We get the master key set from my guards and unlock every closet and locked room we can access, though we can't go into people's private quarters without a reason.

I think about disturbing Aldric, too, but in the end, let him sleep. He can barely hold his illusions anyway.

After the first hour, we meet back in the mages' common room.

Sabella joins us.

And we find in short order that none of us have found anything.

So we set out again.

And come back after the second hour.

And then, Caleb and I go back out as ourselves, with our guards this time.

I don't want people to assume that there's trouble, but there is.

And I'm watching Caleb growing more and more agitated.

It's the dead of night before we stop searching.

And we're back in the mage's common room again.

Caleb's pacing, restless, his hair a mess from running his hands through it. Spectacles slightly askew.

He sees me watching, stops, and stretches.

And I sigh. I'm exhausted. I know he's exhausted. And I'm trying to gauge the urgency. And I'm trying to weigh the politics.

"I'll order a full search of the palace in the morning," I say.

"And what if that's too late?" Caleb asks. "Tor, something happened to her. I know something happened to her."

"Something might have happened to her the night before, if you haven't seen her since then."

Kian, restless on a chair near the hearth, says, "I'm going to keep searching."

"Yes, do that." Caleb looks to Sabella, who's hunched across from Kian, her face in her hands.

"I'm not sure that I can stay awake," she says. "I will try."

Caleb rubs his hands together. The night air in the palace has grown chill. "Gods, no, go sleep. We all should sleep. And maybe this is what Nikolai wants, too—wants us all exhausted. Oh gods, we should all sleep."

"I'm not sleeping," Kian still insists. "I'm fine. Just, I need to sit for a little more."

"Fine, keep searching when you can," Caleb says. "Tomorrow, you'll rest during the day." He braces his hands on his back, and I know it's hurting. I feel a twinge in my own back, and I ache to be able to ease his pain.

"Be careful, Kian," Caleb says.

"I know." And despite Kian saying he needs to sit, he pushes up again and reweaves his illusion on the way to the door.

He is loyal. He is unfailingly loyal to his friends. And I know he's hardly ready to be the palace mage that Caleb just made him, but...maybe he's readier than I'd thought.

I move behind Caleb, kneading at his shoulders, resting my cheek against his hair. "We can't do more tonight without causing chaos."

Caleb leans back against me.

"Nikolai is toying with us. Again. But he's playing with her life. Gods, Tor." He turns against me, leaning into me. Bracing himself.

He's at the end of his ability to deal with this.

As am I.

Gods, as am I.

Caleb told me to trust him, but it's been in the back of my mind these last hours of searching that he told his apprentices how to get past the palace guards.

And that Aria is gone, the day Nikolai's letters have become a threat found in our nursery.

Unless that threat was there all along? We haven't been in the nursery since the Festival started. We've both been too busy.

How are we going to care for the child, when it comes, if we're always so busy? How did my parents—

I swallow.

And I'm swaying on my feet, and Caleb is, too, both of us holding on to each other. Keeping each other upright.

I slide my hand down his shoulder.

"Bed," I say. And he's probably not wrong that Nikolai wants us to be without sleep. Wants us distracted and unfocused.

Caleb pulls back to look at me, his mouth pinched tight with worry. But he nods.

Slips his hand into mine. And lets me guide him toward our tense guards by the door.

We're quiet on the way back to our apartment.

Quiet as the guards move in ahead of us to clear the rooms, though Caleb's hand tightens in mine.

"Clear," Kas says, coming back into my study. "Sire, I'm stationing two men on the other side of your study door leading into your father's apartment."

I nod. We will be as fortified as we can be tonight.

And though I'm still bone weary, I don't know how I'll sleep.

And tomorrow?

Tonight, the court found a reason to celebrate again. To celebrate the coming of an heir.

The Harvest Feast is about renewal and abundance for the year to come. What better abundance than a child on the way?

What better omen of the year to come?

How can I break that renewed hope by ordering a palace wide search for an apprentice weaver? To remind them that there are still enemies among us.

And I'm afraid, I'm very much afraid that they won't look to Nikolai as the threat, but Aria. To all of the apprentices.

But we've all spoken to enough of the staff tonight that I know the rumors are rampant already.

I sigh, deeply, too exhausted for a moment to move.

The guards leave, taking up their places for the night.

Then we're alone.

Caleb doesn't move toward the bedroom yet.

"Tor. If he has Aria—"

"I know."

He turns to me, letting go. "No, you don't. I'm afraid for her, yes. I'm so afraid for her. But if he turns her against us, if he can control her—Torovan she's so strong—"

"Caleb, I know."

And that's been churning in the back of my mind, too, a quiet and rising panic.

I can't tell Caleb that I'm still afraid that Aria might be a traitor.

I can't do that to him.

But if Aria left on her own will or was taken by Nikolai or our other enemies, does that make much of a difference if we have to face both Nikolai and her in a fight? If he ends up controlling her?

Is she strong enough to withstand that attempt at control?

I wasn't. Not on my own.

Caleb drops his illusion, but his body language doesn't change. I know when he's Caleb, and when he's not.

And I now understand the drain wearing an illusion can be.

"I told Morgan I'll train him to be a weaver," he says, and finally heads toward the bedroom.

"Morgan." I blink. "My guard? Is now the time, Caleb? You should wait until—"

Until after the child. Until life is less complicated, less dangerous.

But it won't be less. It just won't be.

"Now is the time," he says firmly. "We need more weavers, Torovan." He pushes into the bedroom.

One of the guards left a lamp on a table beside the bed. And I can see the strain in Caleb's neck, the pinch between his brows.

His hand on the back of his neck, he turns to me. Just… looking. Like he's lost. Like he doesn't know what to do next, even just here, even now.

I pull him close, and he wraps his arms around me.

I haven't let go of my vigilance with my weaver's senses, and I know he hasn't, either.

I know we're both thinking about the unreality weaving in the nursery.

Nikolai could have been in our bedroom, too.

"Is there anything here?" I ask quietly. I can't feel anything, but his senses are so much more honed than mine.

"No," he whispers. Then, "But everyone knows now."

About his pregnancy.

"Torovan. We're losing in every direction."

"It was good to tell them," I say. "I'm glad we told them."

"I didn't mean to. Not yet."

"I know."

And we're quiet a moment, holding each other in the mostly dark, mostly cold. The small hearth in the bedroom dimmed, too.

"Barella will have its heir," I say, "and the people are glad of it. And glad for you. And glad for us. That's good, Caleb. I know that's good."

But I'm trying to brighten a dark room.

"The mage trial is supposed to be tomorrow," he says. "Should I still compete in it?"

I don't know. I don't know what will happen tomorrow.

But I have little hope that Aria will show up on her own.

And I have a growing sick feeling about what will happen because of it.

We might not have need of a mage's trial.

We might have a trial of our very own.

"We'll see," I say.

CHAPTER 35

FIRE

CALEB

I sleep restlessly, and both Torovan and I wake early. We're quietly getting dressed when there's a knock on the bedroom door.

"It's Morgan," I hear through the door. "Kian is here to see Your Majesties."

I move to open the door. We're dressed enough. And I want to know what Kian has to say, either way.

"Not in the bedroom," Torovan growls, pushing out past me, tucking in his undershirt. "Morgan, bring him to my study."

"Yes, Sire."

I'm pulling on my coat when Kian comes into the study, looking haggard, his eyes dull.

"You found nothing," I say.

He shakes his head. "No. I'm sorry, Caleb. I looked all night—"

"No, gods, Kian. You did well."

He straightens a little. "What should we do today, will you call in the guards?"

I look at Torovan. And, though sleep is still fogging my mind, it's still clearer than the night before.

I know ordering an all-out search will send the palace into a panic.

I know that.

But still I'm going to ask.

I open my mouth.

"Oh," Kian says, and reaches into his coat. Which is rumpled now, still what he was wearing from the night before. "Someone asked me to give you this on my way up here, Caleb."

He pulls a folded sheet of paper from his coat pocket.

Sealed with black wax.

I start, and Torovan lunges to snatch it from Kian's hand.

"What—" Kian stumbles back a step.

But then Torovan shouts and trips backward, too, shaking the letter in his hand.

It flutters down, while a weaving surges out of it and writhes up Torovan's arm.

Kas bangs back in from the corridor door, with Morgan and Reveyan on his heels.

But there's nothing they can do.

I throw my senses wide and grab the weaving halfway up Torovan's arm. It's like the trap on the letter from yesterday, normal threads mixing with sinewy soul threads. Except this one is starting to catch fire while it winds up his arm.

Shit.

Torovan's scrabbling to grab hold of it, I can almost feel his effort, but he's panicked.

I wrestle the weaving away from him, out into the air in front of him, and carefully and viciously begin to unravel it.

"Who," Torovan gasps, "who gave it to you?"

"I—" Kian stammers. "What was—"

He doesn't know about the letters. About Nikolai's threats.

We hadn't told him or Sabella.

We'd been fully focused on Aria, and...well, it had seemed too private, too raw. Too close, after finding that letter in the nursery.

Something not to trust anyone with but Valtair.

"It's from Nikolai," I say, still focused on unweaving the interwoven threads of the trap. "Quiet."

And they all stay quiet, though the guards move to help Torovan. And I can't spare a look for the damage on his arm. I can't think about it.

Then the last of the threads comes loose, the normal threads of reality snapping back into the whole of reality around us. The soul threads shuddering before they start to fade.

I crouch with one hand on the floor to brace myself, panting.

And finally look up to see scorch marks all up Torovan's sleeve.

Morgan is trying to roll up his sleeve, and Torovan's fighting him.

"You're not fine," I say, launching up.

He glares back at me. "What does the letter say?"

I look down at the floor between us. And the letter, the seal partially broken, is still lying on the floor. Singed on one corner.

That hadn't burned.

Last night, Torovan handled the other letters he had just fine, and they'd only attacked when I'd touched them, or tried to weave them.

This time, though—I think this letter was meant for me, with the trap tuned to him. This was meant to make me watch while Torovan suffered.

My hands curl into fists.

Then uncurl again as I stoop to pick up the letter.

"Caleb—"

"The traps are gone," I say. I straighten slowly as I unfold the paper.

I have what you want. Come alone, or your weaver feels my wrath.

I look up at Torovan.

He stares back at me.

"Well?" he asks.

I read the letter out loud, and he swears. Then hisses as Morgan dabs at one of the rapidly blistering burns.

"Valtair should look," I say, seeing the burns, and then quickly add, "He needs to know about this."

Which is also true.

But I don't want to bring one of the palace elemental healers into this, not and have more rumors of misfortune during the Festival. And not without knowing who to trust.

But Morgan's head snaps up. "I—I can—I'm trained to help with wounds and burns." He turns to the other guards. "Can you get a basin and water, and bandages?"

Kas looks to Torovan, who bites out, "Go."

Kas and Reveyan retreat, and Morgan looks to me, looks to Torovan, looks to Kian.

Swallows.

"I—I have elemental healing," he says. "Let me lessen the wounds, and I can heal them completely when they're wrapped."

Is Morgan from a noble family? That he feels he has to hide this? I don't know his background.

But he knows Valtair is also an elementalist. I saw him move to quickly cover for my slip in asking for Valtair.

How does Morgan know about Valtair?

And if Morgan knows, does Nikolai know?

What else could Nikolai use against us?

I raise the letter again, trying to read it through the haze of my pounding heart.

This letter was meant for me. Nikolai wants me to come. He has what I want.

Aria.

And he'll hurt her if I don't come alone.

Or does he mean he'll hurt Torovan? Is Torovan "your weaver" to Nikolai?

"Yes, do it," Torovan says to Morgan, who moves to grip his arm. Torovan hisses but then lets out a breath—Morgan must be doing something to calm the pain.

Torovan stabs a glare at me. "You can't go to Nikolai. You can't even think on it."

"He has Aria," I say.

"You don't even know that, this could be another mind game—"

"Of course it's a mind game!" I shake the letter, flapping it in the air. "It's all mind games. *All* of this is mind games, that's his battlefield, Tor, it always has been! And your mother's!"

He grunts as Morgan shifts his grip on Torovan's arm.

Then, Morgan lets go. "Does it feel better?"

Torovan clenches his hand as he looks down, releases it again. There are still red marks on his arm, but they're not as angry as they were.

"Good enough," Torovan says, and rolls down his scorched sleeve.

He'll need another shirt.

"I have to go," I say.

"He didn't even say where, Caleb."

Torovan starts toward the bedroom, and I follow. We all do.

"I'll go with you," Kian says.

"No. Neither of you are going."

"Then you're just going to let him have Aria?" Kian asks, his voice cracking.

And I see the tightening set to Torovan's shoulders.

I grip his arm before he turns into the bedroom doorway.

I know what he's thinking.

And *no*. No, I will not let him do what he's thinking.

"No, Torovan. Gods. You can't go! If you're even thinking that—"

"Caleb, if you leave, this palace is defenseless. Nikolai will take it. Can you tell me I'm wrong?"

I stare at him.

Because no, I can't. I told my mother as much.

I know it's true in my bones.

Either Nikolai, or the Dowager's people. The Akreans have a weaver in Lady Denya, if she wishes to act. She's more an enemy under the truce of a mutual cause than an actual ally. Or maybe the Dowager Zinara has other weavers here, set to attack and overwhelm the palace if I'm not here.

Or, they don't even have to be weavers.

Elementalists. Or people with knives.

Or Nikolai could still be here himself. *With* a controlled Aria.

He's not wrong. I can't leave.

I meet Torovan's eyes. "But you can't go."

He heads into the bedroom, yanking open his wardrobe doors.

"I'll take Kian." He glances to Kian, and Kian nods quickly. "I'll take Aldric, and some of the elementalists. I'll take a troop with me. Two."

He looks up, and I see something more in his eyes now. A need to fight back, to have a direction, to prove himself.

He needs this, as much as I need to find Aria, too.

But is he strong enough to face Nikolai, even with all of that?

It's a trap. Of course it's a trap. It's a trap if I go, it's a trap if I stay. It's a trap if he goes or if he stays.

And I need to get Aria back. She can't be controlled by Nikolai. And she's my apprentice. Gods. My responsibility. If anything happens to her, if anything *more* happens to her—

Nikolai must be stopped.

We have to find where he is.

We have to know, either way. We have to go to him, or draw him out.

We have to fight him.

And now do I have to choose between my apprentice and my husband? Another impossible choice.

But we *have* to confront Nikolai. This just can't go on.

Torovan knows that, too.

His gaze on me is steady.

Whatever Nikolai planned, there's a chance the trap will be sprung outside the palace, and there's a chance it will be sprung within.

That Torovan might be attacked if he goes, or I'll be attacked if I stay.

But if we do nothing, then the threats continue. And Nikolai chips away at us, piece by piece by piece.

While we slowly lose our willpower to our fears.

And no, this is not a good plan right now.

I wet my lips.

But Nikolai was here, in our apartment. That unreality weaving was in our *nursery*.

That letter was in our child's crib.

This can't continue. It *can't*.

Torovan's not the man he was six months ago. He's stronger than that. Even if he's had his moments of faltering, he's *strong*. I know he is.

I know him. And I love him.

And this is about more than Aria just now, too, it's about making a show to our people, to our enemies, that we're fighting back.

The court united again with us over my pregnancy. Over a future heir. And maybe they shifted to celebration again, but the threat of an enemy in our court didn't just go away.

And the people have been slowly giving in to Nikolai's influence.

That is the threat they don't know. And don't yet understand.

That is the threat we have to stop, too, before it swallows our kingdom whole.

But that can end today, too.

I brush past Torovan into the bedroom and grab my master weaver's medallion where I left it beside the bed.

I loop it over my head, and it settles over my heart.

"Okay," I say. "I'll have Sabella here with me."

She isn't strong, but she is steady.

"I'll leave as many of my guards as I can," he says. "And your guards stay with you."

I nod. "And leave me the master elementalists."

There are three left in the palace.

And the palace has its own garrison of soldiers.

And it has me.

And though fear gnaws at me, though fear is threatening to close up my throat, I know we must do this.

I know we can.

Torovan nods, and I move to help him pull on his coat over his still injured arm.

"Sire!" I hear Kas call from out in the hall. "We have the basin. Morgan—"

Morgan, who's listened to all of this with a grim set to his face, steps back into the hall. "It wasn't as bad as I thought. We don't need to clean the burns, they faded rapidly. It was more of an illusion of danger."

Kas looks at us, his jaw jutted to one side.

"Huh. Okay. Sire—you don't need the water?"

"No, Kas. Get Valtair. He should be here—then we must talk. Quickly, now!"

Kas salutes and hurries out again.

CHAPTER 36

REASONS NOT TO DO THIS

TOROVAN

"Have you found her?" Valtair asks as soon as he enters my study.

Caleb is Irava now, and she's restlessly moving around the room, not quite pacing. Kian fidgets in place near the hearth. He still hasn't slept, and he won't get sleep anytime soon. And Morgan—I asked Morgan to stay.

He did ease the pain in my arm, though the burns are still throbbing, a dull ache.

A reminder that my enemy won't stop until I defeat him.

I didn't know Morgan was an elementalist, though I understand why he hid it. His family is high nobility, and even though few people in the palace know his heritage, it's still frowned upon for a guard to be an elementalist.

Magic is seen as volatile; guards are supposed to be steady.

And so are kings.

"No, we haven't found Aria yet." I move around my desk and hand Valtair the last letter.

He takes it, eyeing the singed corner warily. "What's this?"

"Just read it."

And I'm glad I changed my shirt, because I know he'd be alarmed at the scorched sleeve.

Valtair reads the letter, then looks up at me, then at Irava.

He folds the letter carefully.

And I know he knows one of us is going to ride out to face Nikolai.

And he also knows it can't be Irava. And not just because she's carrying the heir, but because she's carrying the safety of the kingdom.

Right now, Barella can afford to lose me more than it can afford to lose her.

"What can I say to talk you out of this?" Valtair asks.

"Should you talk me out of it?"

He pinches his lips tightly.

He once told me my kingdom needs a king that actually rules.

And I have been ruling. I have been doing all I can, I have been giving my kingdom all I have.

Maybe too much.

So much that I haven't been giving my wife all she needs, too. Haven't been giving her enough of my time.

But now, I have to give more of myself to both my kingdom and my family.

I will not let the man who killed my father keep threatening everything I love.

Visions of cutting Nikolai down with a sword, with a dagger, with my willpower—any way I can—fill my mind.

And I keep them there, letting them harden my resolve.

"This is what Nikolai wants," Valtair says. "It's obviously what he wants."

I glare him down. "And I want him stopped."

But Valtair is immune to my anger and glares right back. "And if he tries to control you again? He will."

"I'm taking Kian," I say, nodding to where Kian is sitting rigidly by the hearth. Not quite trying to be invisible but not daring to interrupt us now. "And Aldric, and most of the rest of the court mages. I'll leave the other master mages here with you and Caleb. I'll take two troops—"

"And if he controls them, too?" Valtair asks, and I see his own panic rising.

He was there when we faced Nikolai before. He was there when Irava and I wove a storm.

He knows what I'm facing, what we're all facing, and Nikolai hasn't been here visibly, no. But his presence has been *everywhere* this last week.

In the attempt on Irava's life. In the letters he sent to me. In the letter in our child's crib, and the letter that just tried to, what, kill me?

In the soul weaving Irava found in her apprentice's mind.

And now, he's kidnapped a member of my court, a powerful weaver, now a court mage. And someone Irava cares about deeply.

He's poisoning the hearts and minds of my people, slowly but surely.

"This won't stop," I say, "until I stop it."

Valtair glares at me a moment more, then sighs.

"Okay. Where are you supposed to meet him? Is he going to send further instructions?"

"I assume he'll expect us to head to his family's estates."

"He expects *one* of you. It says to come alone." Valtair rubs at his eyes. "And, assuming *that's* not the trap, and he wants to get you away from the palace? What if he attacks here at the palace instead? With Aria already under his control? Which— which is why Irava needs to be here."

I nod tightly. Not looking at Irava. Not paying any attention at all to the clenching of my heart.

Because she hadn't seen the dagger that was thrown at her. And I was the one who caught it.

But I'm leaving now, and if another dagger is thrown, I won't be here.

"You'll have the master elementalists," I say, "you'll have Morgan and the rest of my guards, except Kas and Drein, who will stay with me. You'll have the soldiers in the palace garrison. And Sabella, Irava's other apprentice, too."

Valtair straightens. "So he wants us split up. That's obvious. His plan is probably changeable, depending on what we do."

"Then we hold strength in two forces," I say, pressing down on my desk. Trying to anchor myself. Trying to steady my resolve.

I need action. I need to get into motion, or I will talk myself out of going.

And this will be a battle of wills more than anything.

My will to protect my family and my kingdom must be stronger than anything.

"And the Harvest Festival?" Valtair asks. "I'm sorry, Torovan, but we still have to consider that if you leave now, that's not going to look good in the eyes of the people. Especially to go after a weaver, who they already fear—"

"So then we make it look good," I growl. "They know someone tried to take Irava's life. We say I'm riding out to defeat the assassin, that assassin being Nikolai."

"And when they use that as an excuse to fear weavers even more—"

"Valtair!"

Irava, finally, moves. She stands beside me, holding steady. "We can find a thousand reasons not to do this. But those reasons won't stop Nikolai from tearing us apart. Or killing us anyway. Valtair, he was *in these rooms*."

"Shit," Valtair says, pinching between his eyes.

He shudders in a breath and looks between us again, looks like he wants to say more, but then shakes his head, until it turns into a nod.

"All right. Fine. Yes. You'll have to address the court before you go, at breakfast, they'll already be in the Great Hall—no. Do that in the courtyard, in your armor. Make an absolute Festival show of it, Torovan. The people will be moved by that, especially after your announcement last night. Both of you. Yes, *yes*, make this about protecting your future child. Your wife. Or husband, if you're Caleb at the time." He nods to Irava. "Okay, we can leverage this."

"Yes," I say. "You control the narrative. Control it while I'm gone. While Irava holds the palace as queen in my absence—support her."

"Of course."

"And manage the delegates." I pause. "And quietly gather a sense of the guests who might be willing to fight if it comes to it, too. If that's where the real trap is. If Nikolai's planning to take the palace."

"I assume the mage trials will be off for today," he says. "If you'll be taking most of the palace mages with you."

Irava blows out her breath. "Yes. Gods. But maybe

watching their king ride out in force to take down his enemies will be spectacle and gossip fuel enough."

She shoots a sideways look at Valtair. "And we have to make sure the people know there's a difference between Nikolai's weaving and ours. I thought they did know, but those lines are blurring in the people's opinions lately. According to my apprentices, who've been gathering information on it." She nods at Kian. And he straightens, nods back.

Valtair sighs.

"Right. Okay. I'll call off the mage trials *after* you start making a visible show of pulling your forces together, Tor. And I'll see what I can do to start seeding opinions in the other direction. More than what I already have been doing."

I nod in agreement to all of that.

And I know this is what I want to do. And yes, I'll have to gather my forces, the troops I'll take with me, the elementalists. I'll have to talk to Aldric, because he won't be happy about this, either.

I have to address my people.

I have to do all the things expected of me and do them well, but—

For a moment, my mind blanks.

This is what I'm pushing for. This is what needs to be done.

It doesn't mean I'm not still terrified.

I feel the burns on my arm throbbing with a low but persistent pain.

"You have the will," Irava says.

I start, meeting her eyes beside me. And take a breath.

I nod. I know I have the willpower.

I *know* I do.

Because not having the willpower to defeat Nikolai is not an option.

I glance at my arm, tugging my sleeve to relieve some of the pressure on my skin.

"Valtair, please start preparations. Alert the town's garrison that we'll be taking two troops." And that left only the palace garrison to defend the palace, after I already sent two troops to the border to Akreal. And I'm beginning to understand the trouble at the border now, too. They want us divided. And Nikolai and my mother must still be working together.

But there's no helping any of that now.

"Tor, what happened to your arm? You're favoring it."

Valtair steps closer. But he doesn't quite reach out.

"I can heal the rest now," Morgan says. Pointedly.

Valtair shoots a startled glance his way. "You healed him? What happened?"

Morgan's eyes flash, his hands flexing at his sides.

And I haven't missed that Morgan looks a little different now, and I know Valtair hasn't, either. Either Caleb already taught him some weaving, enough to weave an illusion around himself, or Caleb wove an illusion or reality around Morgan, too.

I watch Valtair's eyes narrowing, an anger of familiarity. I've seen signs of tension in their interactions before but usually ignore it. Whatever is between Valtair and my guard is not my business.

Unless it hinders what I need to do.

I hold up my arm. "Morgan?"

Valtair turns his narrowed look to me. "What happened, Tor?"

He nods at the letter, which he set back on the desk. "I noticed it was scorched."

Morgan carefully rolls up my sleeve and lets out a small sound. I look down to see the burns much angrier than they'd been before.

Valtair hesitates, glancing briefly over his shoulder at Kian.

"Kian," I say, "will you go tell the guards to alert the town's garrison that we'll need two troops? Then come back."

Kian shoots up off his chair, his nervous energy finally finding an outlet.

"Yes!"

He runs out before I can say more.

Valtair huffs a not-quite-laugh, glares at Morgan, then turns back to my arm.

"I can fix it," Morgan says through a tight jaw.

Valtair regards him for too long a moment, then steps back.

And I'm growing impatient with this, I need to get on the road. To get into motion.

Morgan leans over my outstretched arm, gently holding it steady, and I feel my arm warming, the pain easing. I watch as the red patches blister, then peel, then new skin grows in, tender but not burned.

Valtair watches, too, and I almost hear his silent critique of whatever is going on.

But I just need my arm uninjured. I don't have time for whatever other feud they've got going on.

Morgan inspects my arm, the heat cooling now, and pronounces it healed as Kian bursts back in.

"The guards are alerting the garrison in town," he says.

I tug down my sleeve.

"Kian," I say. "In the top right drawer of my desk are court mage medallions. For weavers. Grab one, please."

Kian nearly runs for the desk, until a look from Irava slows him. And despite everything just now, I hide a smile. Meet Irava's eyes, and her troubled gaze softens.

Kian has been wanting this medallion since the moment he started his training.

He pulls one out and skips back around to me, holding it up. "This one?"

They're all identical.

"Yes."

I don't have to ask him to put it on, he loops it over his head, lets it settle over his heart. Looks up to Irava's medallion, then back to his.

I give him the oath of a court mage, and he repeats it and beams, then turns to show Irava.

Valtair, his arms folded now, has resumed glaring at me.

But Morgan has finished, and it's past time we all get moving.

"Morgan, if there's trouble at the palace, and you can help—"

He knows in which way I mean. With his elemental healing.

"Of course, Your Majesty."

I glance at Valtair, but he doesn't, at least, protest that.

Irava steps in front of me. Looking into my eyes.

Then reweaves her illusion into Caleb.

His brow furrowed, his lips parted.

And it's that look again. Studying me, like it might be the last time.

I tuck his hair back, trace his jaw, trace his lips. He reaches up to run his thumb across the stubble on my cheek. The friction sending a jolt straight down to my stomach.

I kiss him. Fiercely.

He is who I'm fighting for. He and the life he holds within him.

This is why I must go.

And this is why he must stay.

Then I pull back, and he does, too.

His expression closing.

As I know mine is.

I turn. "Morgan, tell Kas—I want my armor brought to the battle room, and have my horse and the mounts we'll need prepared." I glance at Caleb. "We'll get Aldric and the mages. Valtair, have everything ready—provisions for ten days on the road."

"Yes, Sire." Morgan hurries out.

But Valtair lingers. And Kian, too, rubbing his fingers over his mage's medallion.

Valtair moves closer to me, too. And I could almost bear that look from Caleb, I've seen it before, I was braced for it. But I don't know that I can take it from him.

Kian, seeing us all draw in, huddles closer, too.

I don't have my father anymore.

And I don't have my mother—not that I ever really had my mother.

My sister, I will do my best to keep my sister safe with everyone else in this palace. I'm riding out for her safety, too.

But Valtair is also my family.

Even Kian—I know he is a part of Caleb's family, the family he's carved out here. And Sabella, too, who is likely waking up now, if she's not already.

And Aria.

And I understand that. I understand needing to protect family.

"I'll bring her back," I tell Caleb.

And he gives the smallest nod. His eyes hardening.

"You have the will, Tor," he says.

I nod. "So do you. Stay safe."

One more kiss on his lips, but not passionate now. Not lingering. A kiss goodbye.

Then we're all moving for the door.

CHAPTER 37

THE SPEECH

CALEB

The preparations have been made.

The palace is stirring with the rumors of what's happening, and now people have gathered in the courtyard outside the palace.

I still get smiles and congratulations just by walking with my pregnancy showing. But now, the mood has shifted to a different kind of anticipation.

Morgan and Reveyan stay close by my side as I follow Torovan out to the palace courtyard. The mid-morning sun catches on his plate armor, on the intricate etched and enameled patterns. Torovan's armor is absolutely the armor of a king.

And that king is about to go to war.

I'm wearing my crown, too. And one of my best coats.

This morning must be about ceremony as much as it's about urgency.

"Caleb!" I turn, seeing my mother approaching, and

though I'm tempted not to let her close, I nod to Morgan not to stop her.

She's wearing her crown, too.

"Caleb, what is going on?"

But she'll have heard the palace rumors, too, that the king is riding out to take down the enemy who tried to kill his husband and his unborn child.

I touch my stomach. And a wave of heat goes through me, a queasy disconnect between what's happening now, and the world I grew up in. I feel conspicuous with my pregnancy showing. More vulnerable than I should be.

I throw my senses wide, looking around—is this feeling because I'm sensing mind control weaving?

But I don't feel anything. Just the cool autumn breeze whipping my hair in the too bright sunlight.

"Are we in danger?" my mother asks. A little too loudly.

I turn back. "No. Not right now."

I don't know that.

Because yes, we are. Every moment, we are. I am.

I lean toward her. "He's going to rescue one of my apprentices. Who was taken by Nikolai."

She gives me an incredulous look. But at least she lowers her voice to ask, "Who, by your own admission, you barely won against before? *You*, Caleb, not Torovan?"

I stare back at her. I know people are watching us now, I've stopped while Torovan's gone on with his guards toward his waiting stallion.

And no, I'm not wearing the heavy ceremonial crown just now, I did draw the line at that, but the lighter daily crown.

I almost never wear a crown at all if I don't have to.

And the court knows that.

My mother looks around her.

And she gathers herself and steps back.

She doesn't have to agree with what we're doing here. But she doesn't know everything going on.

And I'm not about to tell her about the letters. I'm not.

I spot Valtair coming out from a palace side door, and he sets himself on a path to meet me. We're both heading again for Torovan.

He's just mounted up, and his huge war stallion, nervous from the rustling energy of the crowd of courtiers and Festival guests, dances back a few steps before he regains control.

He looks down at me, his face stern. His helmet is secured behind him, not yet on, and he's pulled his dark hair back into a tidy battle braid.

His court mage's medallion is shining over his plate armor, higher toward his neck than his heart with the bulk of the armor pulling it upward. But the effect is the same.

This king is a weaver king.

He's a battle mage.

And he's going to war.

"The rest of the provisions are being loaded," Valtair calls up to him. "We'll have everything ready within the hour. The mages are being fitted into their armor now."

I have armor, too. Every court mage does, in case those mages are needed to defend the palace.

Not that that happens often.

And right now, I'm not wearing mine.

Because that was another hasty discussion between Torovan, Valtair, and me on the way down to get Master Aldric.

I need to show the palace that all is well here. That I am holding the authority I have with ease.

Torovan needs to show them that he'll fight for it to remain that way.

If Nikolai is playing on the level of people's perceptions, we must play that game, too.

Torovan nods to Valtair. His horse dances backward again, and I step back a few hasty steps so he can turn his restless stallion in a circle. Around us, his two guards are mounting their own horses, and Kian bounds onto his own. As an apprentice, he doesn't yet have palace-commissioned armor, but as the son of a general, he has his own.

Torovan rests one hand on the pommel of his sword.

And maybe Barellan kings aren't encouraged to carry swords in their palace, but that doesn't mean they don't know how to wield them.

"People of Barella!" Torovan shouts. And I hear the small catch in his voice, the nerves. I pray to all the gods that he'll make this speech what it needs to be.

"Our enemy has invaded our palace and our hearts. He has sought to turn us against each other. He has tried to kill my husband, and my child." He looks to me, and his look is scorching and raw. He's wrestling with his horse again in his own tension.

"He has tried to kill *me*. Nikolai Metrial has sent threats, and he's set dark weaving traps. He is our enemy! He is not a weaver at all, he's not fit for the name. He is a soul mage, and that's all he will ever be. So we ride now to rescue a court mage he has kidnapped, and to end this tyranny for good!"

He's straining for words, I know him, I know he thinks he's faltering, but he's doing so well.

He surveys the crowds, which are mostly silent.

Looks back to me. "I will return with Nikolai Metrial," he says. Like a solemn promise. "That will be my gift to our child. Our child's safety."

I swallow hard.

I didn't know he would say that.

There's a beat of shocked silence.

Because despite everything, the Metrial family still holds high sway in this kingdom, it's why they've been untouchable.

But then there's a rumble among the courtiers gathered, and then a roar.

I catch my mother's eye again, and she jerks her head toward Torovan, then looks pointedly back to me.

I suck in a breath. Then do my best to pitch my voice to carry. "And I'll keep the kingdom safe until you return. Safe for our people, and safe for our child."

I press my hand over my master weaver's medallion and bow the slightest bow to my husband.

He presses a gauntleted hand over his medallion and bows back to me.

And the crowd *roars*, stomping, the flagstones trembling beneath my feet.

Valtair steadies me.

"We still have an hour yet," he says into my ear, with some dismay. "The supplies aren't ready."

But Torovan dances his stallion around again, then, with his guards and Kian kicking into a gallop behind him, thunders out the palace gates.

I hope he's going to the garrison in town, to wait until the mages and the rest of their supplies catch up. I know he won't ride out ahead of his small army. But.

Gods, but that was the right exit.

It was.

I spot someone hurrying toward me, let through by the guards.

Elsira. Coming not from the palace, but the town. She's dressed in trousers and leather hunting gear.

She was out on a *hunt?*

"What's happening?" she gasps. "Torovan—gods of winter, Caleb. He's in armor. Is it our mother? Is it—"

I grip her arm, surveying the roar around us. They're still cheering after Torovan, but some are focusing back on me.

I let go of Elsira and step forward, raising my hands. "Our best defense is our festivities!" I shout. "We won't be holding the mage's trials today, as many of our mages are riding out, but I welcome you all to the Great Hall for ongoing celebrations!"

Of which no doubt palace staff will scramble to provide.

I turn to Valtair and mouth, "Rain provisions."

And he nods. There are alternate plans for bad weather, that will be enough for today.

And I'll have to be on and visible all day. Have to be.

In the absence of Torovan, I am the king in Barella.

My hands are still up, and I shout, "Let's show our enemy what we think about threats in Barella! We still carry on!"

That gets another roar. And people turn to go back into the palace, now that the show of Torovan riding out is over.

"Caleb," Elsira says, and she looks near tears. "What is happening?"

I loop her arm in mine and start for the palace. Valtair hurries ahead to start giving orders, and Morgan and Reveyan fall in ahead and behind us, with Elsira's guards.

"Nikolai threatened us," I say. "He's taken Aria, and Torovan is going out to meet him."

"What!"

I squeeze her arm, and she gives me a baleful look.

"You didn't tell me," she hisses.

And I swallow. Because no, we didn't tell her any of this. We didn't think that—

I swallow again, to settle my stomach.

I know what it's like to be a princess in my mother's household, overlooked and disregarded.

"I'm sorry, Elsira. We have to be at the festivities today, both of us. But—let's go to my study, catch you up."

She nods, her lips pulled tight.

CHAPTER 38

THE SECRET

CALEB

I manage to fend off my mother again, saying I need to discuss family business with Elsira. And she does understand that. Even if she is also my family.

Elsira's calmed to a deadly chill by the time we reach my study in the mage's quarters and pass through the common room. Which feels far too empty.

Sabella's coming in from the direction of the mages' quarters when we arrive, though. She eyes my crown, then Elsira, and bows.

"I'll stay close," she says.

"Thank you," I say, with feeling.

We filled Sabella in on Torovan riding out earlier, after we told Aldric. And when I have a spare moment, I'll give her a court mage's medallion, too—the court will need to see that. To know she has official approval.

And she needs to know that, too.

"We should be meeting in Torovan's study," Elsira says as

she looks around my cramped space, tugging off her leather gloves.

She levels her gaze at me, glances up to the crown.

But then she shrugs and sits.

And as quickly as I can, I tell her all I know.

She gets more hunched as the details go on.

"He was in your rooms?" she asks, gripping the arms of her chair.

"In our nursery."

She pulls a face that's all rage. "I will kill him. I can't believe—"

She shuts her mouth. She's said it often since finding out just how rotten Nikolai and her mother were. She once defended him to me.

Elsira looks away. "I will kill him."

Said with absolutely no inflection.

And I believe her, if she ever has the chance.

She waves for me to go on and stops me again when Torovan makes his speech.

"He shouldn't be going. He shouldn't have left you, left *us*, and he shouldn't be going to face Nikolai without you."

"I know."

"Then why did you let him—"

"Because there's no good answer. Because I have to be here. Because what if the trap isn't an ambush out there, but an attack on the palace here?"

It's what I keep telling myself.

I sit back in my chair.

Then decide I can't sit still another moment and get up to pace to the window.

The sky is clouding to the north, where they're going,

looking like the day will turn to rain. And that will not be a pleasant day on the road.

Not that today was ever going to be pleasant.

"Caleb…"

I turn at the tone in Elsira's voice. It sets the hairs on my arms on end.

"What?"

She opens her mouth, closes it again.

"Elsira, what is it?" I can't take any more disasters today. No surprises, none.

She hunches her shoulders, then says in a rush, "I'm an elementalist. I haven't told anyone, so please—please don't. Not anyone. Not Torovan. I can, uh, move the earth elements."

She holds up her hands.

And I take a step back, I'm so unprepared.

"You—you're—but you're royalty—"

Her smile is bitter. And she doesn't dignify that with an answer.

"You're sure?" I ask.

She rolls her eyes. "Gods, Caleb, of course I'm sure. Are you sure you're a weaver?"

I wave incoherently, trying to pull my thoughts in this new direction.

"I want to help," she says, "if it comes to it. I—I'm not very experienced yet, I only figured it out after Mother—after she left."

Gods. I've heard of that happening, sometimes, where someone has dormant elemental abilities but only manifests them after trauma.

"Does anyone else know?" I ask.

"No. *Please* don't tell Torovan."

"I won't. Of course I won't. But—"

But she took third-place in the archery competition. And I hadn't seen her do anything with a bow until a month ago. I thought I just hadn't been paying much attention.

And she's suddenly interested in hunting.

I rub at my temples, upsetting the crown. I make a face and start to lift it off, but Elsira shakes her head.

"No, you need that now. That's your armor, Caleb, if Torovan has his. Don't take it off."

"I'll have to sleep—"

"You know what I mean."

She sits back, looking tired, and I face her across the small room.

"What can you do, if it comes to it?" I ask.

We should be having this conversation with the master earth elementalist still in the palace. He's older than my grandfather, but I've seen him move the earth in calculated, terrifying sweeps in practice.

"I...can make the ground shake. Sometimes. I can nudge things of the earth." She chews on her lip.

"Like arrows?" I ask.

"Huh. So, and I can make stone go a little soft, but I haven't found anything useful to do with that."

She's been teaching herself.

And I know what that's like, to have a magic you know won't be approved of.

But I wanted to be a weaver. She certainly didn't ask to be an elementalist. Not when she's a princess.

A part of me wonders just what the Dowager Zinara would think now if she knew her own blood might carry elementalism.

But she'd probably blame it on her late husband.

"Okay," I say. "And when you're doing what you're doing, can you be precise—no, that's a bad question, I know where you placed in archery."

"I would have placed first," she says, carefully folding her hands in her lap. "I didn't want to look too good."

I believe her.

Elsira is the heart of this palace, but also part of its strength. She did not fall apart when she found out about her mother.

She lifted her chin and carried on. She's been helping Torovan with the work of shifting more power to the common people, helping make education plans, talking with various Council members about logistics.

And she's steady, and doesn't make waves. She's far too easy to overlook.

I have to do better.

"I'm sorry. For not bringing you in on all of this. We only knew most of it last night, but—"

I half expect her to shrug it off, but she nods. "Thank you. And Caleb—use my skills if you have to. If it's worth exposing my being an elementalist, do it."

If it's worth showing that not only is there a weaver among the Barellan royal bloodline, but an elementalist, too.

I make a face.

"This has to change. We've changed a lot, Elsira, but this—this prejudice against magic you're born with—"

"I know," she says. "We have to defeat Nikolai first. And my mother."

She gives me a level look. "I want to be there when we take down our mother."

"I won't let Torovan say no."

She almost smiles at that. Then pushes up. "Come on. Back to the Great Hall, you have to be the king, and I have to be a princess." She slants a look at me. "I'll be close, too. And watching. If Torovan hadn't caught the dagger—well, I saw it, I was going to try. And I've sort of got that, too, I've been practicing the last few days, since the first feast."

She pulls a dagger hilt from her belt, which looks ordinary from the handle. But the blade itself is dull and blocky, like it was only partly formed. She did this with her magic?

"I practiced today until I can sharpen or dull a blade. Mostly. It would still hurt if it hit you and it's dulled, and might still cause injury, but it wouldn't kill you. Not with the blade, anyhow. It's something."

She shrugs and puts her dagger back in her belt and marches out.

Okay.

Okay, one more elementalist.

That's one more we have to defend the palace, if we need to.

Shaking my head, I hurry to catch up.

Chapter 39

Riding Out

Torovan

I wait in the town with the cavalry garrison bustling with last-minute preparations. I wait until the mages ride down with their battle armor and their nerves. I wait a bit more as extra horses are tied to our company as relief mounts, though we'll be riding hard.

And then it starts to rain.

When he arrives with the rest of the mages, Aldric, to his credit, doesn't complain. He has never been anything close to a battle mage, and I know he's had his aches lately.

But in his light mage's armor, he does look regal. He does sit tall in his saddle.

He holds my eye and nods. He will ride out with me, despite his age, despite his lack of practice as a battle mage.

He'll stand with me.

And for that—for that, he wins a little more of my respect.

And then, with my shout, and a scattered cheer again from the people gathered in the town, we set out on the road north.

The send-off bolsters my spirits enough that for the first

few miles of the ride, at least, I'm not thinking about how we're riding into a trap.

We ride through rain on and off all the first day.

And the need for action numbs into the steadiness of hoof-beats on the road toward Nikolai's family's estates. The clatter of our column echoes off low hills around us. The clank of plate armor that's growing heavier by the minute.

People still out working the unharvested fields for a late harvest stop to look up at us as we pass.

There are a few scattered cheers nearer the palace. People who might have heard some of what's going on at the palace.

But there are less cheers the deeper we ride into the countryside.

Will Nikolai even show himself?

If I don't come alone, will he even show up at all?

That is the fear that gnaws at me as we camp outside a small village with a post station to freshen our mounts.

I don't exchange my stallion, though. The short night's rest will be enough.

We camp in coffin-sized tents as it drizzles throughout the night. And every time I close my eyes to sleep, I see Caleb back in the palace.

Caleb under attack, because I left him there. Because I thought coming to Nikolai and taking much of the palace's defenses with me would be a good idea.

Did I make the right choice, leaving him to hold the kingdom while I chase after what might be nothing more than bait?

But the next morning, with my breath misting in the crisp autumn air, I look ahead at the road stretching toward Nikolai's family lands, through autumn-gold fields.

And my resolve, again, firms.

Riding beside me, Kian shifts in his saddle, his young face set with a determination that's growing less fierce the farther we go. And settling into an anxious exhaustion.

He's been quiet since we broke camp, but I know from Caleb that he always asks questions, always wants to know what's ahead, and always wants to dive in.

So I'm not surprised when he asks, "So am I just a court mage now, or can I say I'm a battle mage?"

I glance aside. "Do you want to be a battle mage?"

He rustles his heavy armor.

And I get it. There's all kinds of glory in the old stories about battle mages winning the day.

What they don't talk about is the days on the road, the chafing of the armor, the weariness of riding in that armor all day, the cold and damp nights. The travel rations.

The fear of what's ahead.

Not that I have much more experience with any of this than Kian. But I can't let my own inexperience show.

"I want to help people," Kian says. "And I want to protect the kingdom."

He straightens in his saddle.

Which, at this point in the road, is a losing battle.

"So, yeah," he says, more brightly now, "I want to be a battle mage. If that's what I need to be."

I look aside again, and this time meet his eyes.

I've known his father the general for years, and Kian from a distance. He was too much younger than me to be a peer growing up at court, not like Valtair.

But he's a court mage now.

And even if we had to rush that, and even if he's not

completely done with his training from Caleb, he has the heart of a battle mage.

I think he's ready.

Well. As ready as I am, anyway. Which is probably not nearly enough.

"So can a single weaver really turn the tide of a battle?" Kian goes on. "Like, did that actually happen when a weaver held off an entire army for three days by making them think they were fighting in a swamp with his illusions and constructs? They kept sinking into mud that hadn't been there before."

"It's true as far as I know," I say.

Aldric, who's been riding in a lull behind us, calls up, "And a battle weaver can change the weather, reshape the battlefield, create illusions of more forces behind them than there actually are, or make their own forces camouflaged."

But that was hundreds of years ago. I know from what Caleb's told me that much of those techniques have been lost to time, along with the soul weaving. Because soul weavers used that destructive magic, too.

"Caleb could do it," Kian says. And with that I hear the silent, "And if Caleb's my teacher, so can I."

I hope he carries that confidence straight to whatever we're riding into.

I hope I do, too.

And I start thinking through all the ways I can use what I know in an actual battle.

I haven't thought it through much before, I've been so busy trying to move the Council, move the people, move the kingdom in the direction I want them to go.

I've been so busy running into the fact that wanting change

isn't enough—the people have to want it, too. And I'm finding that's going to take more than telling them they can have it. That's going to take showing them why it's good. And that they can trust that this change will last, when so many of the nobility have failed them before.

"You caught a dagger," Kian goes on, and I blink, focusing back on him. "That feels like a battle mage skill."

Behind me, I hear Aldric's huffed out cough.

"What?" Kian turns around. "If you can catch daggers or arrows on the battlefield, that could turn the tide, too. Can you teach me how to do that? I've been wanting to try, ever since—"

"Of course," I say. "Though that was more instinct than anything, I'll have to work out what I actually did."

"Oh, well, I saw what happened, I saw that you grabbed the blade inside a—"

Kas, riding ahead of me, holds up a fist. "Ahead!"

He stops, and we all stop, rolling back through the column, as a bend in the road reveals two figures standing in the road ahead of us.

I squint in the mid-morning sun.

Then still as I see them.

One is a man with brown hair dressed in a fine blue coat. Even from this distance, I can make out Nikolai's arrogant posture, the way he stands like he owns the world around him. Beside him is a young woman, long black hair loose around her shoulders, the hem of her red skirt obviously muddy even from this distance.

My gut tightens. Did he drag her here? Did he abuse her?

"Aria!" Kian gasps, his horse dancing sideways as he fights the urge to spur forward.

I hold up a hand to keep our column stopped, my mind racing through possibilities. This is too convenient, too exposed. Nikolai wouldn't just stand in the open unless he was confident about the outcome of this encounter.

And is it actually Nikolai, or an illusion?

I throw my senses wide and try to sense ahead, but the distance is far.

"Steady," I say to Kian.

And I don't say that we still don't know if Aria is here with Nikolai willingly, or under coercion. Because despite Caleb saying to trust him, that he knows Aria, we can't afford to assume.

My hand is still out, waiting to see what Nikolai will do.

But he seems to be waiting for us to come to him.

And—should I just attack now? I'm struggling to reach that far with my senses, could I reach that far with my weaving?

Can he reach that far with his?

But then, we were just talking about battle mages, and I know it's possible for a weaver to influence an entire field of battle, not just the people immediately around them.

When we get through this, I will need to start training.

"We approach carefully," I say.

I signal to the guards, and our formation shifts subtly—still advancing, but ready for combat. The elementalists spread out slightly, going off the road to either side, giving themselves room to maneuver, room to see.

I see fire crackling, air gathering between their fingers.

Slowly, we advance.

Nikolai raises one hand in what might be a greeting or a warning. His voice carries clearly across the distance between us. That's likely some form of weaving, too.

"Torovan! How unexpected! And you didn't come alone! But now that you're here, we can talk."

His reasonable tone makes my skin crawl. This is the man who murdered my father, who tried to control my mind, who's been terrorizing my kingdom for months. And he wants to *talk*.

"What do you want to discuss?" I call back. "How you've been threatening my husband?"

But will he hear me? My voice feels thin and thready, carried on the wind.

We continue riding forward, slowly.

This is a trap—of course this is a trap.

"How you kidnapped an apprentice of my court?" I continue, despite not knowing how to make my voice carry farther.

If Nikolai can't hear me, at least my own people can.

I'm calculating if I should try to do something like how I caught the dagger in the Great Hall, with constructs of air, except, could I hone them tighter and sharper, could I make them into blades, could I slice his throat where he stands?

Do I dare try that for the first time just now?

We are closer now, though, and I can feel the sense of Nikolai's reality ahead, still faint from the distance, but there. It is actually him, not an illusion, a ghost on the road. And it's actually Aria, too.

And part of me is relieved, so intensely relieved, that Nikolai is here now, and not at the palace where Caleb is.

Caleb is safe.

That's all that matters.

I can fight, whatever happens today, knowing he's safe.

"Actually," Nikolai calls, "I want to discuss your family's safety."

I draw a long breath and let it out again. We're all still moving, slowly, forward.

And as we get closer, I see Aria looks more defiant than controlled. Her chin raised, her shoulders set in a line of stubborn resistance.

Her cheek is bruised.

Gods, if he did lay hands on her.

Well. I was planning to kill him anyway.

But her defiance now, does that mean she's not under his control? She's looking defiantly at *me*.

Or is she controlled completely?

Or was Caleb wrong? Was Aria Nikolai's agent all along?

"Aria!" Kian shouts, his horse dancing as he strains to hold it back. Or hold himself back.

Then he spurs forward.

Chapter 40

A Battle of Wills

Torovan

"Kian!" I yell. But he's already riding at a fast gallop for Aria, shifting in the saddle like he means to scoop her up without stopping.

Shit.

In his armor, he's more likely to hurt her or be hurt himself.

Kian has read entirely too many stories.

I glance to Nikolai to see the air shimmering with threads of void, of darkness, of control. I can see them this time. This time, this fight, I have the willpower and the training to see them.

And they're like Caleb described. Like tears in reality, not reality itself.

Mind control threads.

Nikolai isn't even bothering with Kian. He's aiming the threads straight at me.

I don't know if it will stop them, but I weave the air in front of me, trying to build up a hardness, a shield. If I stopped the dagger aimed at Caleb by hardening the air, can I stop these threads, too?

"Torovan," Aldric calls. "He's not aiming at you! Widen the shield! Take my will!"

I feel his willpower thrust at me, and scramble to hold both it and my shield, to integrate his strength into mine. I've practiced this with Caleb.

But, as with everything else, I haven't had as much time to practice as I'd like.

But Aldric's willpower bolsters my own just as Nikolai's threads reach me...and move past me, slipping aside, aiming for my guards. Aiming for the soldiers and the elementalists.

I watch Kas ahead of me twitch in his saddle as if struck.

A court mage with fire crackling between his fingertips turns toward me but doesn't hurl it. There's an intense strain in his eyes. He's fighting against his own will.

The fire within his hands grows brighter.

But he's not throwing the fire yet.

How long will that hesitation last?

Can I hope that my people will be able to hold Nikolai off? We all know this is what we're dealing with now, he's not taking anyone by surprise this time.

I try to widen my shield, as Aldric said, to protect Kas.

Will Nikolai's desire to see me harmed overtake my people's desire to protect me? To protect each other, to take down this mage who's standing against us?

The elementalist hurls the fireball at me.

I jab my heels into my stallion's flanks and surge forward, away from the fire, and lean into a gallop toward Nikolai. I take my woven shield with me.

Ahead of me, Kian's off his horse, frantically defending himself against Aria's weaving.

But at least she's weaving normal reality, not trying to weave his soul.

Nikolai watches me approach, not moving, not showing anything like fear. He's just grinning at me, his sun-tanned cheeks pinking in his excitement. The hoops in each ear glinting in the mid-morning sun.

I draw my sword.

And two things happen at once.

Where there was just countryside a moment before, the ground around the road rolling down into the fields, now there are people. More than two dozen, all armed, and charging straight for me.

I'm looking everywhere at once as I'm suddenly surrounded. I didn't feel these people.

Are they illusions?

But no. No, I sense them now. He was hiding them beneath an unreality weaving, wasn't he?

Nikolai isn't just skilled at mind control weaving, and how have I forgotten that in these moments now?

Nikolai is a battle mage.

And he's warring against *me*.

The second thing that happens is Nikolai launches an attack of his soul magic straight at me.

My woven shield has faltered, and I don't have time to deflect.

I'm reining in instinctively, trying to gather my mind and my will again to weave another shield, but between that moment and the next, Nikolai's threads reach me.

I feel them in the air and know what they are, the threads

trying to enter my mind. Slipping through the cracks in my fear.

My fear rises to terror.

Vaguely, I hear someone shout. Kian, maybe.

I watch Nikolai's new fighters not engage me directly, but swarm past me, toward the mages behind me. Toward my guards, and Aldric.

I'm still holding Aldric's will. And I think, through my haze, that I probably should release that. I just manage to wrench his will from mine and send it back to him.

But Nikolai wants me to turn and fight with his new forces. To use my weaver's abilities and senses to slaughter my own people.

He's trying to show me that I want that, too.

My horse turns back the way we came, takes two steps forward.

Then I pull back the reins and stop it.

Of course I don't want to fight against my own people.

But what if this is the only way to stop Nikolai? To fight my people?

No.

No, that doesn't make sense.

I'm panting. Straining. Because yes, it does make sense.

All the sense in the world.

I jerk my stallion's head around again, back toward Nikolai.

That makes sense. Nikolai is my focus.

I must stop him. I must take him down.

To protect my husband. To protect my family—

I stop again, holding the reins tightly in one hand, keeping my nervous mount from moving forward.

Caleb knew I was walking into a trap and didn't stop me.

He knows how weak I am.

He wants the kingdom for himself.

I shake my head. No. Gods, no, these are Nikolai's thoughts, Nikolai's lies, how can he think I'd believe them?

I urge my horse forward again toward Nikolai, but stop a few steps later.

Caleb knows I'm not strong enough to rule my kingdom. He hasn't taught me all of what he knows because he knows I can't handle it.

He didn't tell me what he knew about Nikolai being in the palace.

He knows I can't handle anything at all.

No.

I brace against this. My whole will surging up because it's *not true.*

Behind me, Aldric shouts, "Give up, Torovan! You don't have the will to fight him!"

Gods. I gave him back his will, but it was too late. Or maybe not enough.

Nikolai has Aldric now, too.

I was a fool to bring Aldric with me. He might have resisted Nikolai before, on the day we fought Nikolai in the Council Chamber, but he's never been that strongly willed. He shouldn't have given me his willpower. But maybe he always would have broken.

And maybe Nikolai thinks Aldric's words will be the words that break me, like Aldric is someone I actually respect.

But it stiffens my back.

Because it's *not true.*

I spur back into a gallop, charging at Nikolai, making riding straight at him my singular, final, focus.

I raise my sword.

Then drop it, yelling, as fire hits the blade.

One of my elementalists is charging at me, his hands upraised and gathering more fire between them.

My horse shies, stumbles, starts to fall.

I have enough wits left to jump clear, trying to roll, but the armor is heavier than I thought, and I land hard. I hit my shoulder, crying out at the crack of pain in my arm.

And I lay, stunned on the ground, trying to catch breath that isn't there. I watch the battle going on to one side. Nikolai's people against...well, only some of mine. Some of mine are fighting with his people.

The elementalists are scattered.

There are bodies on the ground. Some of Nikolai's people, some of mine. More of mine.

I find Nikolai to my left, closer now—but I came closer to him. Kian is struggling against a binding weaving that Aria has around him.

And I see the thick soul weaving threads that Nikolai has between himself and Aria, and that...that almost feels like a relief.

And proof that Caleb was right. That Aria didn't come on her own will.

Is that anything to hope in now?

Nikolai starts toward me, his mouth tight in concentration.

I finally pull in breath again and struggle to push up, falling as I try to put weight on my left arm.

Is it broken?

No, I don't think so, but it's still not good.

I push up anyway, standing to face Nikolai.

My sword is gone, lost somewhere behind me. My horse is up again, but galloping away from the fighting, into the fields.

Barellan war horses are trained for magical attacks in battle, yes.

But not this much chaos. Not this much fear.

Nikolai's not trying to weave me now. He's just approaching.

"I'll kill them all," he says. "Or, you can come with me. I just want to talk."

This doesn't look like just wanting to talk.

"You tried to control me," I say, and my voice comes out hoarse.

"You were attacking me," he says.

He's close now. And I'm calculating if I have the strength to lunge at him.

If I have even a chance at taking him down.

Then I remember that yes, I am a weaver, and weave the air in front of me into the blades I was thinking about before, shoving them toward his throat.

Nikolai raises one hand to stop them. He doesn't try to unweave them, just puts a shield of reality around himself.

He grimaces, his eyes sparking.

Then sends his soul weaving toward me again.

My knees hit the ground beneath me.

How had I ever thought I could face this man?

Even with all the forces behind me, with Kian, with Aldric, with the court mages at my back, and the soldiers—

I'm not strong enough.

Maybe not even Caleb is strong enough to face him.

Nikolai's grown in power.

Or maybe, I've just grown weaker.

Maybe, my trying to change the kingdom has only exposed my own weakness.

I'm a failure.

I'm hardly fit to be a king.

I stand up. "No."

He's in front of me now.

"No! It's not true! None of that is true!"

"You told Caleb about the letters?" Nikolai asks. "Then you are weak, Torovan. You don't care for his own life. You don't care if he dies."

"Of course I—"

I shake my head. And try to sort through the tangle running through my head, I know it's his mind control threads, I know it. And I try to find then within my thoughts, try to grab hold of them, try to expel them.

My mental hands slide off.

Which is what Caleb described when we fought Nikolai before.

How he defeated Nikolai—the only way he defeated Nikolai—was by sharing a truth so potent that Nikolai couldn't show it to be false.

By showing me who he really was. All of who he was.

But I'm here right now, and I don't have more of myself to show.

I'm all of myself here, fighting with all of my will.

And it's just not enough.

Not enough to defeat the man who murdered my father.

How could I have even thought to try?

So foolish.

So stupid.

I close my eyes, baring my teeth.

"It's better this way," Nikolai says, and it's almost gentle.

Is it gentle?

Or am I hearing it as gentle?

He moves behind me, and snaps something cold, metallic around my wrists.

"I just want to talk," Nikolai says again.

And what if it's true?

He hasn't killed me yet, though he has killed some of my people.

But, if we're in a battle, that's reasonable, isn't it?

No. It's not.

I can't imagine I want to hear anything he has to say.

Not after the letters.

Not after my father.

Not after he tried to control me before.

I feel a tightness around my arms, my chest, and see his threads of reality binding me. Normal threads, but my thoughts slip away from trying to unravel them.

I look back to where the fighting is and see my people—too many of my people—on the ground.

And those still fighting, quickly being outmatched. Some still by my own people.

I look to Kian, who's fighting within Aria's bonds, unsuccessfully.

And Aldric, who's standing rigidly. Fighting his own inner battle. At least he's still fighting back.

"See?" Nikolai says. "It's no use to fight. Just come with me. I just want to talk. Your family is safe. Your weaver is safe. His child is safe. That's all you want, isn't it? That's all you care about. So, I'm telling you they're safe, if you come with me."

Nikolai pulls me toward him. Toward, I see now, two carriages coming down the road ahead of us.

"Tell your people to stop fighting," he says calmly. "We just want to talk. They stop fighting, and your family stays safe."

I turn back to where my people are still fighting.

And—and this is wrong. I shouldn't tell them to stop. But I shouldn't tell them to keep fighting, either, I know we're outmatched. I know I made a mistake in coming, in thinking it was possible to fight Nikolai at all.

But I shouldn't tell them to stop.

So I gather my will, gather just enough to shout, "Run! *Run!*"

I see one of the elementalists start. See me. Freeze.

"Tell him!" I shout. "Tell him what happened—"

Nikolai cuffs my cheek, and my head whips to the side. I stumble, my hands bound, unable to check the damage.

But manage to stay on my feet.

And when I look up, I see some of my people breaking off, riding off if they're still on their horses, or running for some of the lingering horses if they're not.

And that small bit of triumph wells up in me, enough to break through enough of Nikolai's fog that I turn back and butt his head with mine.

I see stars. And he staggers.

I surge forward—but trip within his woven binding, and fall down hard again on my shoulder, crying out.

It's no use.

I failed.

I am a failure.

I'm too much of a failure to ever be a good king to my people.

A good husband to Caleb.

A good father.

I couldn't stop Nikolai before.

How could I have ever thought I could?

I thought—I thought I would be enough. That I'd learned enough. That I wanted to protect my husband and my child and my kingdom enough.

That all of that would be enough.

But no, I don't have the willpower.

I close my eyes, shuddering.

"Caleb," I whisper. "I'm sorry."

Chapter 41

Holding Court

Irava

It's evening of the day that Torovan rode out, and the palace is festive. The courtiers have been festive all day. They've treated him leaving to fight Nikolai like a trial of strength he's already won.

And I'm wearing my crown all day, I'm holding the burden of a kingdom, I'm watching the people look to me to set the direction and the tone, and I'm...starting to understand.

Yes, I've been beside Torovan while he's at Council meetings, or while he's talking with ministers, or delegates, or traders, or generals.

I've listened while he rants about this minister or that delegate who are making problems for him.

And then I've gone off into my own world of being a master mage, and training my apprentices, and leaving him to his work.

But I've spoken to so many people today who wanted reassurances of Torovan's success, and that he'll return triumphant before the end of the Festival. I've had to carefully fend off people who thought that if Torovan told them no to something, that they'd be able to get a yes from me.

I finally pulled Valtair to my side halfway through the day, letting him take half of the answers, because my head was full. So very full of all the people and all their problems and all their joys—I'm still getting congratulations, too, and even that is wearing thin.

Maybe especially that.

Because I'm not wearing an illusion right now. None at all. I'm myself as Irava, and my pregnancy is showing.

And that is...terrifying.

Right now, I'm sitting at the high table for the night's feast, sipping grape juice as the people eat and roar in laughter and gesture to each other.

It feels utterly wrong with the worry churning inside me, and yet I smile, because the kingdom needs to see it.

And I'm starting to understand that, too.

Torovan's been carrying this weight for months.

It's been carving him into the person he needs to be. And pulling him away from the person I want him to be.

But being a king is who he is.

It's who I am now, too.

I'm sitting in Torovan's place at the table, and everyone to my right is shifted a place over so there's no gap in seating. Elsira to my right. Valtair to my left. My mother beside Elsira—and she mostly has kept her distance today, though I know she still wants to talk.

But I think she sees that my visibility in the court, that holding the crown steady, is more important just now.

Valtair leans in.

"Lady Sima wanted to call a session of the Council for

tonight, but I fended her off. They don't like that Torovan acted without them. But I know, and you know, and he knows that if it had taken a Council vote, it would have taken a week to act."

Gods of all the seasons, I can't handle a Council meeting tonight on top of everything.

"But, we'll have to meet tomorrow," he says. "I could pause that for a night, but not more."

I nod. And my eyes are still on the festivities happening around us.

But my mind is with Torovan, on the road, thinking through every possible detail and danger I can imagine. And how he might deal with them.

How he might deal with Nikolai.

In everything he's learned these last months of coming into his own as the king, has he gained advantages over his mind and his willpower that Nikolai can't exploit?

I've played so many scenarios through my head that they're blurring together.

Nikolai trying to control Torovan again, and Torovan holding steady.

And Torovan giving in.

And Torovan prevailing with the numbers of his force, the strength of the elementalists behind him. The strength of his troops.

Kian striking down Nikolai before Nikolai can have a chance to control anyone.

Aria breaking free from Nikolai's hold and cutting him down herself.

Nikolai striking first and with overwhelming force and Torovan...failing.

I get to that version, again and again, and run it all through again, stubbornly shifting to different outcomes.

Because I know my husband. And he's stronger than he thinks he is.

I don't know the scenery, I don't know where the confrontation will take place. I don't know if it's happened already, or will happen soon. I don't know if it will take him all the way to Nikolai's family's estates.

But we've heard nothing yet, so whatever happened or will happen, it's not happened close.

Valtair's hand closes around mine, and I look up.

He doesn't give me reassurances. And I don't give them to him.

But I keep my hand in his, that's reassurance enough just now, and nibble at a buttered roll.

And maybe I can hope that Torovan will be home before tomorrow, and he can deal with the Council meeting.

Yes, I'll cling to that.

But I'm the master weaver, I should be riding out to face our enemies.

And he should be here to face his rivals in court.

These are our places we've carved out for ourselves.

Yet he's riding out, and I'm holding court.

But maybe I'm stronger than I think, too.

Maybe willpower isn't just the will to protect or defend with magic, but defend through the everyday and ordinary, too. Carrying on in the face of danger is a powerful illusion.

"The fifth and sixth garrisons are on their way in toward the palace," Valtair says in my ear. "I got word before dinner."

We'd decided that this morning—we need more troops at the palace. Even if they aren't ultimately used, they'll be here.

I nod.

"And...the combat trials are tomorrow. It's traditional for the king to fight in them. And I know that's not practical, Irava, even if you weren't pregnant, you're not trained for physical combat, I'm sorry—"

"Do the rules say anything about using magic?"

He pauses. "Everyone just assumes that a Barellan king won't have it. And there have been a few elementalists who've fought in the trials, I don't think it's against the rules." He dabs at his mouth. "But there was a soldier who was secretly a fire elementalist being booed for burning the arm of his opponent."

Valtair looks at me askance. "Mages are always set apart. Always."

I meet his eyes.

I do know.

And do I really want to remind the people right now of how lethal weavers can be?

Torovan hadn't done that in riding out. He'd reminded them of how lethal a *king* can be. With his armor, and his sword, and his family's history.

"I was going to suggest," Valtair says, "that you have a champion fight for you. It's not typical, no, but with everything going on—"

"I'll fight," I hear behind me. And I look back to see Morgan, his cheeks splotching as if he's only now realizing what he said.

But he pulls himself up and says more formally, with a short bow, "It would be my honor to fight for you, Your Majesty."

He's not looking at Valtair. Pointedly so, I think.

Valtair is very pointedly not looking at him.

What is between these two? I saw how Morgan protected him earlier, used his own magic when I'd slipped and almost revealed Valtair's magic to Kian.

I can trust Kian, but Kian sometimes blurts out whatever's in his head.

Morgan protected Valtair's secrecy at the expense of his own. Because no, guards really aren't supposed to have magic, either—though I offered to train him in weaving. And he accepted that offer.

Are Morgan and Valtair acting weird around each other now because I wove Morgan into his own body?

"Yes," I say to Morgan. "You may fight for me in the combat trials."

Morgan grins, as if this is a great reward. "Thank you, Your Majesty."

And maybe his need for this is more than to help in this moment. Maybe he wants to test himself, to put his new body through its paces.

I know he feels stronger. I know he needs to expand into that feeling.

I know.

I shrug my shoulders, reweaving my illusion as Caleb around me.

If I can find a spare moment, maybe—maybe I can just think about reweaving my reality around my growing child.

Just think about it. Just think it through.

Maybe.

CHAPTER 42

WEAPONS

CALEB

Torovan's not back that night.

He's not back when I wake at dawn.

And the Great Hall the next morning, and the people's expectations of me, which I'll have to carry again today, have never felt more imposing.

The mood of the court today, maybe picking up on my own nerves, is more subdued than the day before.

Are the people realizing that their king, after all, is human?

That there's a chance he won't win this?

But I can't think it. I don't dare to think it.

And still, I feel like I'm holding my breath.

We all sit to breakfast, Valtair, Elsira, my mother, and me.

And it's starting to feel rote, like this is the only thing holding back the kingdom from the chaos of panic. The four of us, showing everyone that everything's still fine.

I spot Sabella sitting at a table near the left center of the hall —good. I'd said the day before about her joining in the palace meals again, and she'd been hesitant about the mood of the court, but agreed.

And I see a noblewoman next to her smiling, shyly, and chatting as she arranges her napkin.

A small tension inside of me eases at that. Sabella's been worried that the court won't accept her as a court mage because she used to be palace staff. But she's wearing her mage's medallion now.

And maybe everything will, in the end, be okay.

"Council meeting in a turn of the glass," Valtair says. "This might be a long one."

"I'll come, too," Elsira says, leaning around me. "I want to know what's happening in the kingdom. I want to be a part of it."

Valtair raises a brow. "As is fitting a princess." But he turns and gives Elsira a tired smile.

The staff lays out the first course for breakfast.

My nausea is less present today, thank the gods, but I'm still not hungry.

Not when I'm thinking about Torovan. And Kian. And even Aldric, and the other court mages, wherever they are now, whatever they're doing now.

I take a dish of steaming porridge from a platter, heaped high with sliced berries on top, and pour milk around the edges.

"When your Council is finished," my mother says past Elsira, "I would like to meet, Caleb, if your schedule allows. I have thought of calling in mages from Galenda, a strictly diplomatic mission."

By which she means, they won't be here to help officially, but they'll be here if I need them.

But they're not here right now.

We have more weavers in Barella, too. And maybe it's time I call them in, too.

Torovan hadn't wanted to cause panic before, but maybe that time is here. And maybe it won't be panic this time, but playing into the heroics that Torovan showed when he rode out. Weavers coming in to protect their kingdom.

I know my mother's help won't come without political strings, though, I know it won't. So I nod and say, "We'll meet with Lord Valtair, as well. He knows the logistics of the kingdom best."

My mother's mouth twitches, but she nods.

There's a scuffle among the people eating and I look up, my alarm spiking, my weaver's senses, always more open now, going wide.

It's probably just an argument. And I'm trying to find the source of the raised voices when a hand grips my arm and pulls me out of my chair.

I twist to see Morgan.

"Get *down*, Your Majesty!"

"But it's just—"

"Weapons are drawn."

"What—"

Around me, my other guards, and Elsira's guards, and my mother's guards are pulling all of us down, while others are drawing blades.

"Don't you move!" someone I don't recognize shouts, and the hall, eerily, goes silent.

"Let me up," I growl at Morgan, who's still holding me firmly down.

"Sire, I can't—"

"Let me *up*." And I carefully weave air into the barest space between his hands and my arms, pushing him apart from me.

I stand.

And my mouth parts as I see people with daggers rushing to grab nobles and dignitaries—gods, is this an Akrean attack?

Lady Denya said her people might not share her own views.

But I spot her at a table to the right, near the front of the hall. She has a knife to her throat, too. And she's watching me with a steady, compressed fury.

A man I've never seen before walks up the center aisle of the hall, his boots echoing on the floor in the sudden hush. He's well-dressed, dark hair pulled back in a neat tail, moving with the confidence of someone used to command. But there's something wild in his eyes.

"What is going on?" I call out, because I have to say something. I have to do *something*.

The man keeps walking, pointing a long dagger directly at me in challenge.

Morgan's hand grips my shoulder, ready to pull me back again at any moment. I don't shake him off.

Is this the man who threw the dagger on that first night?

I can't tell. There's no way to tell.

Cold sweat washes over me. Could this be Nikolai? Here, and not meeting Torovan on the road?

Is this man's appearance an illusion?

He stops, waving his dagger around.

"We are liberating this kingdom!" he declares, his voice ringing off the stone walls. "We're liberating this kingdom from the tyranny and the danger of the weavers!"

His accent—it's light, but I recognize it as from north of

the palace. Could it be from Nikolai's district? Nikolai himself doesn't have that accent.

My stomach churns.

No, I don't think this is Nikolai. The man's waving around that dagger in a graceless manner.

And this whole thing, his other conspirators holding knives to the throats of nobles, this isn't Nikolai's style. Nikolai likes to control from the shadows.

But *yes*, it is his style. Is this man being controlled?

This is a rebellion. People from our own kingdom who have been turned against us.

The man turns again toward me, glaring at me with the burn of hatred. He holds the dagger out again, pointing toward my head.

Morgan pulls me back again before I can look for soul weaving. "Your Majesty—"

But it's Reveyan who stops him. Who pulls Morgan away instead and gives me a grim nod.

Morgan wants to protect me, yes, but my job is protecting this kingdom right now.

And I am this palace's main defense. I can't be that defense by hiding behind a table in the middle of a coup.

I squeeze my hands into careful fists and then release them.

I count at least twenty men, and a few women, with daggers. All dressed as courtiers. But I think very few of them actually are. And with so many people coming in and out of the palace during the Harvest Festival, no one would think to check.

But that's twenty daggers at people's throats. Could I neutralize all of them before anyone's killed?

I see Lady Sima at one of the tables nearest the high table, her head tilted back, glaring at me with steel pressed to her throat, too.

And—and gods. Sabella.

There's a dagger at her throat.

I look back to the man in the center, who seems to be waiting for my attention to continue his little act.

He smiles. "Good. Now let's discuss the future of this kingdom."

CHAPTER 43

YOUR ATTENTION IS REQUIRED

CALEB

I don't know what to do.

My ears are ringing. My pulse kicking to a gallop, my eyes going everywhere, seeing every dagger, and every face that wields the dagger watching me. Just waiting for me to make a move.

And every face with a dagger pressed to their neck watching me, too. Praying that I don't get this wrong. Pleading with me with their eyes. Or trying to urge me on with their rage.

I can weave without holding up my hands. But it's harder to get precise movements, and I need to be precise.

I *absolutely* must be precise, or it will be so many lives on my hands. And if the Akrean delegate dies here today, could that be the start of a war?

Is that what this is about, too?

I don't know. But I know I can't fail here.

Valtair stands back up, too. "There is no tyranny of the weavers," he calls out. "You are acting against your rightful kings!"

Morgan's still near me, tensed, just ready to spring and pull me down again, though he's keeping a respectful distance now.

I almost wish he wasn't.

I turn back to the man in the center. "We are kings first," I say. "But yes, we are weavers. And by being weavers, we have kept this kingdom safe."

"You're on the wrong side of this, weaver," the man says, pointing his dagger at me again. "You shouldn't have come to Barella."

Morgan moves closer, and that's a reassurance at my back. Reveyan is not stopping him now.

"And what's the right side?" I ask. "The side where Nikolai Metrial controls the court, and the king? Is that the only weaver you support?"

"We don't support any weavers!" the man shouts, and turns as his other conspirators echo in agreement. "We support the natural order of things, and reality only as we see it—"

"For gods' sakes," Valtair says, "you're doing exactly what Nikolai Metrial wants! You don't see that, but he wants you to think that—"

I brush Morgan's arm behind me, and he immediately pulls me down.

"Hey!" the man shouts.

I grip Morgan's shoulder and lean to whisper in his ear.

"Can I make an illusion around you that you're me? It won't change your reality. Then I'll look like you."

I pull back, and his eyes flash. He nods.

And I do it.

"Your *Majesty!*" the man calls. "Your attention is *required* at this meeting of your people!"

I finish weaving the illusion around Morgan that he's me,

and he touches his face, his fingers going through the spectacles.

I pull his arm back down, lean in again. "Say your guard pulled you down, apologize, then taunt him for waiting until Torovan left to spring this."

"I—I don't—"

Shit, I forgot the voice. I fix that, weaving the illusion of his voice into mine.

I push him upward, and he stands, tottering a moment before he regains his balance.

My mother, beside me, stares at me. She doesn't ask what I'm going to do.

She only nods.

So I reweave my illusion around myself into Morgan.

And stumble upward, trying to look shaken, like I was just fought off.

I approach Morgan again, but he senses it, turns, and shouts, "Back off!"

Good. Gods, good.

I stumble backward, and almost actually trip before Reveyan catches my arm.

I look to both sides of the dais that the high table sits on. And no one but the guards here are armed. The conspirators' group hasn't yet dared to approach the guards, the cowards. No, they're just holding the nobility hostage. But the cloth on the table is thick enough you can't see through. No one but those behind the table saw what I just did.

Morgan, gripping the table with a death grip, starts stammering about Torovan and courage and how these people are idiots.

That could be better, but it's what I have. I need eyes to

not be on me as I try to weave in this room. As I try to get a sense of how to take all of the attackers out without anyone getting hurt.

Elsira, still on hands and knees behind the table, lunges at me before I step off the dais, and catches my ankle.

"Morgan," she hisses. Though I know she saw who I am. "Where are you going?"

"Not far," I say. Then pause. "Be ready."

She swallows, but nods.

And turns to peak over the table again.

I don't know what she'll do, or can do, in this crowd. But she's a weapon no one else knows I have.

I ease past Reveyan, who makes a show of pushing me to the side, like I just endangered the king.

Valtair's joined the actual Morgan in hurling insults at the leader now, and the man in the center is fully engaged in this battle.

I move toward the side of the dais. And finally I can see the full hall again.

Nothing yet has changed.

I ease past the end of the table, toward the wall. Aiming to take up a guard's position here.

A few eyes flicker toward me, as one of the only things moving in this hall right now.

One of those who turns is the man holding a dagger to Sabella's throat. He tightens it, and I watch her tilt her head back to keep from getting cut.

Oh gods. Gods.

I have to be so careful here.

Sabella's eyes meet mine.

And something hardens in her expression.

She knows I'm not Morgan. She knows it's me.

Maybe it's the sense of the child, as Torovan said Aldric could feel. More than one set of possibilities within me.

Maybe she just knows me.

But I watch her face subtly change.

And then I feel it.

This hall should be teeming with fear, with anger, with the ice of terror, with the determination of those holding their captives. All of it.

But my sense of reality around me feels muffled. I've been too distracted to feel it before, but I sense it now.

There's a weaver here who can weave unreality.

Is Nikolai here after all?

The man in the center shakes his dagger at Morgan and marches forward.

That man—that man, I decide, is the distraction.

Reveyan steps up and pulls Morgan back now.

With two distinct armored clanks as something Morgan's wearing beneath his illusion—maybe his sheath—clanks with Revayan's sheath.

Oh, no.

Did anyone else hear that?

My guards are moving forward now, moving to intercept the man marching on the high table.

But he holds up a hand and shouts, the people holding their hostages throughout the crowd holding them tighter.

I need to break this fight, and break it now.

I open my weaver's senses as wide as I can, trying to find the anchoring thread of unreality. I feel toward the corners of the room first, but it's a large room, full of so many people and their possibilities, even if they're muffled right now.

I'm struggling to find anything solid and defined in this chaos.

I pull back, then try to let my thoughts spread wider, to take in the room as a whole, to find where the unreality feels most concentrated.

There's a point, yes.

And I follow it, slowly, toward its center.

Toward...Sabella.

I watch as her hands twitch.

And though the unreality weaving is still active, it covers such a large area that I can still feel something beneath it.

With my senses wide open, and knowing what I'm looking for, I see the ghosts of threads around her. Threads like numbness, like void, like reality hollowed out and twisted.

I know that feeling too well from fighting Nikolai.

I felt the ghost of that feeling inside Sabella's mind.

Oh, gods.

The threads coming out of her are delicately touching some of the people holding daggers. Not all of them—maybe half. The threads are subtle, precise. She's not controlling them completely, just...influencing their will.

Sabella knows how to soul weave.

And for a moment, my entire world freezes on that thought.

Is it possible that she's still being controlled by Nikolai?

Is it possible he got to her again, or that I didn't fix all the traces of mind control I found in her?

Or...or is it possible that Nikolai was never in the palace at all?

"It's not your palace!" Morgan calls from the high table, fighting Reveyan off to rush forward and brace against the table. His voice—my voice—wavers slightly, but he's pulling this off better than I'd hoped. "And who would you have as your king? Someone who can't fight your enemies? Someone who can't protect you?"

Someone in the crowd, one of the people holding the knives, shouts back, "They are controlling us! Torovan is making the nobles give up their power—surely that is evidence of mind control!"

Oh these poor deluded fools.

I watch as Sabella thickens her dark threads toward the speaker, reinforcing their conviction.

Sabella. My apprentice. My friend.

This woman I trusted with my secrets. I gave her a court mage's medallion last night. She's *wearing* it today.

She's a soul weaver.

And now, I have a better idea of what I'm facing.

But she knows who I am, and she hasn't tried to call me out yet.

What does that mean? Can that possibly mean she's not working with Nikolai on her own will? Can I hope that?

But I don't dare hope.

And from the mind control threads, I can see that some of the attackers are being influenced by her, but others aren't. Some are here by choice, believing their own rhetoric. Others are being nudged, their fears amplified until they act.

I can't defeat dark weaving directly—I learned that fighting Nikolai. But I need to act before this gets worse.

From my new vantage, though it's not the best vantage, I count the visible daggers again. I counted two more before that I don't see now, but then, I could see better from the high table. But I couldn't weave from where I stood while everyone was watching.

I do my best to fix in my mind where the other daggers were, where my blind spots will be now. I push my senses to their limits, trying to pinpoint the greatest points of fear. Of malicious intent. And I do think I find the other two attackers with their hostages.

The leader is moving toward the high table again. Shouting something I'm no longer trying to follow.

I have to act now.

I don't move my hands. But I mark every place where the daggers are, narrow my eyes in focus, and shift reality over each of them, pulling down the threads to weave the daggers into flowers.

The effort, so many points of focus at once, drains me quickly, and I sway.

But I know it worked when I hear the shouts.

Chapter 44

The Symphony

Caleb

The conspirators who once held weapons are now waving around flowers, petals scattering to the stone floor.

Morgan looks at me, his eyes wide, then quickly holds up his hands like he's actually weaving the transformation.

The hall erupts into chaos.

Many of those who'd been held hostage stumble away from their stunned captors. Or turn to attack on their own.

Some of the captors, though, think too quickly and try to wrestle them back under control.

But the guards around the hall, who hadn't dared to move before, now rush in to grab the conspirators.

I focus on Sabella, whose "attacker" abandoned her completely.

But then, she was never really under his control. He was under hers.

I'm readying a binding weave, but she stands and hurls her

own binding at me. It's a traditional weaving, not soul weaving, and I deflect it easily enough, but gods.

What if she hurts my child?

I step back, my hand instinctively moving toward my stomach before I catch myself. I'm still supposed to be Morgan. I should probably be rushing in with the rest of the guards, but I'm slowly freezing up. Backing until I feel the cold stone of the outer wall.

This isn't the same as the fight with Nikolai. I can't give everything I have—everything isn't mine to give anymore.

And Sabella was my friend.

She was my apprentice, I taught her—but how much did she already know?

She's soul weaving.

I don't want to hurt her, but I have to stop her.

My throat closes as she points directly at me.

"There! That is actually the king! Take him, before he kills us all!"

I freeze. Would the people actually believe that? That I'd do that? That I would kill them all?

But she's sending out soul threads again to reinforce her claim.

Some of the conspirators in the chaos stop, turning to charge back at me with their fists raised where their daggers used to be.

Some of the nobility turn, too, caught in the fray. They turn toward attacking *me*.

I react without thinking, weaving a glass wall out of the stones in the floor in a half circle around myself.

My attackers run into it, hard enough that I wince. I'm still staring at Sabella through the distorted glass, this woman I trusted, who I brought into my training because I believed in her.

I have to make a choice.

I can't protect her if she's being controlled, but I have to protect myself and my kingdom. I can't let this kingdom fall today.

Not to this.

Not now.

My throat burning, my eyes starting to burn, too, I drop all my illusions, because I need my full concentration for this fight.

I point at Sabella through the rough glass.

"Sabella is the soul weaver! Guards!"

Reveyan draws his sword without hesitation and rushes toward Sabella, his blade flashing. But Sabella stops him with a soul thread, freezing him in place like a statue.

I lash out with the full strength of my binding weaving again, but Sabella deflects it, slips away.

Her control has always been formidable, but now, I don't find her willpower lacking, either. That must have been a feint all along.

Or maybe, like Nikolai's weaving, something in her normal weaving is lacking, while her soul weaving roars out in strength.

Any hopes I have that this isn't what it looks like, that Sabella isn't a dark weaver herself, on her own will, are fading fast.

I trap Sabella inside more walls of glass as she tries to back up.

She weaves them into paper and smashes through them.

People are scattering now, realizing this is a fight between weavers. Chairs scrape against stone, voices rise in panic, and someone screams near the doors as the crowd surges toward the exits.

Morgan, whose illusion dropped when I dropped mine, dashes to my side.

Sabella hurls spikes at me, jagged constructs she's weaving from the air. They shatter my reality construct wall, scattering glass across the floor around me.

I unravel her spikes into harmless flowers before they can reach me—my mind is still on the flowers.

I can't send the spikes back to her, though. I don't want to harm the people still around her, though the area is rapidly clearing.

But the fighting continues all around us, guards chasing the conspirators, capturing some.

I hear another scream.

I glance, but I don't see the leader.

But then, that man truly wasn't the leader.

The leader here is Sabella. Or maybe Nikolai, wherever he is.

And I'm increasingly certain that's not here.

But are there any other mages or weavers among the panicking crowds?

I don't know.

Sabella's are the only soul threads I see.

I weave another wall of reality in front of me again, to buy time to think.

And if we win today, do we really win?

The people are seeing a fight between weavers.

They're seeing my apprentice betray us.

They're seeing that weavers will all lose control, or betray us in the end.

Even my fighting now—it's desperate, and I don't know that it's enough to turn the fears.

And why?

Why would Sabella do this if she's not being controlled?

She's not nobility. Why would she be fighting on Nikolai's side?

Sabella shatters my wall of reality again.

"Morgan!" I shout. "Dagger!"

I hold out my hand to him, and he unsheathes his dagger from his belt and gives it to me.

I stride past the fallen glass, unweaving it into dust, my dagger in one hand, my other outstretched to unweave Sabella's attacks.

My energy is draining fast.

Then Sabella turns and hurls a spike past me.

I hear a cry, and whip around.

Morgan staggers, the spike jutting out from his shoulder in a crack in his armor.

No. *No.*

She does *not* get to hurt my people!

But before I can rush forward, before I can even think about gathering the courage to take her down, Sabella hurls her next attack at me.

And this time, it's her soul threads.

I shudder, stiffening, reaching for the slippery tendrils, unable to touch them.

I am failing. I am failing at everything I am.

I'm not the man I should be. I don't even have my illusion around me just now.

I'm not a protective father, I'm battling here, putting my child in danger.

And I sent Torovan into a danger that I should have faced.

I didn't even see my apprentice was working with my enemy, oh gods. I didn't see.

But Sabella is crying. Even through the rush of thoughts that I know aren't mine, I see tears streaming down her face.

Even as her face is contorted in rage.

Is there hope? Can I have any hope at all that she's not, in her heart, my enemy?

I take a step forward.

I am *not* a failure.

I am—

She bares her teeth and sends more threads at me. Shouting, screaming, pushing me back with the force of her fury.

I stumble, fall to one knee, and feel someone else beside me now—Reveyan, broken free with Sabella's concentration all on me now.

He starts to drag me backward on the cold stone floor, but I—I'm the one who takes my dagger and slashes his arm.

It startles me.

I didn't think. I didn't even think, and I stare at where my blade carved a deep furrow into his leather armor. Did it go all the way through, did it pierce his skin?

Reveyan stares, too, then looks up at me with burning eyes.

"She's turned the king! Sabella turned the king!"

Turned me, he means.

Sabella is controlling me.

I need to stop—gods. If she takes all that I am, if she takes all of my power, if she takes—

I open my mouth, then hunch down as I feel more of Sabella's threads worming into my soul.

I can't breathe.

I can't think.

Torovan!

He's not here.

And how am I this weak?

How could I face Nikolai before, but not face my apprentice now? Or his apprentice?

Sabella crouches in front of me, and no one is stopping her.

Reveyan is frozen again.

And I'm fighting—I'm fighting...what?

I have failed at everything entirely.

What is there left to fight?

I don't have the will to stand against our enemies.

Torovan didn't trust me, Sabella was plotting against me, my mother doesn't even trust in me, she wants to drag me home.

She'll certainly take me home now.

I can't pull myself around me, I can't have the body I need right now, I can't—

I need to—

I shut my eyes.

Breathing as Sabella's threads burrow deeper into my soul. Nearer and nearer to my child.

"Just give in!" Sabella screams.

But I listen to the symphony that is my soul. Like I did with Morgan.

Like I did with Sabella, even, before.

My symphony now is jagged, a hundred instruments out of tune. And they're all, they're *all* screaming.

And my child, those possibilities still safe inside me, will feel that screaming soon. Might be feeling it now.

My muscles tense in my strain.

And I react with everything left in my soul.

She will not take my child from me.

"Just give in, Caleb!"

And she will not turn me against those I love.

She can't use me like this.

I fold myself around my child, then pull *everything else* through the symphony I know I should be. Reweaving my body around my soul. Anchoring in my body. Shoving the threads of my soul back into their harmony.

Forcing Sabella *out*.

I blink, panting, my hand tight to my stomach. For a moment desperately searching the possibility within me, to know that it's still safe—but it is. The child is there. The child is well. The child isn't even disturbed, their own harmonies as steady as before.

I gasp out, a silent scream.

Then look up, my hazy vision resolving again into the world around me.

Sabella stares, tears tracking down her cheeks, her eyes wide. Then she scrambles back as I launch up, screaming. Forming a dagger of glass in my hand, slashing at her.

"You can't have me! You can't have my child!"

She freezes.

Goes completely still.

Stops fighting.

Reveyan and a bloody Morgan close in, Morgan holding his injured arm to his chest.

I weave a binding around Sabella, and now she does start, and tries to fight it, but her weaving can't cut through mine.

My will is stronger, centered as I am inside myself.

I wove myself. I wove my body.

I am *myself.*

I am myself, and the child is still fine.

More guards close in now, and with her hands bound, Sabella's attempts at weaving aren't nearly as effective. The soul threads lash out, but don't attach. The guards that the threads hit pause for a second, then shake them off.

I tighten my binding weave around her throat, watching dully until her eyes lock back on me and she stills. Her glaring eyes still streaming.

"Caleb!"

I shudder and turn to see Valtair. He's beside me now, gripping my arm.

"Can I—" he asks.

I know he wants to look within me, to see if I'm injured. If the child is okay.

Did he see what I did to reweave my body? But he'll be able to feel what I did.

I know the child is fine. I can feel the child is fine. But still my fear shoots up into my chest, blooming into heat.

"Yes, please," I say, but I clamp my jaw down on more. I won't ask him out loud, I won't expose him even in my fogged thoughts just now.

But he nods, and his eyes go distant as he senses with his elemental magic.

"We'll take her to the weaver's cells," I tell the guards, my throat tight and hoarse. I loosen my hold on Sabella's throat, but only just enough for her to breathe.

I have to follow them down to the cells. I could knock Sabella unconscious, but that's always risky, and I don't trust myself to handle that just now. But even still—even still, I want her awake. I want to know *why.*

Why would she do this?

I want to examine the threads of her mind and see if she's still being controlled.

I want to hope.

I still, even now, want to hope.

She begged me to give in like her own life depended on it. Like everything depended on it.

Valtair grips my arm more tightly. "You're fine. But you need to rest. And I need to know what you did. And we probably need the healers."

I look to him, fighting for breath. Then take in the chaos around us.

The guards have herded more than a handful of the conspirators together in one corner of the Great Hall. Now, they're holding them at sword point. And the doors are open —most of the courtiers have gone out.

"Your parents," I say with a start, turning back to Valtair. "Were they among the crowds, I didn't see them."

"No, they've been taking breakfast in their rooms, thank the gods."

I nod.

Have any of the conspirators escaped?

I feel the weight of the crown I'm still wearing. It hasn't fallen off.

I carefully adjust my spectacles, which did go askew.

And run my hand down my swollen belly. I'm not under any illusion now, though I'm fully Caleb. And showing as pregnant.

"Caleb," Valtair insists.

Torovan's still not here.

And in his absence, I'm still the king.

And even if I feel shocky, even if I don't have words right now, I have to say something. Have to show the people that they will be safe.

"My mother?" I ask Valtair.

But I spot her, standing behind the dais with Elsira.

Elsira, who's looking entirely stricken.

Had she helped in that fight? Had someone seen her?

I wet my dry lips. I have to tell the people that I will protect them.

But there are bodies on the floor.

This was not a full victory today.

Still, I call out, "People of Barella!"

And the guards, the courtiers yet in the hall, slow.

I flex my hands and realize I'm still holding the glass dagger. I drop it, unweaving it before it hits the stone floor. I'm almost waiting for the clatter that doesn't come.

Sabella isn't fighting her guards anymore. She's just watching me. Her whole body radiating anger.

I look up to the other waiting, expectant, scared faces.

"They didn't win," I say. And realize just how tired, how breathless I really am. "I'll protect you. I will *always* protect you."

Then, because I know I'll need to sit soon, or lie down, and the feeling is growing in urgency, I wave at the guards holding Sabella.

"Go!"

CHAPTER 45

HANDLE IT

CALEB

My willpower feels scraped raw, like I've been fighting for hours instead of minutes. The child shifts inside me, and I press one hand to my stomach, trying to steady myself.

And panic rises above the exhaustion.

Yes, I can feel the child is fine.

Valtair even confirmed everything's fine.

I know that. Their harmony feels in sync with mine. More in sync now that I've pulled my own harmony into tune.

But what did I actually do?

I feel the way my clothes brush against my skin as we walk down to the cells beneath the palace.

My body is definitely a man's. But where my child is, my body is still holding apart, holding my child safe. I will be able to bear this child. And birth them.

I probe the inner threads of my body, searching it all out. Until I look up at the guards' agitation ahead. Sabella is starting to fight them again. I gave her just enough room within the binding weave to walk, but she's straining at the binding again now.

I narrow my eyes and tighten my grip on the binding again, making it barely loose enough to breathe up top.

I'm still hovering between the rage of her betrayal, and my own private, desperate hope that it's not as bad as I think. That there's somehow a reason she'd do this to me. To all of us. To the kingdom.

Valtair is walking beside me, staying close. Somewhere in all of this, he holstered a dagger to his own belt and he's gripping the hilt with deadly intention if Sabella breaks free. If anyone else tries to attack us.

And will there be more attacks? Was this one wave among many?

I hear another sharp inhale ahead and expect to see Sabella causing more trouble, but it's Morgan, who'd stayed near Sabella. He drops back, a hand pressed to his shoulder. He stops to look at it.

His hand is covered in blood.

Gods, in everything that happened, I'd almost forgotten that Morgan was wounded.

I hold up a hand to stop the guards.

Valtair catches Morgan's arm, looks between his eyes. And Morgan, reluctantly, meets his.

Valtair half turns to me. "Are you all right to go ahead? I need to—"

"Yes. Handle it."

"Caleb, just secure her. Question her after you rest."

"I have to know if there will be more attacks—"

"Gods, Caleb. We're braced as well as we can be. I'll question her after I do this. You have to *rest*."

"She won't talk to you," I argue back, "but she might talk to me."

"We don't know anything right now," he says, probing at Morgan's would. "We can't assume anything."

And will Torovan come back to this mess? Will he search for Nikolai on the road and not find him, because Nikolai's still here, lying in wait for the next round?

Or did Torovan find him?

Was the trap that they both were a trap?

"You can't protect anyone if you pass out, Caleb," Valtair snaps. "Get her in the cells, rest. I'll find you when you wake. The faster you recover, the faster we're protected again."

Frustrated, I grip his arm and let go. I check the binding I'm still holding on Sabella. She's turned around ahead of us, she hasn't been watching, but I know she's been listening.

"Wake me if there's more trouble," I say.

"Yes. I will."

Reveyan drops back and gives me his arm.

I'm barely standing now, and struggling for breath.

Whatever I did, everything I did, it took all I had. And keeping Sabella secure now is taking more than I have.

I see Sabella into the cell, keep her bound with my weaving until her hands can be bound properly in tight iron mittens, a blindfold tied around her eyes, both of which are standard for weavers. The weaver's cell is isolated, the walls immensely thick, and one of the master elementalists has already been called down for the first watch. There will be no less than ten guards at any time.

The guards will have to feed her, give her drink. They'll probably wait until I wake again.

So even though I'm swaying, I say, "Give her water now."

I'm still holding my binding on her as one of the prison guards approaches, glances at me, then carefully tips a flask against Sabella's lips. She splutters but does manage to drink.

"Okay," I say. "I will come back. Wake me at any sign of trouble."

I think to stay a minute, to try and ask my questions, but I'm struggling to keep myself awake now.

So I carefully let my weaving binding on her go.

Sabella shudders, but she doesn't attack. She stumbles a step backward, until the back of her leg reaches the cot.

My hands twitch, and I know the precautions are dire. But she just tried to overthrow the kingdom.

To kill me, or take over my mind.

The cell is, at least, clean.

There's a cot in one corner, and a waste bucket with a lid.

There are no windows, but the barred window on the cell door, and the corridor beyond is torchlit.

I hesitate at the door, watching Sabella sit slowly on the cot, her bound hands awkwardly in front of her, looking exhausted.

And despite my own exhaustion, I ask, "Where is Nikolai?"

She looks up, but she can't see me through the blindfold. She might still sense the threads of me with her weaver's senses, though.

I tense.

But she says nothing.

And she doesn't try to weave.

"Is he in the palace? Is he here? Is he controlling you?"

She drops her chin again and scoots back on the cot to slump against the wall, her short hair falling over the blindfold.

I step away from the door and look at the guards. "I mean it, send for me the *moment* there's any sign of trouble."

"Yes, Sire."

Elsira catches me on the way back through the palace, trudging up toward my apartment.

"I'm sorry," she says, coming close, speaking low. "I'm sorry, I didn't help, I could have helped—"

I wrap my arm around her, as Torovan does, and she leans into me, just a moment.

"I froze up," she says, her voice tight with anger. Anger at herself. "I won't freeze again."

I'm tired enough that I hardly have the energy to muster up a response.

But I squeeze her shoulder as we enter the corridor for the royal apartments. "I have to rest. Hold down the kingdom? With Valtair? Until I'm up."

"I will," she says. She still looks like she wants to say more. Reprimand herself more, maybe.

"And if Torovan comes back while I'm—"

She huffs out, her gaze shifting from her own inner battle to take me in. "Yes, of course, I'll wake you."

But I see her concern now. I'm not sure she actually will.

But she leaves me to my rest.

The apartment I share with Torovan is silent, chilled.

I haven't seen Morgan or Valtair again, so it's Reveyan and Chiran who clear the space, then Reveyan who hesitates before helping me out of my coat.

"Your Majesty," he says. "Call with any need."

My mind is buzzing enough that I'm not sure I'll actually sleep, and it's still only morning. But I'm out before my head hits the pillow.

CHAPTER 46

SOMEONE TO STEADY US

CALEB

It's evening when I wake, only the afterglow of sunset coming from the windows.

I lay in bed a long, hazy moment, startled at the feel of my body. Stretching into it.

It's mine. My body is *mine*.

Can I weave myself back and forth between my realities now?

I don't know. I don't know exactly what I did.

I push up with a start, trying to blink myself awake. I wove my reality during the fight.

And now I'm remembering the reason I was sleeping during the day.

The rebellion. The...the coup.

I'm still dressed from this morning, if rumpled, but head out for the corridor anyway.

I find Morgan with three other guards outside the door to Torovan's study. He's changed into fresh clothes and armor, all signs of his injury gone.

"Torovan?" I ask.

"He hasn't returned yet," Morgan says. "Lord Valtair wants to see you when you wake. And the kitchen is only waiting, and they'll send up a meal."

I hesitate. Do I go see Valtair now? Or—or I should call him to me. Gods. Yes. I'm still the king.

But.

"I need to see Sabella."

Morgan looks to Reveyan, and they silently fall into step ahead of me, the other two behind.

Valtair will have to wait.

Sabella is lying on the cot in her cell when I arrive but sits up when she hears us.

I motion to the cell door, and the prison guards reluctantly open it.

I grab a wooden chair that's set outside and carry it in.

"Secure the door behind me."

"Sire." A small protest.

But the eyes of the guards are angry.

Their palace was attacked, too.

Their king.

And—gods, Valtair had said he'd try to talk to Sabella. Maybe I should have seen him first. A lot could have happened in the hours I was asleep.

"Has anyone else been here?" I ask. "Valtair?"

"He was here. The prisoner didn't talk."

Okay. Well. That answers that question.

Sabella is sitting at the edge of the cot, listening as I set down the chair and sit heavily.

I'm rested now, but my body feels like I've been running for hours.

My stomach growls.

But I need answers before I eat, I have to know. I have to know if Sabella was under Nikolai's control, if she still is.

There wasn't another attack in the palace, or my guards would have told me.

But will there be?

"I'm going to search your mind," I say.

She says nothing.

So I take a breath and carefully, from across the room, do my best to look.

It was much easier when I was touching her head before, but I still manage.

Then, after a few moments, pull back, letting the threads of her mind go. My heart sinking.

Nothing. No signs other than what I saw, and fixed, before. Unless I didn't fix it. Unless I only broke her more.

But, no, I can't think that.

I know it's not true.

What Sabella did in the Great Hall, that was all her.

"The letters," I say. "Were they sent by you? The weaving, in the nursery?"

She says nothing.

"Does he have something over you?"

Nothing.

"Is he going to meet Torovan, will Torovan find him? Or is Nikolai in the palace now?"

Nothing.

"Sabella, give me a reason to understand anything you've done! Please! You are—you were—my apprentice—"

She hunches. But still says nothing.

And she's not even braced.

She knows I'm not the kind of person to question someone with force. I had to check her mind for signs of control, yes, but that's the worst I'll do. That's the worst I'll let myself do.

And I know she's not the kind of person to give up who she's loyal to.

But I know now she's not loyal to me.

So I stand and carry out the chair.

I'll have to figure out what to do about her later.

Or, more likely, Torovan will.

No—no.

This one will be my decision. She's my apprentice.

Torovan will understand that need.

I might not question her with force, but she did attack the palace. Attack my people.

Attack me.

My throat tightens.

I carefully set the chair back in its place outside the cell. I wince as the door clangs shut, the guards locking it again.

"She's had food and water?" I ask quietly.

The guards don't look happy about giving it to her, especially having to work around her hands in the mitts, but they nod.

I rub my face, then head back up to find Valtair.

Who, a guard tells me when we reach the main floor again, is already waiting in Torovan's study.

But it's my mother who finds me on the way back to the stairs, and I know I can't fend her off forever.

I know that.

"Caleb," she says, looking me over with a critical eye. "I've sent back to Galenda for three of our weavers and three elementalists."

I breathe out. It's what she'd been talking about before Sabella's attack. "Who?"

She names some of the mages in Galenda's court that I know, one I grimace at, and a few I don't know.

But I nod.

Is this the right move? But we need help. And yes, I'm going to ask Valtair to call in the Barellan mages, too.

But will it all be too late? It will take almost two weeks for any mages from Galenda to arrive.

"They'll only be visiting the court, of course," my mother goes on, "to learn from its master mages. Purely an exchange of information."

She smiles tightly. And the one name I grimace at, a weaver who I swear illusions himself every day to be the most hand-some he can be, and uses that to *every* advantage, is not someone I'm looking forward to exchanging anything with.

But he is a good weaver. I've studied his public weavings and used some of his techniques in my own weaving.

And I can't afford right now, Barella can't afford right now, to turn away help.

My mother follows me into Torovan's study. I glance at her, but don't ask her to leave.

Valtair and I both grew up in palaces and around rulers, but neither of us were trained to be kings. And my mother might try to bend everything she does to benefit Galenda's interests, but she's ruled for half my lifetime. She does know how to handle a crisis.

And I *can't* afford to turn away help. No matter if that help is from my mother.

Valtair looks up from sorting a mountain of papers at the desk.

"Would you believe the nerve of sending a complaint about the safety of the court to a king who's already ridden out to defend it?" he asks, jabbing a finger at the offending letter.

But he rises, seeing my mother, and braces against the desk as he stands.

"Queen Sevine. Caleb. We've rounded up some of the conspirators, but at least five that we know of got away. I questioned Sabella—"

"I know," I say, "I just did as well. She said nothing. But I did check, and she's not under Nikolai's control."

Valtair frowns, but then sighs. "No other signs that we'll have another attack, or attempted coup, or whatever that was. One of the conspirators was killed by a guard. And there are injuries, some of them severe. But, no one else has died yet. There is that. I've been doing all I can to control the fallout, but many of our guests have left this afternoon." He glances to my mother. "Will you be leaving soon, Your Majesty?"

"No. I'm not in the habit of abandoning my allies when they have need." There's steel in my mother's voice. And she nods to me.

Valtair steps out from behind the desk and waves me to it, but I hold up my hands.

"I need to eat." My voice goes hoarse, and I cough to clear it.

Valtair crosses to the door and leans out, snapping to the guards to bring up a meal. He comes back a moment later.

Then he stands in the middle of the room, regarding me.

"We were attacked here, but not by Nikolai," he says.

And I know what he means. I thought about it before, before I had to rest.

"I didn't send riders after Torovan," he says.

And I slowly nod.

He made that choice while I slept, and if I hadn't slept, I might have been tempted to go myself, to ride hard after Torovan and the others, because I'd barely defeated Sabella on my own.

Barely.

But though the situation has changed, the level of threat hasn't. Sabella might be Nikolai's only apprentice, or accomplice, or whatever she is.

But the palace here is still under threat. And I can't leave.

Even if Torovan is still likely riding into a trap.

And can I say for certain anymore that Aria isn't with Nikolai, too, can I?

Can I assume anything to be true?

The doubt, the punishing doubt that chilled me during my fight with Sabella worms its way back in.

Because how did I not see this?

How did I not know?

I've seen Sabella every day for months.

And I shouldn't have slept after that battle. Not and left everything to Valtair.

But then, maybe that was best after all. I'm hardly fit to run an entire kingdom. I'm just a princess who became a king because I fell for a king, it's not anything I've actually been trained for. I'm a weaver. I'm a mage. I belong with my apprentices and in my studies, but I have *failed* at all of that.

I open my mouth. I'm going to step back as much as I can. Let Valtair run the kingdom.

"No," Valtair says, watching me. "You don't have the luxury of self-pity just now." His voice is hard and brittle, which isn't like him.

Then I realize he's saying it to himself as much as me.

He presses a hand to his forehead, bracing himself.

I can't set all of this on him. I can't.

"My father," he says. And *ah*, yes, that tone would have been Count Valtair's. "He was giving me advice this afternoon —he was upset that he wasn't there to help with that attack. Gods." He sighs. "His advice, though even he didn't like it, was to wait for Torovan to return. And I agree, I don't want to send word and distract Torovan's resolve, I know that's important to his willpower. So, we have to wait."

"The delegates," I say, moving reluctantly toward the desk. "Are they leaving, too?"

"Most of them. But the Akrean delegation hasn't made any move to leave yet. Whatever that means."

I doubt it means anything good.

"May I suggest," my mother says carefully, "that you not make any more public fanfare about this? Go to dinner tonight. Your guards will be on watch. The court that remains will need a show of normalcy now, more than anything." She eyes the weaver's medallion still resting over my heart. "Wear your medallion."

"Dinner..." Valtair says, looking at the slow glass on the side shelf. "I just sent to the kitchens. But a public dinner is still possible, I think. If the staff have finished, uh, cleaning the Great Hall. Kitchen staff has just been sending up meals as requested. But, like I said, many of the guests have left."

"But your court remains," my mother says. "And they are the ones you need to show loyalty to now." She looks up at me. "I have been fortunate not to have an attempt on my life as a queen. But I have prepared, of course, what I would do in that instance."

I nod.

And look down at the mess of papers on the desk. "Can the complaints wait?"

Valtair huffs a sigh and nods.

I hold out my arm. And Valtair, smiling a bit wistfully, takes it.

I think we both need someone to steady us just now.

Gods of everything, I want to go after Torovan. With all I am, I want to go after him.

It's dawning on me, with a creeping, bone-gnawing dread, that if I was almost not strong enough to defeat Sabella, if she made me turn on Reveyan, even, if she knows my weaknesses that well that she can so easily exploit them—how is Torovan supposed to stand against Nikolai at all?

Or was it because Sabella knows me so well that she could play so heavily on my guilt?

The palace is quiet, the few courtiers we come across subdued and nervous, as we make our way downstairs. We'll have to check on the staff, then see what can be done about a proper dinner. Something, like my mother said, to show we're carrying on.

And maybe we should have sent the guards or palace staff ahead to do this, but this feels important, too. Even if we're still not sure the palace is safe.

If there's another threat—I'm still the most potent defense we have.

We're nearing the Great Hall when a man strides toward me from the palace entrance, followed closely by two guards.

He's wearing the medallion of a court mage.

And his face is covered in blood.

CHAPTER 47

THE MESSENGER
CALEB

The man coming toward me has a cut on his forehead, one half of his face smeared with dried blood. But I know him. Oh, gods.

"Rani!" I rush toward him. My elementalist friend, who rode out with Torovan and the others. "Where is Torovan?"

Rani is shaking, very obviously exhausted, and Valtair swears, shifts to help catch him as his knees give.

I follow Rani down to the floor, the stone cold and unyielding. "Gods. What happened? You were attacked? By Nikolai?"

He's nodding. "He turned our own people against us, and the king." Rani looks up somewhere between Valtair and me, but he doesn't meet my eyes. "He told us to run."

My stomach goes to ice.

"And where is Torovan?"

Now he does look up. "We couldn't fight him, Caleb. We weren't strong enough. None of us were. He was inside our heads, gods, I threw fire at Drayan. I *burned* my best friend, and he—he—"

Rani shakes. But draws in a shuddering breath. "We had to get away so we didn't continue to attack. I rode ahead of the rest, my horse was faster, though it went lame before the gates, I'm sorry—"

"How many with you?" Valtair asks.

Rani focuses on him. "Eight. Me, two other elementalists, five soldiers. Most of us are wounded. They're not long behind me, maybe at the gates now."

I look up to one of the guards who came in with Rani. "Go. Look for the others." He hurries off.

"And Torovan?" I ask, clenching my hands together. I'm still kneeling on the floor, but I ache to launch up, grab my horse, and not stop until I find him.

"Nikolai has him. And the other young weaver, and Master Aldric, and—and if there was anyone else left alive—"

"And Aria?" I ask, forcing that out, forcing out any sentence that's not about Torovan. "Did you see her?"

"She was with him," Rani says darkly. "She was fighting *with* him." The look he sends to me is angry, accusing. Like this could have been avoided if I'd only gone with them.

Or maybe seen what was happening with Nikolai's influence before.

And maybe that's all true.

But, I know now that if I had ridden out with Torovan, the palace would have been lost.

And now—now I have a choice.

I rise, slowly, steadying on my mother as she gives me her hand up.

I meet her eyes.

She wanted me to go back to Galenda, will she stop me now?

Her eyes fall to my stomach.

And no, no I don't just have myself to think about.

But I have a whole kingdom to think about.

And I will not—I won't let Torovan stay in Nikolai's hands. I won't let him be controlled.

Will I be strong enough to stand against Nikolai on my own?

I barely defeated Sabella.

But...I did.

My body now is my own as Caleb, and I still am Caleb right now, not Irava. And I've already revealed my pregnancy to the court. I don't need an illusion. I can bring all I am to bear on this.

Everything. Everything, but what I need to give my child.

Who deserves safety, yes.

But who won't have that until Nikolai is a threat no more.

Valtair's mouth is pressed tight and grim. He knows what I'm thinking.

And what if I ride out, too, and there's yet another weaver ready to attack the palace?

I can't assume at all that Sabella was Nikolai's only apprentice.

I turn to Reveyan. "Go. Get Elsira. Meet us in the second room beside the Great Hall." Where Torovan hid the letters.

Because it's closer than Torovan's study or my study in the mage's quarters, and because I don't think Rani can take much more before he collapses entirely.

We make it to the meeting room where Rani slumps into a

chair. It's Valtair who eases the full story out of him, because Rani has decided he's done looking at me.

I understand why when he says that Drayan was killed in the attack. And I understand the anguish in his eyes. Drayan, an earth elementalist, was more than a friend to him. Maybe more than a crush. Even if, from every interaction I'd seen with them before, I don't think Drayan returned the same love.

"I don't know where Nikolai took them," Rani says finally, exhausted. "I don't know if they're all alive yet, those that were left. I don't know. But—I want to go back. I want to destroy that bastard weaver."

"That enemy of the king," Valtair corrects quietly. Rani stiffens. Bows his head.

And this is bad, if even Rani is repeating these prejudices against weavers.

"Forgive me," he says tightly. "But I want to go back with you."

We all jump as the door to the meeting room bangs open and Elsira hurries in.

"I want to go, too," she says. She's fastening an archery guard on her forearm. She has an unstrung bow already strapped to her back.

I stand. "Elsira. No. You have to hold the palace."

She's still fastening the guard.

"Caleb. I am going with you. I won't let Torovan—"

I move in front of her, brace her shoulders. "If we fail, Barella needs a queen."

Elsira stills. Her eyes are burning, and I know she wants to protest.

But she was raised the daughter of a queen, too.

And maybe I don't have the experience, or the training to rule, but I still understand necessity.

I glance up to my mother, I can't help it. She nods. But she doesn't say anything. She's here, but I have the dizzying sense that she's here to support me as a king in Barella, not try to command on her own just now.

Elsira closes her eyes.

"Gods, Caleb. Don't fail."

"I won't," I say. Though not with as much confidence as I'd like.

I turn to Valtair.

"Valtair—who can we spare?"

He starts ticking off the resources we have left. And it's not much. Rani fills in who he thinks from his party are well enough to return, and it's maybe half.

We have a few older master weavers.

We have my guards—Torovan left me the majority of the palace guards. But some of them must stay at the palace. We can't leave the palace entirely defenseless.

And we'll be leaving the palace without a weaver.

Gods.

We'll be leaving the palace with *Sabella* in a cell.

I think briefly, ruthlessly, if I should order her execution. Just to keep her from escaping and causing havoc. The weaver's cells hinder escape, yes, but a determined and strong weaver could get out.

And Sabella's not weak.

It's impossible to hold a weaver for long without another weaver to help confine them, or at least deter them from trying to escape. I sent down a master elementalist while I had to rest, but that was temporary, I was always going to have to keep an eye on Sabella.

But I almost throw up at the thought of execution.

No. No, I can't do that. I can't think about it.

I still can't look at her and not see my friend.

"We'll leave Master Gardin," I say. A water elementalist, but not an adept healer. But of the court mages that are here, he could deal with Sabella the fastest. And he's the most stubborn of the master mages. I can only hope that he wouldn't be controllable.

I have another thought. "Valtair—your father. We need people like your father to help guard Sabella. People who are least likely to be swayed."

Valtair snorts. "Yes, that would be him."

"I'll take my turn," my mother says, surprising me. She raises her brows at my look. "I can fight. I have learned that."

And if she is controlled?

But then, my mother is as stubborn as they come.

And I don't have many options.

"Okay," I say, a little shakily. "Find more to help. And leave the injured elementalists near the cell as well, where they can help if needed. I hate to do this, Valtair, but—"

He holds up his hands. "But we're at war."

"I'm taking Morgan, and Reveyan, and Chiran, and Islon." My four guards.

"Take the remaining soldiers of the garrison," Valtair says.

"No. You need them. And Valtair..." I meet his eyes. "The leaner we travel, I think, the better. I'm the one who needs to stop Nikolai. If I take as many as I can with me, he'll only turn them against me, and have more for me to fight—"

"That's true," Rani says. "Less will be more here." And he shifts, like he's not even sure he should go. "But I want to—"

"Yes, you're going," I say. And he nods.

"Gods," Valtair says. "Fine. Will you ride out in the morning?"

"Now," I say. "Tonight."

And I start for the door, my focus narrowing to a single, burning point.

Find Torovan.

And defeat Nikolai.

Whatever that means. Whatever it takes.

"Caleb—" Valtair heads after me. Catches my arm to stop me.

He lowers his voice. "No, there was nothing wrong with the child. But I know your energy isn't fully back. I know what this morning took out of you."

He hesitates. And I know he's going to offer to give me his strength. Like he did that day when Torovan and I wove the vortex.

I grip his arm back. "No."

His whole body is taut, poised, his fingers digging into my arm.

But finally, he takes a step back.

"Both of you come home," he says. "I'll go and start the arrangements. Caleb—"

He bites his lip.

And I wrap him in the tightest hug I can manage.

He crushes me back.

"Both of you come home," he says again. Then lets me go and strides away.

Chapter 48

The Room
Torovan

I've been laying on this bed for what must be hours, staring up at the ceiling of rough-hewn planks, trying to think through how to get out of this disaster.

The room they've put me in is comfortable enough. Better than a dungeon cell, certainly. There's a bed with clean linens, a washbasin with fresh water—there's even a change of well-made clothes folded on the single chair, though I doubt it would fit me well. The windows are too narrow for escape, set high in the thick stone walls, but they let in enough light to tell me it's afternoon now.

Maybe I should be grateful that Nikolai's people aren't trying to beat me, or starve me.

But it feels like a cell would be more...clear.

I'm not sure what Nikolai wants with me. He hasn't tried to control me again, that I know of.

He said on the road that he just wanted to talk. That my family would be safe if we talked. But then his people brought me here, and he hasn't come. Or brought me to him. Nothing else has happened, and it's starting to drive me mad.

I don't know what he's done to my people, to the elementalists, to my guards. To Aldric.

I don't know how many got away.

And I don't know what he's already done to my mind. I don't know if I'm already doing what he wants. By not—by not what, not pounding on the door, not screaming at him? Not demanding the answers I need?

Well, I did that at first. I screamed until my voice ran hoarse. I hollered. I threatened. But no one came.

I try to run through my mind how I felt the first time he tried to control me in the Council Chamber, and how I felt afterward. And compare that to when he had his soul weaving in my mind on the road, and now.

I felt the difference on the road, yes. I knew his soul weaving threads were in my mind.

But right now, I can't feel anything different.

Has he gotten good enough that I wouldn't feel it if he didn't want me to?

That first time, in the Council Chamber, I hadn't known he was controlling me at first. I'd felt rage, yes. So much rage. But then, my life had been built around rage.

This time, his lever is my guilt.

And I still feel that in waves so intense it's painful.

Whatever else I am now, I know I'm also bait to draw in Caleb.

And that is my worst fear.

That Caleb will come.

That if I'm locked in this room, he'll be alone in facing

Nikolai, or maybe he will have Sabella with him. But will even that be enough?

How do we fight an enemy who uses our very souls against us?

And—and I don't want Caleb to see me like this.

I'm disheveled but not injured.

But I'm in a cage.

I can't leave this room—I did test the lock.

And I know that Caleb can get through locks with his weaving, but I've been too busy to ask him to show me how. Why would a king need to unlock the doors in his own palace?

And suddenly, I am tired of laying down, tired of inaction, tired of the walls of this room, tired of the gnawing fear.

I sit up and swing my legs over the edge of the bed, running my hands through my hair. My fingers catch on tangles.

Which for a moment feels like the straw that will break me. Of all things, my snarled hair.

What would Caleb think of me now? A king who can't defend his kingdom, who went down on his knees on the road, who can't get out of a locked room with all the magic at his command, who is brought low by the lack of a *fucking hairbrush.*

I squeeze my eyes shut, just breathing.

And if Caleb comes here, the palace will be without a weaver.

Will Nikolai wait until Caleb's here, then ride back to take the palace?

That thought consumes me for moments in a trembling, vicious fury.

And I realize I'm losing hope that Caleb can defeat Nikolai at all.

He'll either be locked here with me, or worse, probably in a weaver's cell. Or...dead.

No. That can't happen.

That *can't* happen.

I won't let it. Somehow. I will find a way to protect him, somehow.

But that Nikolai hasn't put me in a weaver's cell tells me how little of a threat he thinks I am to him.

And I sit, exhausted, in the utter ruins of my failure. As a husband. And as a king.

Until I can't stand myself anymore, and get up.

Because I'm not going to gain the willpower to get out of this by telling myself I can't.

I have to focus on what I can control.

I pull to me every lesson Caleb's ever given me on focusing my willpower.

And I move to the center of the small room, raising my hands the way Caleb taught me. I close my eyes and reach for the threads of reality, feeling for that familiar sense of possibility, of potential waiting to be shaped.

I start with something simple—a small falcon construct, which has become easy and familiar.

The falcon takes shape slowly, my willpower threading through reality to give it form and flight. It's less sure than I usually can manage, and clumsy compared to anything Caleb could make, but it holds together. The falcon circles the room once before I let it dissolve back into nothingness.

It's something. It's a weaving that I can do. And it's better than laying here doing nothing.

But it's not good enough. Not nearly good enough to face Nikolai.

I can't defeat him with semi-illusory birds.

I try again, this time attempting the blades of reality that I tried to hurl at Nikolai on the road.

But the weaves almost fall apart in my hands, and I have to scramble to keep them steady.

I manage, but I end up panting in the middle of the room, my brow prickling with a cold sweat.

I don't have the concentration just now, consumed as I am with everything else.

But I won't do Caleb any good if I blow myself up.

And then I spend a solid few minutes wondering if I *could* blow myself up, if Nikolai's near me. If that's a last resort solution.

Could I give my life to save my husband's?

To be able to save Caleb, at least, from whatever Nikolai has planned.

But that's a terrible idea.

Even if I'd defeat Nikolai, there's still my mother to deal with, too.

And if Caleb is the best defense this kingdom has against Nikolai, I'm still the shield it needs against my mother.

I close my eyes, trying to steady my ragged breathing.

And then try again.

This time, I manage to weave the blades of reality into existence without my weaving falling apart. But it's too much to hold yet, and I quickly unweave them.

And that's the problem, I haven't practiced as much as I should. I've been able to act instinctively, out of surprise, but deliberately controlling anything is hard. Controlling it while my will is weighted with my fear feels impossible.

I'm like Caleb's apprentices, all with their weaknesses. Aria with her lack of control, or Kian rushing headlong into a battle he hasn't assessed yet.

My weakness? I've been too busy to train.

But—but I've also been avoiding Caleb these last months, as he's been avoiding me. If I'm being honest with myself.

I don't like to see him folding in on himself, and I haven't known how to help him.

Maybe I can't help. Maybe we just have to wait these months of his pregnancy out.

Just wait.

And maybe I've been too patient, maybe I haven't shown him I desired him enough when he's Caleb. I don't care what shape his body is beneath his illusion, I just want *him*.

But he cares what shape his body is in.

And I don't know enough to help him fix that.

I can turn the direction of a kingdom, but I can't help my husband feel comfortable in his body.

And I'm part of the reason he feels that way. I shouldn't have agreed to try for a child, for him to carry that child, even if it was something I wanted, too.

But then, that was also his choice. Should I have tried to take that from him?

I bare my teeth and weave the blades of hardened reality again.

How did Caleb get so powerful? Is it just raw talent, or something more?

Can I somehow increase my power now? Can I focus my will? Can I find a way past the fear?

Caleb defeated Nikolai before by laying out a truth that no one was expecting, a truth that Nikolai couldn't subvert and twist.

But where can I find that within me?

I've never not been who I am.

I was a prince, my father's heir, and now I'm a king.

I'm a weaver, yes, and I'm a court mage.

I...I am not my mother's son.

I am Caleb's and Irava's husband.

I will be the father of our child.

What among these truths can I embrace more of?

I'm already all of these things.

And I can't let Nikolai take them from me. I must find a way. I have to defeat him, before Caleb comes. Before Nikolai has a way to control both of us without his threads, threatening us with each other.

Because that's the pit that's been yawning within me.

That's what he did with his letters. With his threats in the crib.

I'm not sure that I could stand against that kind of threat again.

The door opens with a soft creak.

CHAPTER 49

STRENGTH OF WILL

TOROVAN

I drop my hands and spin to face the door, tensing for a fight.

Nikolai's slipping in, like he interrupted something sacred, and I feel my face burn knowing that he saw my weaving.

He grins. Like we're friends.

He did tell me he just wanted to talk, but—of course I can't believe that.

This is the man who killed my father, and tried to control me. Who just tried again this morning.

He's cleaned up since our battle. His brown hair is neatly combed, his clothes fine but not court wear, the sort of thing a high noble's son might wear to an informal dinner. He looks younger than I remember, almost boyish, though I know we're of a similar age. And that look of innocence somehow makes it all worse.

"Torovan. Don't let me interrupt you."

I watch him warily. "I'm done."

He shrugs, sauntering toward the cabinet along one wall. I checked the drawers—they're full of blankets that smell like they've been in storage for years.

Well. At least I won't freeze to death in this room without a fireplace.

"I hope you've found the accommodations acceptable," Nikolai says.

What game is this?

I track him around the room, every muscle in my body ready to spring.

His smile widens. "I just want to talk. Remember?"

"Then—" I spread my hands. I don't know how to play this. I don't know what he wants. "If you wanted to talk, why did you threaten my husband?"

He shrugs. "To get your attention. I did."

He's acting casual, but I'm noticing the little signs of tension in his stroll around the room. The stiff way he holds his neck. The restless movements of his hands on every object he comes across.

Is he weaving?

But I don't see it if he is.

He's trying to play his head games again, even if it isn't weaving.

Nikolai turns to face me, looking between my eyes. Like he's searching for an answer I haven't yet given him.

"You were in my apartment," I say.

He smiles. "Was I?"

"You left a letter threatening my *child*, Nikolai, you just turned my forces against me on the road. Why the *hell* would I have anything to say to you—"

"Ask me what I want."

I splutter, shaking my head.

"I want your kingdom," he goes on, not waiting for me to ask. And his smile widens.

"You can't have my kingdom!"

My fingers twitch. Do I even dare to think I can form my blades again now, with my hands down, when I was struggling to before?

And he just came out and *said* it. He's not even denying it. He wants my kingdom for himself.

My hands twitch again, but then I can't move them. And I see Nikolai's weaves now binding them. Holding my hands to my sides. Holding my fingers tight together.

Nikolai's grin widens into the viciousness I remember. He's done playing whatever game he started here. "I thought once I might catch your eye. Be your king."

Caleb told me he saw that, though I only had eyes for him.

"Two powerful weavers, ruling the kingdom together," he goes on.

I try to probe at the weaves on my hands with my mind. But I need my hands to pick the threads apart.

A chill is slowly creeping up my spine, and with it, the rising, relentless, panic.

"Is that why you tried to kill Caleb?" I ask. Something, anything, to interrupt the rising panic.

He shrugs.

And he's not answering my questions, while I fear I'm very much answering his.

I need to hold myself together.

But this man—this man holds me between rage and terror. And he knows it.

He's using that to his utmost.

"Caleb has his purpose," Nikolai says.

"And what is that purpose to you?"

He stops in front of me, facing me. "I have decided that the path to power is not to control you. It's to control those you love."

And that I've already figured out.

I am barely restraining myself from lunging at him. Even if I know I can't move my hands. Even if the weavings binding my hands to my sides will probably make me fall. It would be *something*.

Nikolai's not afraid of me.

He knows he can best me in a fight between just him and me. That is achingly obvious.

"You're still working for my mother," I say instead, watching his face.

Another shrug.

He steps closer still. And I can smell cloves on his breath. Bitter wine.

"I'm going to raise your child."

My throat closes. "What?"

He nods as if we're discussing the weather. "It's not uncommon for noble households to foster children for alliances. Like your marriage. It's political. This is what's going to happen, Torovan. You foster your heir with me. I will care for that child as my own. See? Your family will be safe."

The casual way he says it, the friendly tone, makes it somehow worse than if he's screaming threats.

I lunge for his throat, in my mind.

But in reality, I sway, then start to fall as he locks my legs together, too.

I crash onto the hard floor on my shoulder, the same shoulder I bruised in the fight on the road.

I clench my teeth to stop a cry but can't stop the pitiful half-moan that escapes.

"Allies don't attack each other," Nikolai says, stepping casually back before he releases me, struggling and trembling on the floor.

I *must* increase my strength.

This monster is not going to raise my child.

He will *not* raise my child.

I roll, and with my hands now free, weave my blades in the air, pushing hard for his throat.

But Nikolai flicks up a hand and weaves hardened air in front of him. My blades shatter against it.

And he smiles.

"Aren't you going to ask how I learned about the child?"

"You must have seen it," I growl, shoving up. My hands tightening back into fists.

"I haven't been in your palace since I left. Your weaver's apprentices are loyal to me."

I swallow.

Does he mean Aria? But he said *apprentices*, plural.

No, he's trying to get into my head again.

I face him, tensed for him to retaliate against me, because he hasn't yet. He's only restrained me.

And I wrack my thoughts for what I can do to attack him right now. To attack him *effectively*.

But what if what he said is true?

What if it wasn't just Aria who betrayed us, but Kian, too, or Sabella?

What if it's one of my guards?

What if it's Elsira, or Valtair?

Gods, no. How can I even think that?

What if he got to them? What if he got to *any* of them?

I know how desperate I've been with his letters, and that threat hanging over Caleb.

What if I wasn't the only one he sent his threats to?

Fear is paralyzing my soul again. And I think he must have done something to me, to make that fear rise up so sharply.

Or maybe, that fear's been there all along.

My mother, after all, murdered my father.

By the hands and will of *this man*. Who says he's going to raise my child. Not asking, *telling*.

And can I stop him? Is Caleb on the way even now, coming straight into this trap?

Nikolai's too strong. He's just too strong.

And now I'm struggling to breathe.

I close my eyes, which is desperation enough with my enemy in front of me, and shake my head.

No. No, I won't let him in my head like this.

No! He can't have the strength of my will, either.

And holding out against him isn't giving in to fear.

"Consider it," Nikolai says, moving toward the door. "I'm sure your husband will see the wisdom in it. What parent wouldn't want their child raised with every advantage? And I do have so much to offer."

The door bangs shut behind him before I can call him every name rising up within in me.

And I'm too proud to shout them at a closed door.

I hear the lock—no, *locks*—click and slide shut again.

Then I sink back onto the bed, my legs unsteady. My hands are shaking now, and I lock them between my knees.

He wants our child. Not just to hurt us, not just as leverage —he wants to raise our child as his own heir, his tool, his weapon.

Is this how my mother takes back the kingdom?

How long will it take, again, for Nikolai to control me and make me a puppet?

How long will Caleb truly last?

How many hearts will Nikolai poison?

He's not saying he'll raise my child in the palace. So does he want to gather his own court, to move the center of power in Barella from the palace to his own estate?

I don't know his plans. But all the horrible implications of them rattle out through my mind.

Our child, growing up with *him* as a parent. Being taught to hate us.

Being taught to control us.

Growing up believing that power comes through control and cruelty. Learning to weave reality to break others instead of protect them.

That, I resolve with everything I have left, will never happen.

Never.

Not stopping Nikolai is not an option.

Not being stronger than him is not an option.

I stand again, more steadily this time, and close my eyes.

I know who I am. I've always known that.

But I have my wounds.

I have my scars.

And I know the man, and the woman, who's helped start to heal them. Who's held me tightly when I start shaking, thinking about my mother. About my father.

I know the man who's patiently—mostly—showed me that I do have the willpower to be a weaver.

Who's taught me.

Who's loved me, despite my temper, despite my flaws.

Who came to expose me in the rumors he thought were true, but instead saved me.

When he comes—and he will come—I will be ready.

When he fights Nikolai, I will be with him. I will match his strength.

And we'll weave the storm together, side by side, strength by strength.

This storm will not overtake my kingdom again.

I raise my hands again, and this time when I reach for the threads of reality, they come to me more easily.

They must.

Because not growing stronger is not an option.

If weaving is rooted in my will, then my will itself will grow stronger.

Maybe I don't have to know how to grow stronger, just will that I do.

I weave the falcon again, my starting point, and it's larger, the detail sharper, its wings cutting through the air with precision.

But that's hardly enough. I need more than illusions.

I weave the blades of reality again, forming them in the air in front of me, pouring everything I have into them.

The blades glint in the air, and I move them slowly to my control.

And it's working.

I sharpen them with my will. I guide them toward the

hutch, and carefully carve down the point of one edge, making it into a bevel.

A thin slice of wood falls to the floor.

But it's not enough. I know it's not yet.

So I'll practice until the light from the window fades.

If I don't already know the weaving methods I'll need, I'll find them.

I'll *invent* them.

I'll practice until my hands are cramped and numb. Until my mind is strained to its utmost.

All I have, for my husband, and my child, and my kingdom.

Caleb once gave everything he had to me.

Now, I will give everything I am to him.

All of it.

And maybe, this time, I will be my king's weaver.

Chapter 50

ARMOR

Caleb

My armor does not fit.

I can wear the shoulder and arm pieces, the legs, but my torso will be unprotected.

Morgan, who's followed me into the king's personal armory, frowns.

So I weave the piece myself. Weave it into a reality where it does fit my shape.

Morgan carefully sets the original piece back down.

"I'll teach you weaving along the way," I say, and head for the door again. The palace staff should have the preparations in motion by now, provisions and horses should almost be ready.

"Now?" Morgan asks, almost a protest. "Shouldn't you spend your time—"

"Increasing my chances of winning?" I ask, and give him a look.

"But, I can't become a weaver in a day—"

I think he might be able to. To a low degree, with no precision. But I saw how he acted during our fight. He was very much the master of himself in that intense situation.

"We'll see."

I stride out, feeling weighted down in my armor, but it's a step toward rescuing Torovan.

I have to get to him. He's alive.

I know he's alive.

Though we're not physically close, I can still feel the resonance between us. And he never has been this distant from me, but I feel it all the same.

Faint, very faint, but there.

Whatever has happened, I can bring him back.

But as I'm sensing that, walking down the corridor toward the palace entrance, I feel something else probing at my senses.

Something that's not me.

I stop. It's a slippery tendril of soul magic.

Coming from the direction of the dungeons.

Shit.

I hurry that way instead. My armor, which I'm not used to at all, weighing me down.

It's more lightweight than Torovan's, and I have more physical strength now in my body as Caleb, gods, but I was only here a month to practice with this armor before I became pregnant. I've barely been practicing since.

"It's Sabella," I say to Morgan, forging through anyway, and he signals in more guards to follow us.

"Is she escaping?" Morgan asks.

I narrow my eyes.

I still feel Sabella's threads reaching out toward me. But she's not trying to manipulate my mind, I can feel that. Just trying to get my attention.

Well, she has it.

"I don't think so."

I find Sabella standing near the middle of her cell, arms still locked together, hands in the mitts, still blindfolded. But there's hardly anything in the cell she can trip on.

She turns toward me when she hears us, and I can't come quietly wearing this much armor. I can see through the barred window in the door, and she can clearly hear me.

"Caleb," she says.

One of the guards rattles the locked wooden door.

"You will address your king as—"

I hold up a hand. "What do you want, Sabella?"

She comes closer to the door, and the guards take up a ready stance.

And I ready my weaving. To bind her quickly if she tries anything.

"You would do anything for your child?" Sabella asks. Her voice is cracked and thready.

She withdraws her weaving from me. And I don't see any more threads coming out of her now, soul weaving or otherwise.

"Anything," I say, glaring at her. Because she attacked me. She attacked me *and* my child.

"You have shut off a part of yourself for months for your child. Just for the *possibility* of your child."

That's not the conversation I want to have right now, or have here. Or ever have with her.

I have to save Torovan. Is she trying to stall me?

She's standing right at the window in the cell door.

I stare at her, my hackles all the way up, wondering what mind game this will ultimately be.

I open my mouth to say I'm done here.

But then she chokes. Folds forward, leaning against the bars.

"He has my son."

My stomach drops. "What?"

"He has my *son*, Caleb."

And I understand. She's asking me if I'd do anything for my child?

Because she'd do anything for hers.

Oh, gods. *Gods.*

And she already has.

This wasn't control by Nikolai through soul weaving. But through family.

"Let me into the cell," I say, and step aside as the guards unlock it.

Sabella is close to the door, but she doesn't move until I nudge her back so I can enter.

"Nikolai was never in the palace," she says quickly, "he was in the town. For months. He comes and goes. He taught me over months."

Close enough to influence. Not close enough for me to find him or notice what was going on—I so rarely go to the town myself. And I had no reason, I thought, to stretch my weaver's senses that far.

"He's had my son for months," she says. "Since—since you offered to make me your apprentice."

Gods of all the seasons.

I squeeze my hands together. This was something else I hadn't seen.

"Take me with you, Caleb."

I swallow hard.

I can still feel the echo of her soul threads burrowing into my mind this morning. I can still feel myself slashing at Reveyan.

And see the rage in the eyes of those she was stoking into violence.

Sabella stands steadily. "He will always hold my family over me, and yours over you. Take me with you, and we will stop him."

But she attacked me. She attacked the palace, she was behind an attempted coup.

"Sabella—"

She stiffens. "I won't apologize for doing what I had to do to save my son."

She had been crying during that attack.

She'd begged me to give in to her.

Gods, she'd begged me before her weaving reached my child.

She'd *begged*.

"If you want me to apologize," she says, "you won't have my willpower. You can't. You *know*, Caleb. You know the needs of a mother. Of a father."

Her son is the source of her formidable will, she means.

And I can't separate her from that.

Not and ask her to fight with me.

I can't trust her, I know I can't.

But maybe I can trust her to save her son.

And I am running very low on resources and options.

"Sire," Morgan says from the door's window. A warning. His own plea.

Valtair had healed his injury this morning, an injury that she inflicted.

Sabella lifts up her chin. "So weave my mind. Know that I won't turn against you. You have my permission. Weave my mind, Caleb."

I take a step back. "I'm not a soul weaver."

"You are," she says, with a bitter laugh. "You wove my mind before. You can do it again."

"But that was with your permission."

But...she's giving permission now.

And was it soul weaving?

I'd pulled her back to herself, not pushed her away from it.

Is there more than one side to soul weaving?

"No," I say. "That's not—I can't do that."

"Sire!" Morgan says, more urgently.

He knows I'm leaning toward trusting her this far. Despite the risks. Because I need to defeat Nikolai. And I have to make this call, and make it soon.

But...but if Nikolai has her son with him, and threatens her son again, visibly, Sabella will turn on me.

I know it as surely as I know I'll have to stop her again. And this time, I might not be able to keep her alive.

Not in that desperate of a fight.

I bite my lip, thinking hard.

Then exhale sharply as an idea, an absolutely crazy idea, comes to me.

"Stay here," I say to Sabella.

She makes an exasperated sound. Because where else would she go, already in this cell?

"Whatever else, Sabella, we will get your son," I say. Which is probably more promise than I can give.

And she slumps, even while her body stays tense. "Take me with you, Caleb—"

"Stay," I say, and stride out. "Morgan—can you run ahead, I want to see the Akrean delegate, Lady Denya."

He gives me a look but takes off at a sprint.

"Reveyan. Get Valtair. Meet me in the same meeting room as earlier."

He sprints off, too.

And I'm left with Chiran and Islon, who press closer as I make my way up toward the meeting room.

Each step growing heavier.

Gods. And I can't handle this, I can't ride out like this, weighed down with so much steel.

I start to unbuckle my armor.

"Sire," Chiran protests. "You will need—

"I have to be able to breathe, and move, and not grow tired just walking." I turn to look at him, at his handsome, gray-stubbled face. "My weapons are my mind and my soul. My armor is my weaving."

Which is also probably more than I can promise.

But it's what I have.

He doesn't look happy about it, but he takes the pieces of armor as I unbuckle them clumsily and hand them over.

I have half of them off by the time I reach the meeting room.

I see Morgan approaching with Lady Denya. And Valtair hurrying toward me from the other direction.

Valtair looks me over, half out of my armor, with my padded garments beneath.

I wave them inside the room and wait until the door is shut.

"I'm leaving Sabella here," I say. "At the palace."

"Yes," Valtair says, watching me closely, because he knows there's a catch somewhere. "We already talked about that—"

"I'm leaving her free." I turn to Lady Denya before I see his protest. "Nikolai Metrial has her child. Sabella is behind the threats we've had in the last week, at least, behind placing them here if nothing else. I want you, please, to watch her. She is a soul weaver, you saw that."

Denya's mouth thins. "I won't directly get involved in the politics of the Barellan court—"

"And if this keeps Barella from falling to Nikolai Metrial, which is one step closer to Barella falling to the Dowager Zinara, too? If Zinara takes Barella, how long do you think it will take her to bring Akreal into her power, too? With the steps she's already taken?"

Denya glares at me. But she drums her fingers on her thigh, looks to Valtair, back to me.

"I felt her strength, your apprentice. It isn't small. But I do believe I can subdue her, if needed. Or at least slow her down. Yes, I do have that experience, as I said, with dark weavers."

"With all my respect, Lady Denya," Valtair says tightly, "Caleb—you want to leave the palace in the hands of a soul weaver who already just tried to take it over, and another weaver who belongs to a rival court?"

"You'll be here," I say. "And Elsira. And Sabella—she knows I'm going to get her son as well, I'm going to try my utmost. She won't endanger that."

I don't know that for certain, I can't know that. But I have to trust that far.

I have to know this palace is safe, too.

"You have my word," Lady Denya says, "on my life and on my god's favor, with all my respect, Lord Valtair, that I am not interested in taking your palace." She touches a pin on her collar, what's probably an Akrean religious symbol.

He nods in acknowledgement, but he's not happy. I know he's not happy.

"Take every precaution you need," I say to Valtair. "But truly, are we safer than with her locked in a cell, thinking her son is in danger now that she's out of play and out of use to Nikolai? Or knowing that her helping now is helping protect her son as well."

"Gods." Valtair rubs at his eyes. But then rolls his shoulders, straightens. "All right. Go—go bring Torovan back, all our people, and Sabella's son. And drive that fucking *monster* into the ground."

"I will."

And that...that is a promise that I can keep.

Will keep.

I finish unfastening the rest of the armor, Islon moving in to speed it up, making another growing pile on the floor. Valtair only eyes it as I head off again.

Back down to Sabella. Because I have to, at this last moment, be sure. And know that she's sure of my loyalty, too.

I approach the cell door again, and she's right there, still waiting.

"Sabella."

She straightens. "Your Majesty."

It hurts, that title. It hurts because I know she never wanted to turn against me. It hurts because I know she did anyway. And didn't trust me enough to help her.

But then, Torovan hadn't, either.

And that's Nikolai's poison.

Making people doubt everyone around them.

And most of all, doubt themselves.

Like I've been doubting myself, too. Doubting Torovan. Doubting my apprentices—and there, I had reason.

I press my hand to my stomach, a reassurance to me, to my child.

Because I know I'm not going to win against Nikolai in my doubts. I can't.

"Open the door," I say.

The guards are reluctant, but Morgan, who was in the meeting room and heard our conversation just now, moves around me.

He opens the door, and Sabella, hesitantly, still blindfolded and bound, steps out.

Morgan looks to me, then grabs the keys from a guard and releases the mitts on her hands and the iron on her wrists. He unties the blindfold.

And I almost hold my breath for an attack, biting my lip, watching for any signs of weaving against Morgan or anyone else. Hoping I'll be able to stop it in time.

But Sabella just stands there, her eyes welling. "You're taking me with you?"

"No. Sabella, I can't. You know I can't. He'll try to use you against me again. I'm leaving the palace in your care. And you have my word, my utmost, all that I am, Sabella, you understand me? I will do everything I can to bring your son back to you." I press my hands to my stomach. "I do understand. You have my word."

She squeezes her eyes shut. "But—"

"But I can't face Nikolai knowing the palace is still under threat. And I can't face him with you, knowing he'll use your son against you again." I hesitate. "Do you know if he has other apprentices?"

She shakes her head. "I don't—I don't know."

"Then I trust you. Hold the palace safe. I'll bring back my husband and bring back your son."

Her jaw is still locked, her eyes growing harder. Like she'll just follow us anyway.

I step toward her, hold out my hands. Despite Morgan's flinch.

Sabella takes them.

Like she didn't try to take the palace this morning.

Like she didn't try to kill me.

Well. But she didn't want to.

"Trust me, Sabella. If you go with me, it lessens all of our chances. You know that, don't you?"

"But you can weave me—"

"I'm not going to weave you against your will. Or, even if you say I can, weave you against your own mind. You said I can't ask you to apologize and still be effective? I can't weave you against your own symphony and think you'll be effective, either. If you're not in your own truth, Nikolai would still turn you against me, even not knowing who you are. Because you wouldn't know who you are, either. You wouldn't be able to stand against him at all."

She shakes with her sob, her hands tightening on mine. A shaky inhale.

She knows this is true.

Better than anyone, she has woven souls against their will. She knows the doubts that bring people down.

She knows the doubts she used to fell me.

She meets my eyes. And she knows what she did. She said she wouldn't apologize for wanting to save her son.

I won't ask her to.

This isn't freedom—she knows that, too.

But it's a step.

"I will hold the palace safe," she says. "On my son's life. For your return."

I nod.

"Bring him—" She swallows, her eyes starting to burn again. "Bring him back to me."

I press one hand to my stomach.

And nod again, holding her eyes until she lets go.

CHAPTER 51

TRAINING

IRAVA/CALEB

I'm Irava right now, but my body is still Caleb's. My legs, unused to a long ride, near shaking on my horse.

I might hold an illusion of being myself as Irava, but I want all of my senses with me right now, all of my concentration if I need it. And I haven't worked up the courage yet to try to unweave my reality as Caleb back into Irava. I think I can do it—no, I know I can. My body and my soul know the way.

But there's a part of me that's terrified I won't be able to come back to my body now. Not after being apart from it for so long.

And...these last months, I've been Caleb more often than I've been Irava.

So.

At least I shed the plate armor. That, at least, isn't weighing me down, though Morgan managed to talk me into wearing some of the guards' leather armor they wear within the palace. Which is at least some protection. Still more than I want, but much, *much* less heavy.

My eyes stay locked on the road ahead.

I will find Torovan.

I will defeat Nikolai.

And I will bring my husband home.

The night before, we rode into the evening, then lit the road with one of Rani's flares and rode partly through the night, only camping when the horses needed rest and we all were exhausted.

Today, we're headed again toward Nikolai's estates, Rani taking us on the same path Torovan took before. But I don't think Torovan is at Nikolai's estates. That's too far.

I've been watching the resonance between us grow stronger the longer we're on the road, so he's not still traveling.

I have to hope, when we reach the end of Rani's guidance on the road, that I can find Torovan by our resonance, too. I can vaguely feel the direction now, and we're still headed the right way.

But though I'm straining this morning, sore from the ride, and hardly with enough rest, I can't slow us down. I can't.

Morgan rides beside me. And to keep my mind from worrying about Torovan, and about Sabella being with Valtair and Elsira and my mother back at the palace, I've been teaching Morgan the basics of how to weave.

"No, you have to sense for the threads of reality around you," I say. "It's like…it's like relaxing. With intent. Don't grab them, let them flow to your will."

Morgan's face is tight with concentration beneath his helmet. And I know he wants this badly. And I know he can get it, I know he can.

But we're trying to condense weeks of study and careful practice into a few hours.

"Like this?" He extends his hand, and I feel the faint stirring of power as he tries to touch the threads of reality around him.

"Yes. Yes! Now pull the threads, coax them into the shape that you want. Something simple, like a pebble in your hand."

I watch, grinning, as a construct of a lopsided pebble weaves into existence in his palm.

"Ah!" he says, like he's shocked it even happened. He holds up his hand, his eyes wide. "Ah, Caleb—"

"I see it! Yes!"

And it's a small point of joy, watching a new weaver start to come into his own.

The sun is high overhead when Rani, riding ahead of me with some of the others who'd been at the ambush, slows.

"Caleb," he calls back, "I think it's ahead. This looks like—yes. It's not far ahead where we came upon Nikolai in the road."

I check and tighten the straps of my armor—and maybe I am glad I have it, even the leather armor.

Sitting back in the saddle, I sense ahead of Rani, reaching out, trying to feel the reality around me. I sense the earth that's lately been harvested. And the long history of fields.

I feel Rani and the two garrison soldiers with him on their own mounts, nervously looking around.

But I don't sense anyone else.

I don't sense any unreality weavings, either.

I glance aside to Morgan, who's moved on to being able to weave the illusion of a leaf.

"When Nikolai tries to control your mind, root yourself in your own reality. Know who you are and know your strengths. That is how to beat him."

Morgan straightens in his saddle and nods.

And even though I don't sense anyone ahead yet, we move forward with caution. Rani and the others still riding ahead, until they signal us to stop.

There are scorches in the grass, a patch where a small fire must have broken out, but someone stopped it.

The ground around the road still looks trampled, torn up.

Rani stares at a broad scorch mark, his jaw tight. "They didn't leave the bodies."

I dismount and move toward the center of where the battle had been.

"Nikolai stood there," Rani says, pointing toward a bend in the road ahead. There's a hill to one side, and a slide into a shallow valley on the other.

I extend my senses again, and I can feel the seething realities here, even days later.

There was panic here.

There was anguish as people were pushed against their wills.

I gently touch the wounded threads in the air. Nikolai was not kind to reality here.

And I sense—gods. I move forward until I crouch on the road, one hand on the ground.

Torovan. He was here. Right here.

I can feel his anguish, too, the echo of his fear.

Can I sense him nearby? Where is he now?

I close my eyes and focus on the resonance between us, then slowly stand. Slowly turn, toward the direction that's been tugging at me all morning.

To the north, I think, and slightly west.

Rani won't know where to go from here. From here, it's all me.

"Mount up," I say.

He's not far.

I know he's not far, with a certainty I can't name.

And I've been trying to think through, in the moments when I haven't been teaching Morgan, or haven't been lost in my own fears, how to defeat Nikolai.

I've been trying to think through what Sabella said, too, that I do know soul weaving.

And what if that's true?

And what does that say about my ability to defeat him?

I struggled to stop Sabella, but was able to once I rewove my reality as Caleb.

Once I rewove the reality my soul needed, once I brought the threads of my symphony into true.

I rewove Morgan's body by listening to his soul.

And yes, I did shift the threads in Sabella's mind.

And though I haven't rewoven my own body back to Irava yet, what makes me know I can is that I'll search my soul to reweave myself then, too.

I'm searching for my truth when I do that.

And finding it.

I'm Caleb again now, and now my body feels *good* in a way I haven't been able to feel in months. And no, it's not the same as before. I'm still carrying my child and all its possibilities within me. I'm still able to have that child when I'm ready, and that is a difference, but one I'm settled with. One that feels right in my soul.

The *feel* of me is right, and that is its own truth.

Something I can anchor and center myself within.

If Nikolai's soul weaving pushes people away from their truths...is there a soul weaving that pushes people towards theirs, too?

We ride on, and I begin to search the reality around me for any signs of what happened since Torovan and his party were taken.

A gnarled tree near the road holds a quiet unease.

A sharp bend and then a dip in the road ahead holds a shudder of anxiety.

Then the fields spread out before us, some already harvested, some being worked now by workers who look as we pass but don't stop.

Should we ask the workers if they saw who passed before, if I can't find Torovan now?

But ahead, in the distance, the blocky shape of a manor house appears, sitting on a hill.

It's set off from the road, but visible all the same.

I feel the resonance between Torovan and me, and it's strong, and it's in that direction.

He's in that house, isn't he? He's there.

And is Nikolai still there, too?

I can only hope.

It's afternoon now, and we're all tired from the journey, from the ride. Morgan, probably, from his strain at learning weaving, too.

Morgan reins in beside me. "He'll be able to see us, if he's watching for us."

There's no cover on the way toward that house.

I nod. No, we don't have the advantage of surprise here.

Or strength in numbers—there's only the few of us now.

But I have my will to see my husband safe. And our kingdom safe.

And Kian and Aria safe.

And, Aldric.

And now to rescue Sabella's son, too.

All of that will have to be enough, won't it?

It will have to be.

We ride on toward the manor house.

CHAPTER 52

THE DINNER

CALEB/TOROVAN

CALEB

We're halfway to the house when we crest another shallow hill, and I rein in again, studying what I can see of the manor and its outbuildings.

I know I'm not going to win this with a fair fight. I know I'm not going to win with a straight-up attack.

I can sense Torovan now like a tug in my chest—I think he's being kept in a room on the second floor.

Can I sense Kian or Aria?

I try for a few moments, precious moments sitting here on this hill as I know Nikolai and his people are watching.

But my connection to my apprentices, though strong, isn't at all what my connection to Torovan is.

And this close, I feel Torovan's will like a crystalline force. He's focused. He's intent.

Does his will feel...stronger?

We ride on, and not long after, see riders coming out from the manor house gates.

I hold my magic ready, my hands with the reins resting on my thighs, ready to drop them and weave when I need to.

"Caleb Ailin?" one of the riders, a roughhewn man, calls from a distance.

It's been half a year since anyone's called me only that, not Caleb Ailin Varandre Braise.

"Yes," I say, and Morgan beside me stiffens.

I don't feel any threads of mind control weaving around this man ahead, or from the three others with him. But there wasn't mind control for every attacker at the palace, either.

"We're to escort you to the house, sir."

As if I'm not a king.

I'm wearing a leather helmet, not a crown.

But everyone in Barella knows who I am.

"On whose orders?" I ask.

"Lord Nikolai Metrial's."

Well, at least he's not hiding.

I nod, and the four riders surround our small party, settling in to escort us the rest of the way.

No one talks.

And though our horses are tired and needing rest again, we move at a brisk pace until we reach the courtyard of the manor house, riding onto cobblestone pavement that's badly in need of repair, with stones missing and grass growing up through the cracks. I slow my horse, taking care of where he steps.

I look around for more of our enemies but see no one else.

The riders who escorted us in are dismounting, acting like they're taking us to visit a country lord, not taking us into a war zone with hostages.

Morgan rests his hand on the hilt of his sword, but I catch his eye, shake my head.

My guards and the few elementalists and me might be able to overpower these riders here, but I sense much more life inside the house, and in the outbuildings, too. Especially the stables. Is that where our people are being held? Or is that where Nikolai's people are waiting?

I look up at the house, and my soul feels the tug of Torovan's soul there.

Since we spotted the manor house, I've been slowly gathering my thoughts.

About no, how I couldn't hold myself against Sabella's attacks on my will, because my sense of self had been fractured.

And when I wove to heal that fracture, I could push her will out.

Nikolai uses soul weaving to impose his will on people and steal their sense of themselves.

And I've been churning on how my soul weaving helped people, Sabella and myself, and Morgan even, know more of who they are.

I think of the synchronicity I felt when Torovan's willpower joined with mine to unweave the vortex churning toward the palace. We'd been deeply tied together, our strengths amplified.

And I gave my willpower to Torovan to fight Nikolai in the Council Chamber. Our combined strength didn't come from one of us controlling the other, like Nikolai was trying to do, but from being laid bare.

When I teach my apprentices, I'm not just showing them how to weave reality, but helping them find their own wills, their own truths.

And there *is* a resonance between us. I feel Kian and Aria here, too, though I still can't pinpoint where. In the house, I think, though I'm still not sure.

But all of that is soul magic, isn't it?

Has soul weaving been a part of weaving all along, but we've only learned to fear the worst part of it?

"My lord is waiting in the house, sir," one of the riders says.

So I dismount. And so do my guards.

"He says only for you to enter, sir," the rider says, as he and the other riders dismount, too.

I glance at Morgan and Reveyan. And the others behind me.

"I'll go alone," I say. "Stay here."

No one protests. No one here is a fool.

Morgan takes the reins to my horse.

And I follow the rider into the house.

TOROVAN

There's a knock on my door.

I start from where I sit on my bed, propped up with a pillow against the headboard. But I haven't been weaving these last minutes, giving my will a break, a chance to rest.

My will has grown. I know it's grown. And will I be ready to face Nikolai again? He hasn't come in to see me all this day. No taunts, no threats.

If he's sensed me weaving, he hasn't shown any signs.

Maybe he wants me to grow stronger. Maybe he wants the

challenge. He's just predatory enough that I might believe that...if he didn't work from the shadows and play mind games.

No, he doesn't want me stronger. He's just...waiting.

And I'm terrified I know why.

I don't think the knock is Nikolai now. He would just come in, like he did before.

And I'm right.

The solid-built woman who enters is the same woman who's brought me food these last days.

Who's brought a wash basin.

Who's emptied my waste pot.

This time, she's come with two other armed men. And my hackles rise as she motions to me.

"Lord Metrial wishes you to attend him."

He wishes me to attend him.

A lord wishes a king to attend on him.

I rise anyway. And hope she doesn't notice the tassels I've been steadily slicing off the tapestries on the walls in my practice.

But she doesn't even look.

This is the first time since I came that they've let me out of this room.

They escort me down the musty corridor, past rooms thick with swirling dust. It's late afternoon, the light slanting toward golden, and the whole place, wherever this is, has a hush. I hear voices somewhere, though. Distant enough that I can't make out whose they are, Nikolai's or otherwise.

I don't think this is one of Nikolai's family's estates, it looks too ill-kept. Almost abandoned. Does this house belong to one of his allies? I don't think we rode far from where he captured us on the road, though my memories from that time are hazy.

And I don't really want to think about them.

I need my willpower focused just now. Because if I see a chance to take Nikolai down, I will take it.

They lead me to what must once have been a grand hall but now feels cavernous and dim. It's lit only by a scattering of high windows, and a handful of oil lamps that cast flickering shadows on the stone walls.

But my foreboding grows as I squint in the dark. I can feel—I know—I know who I'll see before my eyes lock on him.

I know the space he holds around him, the gentle reality he commands.

I've known that since I've known him, even if I've never felt it this way with my weaver's senses before.

He came.

He's here.

Caleb.

And across from him, in the center of a table that's been spread with what looks like a decent small meal despite the surroundings, sits Nikolai.

My heart falls like a stone.

Caleb's eyes meet mine, and they're hard in a way that makes my chest tighten.

Is he hurt? He doesn't look hurt.

But something is different. Something's shifted. He's wearing the leather armor of a palace guard, his pale face a little burned from the sun. His hair flattened like he just removed a helmet—and I see the helmet next to him.

Why, by all the gods, is he eating dinner with Nikolai?

"Sit," one of the armed men with me says, and points to a place beside...not Caleb, but Nikolai.

I swallow. And slowly make my way to the table, pulling out the chair. Sitting beside this man I want to kill.

But does he hold some threat again over Caleb?

I can't strike out without knowing.

"Torovan," Nikolai says pleasantly. But I hear the edge. "How good of you to join us. I was just about to explain to Caleb the terms of our arrangement."

CALEB

I'm half afraid the food is poisoned, but Nikolai's been eating with relish. As if he's not holding my husband hostage. As if I just came to dignify him with a visit.

So, carefully, I cut into the roast hen and begin to eat. There's no weaving within the food—that, at least, I checked for.

And I know Nikolai noticed. I didn't miss his smug smile.

The staff brought me fruit juice instead of wine. And that detail, while I'm glad of it, twisted my insides. And earned me another smug look from Nikolai.

He's chatted about the countryside. About the harvest. He's asked me how the Harvest Festival is going.

The *nerve* of him.

As if we've known each other for years. And been friends for years.

As if he hasn't hated me from the start.

As if he hasn't threatened me or my child. Or taken the son

of my apprentice, and then bent her own will against me, used her to start destroying Torovan's and my trust in each other and in ourselves in my palace.

I haven't yet seen any signs of Torovan here, and I start to ask about him again.

But Nikolai holds up a hand.

"All in good time."

I'm done with this game.

But I can't know what traps Nikolai's set in place, what measures he's taken to hurt Torovan if I try to attack him now.

I'm about ready to storm upstairs anyway.

But then, I feel Torovan coming closer. The sense of him grows stronger until it's right here.

He's here. He's just now walking into this hall, looking a little rumpled and disheveled. Still wearing the under-tunic and trousers from the armor he rode out in. His hair mussed but bound back behind him, clasped with—with what looks like a tight weaving.

Did I teach him how to do that?

One of the men guarding Torovan waves him to the table, but beside Nikolai, not me.

And that's another threat.

"Torovan," Nikolai says. "How good of you to join us. I was just about to explain to Caleb the terms of our arrangement."

Whatever arrangement that is, it can't be good. I watch Torovan's eyes flash with a rage he quickly suppresses.

I reach out with my weaving as he nears the table, looking into the symphony of his soul. To see if it's been altered.

It...it has.

But not in the way I'm fearing.

His soul feels stronger, brighter in a way I haven't seen.

There are scars there, too, from Nikolai shredding into his thoughts.

But I don't repair them. And Torovan's symphony seems to have flowed around them. He's still holding himself true.

Torovan gives me a small smile and sits beside our enemy.

"Eat, Torovan," Nikolai says, and passes him a tray of meats.

Torovan takes it, and eyes the half-eaten food on my plate.

Then he begins to heap his own plate.

Nikolai nods, then waves his fork between us.

"I wanted you both to be here, to know the good news, but I have agreed to foster your child."

I start, my last bite sitting painfully in my throat, but he goes on, "It's really the only way to ensure lasting peace in Barella. I'm even willing to teach him that the common people should, in the end, have more say in their lives. Isn't that what you want, Torovan?"

Nikolai's not weaving Torovan's mind now, I know that.

He's not trying to weave mine.

And with Torovan here, does Nikolai think he could stand against both of us again? What threat is he still holding over us?

Nikolai meets my eyes.

"My people have instructions," he says, "if I'm attacked, to kill everyone else on this property. Your apprentices, all of your mages, your soldiers, your guards. I think they're important to you, are they not?"

"Where is Aria?" I ask. I hadn't asked before, I hadn't wanted to distract Nikolai from my goal of finding Torovan. "Where are Kian and Aldric?"

"Safe," he says. "Like you are both perfectly safe. I only

want to have a talk, and a meal, and we'll all leave here much more secure in our safety and our futures."

"You're not raising our child," Torovan says in a low voice.

"No," I say, watching Nikolai. "He doesn't want to raise our child. He wants to give our child to the Dowager Queen."

Nikolai shrugs, taking another bite off his half-eaten plate. I've only picked at my food, but he's devoured his.

"I see no political difference. The child would be properly educated and be prepared to rule in their time. And as I said, Torovan, we can even teach this child about your reforms. Within reason."

As if my child is a dog he wants to train.

I take another bite, too, trying to buy time to think.

From the tightness of Torovan's anger, Nikolai's brought this up before.

"May we stay the night?" I ask finally. "And consider your proposal?"

Nikolai nods, as if he was expecting this. He wipes his mouth. "Torovan, is your room adequate? Of course it is, it's a suite for honored guests, though the house itself isn't what it used to be. But you can stay there." He turns back to me. "By the way, Caleb. I haven't mentioned that Akreal has been sending me its weavers. They aren't wanted there, so I have been offering to take them in. Training them. They will be of good use to Barella, I think."

He has weavers. He has more weavers loyal to him?

I stiffen in my chair, meet Torovan's eyes.

"You may meet some of them tomorrow. You can add them to your apprentices as well."

And this is why he's not afraid of us.

This is why we're eating a meal at his table, a meal I'm sure is not poisoned. Why would he need to poison us?

He's already threatened our people. And now he's threatening the kingdom, because he's controlling those weavers, isn't he? One way or another, he is.

Did Lady Denya know about this?

I don't know. And now I have the uncomfortable thought that I hope Sabella is enough to overpower her if she did.

"I am only wishing to serve the kingdom," Nikolai says, looking between us. "I have only ever wished to serve the kingdom."

"And you thought you were serving the kingdom by murdering my father in his bed?" Torovan asks quietly.

"We all make mistakes," Nikolai says.

Torovan twitches, like he's barely restraining himself from attack.

And I tense, too.

There's a chance Nikolai's lying about the threat to our people.

But I don't count on it.

I can't.

And Torovan lets out a long breath, and eases his tension, too.

We just need to get together, alone.

Because I *have* been thinking about soul weaving.

And if Nikolai's raised the stakes with his weavers now in play...I have something I want to try.

CHAPTER 53

SOUL WEAVING

CALEB

Nikolai's people lock us in a room, the fading light of evening the only light out a narrow window.

Too narrow to climb out through, even if I hadn't been Caleb right now. Even if I hadn't been pregnant.

The bed is rumpled.

And there's a feeling here, a sense in the room of increasing...wholeness.

I turn to Torovan.

"You shouldn't have come," he says.

I'm still sensing the room, sensing to make sure there's no malicious weaving here. I see a flurry of charged reality around the tassels in the wall tapestries. Around the edges of the furniture, which are all shaved into untreated wood. Some smoothed into rounded corners.

"Caleb," he says. "I said you shouldn't have—"

"Of course I would come." I feel the realities of two of the guards who brought us up still outside the door.

Listening?

Probably.

So I weave a shell around us, which I won't let sound pass through.

Not unreality. But, a filter of reality.

Torovan feels it, because he looks around himself.

"It's safe to talk?" he asks.

I crush him in a hug, and he rocks back, taking a step before he catches me, rights his own balance on me.

With his hands on my arms, his eyes widen.

"You—you wove your reality. You're—"

"Yes."

He grins. "Gods, Caleb, you did it!"

Like this, right now, is the most important thing in all the world.

Gods, I love this man.

I pull back to look at him more fully.

"Your will is stronger," I say. "I can feel it, Tor. Gods, I see what you've been doing all around the room, *what* have you been doing?"

He gives an embarrassed shrug.

But his eyes on me are intent. "He's not going to win, Caleb."

"No, he's not."

His eyes flick between mine.

His brow furrows.

"What happened?" he asks.

So I tell him about the attack at the palace. About Sabella.

I watch his hands tighten into fists.

"I will kill him," he growls. "I will *kill* him."

I take one of his hands. And I feel the symphony that is

him start to grow discordant. Grow less sure as he thinks about Nikolai.

I wrap both of my hands around his.

But he focuses back on me. "You wove yourself *during* the battle with Sabella? That's how you defeated her?"

"Yes."

I'm staring into his eyes. Does he understand that significance, too? But he doesn't have all the pieces.

"When I wove Sabella's mind before, when I was checking for mind control weaving—that was soul weaving, Torovan."

He rocks back. "No, you weren't trying to control her."

"But it was still soul weaving. I think—in our fear of the mind control weavers, we've forgotten something vital. It's—it's how I saved us from Nikolai in the Council Chamber. Torovan, I wasn't just stating my truths. I mean, I was. That was part of it. But those truths—that is soul weaving." I swallow. "And...can I weave you?"

His eyes flick between mine, and I start to see fear there before he blinks.

"You want to control me?"

"No. And I think—I think whatever you've been doing here—"

"Practicing. He said he wanted to raise our child, Caleb. You heard."

His voice breaks, and I press my palm to his cheek. Against the rough stubble.

"He can't have our child," I say.

He shakes his head hard, leans into my touch. Closes his eyes, and twin streams flow down his cheeks.

I don't know what happened here yet, I don't know what Nikolai said to him.

But the energy of this room, the reality seething here, is of a man who's determined to be more.

To be fuller than he was, more rooted in himself and more embracing his own possibilities. At any and all costs. To any and all gains.

And he's done that. That is so very clear.

The way he's carrying himself is even different.

Like the mage's medallion on his chest—they left that when they took his armor off, or he took it off—holds a greater truth for him now than it did before.

"You were soul weaving," I say.

He flinches.

"No, Tor. This is what I mean. You were increasing your willpower? Increasing your strength? Focusing on your truths. Yes?"

"I was practicing. But...maybe."

I stretch up and kiss him, and he makes a noise, grips the back of my neck, kisses me back like he's been drowning.

And my body responds, heat flowing in ways it hasn't in months.

I bite my lip as I pull back, resting my head against his.

We can't be together here, not now, not yet. Not when we have to be alert. Not when I have to try what I need to try. To know if it might work. To get us out of here. To stop Nikolai so he doesn't hurt anyone else.

Much as I want to be with my husband in the way I've needed to for months, I press my hands to his chest. Fight against the urge.

"You wove your soul into your own truths," I manage to get out, trying to yank my mind back to this singular focus. "You strengthened your symphony of your soul threads. And

—Torovan—I think that might be how we break his hold. In ourselves, and in others. I want to try to heal the wounds he wrecked through your mind. To strengthen your soul, too. I want to see your truths so you can see them more clearly. If you'll let me. And then...I want you to do the same to me."

His fingers tremble in my hair. His eyes are wide, his breaths shallow.

This is what he fears above all. Losing control.

What was almost taken from him.

So I give him my willpower. He can weave me first.

He looks around him, seeing what I'm doing, his brows knitting.

"Caleb—"

"Take my willpower. And then, I'm going to talk you through how to weave my mind, and my soul."

He shakes his head.

"Caleb—"

"I trust you, Torovan."

He takes my will. I feel my power flowing into him, and he draws in a shuddering breath.

We've done this before.

In casual practice. Which, true, almost always ended in bed.

But this is different. He's stronger now. And he's far, far more attuned to his magic than before.

If he's spent all of these last days strengthening his will, honing in on who he is and what his power really is, then his understanding of weaving and his precision has grown, too.

You can learn weaving in books, yes.

You can learn from a teacher.

But you will learn most of all from yourself.

And now he's holding all of his will, and all of mine but what I need to live.

His lips are pressed tightly together, and I see his eyes shining in the dimming evening light from the window.

"Can you see my symphony?"

He's quiet, and I know he's looking.

His chest lifts, then he says a reverent, *"Oh."*

I grin. Oh, yes.

His lips are parted as he looks all around me. "This is what you see all the time?"

"Not all the time. But if I look, yes. And my ability to see it's grown stronger. Lately, but I only really started to see it after the first time we fought Nikolai."

His eyes meet mine. Then he looks around me. "I see your threads. In your thoughts. Is my looking hurting you, Caleb?"

"No."

He reaches one hand toward mine, and I grip it, while he holds up the other near my head. Not quite touching.

"What do you see?" I ask.

He squints.

"You're a song. Like, the most complex song I can hear, in so many harmonies. And oh, gods, the child."

"The child is safe."

"I know. I see. But if I touch any of your threads—"

"You won't harm the child."

His mouth pinches like he wants to argue. But then he nods. "No, I won't. Caleb, should I be looking for signs of mind control?"

"I don't think so. And I'm not even sure you need to look for anything off, or out of true. But—Tor, can you hear my truth? Can you see my strongest threads?"

He looks around me again.

"When I wove Morgan, that's how I found the truth of the body he needed. I heard his symphony. And brought his body into harmony with it. That's how I wove mine."

Torovan shudders. Then reaches out. "This. This is your truth."

My breath catches. Love like a warm summer breeze, delicate and gentle, hums in my soul.

"And this."

Another thrum in my soul.

"This, I think, means you never give up. And you don't, Caleb. You don't *ever* give up. You didn't give up on me. Even when—" He swallows. "Even when I was keeping the letters from you."

I squeeze his hand.

"I love you," he says. And with this awareness, with him holding onto me, with him seeing my threads, the threads within my soul thrum louder with that love. A feeling so intense I almost can't breathe.

"That—that did something," he says shakily. "It shifted some of your mind threads. Caleb—"

But I feel stronger. I feel the cracks in my soul aren't as wide now.

All of my doubts from our ride on the road, all of my fears in my rush to get here, feel less urgent.

He looks me in the eyes again. "I *love* you, Caleb Ailin Varandre Braise. I love that you want to protect me. I love that you're trying everything you can to be who you are, and have what you want, all of it. You are *strength*, Caleb. A strength I don't have."

I feel the warmth, the soul hum, increasing until he gets to that part.

"No, Tor. That's not true."

"It is—"

"*No*, Tor."

He stares at me, lost a moment in his inner battle. Then he hands me back my will. And hands me...his.

"Weave me."

I take his will gently. Cradle it inside my own soul, because I know how hard it is given.

I know the trust he's giving me.

And I open my eyes to his symphony.

He is the brightest song and the deepest ballad.

He's a heart after my heart, and all his own.

He's been wounded, yes.

And maybe the feeling of weaving Sabella's mind hadn't sat right with me, because I was moving threads, but not moving her soul itself.

This is weaving, but it's not weaving. I can see his threads, but it's my soul doing the magic.

"I love you, Torovan Braise."

He shudders. And now his eyes are running freely again.

"I love that you will never, ever back down."

He laughs. "That's what I said about you—"

"But it's your truth, too. I love that you want to heal your kingdom with all that you are. I love that you see me, no matter what body I'm in. I know that, Tor. And I'm sorry for that wound, that was mine, I didn't want to give that to you, too."

I feel my own soul energy lessening, and, okay.

That's still a wound.

But I can weave my own soul, too.

I'm myself. No matter who I am, I'm myself.

And I know that, too.

I steady. And watch his symphony continue to grow, to gain more nuance, more complexity, more wholeness as the parts that were dimmer brighten.

"I love that you want to protect me, too."

"Even if I'm lying to you?" he murmurs.

"I can't cast that blame."

He coughs. A sharp bark of laughter.

And something else eases in my soul.

He's not holding that against me, my lying to him when we first met. I hadn't thought he was, but, well, some part of me was still afraid of that.

Afraid that when I couldn't be with him in my full body as Caleb, that I was still living that same lie a little.

And that he'd hold it over me.

I let go of my sight of his soul, because it's becoming too beautiful for me to stand.

I give him back his will, gently, and wrap my arms around him, and he wraps his around me.

I can still feel his symphony. Weaving in and around my own.

We're stronger. I don't even have to look to see that, to feel that.

"This is how we fight Nikolai?" he asks. "By knowing our truths? I hadn't thought—Caleb, I hadn't thought I had any deeper truths."

I brush his cheek. Because I don't have words, no words left at all.

And kiss him again.

When I pull back again, I say, "I think this is how we free

the people he's controlling. We see their strengths and echo them back to them. If he's fighting with fear, well, we'll fight with every good thing a person can be."

"You think that will work? That won't just strengthen the wills of our enemies?"

I bite my lip. "I...don't know." I step back, out of his embrace, though I'm still craving the warmth. But it's heating into need again for me, and I have to think.

"I didn't feel him weaving during dinner," I say.

"No, I don't think he was."

"So whoever he's controlling here, I don't think he's controlling them all the time. He does have to sleep. And maybe he can shift people's threads out of their truths so they're not a threat to him, so that they follow what he wants, or—or maybe they're just afraid of him, like Sabella. And when he needs to control them more directly, he can actually bend their wills." I pause. "Fear is a powerful incentive."

Torovan grunts. Runs a hand over his face.

The light from the window is almost gone.

He turns back to me.

"Do we do this under cover of darkness?"

I can't think of a better time to try, when we're both still full of our own willpower, our own strengths, our own truths.

Nikolai said if we attacked him, he'd harm our people.

Well, we'll just have to find and free our people first.

I think a moment. And mentally add the Akrean weavers, if they're here, too. Anyone who's ever been harmed or manipulated by Nikolai—these are the people we need to find.

I kiss him once more, for all the luck we'll have.

"Let's go."

CHAPTER 54

BINDING

CALEB

Nikolai thinks our fear will hold us, but he certainly doesn't think this room will hold us on its own. The door only has two locks. He barely even tried.

"Do we try to soul weave everyone?" Torovan asks in my ear.

I hesitate, not yet reaching for the locks.

Would it work on everyone, controlled by Nikolai's soul weaving or not?

Sabella hadn't been controlled by Nikolai when she attacked the palace, not by mind control.

But...but I had woven Sabella's mind. And that hadn't stopped her from attacking the palace. Not when she was still bent on saving her son.

I swallow a tightness rushing at my throat. And how many more of Nikolai's followers has he threatened, too?

We won't have time to figure it out. Not now anyway.

We have to get out and find our people before Nikolai knows we're out.

"No," I say. "Not everyone. Do you remember how to bind someone with a weaving?"

"Yes. Though I didn't much practice after you taught me." He grimaces.

"Bind me now."

He hesitates, but then I see his threads reaching out, tightening around the whole of my body, closing in until I can barely move.

He's immensely careful about it, closing very slowly.

Then he lets go.

"You bind them," I say. "I'll knock them out." That takes more precision by far, and that I haven't taught Torovan yet. He's gained that precision in the last few days, but we don't have the time to practice now.

"There are two guards at the door," he says, turning back to it.

I'm still holding a pocket of filtered sound around us, so the guards won't hear us.

I hold up a hand and drop it now, extending my senses past the door.

Yes, I still feel the two men on the other side of it. I widen my senses and feel more people in the rooms around us on this level, but the farther I sense, the less clear my picture is.

I reach again for my sense of Kian and Aria.

And, here now, I think I feel them downstairs, though I can't say exactly where.

But that's where we'll need to go.

"Okay. Ready?"

He nods.

I hover my hand in front of the door and sense for

the reality inside the locks. And instead of making them click, that satisfying opening I usually do, I ease the bars over.

Then I feel for the handle in the near-dark and slowly open the door.

There's lamp light in the corridor, though it's dim.

And only two guards? I'm almost insulted.

Torovan, behind me, twitches his hand now that he can see the guards. I feel his threads gathering to bind the two guards even as I'm weaving the air away from their mouths so they can't cry out.

Both struggle as Torovan wraps them tightly in his bindings.

Then I weave the air inside their bindings in a way that Aldric showed me, changing the reality of the air within. The two guards slump, and Torovan lowers them as quickly as he can to the floor.

They'll be out for at least an hour.

"Don't breathe that," I whisper as we step past the guards, and Torovan releases his bindings.

He looks down, moves more quickly.

There are more people in the rooms off this hall, but I need to get to Aria and Kian before we can circle back and see if they're ours, too. I have to know they won't be used against us, because they're the greater threat by far.

Unless Nikolai will bring his Akrean weavers into play right now, in which case...

In which case I'm not going to think about that.

I weave the reality around Torovan and me, muffling the sounds of our steps. He twitches when he steps on a creaky plank, but I wave at him—we're fine.

We're halfway to what I think are the back service stairs when a door flings open and a stocky woman steps out.

Torovan's mouth tightens. Does he know her? Was she one of his jailers?

She turns to go the other way, then stops, turns toward us.

She opens her mouth, but I have her air in a moment, and Torovan has her bound.

We're laying her out when a second man comes out.

"Adina? You didn't close the door—"

He gets off a shout before I can take his air, too.

Torovan binds him, and I have him out in seconds, but they're precious seconds, now.

"Run!"

I'm not sure where Nikolai is in this house. He could be in any of these rooms, though I don't sense his malice nearby.

But then, it's a lot harder to sense anything certain through walls, or where you can't see.

We run down the rest of the corridor, and I'm still weaving the reality around us, trying to muffle our steps. But another door opens near the end, and lamplight floods out.

There is no time, with any of them, to sense if they're under Nikolai's control.

So we bind and incapacitate the next man.

We reach the back stairs and thunder down. Because now it's a race against time.

I half expect Nikolai to be in the corridor below, just waiting for us to run into his trap, but no, we meet more people armed as guards.

And take them down the same way.

At least we're good at that. We're moving in sync again.

And that raises my hope.

Torovan moves to the end of the short service corridor as I step over the unconscious bodies.

"Where is Nikolai?" he asks, his voice tight.

I focus again, stretching my senses through the estate around us. I don't have a connection to Nikolai, but the feeling of malice is stronger here than it was before.

Is he near?

"I don't know."

We just have to press on.

I turn in the corridor we're in now, lit by a single oil sconce on one wall. There are several doors and another short corridor leading off of this one.

I sense Kian and Aria closer here. Well, and if there were guards in this corridor, they were guarding something.

I head down the short corridor, and Torovan follows, his hands already up to weave the bindings again.

A shout comes from the way we just came from the stairs. Shit.

I look back to Torovan. "Can you bind them and change their air?"

"Don't know the air."

"Then just...knock them out. However you can."

There's no time for more.

I rush down the rest of the short corridor and, finding two locked doors, try to sense what's behind them.

I feel Kian close, like he's hovering behind the door, trying to listen to what's happening out here.

Does he sense me?

I weave the lock on that door and carefully push it open, in case he tries to attack me.

"Kian!" I hiss.

Kian's hands are up to weave. There's no light in this room, only the dim light from the corridor behind me.

He's staring at me, but his hands haven't gone down.

My hackles rise. "Kian?" I ask again.

And finally, he shakes himself. "Caleb?"

"Kian, are you well? I must check you—"

"Caleb! Gods, you're here? It's—it's actually you? They have the king—"

"I know." I move inside the room, swinging the door shut again.

And barely have time to sense a binding weave coming at me from within.

I deflect it before it reaches me, then fumble after it in the dark, catch it, trying to unweave it without seeing.

"Aria!" Kian yells. "It's him!"

He shouldn't be shouting.

But I feel him moving, and I follow.

I weave a small illusion of light in the air. It's never been easy to hold light, as light is a seething, volatile reality, and always on the edge of unraveling or exploding. But it's enough to see by now if I concentrate.

Enough to see a disheveled Aria huddled in the corner, glaring at me.

"Traitor," she hisses at me.

"No, it's him—Aria—"

She looks to Kian, back to me, her jaw tight, hands up and ready to weave again.

Gods. My stomach tightens.

I don't sense any of Nikolai's threads coming into the room from elsewhere. But when I look at Aria's symphony, it feels...jagged.

"Aria? It's me, it's Caleb." I try to brighten my illusion of light and manage it a little.

She stands fully, takes a step closer.

I don't dare try to weave the threads of her soul, not now, now when I don't know what's happened to her. And that, suddenly, seems like a vitally important part of this.

I can't weave a person's soul without permission.

I can't.

Because that, too, would be no better than Nikolai.

Aria's lip trembles, then her face crumples and she launches herself at me.

I almost flinch to weave again, like she might attack me, but she throws her arms around me.

Then flinches back, yelling.

"It's not him!" she shouts. "He doesn't feel like, it's Nikolai—"

I catch and unweave the chunk of solid air she throws at me.

Kian turns to me, uncertain.

And—oh, gods.

Had Nikolai pretended to be me? Was that how he got her out of the palace? Or had Sabella done that?

I don't know. But she wasn't expecting me to actually be built like a man.

"I wove myself," I say. "I wove myself in the palace, I rewove my reality as Caleb, Aria, look at my soul, can you see my soul threads?"

And I reach within me, plucking on the strongest threads. Trying to amplify who I am into the room around me. Hoping it will do any good.

Aria stills again, trembling.

"I'm sorry," I say into the near-dark.

And we don't have time for any of this, but I'm going to make the time. We have to have the time.

"I'm sorry I couldn't keep him from taking you."

Her face twists. "Sabella led me to him in the town. And said it was you."

I swallow. I don't want another of Sabella's sins weighing on my soul.

Another of Nikolai's sins.

But I nod. "She is his apprentice, too. He has her son."

"What?" Kian asks. "Where? Is he here?"

"I hope. I don't know, but I hope, and we have to get to him again before Nikolai does. We have to get to all of our people."

Aria bites her lip, still staring at me like she doesn't believe I'm real. "I won't—"

Torovan bangs into the room, and we all, for a moment, freeze.

Aria looks between him, and me, then covers her mouth with a cry.

"Caleb, there's more guards," Torovan says. "There was an elementalist."

"Did you—"

"They're all down. I wasn't gentle."

And how many does that make so far? Are we taking down Nikolai's people one by one, will that be enough?

"Aria, let Caleb fix you," Kian growls. "Like he fixed Sabella..." But he trails off. Because obviously I hadn't fixed Sabella.

Aria shrinks back, and probably rightly so. My shoulders twitch with the tension I'm trying not to show.

Kian swings back to me.

"Then weave me," he says. "Nikolai got into my head, too."

I swallow—and is there time?

Torovan's watching the corridor.

But I delve into Kian's symphony. It's not all as it should be, and I don't have time for subtlety now. I tug on his threads, pulling them into true where I see they're not, though some don't want to move as easily as others. In his mind, I find the scarring of mind control, like I'd seen in Torovan's. Like I'd seen in Sabella's.

Kian shivers. I find his strongest threads and resonate with them within my own. His strength and his courage and his absolute determination to be the best he can be.

Kian straightens, dragging in a breath. His soul moves into a better harmony, if not completely whole. But I watch him watching me do this. And that's why he wanted to know.

So he can help Aria, too. Because she does trust him.

And now, he starts to weave himself.

The threads in his soul strengthen. And the threads of his mind, the ones I couldn't budge, start to move back into true.

But this sort of weaving, I'm finding, takes time. Takes the need for a person to resonate within themself.

This isn't going to work how I'd thought. Did we just start a fight we ultimately can't win?

"Caleb," Torovan insists.

"I'm okay," Kian says. "I—I—"

He's crying.

But then, I know that feeling, too. I grip his shoulder, but don't touch Aria.

She's huddled to Kian, though, watching us all warily as we move to the door.

"What did you do?" she asks. "That was more than his mind."

"It's soul weaving," I say. "But, the good kind."

"There's a good kind?" Her voice ends on a squeak. She watches me like I might still be Nikolai, might try to attack her at any moment.

Torovan eases the door open. And then braces himself, his hands up.

There are two more people running toward us.

We take them down.

"Master Aldric is in the next room," Kian says, and I breathe out. Okay.

Aria is still shrinking away from me, and—and god. That's a wound Nikolai made that won't quickly heal, will it?

I swallow.

"Kian, do you know where they're keeping the soldiers?" I ask. "The elementalists?"

"I—I think in the stables? I heard someone talking about the stables."

"Weave me," Aria croaks, gripping my arm. "Caleb? Weave his shit *out* of me."

I meet her eyes.

"You're sure?"

She nods.

I don't touch her mind. I don't even touch the threads of her soul, jagged and discordant as they are right now.

I only look for the strengths I know are there. To who I know her to be.

And then find those same resonances within myself and pluck the threads in my soul instead.

"You're stronger than anything he can throw at you."

"But he—but I—"

She's crumpling.

Torovan rushes down the corridor again, and I vaguely hear voices.

He needs me.

But so do my apprentices.

And I have a hunch what Nikolai's levers over her are.

"You can *never* let me down, Aria, not in who you are."

"But I lost control, and I couldn't tell it wasn't you, that he wasn't you, and I thought you said we were going to fight him, fight Nikolai, I mean. Then I got confused, and I wanted to fight *with* him, Caleb, I fought Kian on the road!"

She's rising again into panic.

I can't help her right now, I'm too close to the source of her pain.

"Kian," I say. He holds her to him, his arm around her back.

And we're out of time. I know we're out of time.

"Caleb!" Torovan calls.

"Go," I say to Kian. "Go to the stables, both of you, get our people free."

I don't know that I'm not sending them straight into Nikolai's arms.

But maybe Kian can help her if she's away from me.

Kian and Aria start to move.

I turn and weave the lock on Aldric's door. And inside, I find him tense, his braid undone, his gray hair loose around him. His jaw set.

Was he controlled by Nikolai, too? Will he attack me?

"About fucking time," he says.

I hold up my hands. "Let me check you."

He glares at me. "Not before we take that shit *down*."

Well. And that's far less restrained than Aldric usually is.

But at least he's aimed in the right direction.

Aldric stalks out after me, and I hurry back toward Torovan.

"Gods," I say, staggering to a stop before I trip on the bodies. Seven of them.

Torovan looks at me, at Aldric, back to me.

Where is Nikolai? Why hasn't he tried to come after us, yet? Where are his weavers, if he says he has them?

The dread in my bones is rising again.

"We have to find Sabella's son," I say.

"Sabella's son?" Aldric asks. He pauses, putting it together. "Then Sabella was his agent in the palace."

"Yes. We have to take away his leverage—"

The door toward the inner house bangs open.

I whirl to see—

Kas.

Torovan's guard. Raising his sword with a yell.

CHAPTER 55

THE TAUNT

TOROVAN

Kas.

He's rushing at me, his sword raised to swing. His eyes wild. Like he doesn't know me.

No. Like he does know me and *hates* me.

I weave a blade of hardened reality and catch his sword on it before he can strike. Then weave his sword in place in the air, like I did with the dagger flung at Caleb at the feast.

Kas growls, trying to pull his sword free.

"Kas."

His eyes won't meet mine.

"Kas!"

I feel Caleb's threads reaching out to him, plucking the threads of his soul.

Kas shudders.

And I reach out, too, to this man who's been by my side all the time I've been the king.

There's a resonance between us, clear to my mind's eye, and strong.

I hold it.

"Kas. Look at me!"

He does. He finally does.

Then looks stricken, looking up to his sword frozen mid swing, his knees buckling.

"No! This was Nikolai, not you! I know you, Kas. You are loyal to the core."

That, said while eyeing the thread of loyalty in his soul, makes that thread stronger. More resonant.

I think I'm getting this.

Caleb calls the soul a symphony.

But, I think it's a river. The river can be dried up or flowing in a way that erodes its shore.

But it can be diverted back to the flow it needs. And Kas's river is flowing stronger again now.

"Nikolai," Kas manages, trembling.

He lets go of his sword in the air.

Caleb takes the handle. "I have it. Unweave it."

The sword is heavier than it looks, and Caleb's not used to that kind of weight. As I unweave the reality holding the sword in the air, the point drops heavily toward the stone floor.

Caleb grunts, but catches it before it reaches the floor, and maneuvers the handle back toward Kas.

"Take it."

Kas looks up.

"I trust you," Caleb says. "Keep him safe."

Kas swallows but reaches for the sword. Shoves it into its sheath.

"Fall in," I say. "Caleb, where next? Do you know where Sabella's son is?"

"I don't even know that he's here," Caleb says, wiping at his mouth.

He looks toward the other door, the way Kian and Aria went.

"There's a boy upstairs," Kas says. "I heard him talking, once, to someone else. He wasn't happy." He narrows his eyes, looks at me, and I see wariness again. "Nikolai used an illusion of you, Sire. When he talked to me."

"He did the same with Aria and Kian," Caleb says tightly. "But of me."

I want with everything in me to charge down that corridor and find Nikolai Metrial, and end his miserable life.

But Caleb is right, we have to gather everyone Nikolai could use to control us. We have to.

"And the Akrean weavers," Caleb says. He presses a hand to his forehead. "Gods. Do we just free some to be controlled again while we're freeing the others? I shouldn't have let Kian and Aria go. Why hasn't Nikolai come after us yet?"

"We'll figure the Akreans out later," I say, and head again for the stairs. I want to find this child and get on with it.

But upstairs, we look in each room and find them empty.

The fear is worming again in my soul.

I catch Caleb's eye.

"He's not here. Nikolai. Or the boy."

Does Nikolai know we're looking for Sabella's son? Does he know that child will be a lever over us as well?

I don't know the child and I don't know Sabella as well as I might. But I'm not going to let Nikolai threaten the life of anyone else's child, either.

"Caleb! Torovan!"

I stiffen.

Nikolai. His voice is distant. Coming from downstairs, I think.

He yells again.

"You're not being good guests!"

I look to Caleb.

And yes, we just wove ourselves stronger. I can still feel that strength within my will.

And yes, I spent every moment of the last few days practicing. Doing everything I could to strengthen my will.

But hearing Nikolai calling out, knowing that we're going to have to fight him, and that it's just ahead, sends all the fears spiraling in again.

I couldn't defeat him on the road.

And yes, Caleb is here just now. He's with me.

But he told me he barely defeated Sabella, his own apprentice, at the palace.

We might have grown stronger, but our enemies have, too.

"Do you hear me?" Nikolai shouts. "Come outside!"

He's choosing the ground. Which means he knows he has the advantage.

He's forcing the fight, which means he knows he will win.

And maybe this was what he wanted all along. Maybe he's playing with us, making us think we have hope, only so he can dash it.

My breaths are turning shallow.

Caleb grips my hand, squeezing tight. He looks into my eyes.

And I straighten again as I feel in his soul the man he thinks I am.

Which might be better than the man I actually am.

But maybe...maybe not.

"You have the will, Tor," Caleb says. "He's not going to win this. He's not going to control you again."

But the words just feel like platitudes now. Like an aching echo of hope in the dark.

Now that I know I'm going to have to face this again.

When I've failed twice before.

"I was wrong," Aldric says, and I turn. "I told you that you couldn't be a weaver. But I was wrong. For whatever it's worth."

He's actually admitting it?

Old anger mixes with old despair and wells up inside me.

But...the old refrain in my soul, that maybe he wasn't wrong, isn't coming now.

Because I know it's not true. Gut deep. To my very depths, I know it's not true.

I already am a weaver. And I know I'm stronger now than I was before.

I touch the weaver's medallion over my heart.

Nikolai let me keep that, and was that meant to be a mockery?

My fingers close around it.

Then I reach into my soul. And feel the harmony of the power within me.

It's mine.

Mine to hold and mine to use.

Mine to protect my husband with, and our child he carries.

Mine to face my enemy and not back down.

Nikolai will never take that from me again.

CHAPTER 56

RAGE

CALEB/TOROVAN

CALEB

The house is empty, though the corridors are still lit. We're nearer the main stairs, but the stairs are open, and that feels more like Nikolai would want us to do, rush headlong into his trap.

So we go back down the service stairs, and wind through the main house, tensed for an attack that doesn't come.

I stop muffling our steps—Nikolai knows we're here. And with his ability to weave souls, maybe he even knows where we are. No matter that he hurts people with his weaving, he does know how to weave souls.

I glance aside at Torovan, then take his hand. Winding my fingers tightly in his.

They fit like they've always fit when I'm Caleb both in my body and my soul, like they haven't fit in months.

Outside, I can hear the late autumn cicadas calling.

It's the only thing that breaks the silence of an empty house.

We reach the front doors I came in through.

The doors are propped open, the cold of an autumn night nipping the air.

And outside, standing back from the house but facing it, lit by the torches and lamps they're carrying, stand Nikolai and his forces.

He's not at the front of his people, as I scan for him, but I find him near the back.

I flick my eyes over the crowd. Some of our soldiers are near the front.

And—gods. There's a boy, maybe eleven or twelve, with pale, cold-reddened cheeks and wind-mussed blonde hair. Is that Sabella's son? I have to assume.

I tighten my hand in Torovan's. Nikolai set the boy right in the front, right in the center of the crowd. Where we will have to plow through to get to Nikolai.

The boy is holding a long, jagged dagger and glaring at me like he's ready to kill.

I swallow and spot Reveyan, and Rani, and my heart sinks even more.

Others are people I don't know, but I can see the threads coming out of Nikolai, sinewy mind control threads to almost every person here. He's not taking chances tonight.

But I don't see Kian or Aria. And maybe we thwarted his plans enough to deprive him of them, at least.

Oh gods, can I even hope?

But as we step out into the yard, I just barely see threads zipping toward me from the side, and before I have time to react, I can't move within a binding.

I shred it, it's normal weaving. But a second binding takes me just as quickly, from the other direction.

I hear Torovan grunt and know he's dealing with the same. And Aldric?

I can't look. I'm shredding out of the binding again, because what if Nikolai knows Aldric's trick of weaving the air into gas, too?

I whip around and see Torovan struggling out of his binding, too, but having a tougher time.

Aldric is...out on the ground.

Gods.

Not seconds into this fight, and we're already one weaver short.

I'm ready this time and shred another binding coming at me, but only just barely deflect a swooping taloned bird as it comes from my other side.

And I have to spin to put up a shield of hardened reality to stop a fireball from Rani.

Yes, I can weave souls, but it wasn't as quick as I thought, or as easy as I thought.

It's easy to control someone, to hit them with fear or guilt.

Far less so to get them to believe in their actual potential.

Torovan cries out.

He's holding his arm, looking down at it, and I see his fingers holding his forearm are red. But he turns, and with a cry, blades of reality spring from the air in front of him, shooting toward the attacker in the shadows.

"No!" I yell, because what if it's Kian? What if it's Aria, being controlled again?

I hear a yelp to my left and spin in the other direction. I can just barely see the outline of a person as someone else tackles them.

Someone out here is still on our side, and I haven't seen Morgan yet.

"You can't fight me," Nikolai calls. "Do you need another demonstration? Do more people have to die because you can't admit that I'm better than you?"

I don't know if he's talking to me, or to Torovan, or both of us.

And there are dozens of people around him. We can't bind them before others attack, we can't knock them out without fear of hurting them.

But I have to get the boy away from them at least. Whether he's Sabella's son or not.

I reach out and bind the boy, gritting my teeth, pulling him as quickly as I dare toward me.

There's a moment of silence, a moment where I keep pulling the boy while deflecting another attack from my right.

They boy screams, and I falter, am I hurting him?

But it's a scream of pure rage.

Then...then the line comes rushing toward us.

I pull the boy all the way to me and see the threads in his mind, the tangle of Nikolai's soul threads fully enmeshed within his own.

There is no time to be subtle, though I'm sorry about it.

I find the connection between my soul and Sabella's still there, a faint ring in the distance. Very faint. And I resonate that toward her son.

He trembles, and Torovan grunts above me as he stops another attack. I duck my head and cover the boy's, and feel something whistle past my ear.

I look up to the shouts, the oncoming attackers have almost reached us. And I bare my teeth in my own growl, throwing up a solid glass wall of reality all around us.

Torovan shouts as one of his air blades hits my wall on the inside and the blade ricochets back toward me.

I unweave it with a thought and turn back to the boy.

I need a few more moments.

"Your mother sent me," I say. "I'm taking you home. I need to weave you out of Nikolai's control."

"She doesn't want me!" Sabella's son screams.

And the force of it rattles my soul.

I don't even know his name. How could I know Sabella for months and not know that? But then, she didn't talk about him more than she had to. And now I know why.

He's still held in my binding, thrashing to get out.

"Let me out!"

I hear thumps against my woven wall, and I have to concentrate to steady it. To hold it against the people screaming, beating against it.

Reveyan—I see Reveyan, and my heart lurches.

There is a connection between us, too, faint but it's been growing this last week as he's been guarding me.

"Reveyan! You know me! You don't want this!"

He shudders.

The attackers have daggers, and they have swords. One is pounding a shovel.

"I can protect your family!" Nikolai shouts, amplifying his voice over the roars of his little, vicious, stolen army. "I can't protect them if you're trying to take my people out!"

He has no people.

The threads spinning out of him show me that.

He has tools he wields.

The attackers hit the wall again in front of me, and I twitch.

It's like the Great Hall all over again. Me holding out against Sabella's forces.

"Let me out!" Sabella's son screeches.

I weave my binding so I can reach for his head.

And I hate this. Oh gods, I hate this, I don't want to do this.

But I reach into his mind, and, resonating the threads of his soul, push Nikolai's threads out.

It works. It does work. Gods, it works.

The boy looks up at me, trembling. And I let his binding go and pull him close to me.

"I've got you. I've got you."

I don't tell him he's safe.

I'm barely holding back the thumps, the roars, the screams against my woven wall.

I look up to Torovan. "Take him."

The boy looks up, and his eyes widen at the sight of his king. He grew up in the palace, he does know who Torovan is, though he left before I arrived.

The boy runs to Torovan's side.

Good. *Good.*

Did I soul weave for good just now? I have to believe that.

I look up and almost recoil at the wall of rage that surrounds us.

Reveyan, still cutting futilely against my woven wall with his sword. What does Nikolai hold over him that would make him turn from protecting me to attacking me?

Rani sends a gout of fire straight at my wall, scattering the people near him.

I do know what Nikolai has against his soul.

I swallow.

To stop this attacking crowd, I have to wrest control from Nikolai. I have to free these people from his control.

But how do I do that, when that takes thought and time? When invading a mind like I just did feels dangerously close to what Nikolai does, even if it was to save that child?

I don't want to do that again.

Will I have to?

But Nikolai's still only trying to control the people he's sending at us, not me or Torovan.

So I hold, desperately trying to think.

But I won't be able to hold long.

TOROVAN

The world outside of Caleb's woven wall is a nightmare. Fists and swords hammer against the clear reality, the impacts shuddering through the stone beneath my feet.

I see the faces of my own people, their eyes glassy and filled with a rage that isn't theirs.

They're fighting against *me*. Did Nikolai use an illusion of me or Caleb with them, too? What is he making them see or think? What is he making them fear?

I'm a weaver, and I know how far he got into my mind. But these people aren't weavers, they don't have even that level of willpower resistance to him.

I want to reach into their souls and show them it's not true. Whatever Nikolai's telling them. The fear isn't true.

But every time I try to reach for that in just one of them, something new startles me. Makes me turn.

I can't concentrate long enough, and every blow clangs with that personal failure.

Again.

My forearm is throbbing with a cut that I don't think is deep, but it's pulling my attention all the same. I almost trip on Aldric.

Then Caleb shoves at me the boy who was at the front—gods—he must be Sabella's son.

And the boy clings to me. I wrap an arm around him but hardly have any comfort to give.

Here I am again, facing Nikolai, and he has the upper hand.

"Caleb! How do we weave them?" I shout. "How did you free the boy?"

But he's braced, his hands out and fingers bent to straining, panting with his effort.

He's turned the wall around us into a complete circle, open to the air above, but surrounding us with glass.

Aldric is down, but I don't dare try to see what happened. if he's still alive.

I'm just bracing, too, waiting for the wall to come down. Holding the child to me, but not knowing how I'll be able to protect him when the people rush in.

I start to give Caleb my will, but he shakes his head.

"No! Hold your will!"

"Did you hear me?" Nikolai shouts, above the chaos. "You can't fight me!"

He's right. I can't fight him. How do I fight him like this? I can try and throw my reality blades beyond Caleb's wall, but how many of these people are innocents?

I don't want to fight my soldiers, or my guards.

The coward, placing them all before himself. Between us and him.

The *coward.*

My anger is heating again, melting the fear that's held me these last moments.

Then I feel the threads, oily and familiar, descending on me.

Caleb wove a wall around us, but not above us. And Nikolai's threads soar right in.

I stagger as they hit me, winding into my soul.

And I can feel them trying to take hold in the same way they did before, but I've already closed those paths to him.

I can't touch the threads, but I hum with the threads of my own soul.

I am a king.

I am my husband's husband.

I am a weaver.

I am *not* going to be controlled.

Right now, I am the protector over a downed Aldric and Sabella's child, too. A child who's been used far too long in this monster's plans.

I *will* protect them all.

Because that's who I am.

Some of Nikolai's threads slip off of me.

But others...others find the fears still there. The fears buried deeper.

The cracks still inside my soul.

Nikolai killed a king.

He lured my husband here.

He captured all of us weavers.

He stole this child, and he can steal mine, too.

And I can't hold out against his threads forever.

I know I can't.

CALEB

My focus is a single, burning point: the wall. Hold the wall round me. Keep the people Nikolai is controlling *out*. Keep Torovan safe.

And my energy is draining.

Is this what Nikolai wants?

This?

To wear us down?

I shudder and try to strengthen, to hold, to reinforce my willpower, enough to hold the wall and try to fight back.

Nikolai wants us diminished. No matter if we die or not, he wants that.

But I can't catch enough of my own willpower, my own breath, to attack.

And I could attack everyone around us...but not without hurting them. Not without killing some, I fear.

And Nikolai knows that.

I don't know how to fight him. My soul is blazing, I know that. I *know* that.

I can still feel the strength from Torovan weaving my soul.

I know he feels it in his, too.

Should we combine our wills, as he wanted to just now? But then, at which target?

How do we take Nikolai down, without him harming someone else first?

But he will keep gaining ground. Little by little.

He'll keep wearing us down.

And gods—I see his threads coming toward us, passing me, to bury into Torovan's mind.

"Tor!"

I turn. Can I weave Torovan's soul, to hold him steady, to push Nikolai out?

Torovan freezes, but every line of his body speaks of rage. And his eyes are still locked past me, toward Nikolai.

He's fighting.

And I have to hold the wall.

To keep him safe while he fights.

Something has to break. And it has to break soon.

I scan the frenzied crowd of attackers, searching for a weakness, an opening, anything.

Reveyan bangs against the wall to my left again, catching my eye.

He's fighting. His eyes aren't wild anymore but scared. He doesn't want to be attacking, of course he doesn't.

"Reveyan!" I yell. And push what little I can spare of my will at him. At *knowing* him.

He falters.

I look into the blaze of his soul and see the depth of his strength. I strike that chord, and he arches back.

Then his whole body shakes as he comes back into his eyes again.

Reveyan looks around. Looks at the sword in his hands.

"Don't kill them!" I shout.

He sheaths his sword. He spots one of the soldiers and wrenches the man back. Spins him to clock him hard on the jaw.

Then moves to the next one.

Okay. Okay, that's something.

But I don't know the others, soldiers from the town garrison. Rani.

"Rani!"

I reach for his soul, but recoil at the fracture I find there.

He's sobbing openly, screaming at me. Screaming at Torovan. But mostly at me.

The noise of all the shouts has become a constant roar, but I pick out Rani's voice among the rest: "You killed him! You *killed* him!"

I swallow.

Yes, I do know what hell Nikolai is using to make him fight me. Me, who let Torovan ride out without me, who let Torovan get captured. And the man Rani loved was killed by his own hands, controlled by Nikolai.

I hear a scream behind me and turn to see the boy rushing at me, tears streaming down his face. Nikolai has his threads in his mind again.

I have just enough time to weave a barrier between us before he crashes into me.

"She doesn't want me because of you!" he screams against it.

I almost lose my strength in the wall I'm holding around all of us. I almost let the chipping swords crack it.

I manage to pour enough of my will back into my construct wall, dropping my inner barrier. I catch the boy, holding him tight, rolling him toward my side when he tries to shove at my stomach. I weave a shield over my belly, and binding around both of us, to hold us together.

"Your mother wants you," I say, and reach to touch the threads of my caring for Sabella within my own soul.

And the threads in my soul that are my deep, growing love for the child that I carry.

The boy shivers violently, and Nikolai's threads slip again.

Then Nikolai withdraws the threads he was using on the boy and sends them again to Torovan.

Torovan braces, face still set, his brow beading with sweat. He's still fighting. And gods but I wish I could give him my strength this time, but I'm barely holding the wall around us.

And now holding a sobbing boy.

I hear voices rising to my left, toward the outbuildings, and look in that direction, but I can't see past the chaos. Reveyan's taken down three men, but then another man slashes at Reveyan's leg. He goes down with a cry.

And the people around him turn to start beating on him.

No!

I try to weave a shield over Reveyan, but then the people attacking him turn to beat against my wall again.

There are so many of them. *So many.*

And Rani screams, shooting fire straight at me again, trembling my slipping control over the wall, making the threads of my reality construct too volatile to hold.

I'm screaming, half in rage, half in despair, because I know my wall is going to come down.

I know I can't save all those I care about.

I know I can't save everyone.

I don't even know if I can save Torovan, or the boy.

Or myself.

Then Rani jerks, stiffening, and falls over.

I spot the weaving around him, and look back to Torovan, but he's still razor focused on Nikolai.

I glance out through the crowd and just barely see Nikolai's grin drop into a frown.

"Caleb!"

Kian. Kian!

He's rushing toward us from the left, with—with Morgan, who's fighting off the attackers with his sword as best he can, with Kian's help.

"Where's Aria?" I shout, stiffening with the fear that Nikolai has her again. That he'll use her against us.

And knowing if he does, this fight is over.

Kian yells, "She's getting the—"

My wall shudders.

Then cracks.

Then falls into pieces, the threads unraveling.

I scramble to pull the threads back in, to weave them into something less volatile. To keep them from exploding around us and killing us all.

I reach around the boy as he ducks under my arm, scrambles back toward Torovan. And I can't track that now—I weave the unraveling reality into an actual metal shield, then have just enough time to raise my shield to stop the shards of reality flung at my head.

There's another weaver.

That attack came from the right this time, away from the stables and outbuildings where Kian came from.

Was Kian wrong, is Aria under Nikolai's control again?

The weavers who first attacked us, they'd stopped, I thought we took them down. Or, someone had.

Was I wrong?

Or is this Nikolai himself, deciding he's done with weaving minds and wants to finish this?

Finish me?

Another man crashes his sword against my shield, and I grunt, weaving a much tighter wall around Torovan and the boy and Aldric and me.

And then finally lower the heavy shield, but don't unweave it. I might need it again.

I'm wearing down. My energy is flagging, and Valtair was right when he said at the palace that I hadn't had enough time to recover from fighting Sabella before riding out.

The night I spent on the road, restless and hyper-vigilant and having to pee every damned half hour, was not truly rest.

I spot the weaver who threw the shards at me in the crowd, an older woman I don't recognize. She's striding forward—she'd been behind Nikolai. And his mind control threads to her are strong.

Her clothing isn't Barellan, but a sturdy common wear. Not court wear like Lady Denya's, but a similar cut all the same.

Akrean. She must be Akrean.

She sends her shards of reality at me again.

There are no tears on her face. I'm not one of her kings, and neither is Torovan.

I doubt she'd shed any tears if we died.

And the boy? Does she know she's attacking a child as well?

Torovan's holding the boy tightly to him now, but he's still wholly focused on fighting Nikolai's control.

And the Akrean weaver is obviously being controlled.

I look around my shield long enough to glimpse at her soul.

She's broken, like Rani. And trying to weave the soul of a stranger on the battlefield isn't going to help just now.

Kian bellows and rushes at her.

Oh, no. But he's not trained for actual war—

Kian has her bound and on the ground in seconds.

And *gods* I am proud of him.

Morgan, fighting beside me, yells, "We freed some of the soldiers, they're getting our horses. The rest—" He rushes to stop a man from attacking Torovan's side of the thinner wall around us.

Torovan is still locked in whatever battle he has with Nikolai.

I look around me, panting. And strengthen my wall as another elementalist rushes at me, shooting tiny, spinning spheres of water toward my head.

The water pings against the wall, ringing it like a gong.

Then splashes onto the ground as Reveyan manages to push up enough to slash the elementalist's legs from behind.

I almost feel the injury myself.

If I hadn't been a weaver, that could have been me.

I've sat in the same common room with that mage for months now. I helped give him his mage's medallion.

Maybe some of the attacks here are local commoners, too. Some might be house staff. Some might be Nikolai's own retainers.

And how long until the people knocked out in the house wake up and join the fight against us?

Morgan said the freed soldiers were bringing horses, but won't they just end up controlled, too?

And there's no way we can run.

We can't run and leave Nikolai still out there, alive and only growing stronger again. Still fighting against us.

Still turning the people and their fears against us.

We have to end this.

Now.

CHAPTER 57

BRIGHT

TOROVAN/CALEB

TOROVAN

Nikolai's will is a physical force against my own, a constant, grinding pressure.

He isn't just whispering doubts now, he's screaming them.

Every fear I have, every failure, every tiny break in my soul, he finds and pries it open.

You can't protect him.

You left him alone in the palace to be attacked.

You failed on the road and brought him here to die.

I see it, a vision as real as the stone beneath my feet: Caleb, overwhelmed, his wall shattering again, a dozen blades finding him.

Finding him. Sinking in.

No!

I can't turn from the vision, but the vision is agony.

But it will not happen.

But the wall around us did fall once, I know that.

I see Caleb distantly, crouching dully, one hand on the ground, his heavy shield propped in front of him now.

I see his threads holding the wall, and he's constantly tuning its strength.

One cheek smudged with dirt where he must have wiped it. His hair mussed, his spectacles crooked on his nose.

He fills out his borrowed leather armor, but he's a scholar and a mage. He's not a soldier.

He's strong, yes, but he hasn't trained for outright war.

I have to help him. I have to get out of this deadlock with Nikolai I'm in and *help him.*

But Nikolai's threads have me locked in place. As soon as I think of moving, his attack intensifies.

I'm vaguely aware of the boy glued tightly to me, too, who's also depending on me.

And my guilt for not being strong enough to fight Nikolai off, to help Caleb anyway, is shattering my soul.

So I reform it again.

Because I'm as strong as I am.

And right now, that strength is holding.

I feel something at my ankle, a pressure against my boot.

The boy?

I can't look down, but the pressure comes again.

And then—willpower flows to me. Just waiting for me to take it.

Aldric.

He's alive, gripping my boot.

And he's giving me his will.

I take what he gives, and it's enough that I can breathe again, can unclench my jaw, can blink, can take a single step forward before the relentless assault of Nikolai's attack locks me down again.

Can I push back?

I have to push back.

Can I weave Nikolai's soul?

But he's not being controlled—he's the one controlling.

Still. He's in my mind.

He knows enough of my thoughts to know what levers to push.

He's focused a lot of attention on me—I can see the threads, just faintly.

But he's also still controlling those near to us who are still attacking.

That's a lot of minds to weave.

"Nikolai," I say. Just a whisper. Will he hear it?

I swallow. And he's not close, and there are so many between him and us, but I try to see the threads of his soul.

Is he still a symphony, as Caleb calls it? Is his river running anything close to true?

I see the blaze of his soul when I look at it, the furious fire within him.

But he's burning so hot I'm not sure I can even touch his threads without being scorched.

"Nikolai," I say again.

And reach for the only thing I can think that might change anything.

That might change something in me.

Because I am strong enough to do this.

And if it took Caleb reaching his deepest truths to defeat him the first time...I have to reach deeper still.

I have to make new truths.

"Nikolai...I forgive you."

I feel, for just a moment, his hold on me falter. Just enough that I can step up beside Caleb and get a better hold on the boy.

Caleb looks up to me, straining to stand beside me, his teeth bared. "We have to end this, Tor. Gods. We have to end this!"

A figure blurs past me, and I focus. Morgan, who I'm just now realizing has been defending my side of the wall against the attackers for minutes. Minutes?

It feels like hours.

Days.

Nikolai screams, and the threads he hurls at me now are enough to make my vision darken.

CALEB

Nikolai weaves his cry into the air around him, his fury like a physical blow.

I shudder a step back, and Torovan just...falls.

No. No!

"Tor!"

The boy's falling with him, but then realizes enough of what's happening to help me catch Torovan, keep his head from hitting the stones.

"You have him?" I ask. "Help me lower him."

Torovan's eyes are open as we both lower him to the stones. He's dead weight, even if I can see his eyes frantically moving, his mouth open and moving like he's talking.

I pour my willpower into him.

Take it. Take it!

I feel something brush against me and I jump, reaching for my sense of the wall—

But I don't feel it.

I let go of my wall when I sprang to stop Torovan's fall.

Morgan's to my back now, still defending us.

The crowd of attackers has grown smaller. So many of them—too many of them—on the ground.

And Kian's caught the weaving of my wall and is unraveling it this time.

I press my hand to Torovan's cheek and look around us, bracing for another wave of attacks.

But...but no one is attacking.

Everyone who'd been screaming and pounding against my wall is suddenly reeling, like waking up from a drunken sleep.

Because all of the threads Nikolai has are now focused entirely on Torovan.

"Fight him," I say, turning back to him. Pouring everything into him that I can. "*Fight him.*"

"I am," he manages. And turns his eyes, just a little toward me. "Take it back, Caleb. Take your will. Take. Him. Down."

He shoves my will back at me, and I don't want it. Not if it means he might lose. And I might lose him.

But if Nikolai's distracted, if he's not controlling anyone else, that means I might have a chance.

If the only person on the line right now is the person I love most in the world.

"Take it!" Torovan cries.

It's a command. A desperate plea.

And I have to trust.

I take my will back in a rush, then turn toward Nikolai and charge.

I dash across the field, my legs heavy, but moving.

The closer I am, the stronger my attack will be.

Will Nikolai divert from Torovan to attack me? To make the people he's controlling attack me?

But Nikolai's attention is fully on Torovan.

And...and Nikolai is crying, too?

Gods, what did Torovan do to make him *cry*?

I weave a binding around Nikolai, but he flicks his chin, and it shreds away.

"I'll kill him, Caleb," he says, his voice strained, almost too low for me to hear. "One more step, and I'll kill him."

I don't stop.

"You can't kill him," I say.

"Do you want to watch me try?"

He sounds...exhausted. There are deep shadows beneath his eyes, ghoulish in the flickering torchlight. The people who'd been wielding the torches have mostly scattered.

Some torches have been planted in the ground.

One or two are smoldering on the ground itself, smoky in the grass still damp from an earlier rain.

The people who'd been behind Nikolai—were they all controlled by him, too?

I see a few still beyond him, watching me approach, their eyes eerily vacant.

Until one man lifts his hands, and I'm not prepared for the reality blade until it grazes my cheek.

I stumble, trip, but manage just barely not to fall.

But I slow my rush, and Nikolai's smirking now even through his strain, not looking at me.

"They're all weavers," he says slowly. "Akrean weavers. They are loyal to me." He pauses. "I'm about to stop your husband's heart."

I swallow but don't take the bait. "Why the hell would they be loyal to you? You're trying to bring weavers down in Barella—"

"I'm trying to bring you and Torovan down. There's a difference. You want to take from us what is *ours.*"

Take power from the nobility?

"You would strip this kingdom and all its nobles of their power until it means *nothing*, Caleb."

I stop, bending over, trying to catch my breath, eyeing the Akrean weavers.

I'm exposed here. Should I weave another wall around myself?

But Nikolai is barely sending any threads to the Akreans, all his focus again on Torovan.

But my energy is draining, too.

"Tell me you'll give me your child," Nikolai growls. "Promise me. Swear on your soul. Swear on anything that means anything to you, because if I don't believe it, I'll *kill him!*"

But he hasn't killed Torovan yet.

And I'm starting to hear the desperation in his voice.

"Why won't he just die!"

The words ring out into the night. And two of the Akrean weavers shudder.

Do I dare step forward again? I don't see any threads to the Akreans now, but as soon as I step, two of the Akreans hurl a binding weave at me.

I unweave the bindings in the air.

"I don't even need him," Nikolai says. "*You're* a king. You could be the regent for your child. Marry me. Or, I'll marry you. It doesn't have to be a choice."

I'm too tired, too angry, too absolutely done with this to argue with him.

I weave reality beside his neck, forming a blade, aiming at his throat.

I push it in.

And it—stops.

The other Akrean weavers are showing more signs of life, now, half focused on me, half focused on Nikolai.

They're shielding him.

He's controlling some of them, but barely. Most have just… just bought into his lies. Whatever those lies are.

It's why he hasn't given a *fuck* this whole time.

He's not scared of us at all.

"This is why you can't win," Nikolai snarls, finally turning to me. "You're not creative enough, Caleb. You never were. You can see what's already there. But you can't weave the people around you to make what you want happen."

I take a breath.

But, I can.

And maybe I've been going about the soul weaving wrong. Here, in this battlefield, I can't weave everyone's souls. And some are too broken to fix quickly. Some might not want to be fixed.

But I can shine like the beacon I am.

I weave my soul.

I weave my heart.

I light my energy on fire, everything about me that makes me *me*.

That makes my apprentices, makes my guards, makes my husband fight beside me. Fight for me. Fight to protect those I love, too.

That makes Sabella trust me to bring back her son, even after she attacked me.

I'm here.

I am *here* because I need to protect my kingdom. And every damned person in it, all of them.

I pitch my voice to carry. "Akrean weavers are welcome in Barella."

Nikolai does a double take.

Because no, he wasn't expecting that.

He narrows his eyes but doesn't look at me directly.

"Any weaver may have a choice to become a court mage," I go on, "or to live as they choose. And I don't care—I truly don't care—if they're soul weavers, too. Because so am I."

I'm a master mage.

And Nikolai...is not.

He finally looks at me. And I watch as his threads, for a moment, falter.

"I know the other side of it, Nikolai. If you're the darkness, I'm the mirror." I step closer. "If you crush their will, I give them space. That's the other side. You can't have a strong weaver without strong will. You *can't*, Nikolai. You can't take their wills and still have them fight strong for you."

Sabella had control.

But not the strength to use it.

Not until she thought her son was under direct threat again, not until she was fighting for her life. Taking that small bit of willpower back to herself.

Maybe that was strength for Nikolai in that moment, but in the end?

I know Sabella is in the palace now, holding back any and all threats that oppose her.

I *know* that in my soul. Because I know her soul, too.

Nikolai pulls his threads back from Torovan and stops, seething, turning to me.

"I have the power, Caleb. I have the willpower to rule a kingdom—"

"You're not going to rule," I say, stepping closer again. "Zinara will rule. You're still allied with her? If you have Akrean weavers? If you—gods—if you're the one kidnapping weavers at the border, your people, not hers?"

And that bit of information clicks everything into place.

"You want to build an army that only you control."

"Weavers are strength," he says. "You know that."

"But you've taken their *wills*, Nikolai!" I throw out a hand toward the Akreans, who are not looking as lifeless at all now. Who are looking between Nikolai and me. "How well do you think they'll serve you? And you get enough people and you'll have to control them constantly."

"I'll train others to control them."

I feel, behind me, my resonance between Torovan and me, the distance between us, shortening. Strengthening.

And I feel, to one side, my resonance with Kian shortening, too.

And to my left. Aria. Who's managed to stay out of the worst of this, but who's coming closer now.

Is she Nikolai's again?

But no, our resonance is still strong.

All Nikolai's threads now are held to himself, held in ready, waiting to spring out at me.

But he hasn't struck yet.

Behind me, Torovan flares into a blaze like I know my soul is still projecting. It takes a few moments, but I see Kian start to blaze in my mind's eye, too.

He's always learned so fast.

Then I feel another, much lesser blaze beside Kian, but still growing.

Gods. Morgan? I think that's Morgan.

"It's not about control," I say. "It's about trust."

Nikolai looks between all of us.

Then all his soul threads shoot out of him at once. Not toward me or Torovan again, but into the Akrean weavers.

Who jolt with the assault but regain their focus quickly.

I don't weave a shield. I reach along the soul resonances between myself and those I care about. And I pour my love along them, and my trust.

I believe in them, because I know them.

And I believe in myself.

After a moment, I start to feel my trust in them come back toward me. They trust in me, too.

Soul weaving. *This* is what soul weaving was meant to be.

Like Torovan and I stood together, side by side, and wove away a storm.

Trusting each other completely.

I feel his trust in me now, comforting as an evening hearth. I know he feels mine.

And Kian. And Morgan. And Aria, where I'm reaching, too.

She's stepping closer now, into the remnants of the torchlight. Her face determined. But then, I don't need to look at her to know that.

The Akrean weavers...don't attack. Nikolai's threads are weakening, thinning, in the blaze of us.

He can't control people who know their truths.

And we're all bright with different truths than what the Akreans have been told. Have been manipulated with.

"You're the king?" one of the Akreans asks, looking at me.

"Don't talk to them!" Nikolai screams, whether at the Akreans or us, I don't know.

"One of them," I say, and nod to Torovan. "He is the king."

The Akrean...kneels. He holds up his hands to Torovan. "Asylum, my lord. Please."

Nikolai hisses and steps back. "I've given you asylum."

"You're a soul weaver," one of the women says to him. But then looks at me. "A—a dark soul weaver."

"I brought you out of that hell of a kingdom," Nikolai snarls, turning around to them. "You fight for me! Kill them!"

Two of the Akreans jerk as Nikolai's threads still reach them. But the others near them weave quickly to hold their arms in place.

"Kill them!" Nikolai screams. He whips around, pointing toward the guards and elementalists and common people he sent to attack us earlier. Who he used as shields.

But those who haven't scattered are watching us now.

And I think we might be blazing enough that even those without weaver's senses might be seeing it.

Nikolai sends his threads at them anyway, and they do take in a few hearts. But they're still much weaker than before.

I step closer to Nikolai still, and so does Torovan.

"I told you I forgive you," Torovan says.

And I jolt.

Was *that* what made Nikolai go crazy and attack him before?

And…Torovan forgives him? For what, for killing his father? For threatening our kingdom? For threatening me and our child?

Gods. I don't.

But Torovan blazes all the brighter for it.

"Because then you can't hold that over me. You can't hold my family. You can't hold my husband, or my child, or my father, or my mother. You can't have them, Nikolai. They're not yours. None of them are."

My breath hitches. And I know I'm dimming a little, my soul rearing up into conflict because no, I *don't* forgive this man. He cannot have that from me, either. That's not his.

But Torovan keeps walking forward. He holds out his hand and weaves a sword-shaped blade of shimmering reality into his grip.

Nikolai starts backing up.

He throws out his hands, trying to catch Torovan in a binding weave, but I reach out and shred the weaving to threads.

Nikolai tries to hurl his own reality spikes.

Kian unravels them, and before I can reach, Aria catches the two he doesn't get.

Nikolai backs up again.

But now the Akreans are behind him.

Clearly not wanting to be on the wrong side of this.

"Surrender," I say. "And you'll live out your life in a place of our choosing, but you will get to live."

I don't want him to live.

But if we have weavers around him trained in the other side of soul weaving...I don't think he'll actually be a threat.

He looks between us.

At Torovan, then me. Then down at my pregnant belly.

Nikolai screams and hurls every thread he has, every soul weaving thread, every woven shard of reality, straight at my stomach.

I throw up a shield wall and pluck every resonant thread in my soul.

Torovan dashes forward and slices Nikolai's throat.

Nikolai's soul threads shudder, flicker, then go out, just grazing against my shield.

His regular threads, his shards, are unwoven by Kian and Aria again before they can reach me.

And for a moment, for a drawn-out moment, everything is still.

The autumn cicadas buzz in the distance.

"You're pregnant?" one of the Akreans asks. "You're the weaver who weaves between a woman and a man?"

"Yes."

"He was trying to kill your child," another says. And then spits on the ground.

And then, one by one, they all spit.

And then kneel.

Torovan, standing over Nikolai's body, trembling, lets go of his blade of reality.

The blood it held on the blade falls to the ground.

He sways.

I jolt from my stillness and let go of my shield wall, rushing to him, wrapping my arm around his back, letting him lean on me. Leaning on him.

"I didn't forgive him," he says. "Not as much as I thought."

Oh, gods. This man.

I press my face into his hair, holding him to me. Trembling. My body not believing it's done.

But it's over.

I check Nikolai's lifeless eyes on the ground, his mouth still open in rage.

I can feel that his possibilities have left him, and only the lingering sense of his fading reality remains.

"Yes," Torovan says, looking up at the Akreans. "You are all welcome in Barella. Let's—let's go back to the house for the night. And then tomorrow, we'll go home."

CHAPTER 58

MY WEAVER

CALEB/TOROVAN

CALEB

In the aftermath of battle, Torovan and I lean on each other on our way back into the manor house.

But everything, it seems, needs to be taken care of at once.

The wounded need tended to, Aldric and Rani and Reveyan among them, and Morgan ends up busy as the only elemental healer we have just now, though he protests that he was never formally trained.

Then one of the Akrean weavers says he can weave reality to heal. And *that* is something I'm going to be asking to learn from him. The Akrean herds Morgan away to one corner of the Great Hall where the wounded are being laid out, barking orders. Morgan, with a look back for my nod, follows.

Sabella's son, who stayed near Aldric when we came inward to fight Nikolai, now lets a shaky Aldric lean on him.

His name, I learn, is Jonan.

Kian is hovering near them, too, and has an anxious eye on Aria, who's helping pile dropped and bloody weapons in one corner. To be cleaned and sorted later.

And the Akrean mages, maybe fearing that if anything happens to Torovan or me that their own fates will fall, too, ring Torovan and me like a halo of guards.

Torovan is still favoring—and trying to hide—his bloody forearm. He didn't let Morgan see it, but I hiss when he removes his hand.

"Tor—"

His shoulders square likes he's going to dig in.

"Morgan!" I call across the hall.

"There are others who need help more than—"

"If you die from an infection, your mother will invade."

He snaps his mouth shut, and holds still as Morgan jogs back over, gives his king an openly reproachful look, and then begins to heal the cut.

"Are you injured?" he asks, turning to me. Looking chagrined that he hadn't asked before. He glances to my cheek, and I touch it, my finger coming away a little sticky.

But the cut's no longer bleeding.

Still, Morgan moves to me, barely waits for my nod, and presses a hand to my cheek.

"Did you take down one of the first weavers who attacked us?" I ask.

"The woman wasn't paying attention," he says. "I knocked her out with the butt of my dagger." He glances back toward the wounded. "She's over there."

I tense. Was she Akrean? Or maybe someone Nikolai brought with him from his own district?

"She's not one of ours," one of the Akreans says, following where Morgan's pointing.

"Torovan," I say, "I think Nikolai was the one taking weavers from the Akrean border. He as much as confirmed it. He wanted to inflame our conflict with the Akreans, I think, and take the weavers for himself."

Torovan's jaw tightens. But then he blows out his breath, glancing toward the still-open doors.

Nikolai is dead now.

Maybe Torovan's mother is still out there, but Nikolai, her sword, is dead.

"Close the doors in between people coming in," Torovan calls. "Let's get the hearth fires built up, let's get the hall warm again."

I shiver, my adrenaline finally fading enough to feel the bitter chill.

I move closer to Torovan, brushing against his own body heat.

While he was talking with the Akreans, I sent some of the soldiers who asked to sweep the house of all the people that we knocked out. Maybe they'd been controlled or coerced, too.

But maybe they hadn't been.

But I see one of the guards I sent coming back from the inner corridor now, with a young man in tow. Tall, lanky, his black hair tousled against his chiseled, light-brown face.

He sees me looking and comes toward me with purpose in his eyes.

Torovan sees the movement and tenses.

But the young man holds up his hands. Bows, even while sidestepping two more soldiers crossing the hall toward the weapons pile.

"Your Majesties, I'm Gardellan Mar. I'm a weaver—"

"You're from the village near the border," I say.

He opens his mouth, nods.

"Are there more?" Torovan asks. "More weavers he took from the villages there?"

Gardellan nods. "Two more, an older man and a woman. They attacked you. They were controlled. But I...resisted Nikolai's control. Mostly."

Then those were the weavers who'd attacked us at the start of the fight.

I look over toward where Morgan has gone back to helping the injured, and the woman he pointed out before.

"So your will is strong," Torovan says, clapping the young man on the shoulder. "Would you like to come to the palace to be a court mage, too?"

Torovan looks to me, but he hardly needs permission for it.

Gardellan looks almost...embarrassed. "I was hoping, uh, yes. I was hoping to get away and come to the palace. And ask you."

He looks to me and bows again. "Master Mage."

Torovan waves to me, a tired smile on his lips. And it is *good* to see a smile, even now.

So I give Gardellan the oath of a court mage.

Then turn to the Akreans. I know Torovan said they could all be court mages, but—but do they want to be?

I don't know what hell they left in Akreal to think that Nikolai's service would be better.

Or, I don't know what choices they had or didn't have.

I'll have to find that out.

But for now, I say, "Come back to the palace in Barella with us, or leave if you want to. You're weavers—your will is your own."

Only two of the Akreans say they don't wish to go to the palace. And the way they're moving, like Torovan and I might change our minds and take them with us anyway, makes me think they hadn't had a choice before.

My jaw tightens.

Nikolai is dead, yes.

He's *dead.* And yes, I did go back and look a second time.

I want to go now and stare into the eyes of the man who killed my husband's father, who caused so much pain in our kingdom, who tried to kill my child as the last act he had in the world.

The Akreans spit on the ground?

I want to spit on him, too.

But, tomorrow morning, we'll burn the dead.

Already, we're unraveling every plan that Nikolai wove in his weavings made of fear.

Those weavings were fragile, in the end.

Tomorrow, we'll send Nikolai back to the gods, if they'll have him.

And the rest of our dead, who are still being counted.

Which others might join in the night, if the healers can't heal all their wounds, or if they're already too far gone.

We won today, yes.

But it wasn't without a cost.

TOROVAN

We're on the road the next morning, a somber and much slower parade than when I rode out.

We left some of our people behind, send up in ash this morning to return to the gods. Some of my soldiers, and the elementalists. One of my guards.

But Kas, his leg half healed and bandaged tightly to keep him from moving it much, not that he's paid any attention to that advice, rides by my side.

And Caleb on my other side, staring ahead, his lips pulled tight. His brows drawn down.

But he catches me looking, and his face softens.

My weaver.

We're bringing back the Akreans who wished to come with us, the weavers taken by Nikolai at the border, and some of Nikolai's own people who have decided to have a change of heart.

Caleb and I went down the lines of all of them this morning, too, soul weaving those who let us to clear the rest of Nikolai's immediate influence.

We couldn't, though, fully clear the trauma.

A few did not let us weave them, which was their choice. Most of those, we left behind. And I truly hope they don't cause more trouble in the countryside, but I couldn't in my heart drag them back to a prison in Barella.

Not when they were likely just longer under Nikolai's control.

Two, though, we're bringing back as prisoners. The woman who brought me my food, who continued to try to attack us after she woke up, and one of the riders who brought Caleb in to the manor house.

And I know from my mother that some people are just... not good in their core.

We ride all day, stopping only for short breaks, at our slower pace, then camp for the night.

We don't have enough tents, so Caleb and I have to share, but...but I hardly mind that.

The feel of him against me.

The smell of horse and road dust and his spicy, earthy musk. He's eaten no cinnamon here, I swear, but he still smells faintly of cinnamon, too.

We're too exposed, too crammed into our tent to truly be together, but when we get back to the palace—when we get back to the palace, I plan to not leave our bedroom for a solid day.

Though I fear my kingdom will have other plans.

CALEB

It's evening the next day when we reach the palace gates. And that night I spent tucked next to Torovan in the tent, with barely enough room to fumble in the dark, and days' worth of fear and need to burn between us...wasn't enough.

Though I savor every moment we have.

Because I wasn't sure we'd have those moments again.

But we're almost home.

Torovan sent riders ahead of us that first day, to tell Valtair and Elsira what happened, and that Nikolai is dead.

And now, as we ride through the gates, all of us dusty and tired and ready for this all to be over, I see Valtair, Elsira, and Sabella on the steps, waiting.

Kian, who's decided it's his job to look out for Jonan, Sabella's son, stands up on his stirrups and waves to Sabella.

"Here! Jonan, your mother is here!"

Sabella puts her hands to her mouth and rushes forward, as Kian hurries to help Jonan down.

But Jonan manages on his own and dashes into his mother's arms.

We managed to convince him, I think, that his mother hadn't abandoned him. But I didn't weave his soul or his mind any more than I had to in that desperate battle. Those wounds will be Sabella's to heal, however they heal.

She looks up to me as I rein in my mount, and get down on shaky legs, the ground unsteady beneath me.

Elsira hurries over, grabbing the reins with one hand, and my arm with the other.

"No trouble here?" I ask.

"No trouble," she says. Her eyes are burning. "You killed him. You did it. You killed him."

I nod to where Torovan is dismounting to an equally fierce-looking Valtair.

"Torovan killed him. But...he's dead, yes."

And on this, the second day after Nikolai's death, I might be finally starting to believe it's over.

I look around to the courtiers gathered in front of the palace, far less than there'd been when we rode out.

I see my mother, and my eyes, suddenly, sting.

And my mother's crossing the courtyard to me, wrapping her arms around me, travel grime and all, pressing her forehead into my shoulder. I feel her shoulders shake, once, before she composes herself and draws back. She cups my stubble-roughened cheek with one hand.

I sniff hard.

"I did it," I say. "I saved him." I look to Torovan, and I know—I *know*—that Valtair's trying to argue him into giving a speech. And I know he will.

Because tired as he is, that's the kind of man he is. That's the king he is.

His people first.

Always.

"And he saved me," I say.

"People of Barella!" Torovan bellows. He's looking for me, and I squeeze my mother's arm before I move beside him, twining my fingers in his. I watch the brilliance of his soul brighten when I come near. And I know my soul is brightening, too.

"Our enemy, who killed my father, and tried to kill my husband, and tried to kill our unborn child, has been defeated!"

He can't say more, because the cheer that goes up is thunderous. Rattling the stone walls and the ground beneath us.

Because of him.

And I know...I know, even if it's only a little, it's also because of me.

I spot the Akrean delegate, Lady Denya in the crowd, and watch as she recognizes some of the Akrean weavers who are just now riding in behind us. She holds a hand to her mouth, and I can see her eyes are shining from here.

That wasn't in Torovan's message he sent ahead. Because that was always going to take more nuance, more explanation.

Denya's eyes move to me, and she gives me a deep and solemn nod.

I nod back. Because she helped keep this palace safe, too.

"And even though we still have those who would stand against us," Torovan goes on, finally, when the crowds start to quiet, "we were saved by our weaver's hearts—that is how we stood against our enemies. And we will stand again! But now—now we have a feast to attend! We didn't get to have our last Harvest Festival feast, to send us off into the next year. Let's—"

And the crowd, in their roar of approval, doesn't let him say another word.

C H A P T E R 59

———

R E S O N A N C E

C A L E B

I'm in his arms, in the quiet, in the softness of our own bed.

And being with him again, being with him in my body now, gods. I'd almost forgotten what that worship felt like.

He's holding me now like he doesn't ever want to let me out of his sight.

Though I know that tomorrow, he'll go to the marathon of Council Meetings both he and the ministers and lords and ladies threatened each other with after the feast tonight.

And I'll be in the common room with my old apprentices, and my new apprentices, and testing the Akreans who've already taken the oaths of a court mage and are now ready to learn the court of Barella, too. And I'll learn from them.

We'll both be doing what we do, because Torovan's the king. And I'm the master weaver.

But he's *my* king, and he's a good king.

And I'm his master weaver, and I'm damned good at that, too.

"Mmm, can we not be busy for a day?" he asks into my hair.

"We wouldn't be us."

He coughs a laugh, and I snicker, but he sighs.

Runs his hands down my arms.

Kisses my neck.

And I know, tired as we are, it won't be long before we're embracing in a different way again.

And one thing, one more thing, one tiny thing in the face of all we've just faced, worms its way into my chest, into my heart, a weight upon my soul.

I turn to him. Press a hand to his heart, and the weaver's medallion he's still wearing.

"Tor. I don't want to have more children."

He grips my hand. Brings it to his lips.

"I know."

I take a shuddering breath.

It wasn't a mistake to want the child growing within me, I want that child with everything I am.

But while I'm still Caleb now, and while I know I will reweave myself as Irava again when I'm ready...I'm not ready.

He brushes back my hair. Leans in to kiss my cheek, but then stops, knowing I'm serious.

Knowing I'm trying to lay out this last thing between us.

I gather myself. "But it's my duty, if I can—"

"It was never your duty." His eyes flick between mine, dark and deep in the lamplight. "Did you think that? Do you still think that?"

Mostly...no.

But also, a little.

"It's your duty to be the man, or the woman, I love. Nothing more, Caleb."

I grip his hand. "I don't regret—"

"I know."

I move closer, leaning until I rest my head against his.

I can feel the resonance of his soul, his symphony quieter now, focused and interweaving with mine.

But his love.

His love is there like the driving note beneath it all.

He doesn't apologize—there is no need.

I don't apologize.

There's been no mistake.

Only two souls who had cracks that needed mending, slowly mending each other.

"What should we call her?" I ask, resting one hand on my stomach. "Or him?"

He's quiet a long moment. Then, softly, asks, "Could we name them after my father? Either Darian if he's a boy, or Daria if he's a girl? I mean—"

I snort.

"And if he figures out he *is* a girl—"

I pull him close, kissing him as thoroughly as my tired body will let me.

Because he is my heart.

All of it.

And I'm all of his, too.

Thanks so much for reading, and I hope you enjoyed *A Weaver's Heart!*

The story continues in *An Elemental Husband,* out in 2026.

Read my next books as I write them on my Patreon!
https://www.patreon.com/novaecaelum

Want to stay up to date on the latest books? Sign up for my newsletter!
https://novaecaelum.com/pages/newsletter

Acknowledgments

To all my patrons who read this first, who supported this book as it was being written, thank you!! I love you all dearly!

Huge thank you to all my readers and everyone who sent the first book viral this year and then demanded a second with this same pair. This book literally wouldn't exist without you, wouldn't have torn my heart inside out again and put it back together more whole than before. You are amazing!

Thanks to Jackie and Ashley, assistants extraordinaire! This whole business would probably fall apart without you.

And to my family and friends who've happily cheered me on! You rock! <3

About the Author

Novae Caelum writes romantasy and epic space fantasy with diverse and inclusive main characters.

Novae's pronouns are he/they/starself. He's transmasc, genderfluid, and ace, and a whole queer galaxy of other things as well.

Novae's fiction has been in Lambda Award-winning and World Fantasy finalist anthologies, and he has short stories archived on the moon!

Novae lives and writes in the American Southwest with his very favorite pup, Major Samantha Carter, who is the cutest.

ALSO BY NOVAE CAELUM

The Stars and Green Magics

The Truthspoken Heir

The Shadow Rule

A Bid to Rule

Court of Magickers

The Nameless Storm

The Second Ruler: Part One

The Second Ruler: Part Two

The Second Ruler: Part Three (forthcoming 2026)

The King's Weaver

The King's Weaver

A Weaver's Heart

An Elemental Husband (forthcoming 2026)

Lyr and Cavere

Good King Lyr: A Genderfluid Romance

The Space Roads

The Space Roads: Volume One

Standalone

Magnificent: A Nonbinary Superhero Novella

The Throne of Eleven

Lives on Other Worlds

Sky and Dew

Visit Novae Caelum's website to find out where to read these titles direct from the author!

https://novaecaelum.com

PREVIEW: THE TRUTHSPOKEN HEIR

THE STARS AND GREEN MAGICS BOOK ONE

A Truthspoken's life is never truly their own. Truthspoken have choices, but the choices always come down to 'is it good for the kingdom?' If not, then it's not a choice at all.

— ARIANNA RHIALDEN, MELESORIE X IN
THE CHANGE DIALOGUES

"My daughter. I've reviewed all available candidates and have begun negotiations with the Javieri family for you to marry their daughter, the prince."

Arianna Rhialden, Truthspoken Heir to the interstellar Kingdom of Valoris, stared at her father with perfect control. Perfect poise. Her breath didn't quicken, her quickening heart rate didn't show—and it slowed again when she willed it. She was Truthspoken, after all. She was in control of her body and her mind.

"Father," she said, inclining her head. "I'd hoped to be consulted on the choice of my future consort."

They were in her father's study. A familiar room, homey in its way. There wasn't currently a fire in the hearth—her father had been in meetings all day—but the beige walls themselves held a warmth, the powder blue, overstuffed couch she sat on knew her form. She'd spent many hours here under her father's training, learning how to read every nuance of a face, a posture, a personality. Learning how to shift them at will and become someone else.

Her father sat back, his narrow eyes sharpening on her. His black hair was bound into a femme-style knot to one side, diamond and red nova heart pins holding it in place. His red lips twitched, and it wasn't in a smile.

Arianna braced herself.

"The Javieri family was the only real choice. It was them or your mother's family, the Delors—and that line is too close to your own. You know the power they hold, and the power they threaten us with. You know your duty, Arianna. You have always done your duty. Prince Lesander is charismatic, she is excellent with handling people, she has as much social training as it's possible to have without being Truthspoken."

He raised his brows. "She's beautiful."

Arianna gave a tight shrug. It wasn't that she didn't appreciate beauty—she did, even if she had little desire to actually sleep with anyone. Or the time to explore if she ever wanted that option. That wasn't the issue, though, was it? She wouldn't have to sleep with her wife, or husband, or spouse, whoever that would be.

She wanted to not be tied to anyone. She wanted to not be forced into a proximity with someone she didn't know.

Arianna was the Truthspoken Heir, and yes, it was her duty to marry. She'd always known it would happen, but she'd thought she'd have more time to train before then. She'd been steadily taking on more responsibilities at the palace. She wanted to go on a tour of the other worlds, solidify her power and persona in the public eye. She didn't want to spend a significant portion of her time entertaining her future wife.

There were very few people she actually liked in the universe, and she was sure that this Lesander Javieri would not be one of them. Hardly anyone was on a level enough to be interesting to her.

"I will, of course, meet with her if that's what you wish," she said.

"Arianna, I've already made the formal overtures to the Javieris. Lesander is on her way. That's a two-week trip from the Javieri homeworld near the Dynasty border. We'll convert one of the upcoming balls into an engagement ball in your honor. That popular band, the Rings of Vietor, will be in the city then—your sister would swoon to line them up for the ball. It will be an excellent opportunity to build your popular image, make your engagement a cultural event."

"Father," Arianna said carefully, smoothing out the edges of her green silk tunic, "is there something I should know, that you're rushing this engagement?"

He'd already made the plans. Adeius, then it was done. She'd have no choice.

Not that she ever had a choice. Her life was her kingdom's. Her life would never be her own.

She met his eyes and saw something there, just a flash of unease, that set her senses on alert.

"The political climate is volatile," he said. "Perhaps more than you know."

She knew a lot. She knew the politics of the Kingdom of Valoris with its one hundred and eighty-seven vassal worlds. She knew the ongoing schemes of the high houses to gain power and potentially overthrow the Truthspoken who ruled the kingdom. She knew the internal tensions around the Green Magicker sect and their need for more power, and the intensely alien Kidaa on the anti-spin border. She knew all of this, and she couldn't see where that added up to her needing to secure an engagement to the Javieri prince in the next two weeks.

"How? How is it more volatile than I know? I've been sitting Reception for the last month, listening to the courtiers' woes. The situation with the Javieris isn't any less stable now than it was a month ago. I've been judging, I've been ruling—"

"While I gather information. While I deal with the Navy and the Army. While I deal with the diplomats and ongoing treaty negotiations. Yes, Daughter, you have been ruling over much this last month, but don't forget, you are not the Seritarchus. You're not the ruler of this kingdom—I am. Power needs to be rebalanced, and this alliance with the Javieris will do that. Can you set aside your dislike for people of all kinds—"

"I don't dislike people."

Arianna stilled as she watched the disapproval on her father's face. She was losing control of her temper. Adeius, she'd been talking over him. She never got rattled enough to do that. She had to stay in control. The Truthspoken Heir must always be in control.

"I don't dislike people," she said again, her tone more moderate this time. "But I truly don't see how an engagement now will benefit the kingdom. It will only take me away from my duties, and you need me—"

"Arianna, I need you to do your duty as the Heir, and at this moment, that is to marry into the house that is most advantageous for the kingdom. You must marry, and you must have your own heirs."

She caught something in his tone, and her focus sharpened. "Is your life in danger? Have you been threatened more than usual—"

He laughed, a jarring, bitter sound. The red nova hearts in his earrings sparked in the light.

He so seldom laughed it gave her pause.

"Truthspoken are always in danger of assassination. The sooner you are married and your heirs are started in their incubators, the better for all of us. If I'm killed, you'll be the ruler. If you're killed—well, your sister isn't ready to rule a kingdom. I'm giving you every chance I can to give you a strong and stable rule when that time comes. May it be many, many long years off."

But she didn't like the edge in his voice. If she was always in control, he—well. He was the Seritarchus. He was control itself.

He stood, tugged down the cuffs of his midnight coat. "Do your duty, Arianna. Marry the prince. If you have to craft another persona for yourself to make it work—do that. Just make it work. The engagement will be in two weeks. Now, if you will excuse me, I have work to do, and so do you."

❧

Dressa Rhialden, second Truthspoken heir to the Kingdom of Valoris, caught her breath as Prince Lesander Javieri entered the reception room. Lesander was grace itself, tall, with pale pink skin, her flame-red hair bound up and cascading around bare shoulders, deep blue shirt and tan trousers cut at just the right angles to show off her curves without flaunting them. Diamond earrings that caught the light. Lips slightly parted as she held out her hands to greet . . . Dressa's sister.

Dressa was trained to never let any emotion show that she didn't want to. She kept her smile open and genuine, if not overly wide. Delighted to meet the prince who would marry her older sister, but not so delighted as to cause an interstellar incident.

Her chest constricted as her sister, Arianna, *the* Truthspoken Heir, took Lesander's hands, exchanging chaste kisses. Arianna was perfectly poised herself, not one of her hairs out of place in her elegant knot, minimal makeup on her flawless, copper-brown skin.

Dressa could be flawless, too. She could be whoever she wanted—but flawless wasn't the persona she portrayed to the court. And anyhow, flawless wouldn't matter here in a political marriage.

And this woman, this prince who almost outshone the Truthspoken Heir herself, was forever out of Dressa's reach.

Adeius, she had no wish at all to be the Heir, but the thought of having Lesander as her wife was so tempting. But she had no wish to rule the kingdom someday. She was perfectly happy to leave that chore to her sister.

"Prince Lesander, it is good to see you well." Dressa's father, the Truthspoken Ruler of the Kingdom of Valoris, stood on the other side of Arianna, hands clasped loosely in front of him. He was wearing his own body today—or what body he publicly showed as himself to the court. Athletic build, long black hair bound in a tight braid down his back. Wearing a ring on every finger and a purple high-collared coat that matched his purple color-shifting lipstick.

Lesander broke from Arianna to clasp his hands as well, though she didn't go so far as to kiss his cheeks, and he didn't offer.

"Seritarchus. I am honored to join your family."

"You haven't joined it yet," the Seritarchus said dryly, and Dressa watched Lesander stiffen the slightest degree.

The marriage, of course, was all politics. Lesander's family was one of a number of high house families actively clawing their way to the highest seat of power in the kingdom—which was right here, in this palace, in this ornate reception room.

Lesander wasn't *quite* the enemy. But she wasn't coming from an allied family, either.

"Of course," her father went on, "after the ball tomorrow evening, the engagement will be formally signed, and we will start the process of acclimating you into our household. Until then, please enjoy your rooms in the guest suites, and make use of every amenity you wish to. The palace staff is at your command—within reason, of course."

The problem with a political marriage, Dressa knew, was no one knew just how the marriage would work out. If Arianna wasn't attracted to Lesander—well, a marriage could succeed without physical love, they did all the time.

Dressa knew her sister, though. Arianna's true wife would be the good of the kingdom, and where would that leave Lesander? Their marriage contract required mandatory exclusivity until they'd pulled their second child from the synthetic womb, whether they themselves consummated their marriage or not.

When Dressa was right there, feeling warmth she absolutely should not feel. This was going to be an excruciating next few years for everyone, wasn't it? An excruciating lifetime for Dressa.

And what was she thinking? There were plenty of courtiers for her to have flings with. Her father would negotiate her own marriage in a year or two, and then she'd have her own spouse to deal with. Lesander was beautiful, yes, but she was one of many, many beautiful people in the Rhialden Court.

Dressa shifted, the slightest betrayal of her agitation, and caught her father's eye—not good. She didn't see her father often these days, and that was by choice. Probably mutual.

"Of course, Seritarchus," Lesander said with a slight bow. "I will only and ever treat the palace staff with respect."

She glanced at Dressa, and the Seritarchus stepped back, waving at his second daughter.

"By all means, greet your future sister."

The words grated, but Dressa didn't let it show. This couldn't work out any other way—she wasn't the Heir, only the second. And High House Javieri wouldn't settle for the second.

Lesander's hands when they took hers were warm and soft. Lesander's smile quirked sardonically at the corners. Her blue eyes flashed with more personality than she was letting show through, too. As a high house prince, whether she was trained in the Truthspoken social arts or not, she certainly wouldn't lack control.

"Sister," Lesander said. "It is good to see you again. You

were"—she bent to hold a hand less than a meter off the floor —"this tall when I last saw you."

"You weren't much taller," Dressa shot back, and Lesander flashed bright teeth before tamping her grin back again and returning to Arianna's side.

As she left, her perfume, like ocean juniper, lingered.

She couldn't stare, Dressa absolutely couldn't stare. Lesander would be her *sister*.

And Lesander would be tied to Arianna, who only seemed to get stiffer and more controlled every year. Dressa couldn't think of a worse fate than being married to her sister—

All right, no, that wasn't fair. She didn't hate her sister, and Arianna was by far the more effective Truthspoken—she could shapeshift her appearance and personality with so much more ease than Dressa. She was born to rule and exuded that birthright in everything she did. It was simply who she was.

While Dressa did her absolute best to flow with the court, laughing and making friends, the opposite of what a future Truthspoken Ruler should be.

But—by Adeius, Arianna could at least *try* to be anything other than cold and calculated. Outwardly, of course, Arianna's public actions would show exactly as much romance as she calculated would help the kingdom. But it wasn't Arianna's image Dressa was worried about.

Why couldn't Dressa marry the prince and they raise the kingdom's heirs and leave Arianna to what she really wanted— ruling the kingdom? Then everyone would be happy.

Alas, alas. Happiness wasn't a thing often afforded to Truthspoken.

Arianna was looking a little wan that night, as she had been for the last few days, which was worrying. Dressa did, truly, care for her sister, petty tyrant though she could be. Arianna should never look other than vibrant—that could only mean enough stress for a lack of control.

Dressa's father stepped closer to her as Arianna led Lesander to a set of chairs. The whole point of this meeting had been for Lesander to meet their family, but also to meet her future wife.

"Lesander can hold her own with Arianna," her father said softly. "She will do well here, I think. Be welcoming, Daughter. That is your role."

Dressa pressed her lips tightly together. Nothing, with her father, meant only one thing, and seldom what it seemed. He'd seen her reaction to Lesander, she knew it. Was this a warning? An admonishment?

She turned to her father. Put on her most vacuous courtly smile. "Absolutely. Of course I'll welcome my new sister."

If he liked Lesander, if he'd chosen her for his favorite daughter the Heir, of course Lesander would do well. And Dressa would watch, every day, as Lesander lived in the royal residence, talking with her sister, attending functions with her sister, and maybe—*maybe*—sleeping with her sister, though that was by no means required and Dressa was pretty sure that would never happen. Well, and maybe that was a good thing.

She strode past her father to take a chair beside her sister, to play the dutiful sister. She always did. She always would—it was her place in the palace court. And truly, she wasn't unhappy with that.

Except for Lesander.

Dressa's eyes kept meeting Lesander's, until she finally looked away, because that could lead to nothing good. The engagement ball was tomorrow night, and they'd all be on full display. She'd better start burying her feelings now.

The story continues in *The Truthspoken Heir*, Book 1 of The Stars and Green Magics series, out now!

The Stars and Green Magics series is a queer romantic fantasy in space, with sapphic princesses from rival families, an ace enby princess falling for her trans man enemy (starting Book 2), a genderfluid king who takes down enemies in a dress, and a nonbinary space lieutenant out saving the day, in a world with space magic and without the patriarchy.